Crimson

DEAD WORLD BOOK 3

JORDAN SUMMERS

Crimson

ISBN-13: 978-0-9904454-3-2

CHAPTER ONE

Gina "Red" Santiago crawled out of the dark tunnel straight into the jaws of hell. The hot fetid breath of the desert hit her in the face as something growled near her ear. The hair on the back of Red's neck stood on end.

Not bad enough that she'd been framed for murder, now she'd have to contend with being eaten alive.

The rumbling growl deepened.

Red gulped and glanced over her shoulder at the men coming out of the tunnel behind her. "Morgan?"

"Don't move," he said.

Morgan Hunter and Demery Wilson's gazes were fixed on something to her left. Red's heart stammered in her chest, as she forced herself to look at what held their attention.

Please don't let it be a bear.

A large canid stood a few feet from her. It dipped its head and bared its teeth. Drool hung from its bottom jaw in long, liquid strings that dropped onto the sand. He was big, but he was alone. Thank goodness! Red's relief was short-lived, as a mixed pack of canids poured over the dunes on silent feet and quickly surrounded them.

"Dung," she muttered under her breath.

"It's okay." Morgan squeezed her hand, but didn't look at her. "I've got this." He rose to his feet and peeled his clothes off. His movements were deceptively unhurried.

The canid beside Red took a step back to assess the new threat. She did a quick head count. "There are too many."

Demery came out of the tunnel and immediately took up position on her other side, so Red was sandwiched between the two of them. He pulled his dreadlocks back and secured them at his nape. As he stared at the circling pack, his dark chocolate-colored eyes took on a red glow and fangs pushed past his blunt teeth.

Without the ability to shape-shift, Red went for the only weapon she possessed—her laser pistol. Morgan stilled her hand before she could withdraw the weapon from its holster.

"Too noisy and far too visible at night," he said. "We don't want to give away our position."

Red's hands clenched into tight fists and her face flushed. They'd removed their indenti-chips so the satellites couldn't track them, then she, Morgan, and Demery had slipped across the boundary fence that divided the republics from the lawless area known as no-man's-land. Thus far, they'd evaded Roark Montgomery and the International Police Tactical Team, but one blast from her laser pistol would change that.

She cursed under her breath at her own carelessness. Red knew better than any of them how IPTT operated. As an officer with the tactical team, it had been her job to enforce the rules.

But there were no rules in no-man's-land. Here her tactical team training was all but useless.

The largest canid, a coyote hybrid of some kind, stilled, sensing a change in its prey. Something in the canine's bloodline had given it added size and darker coloring from the rest. It watched them for a few seconds, then yipped excitedly. The sound spurred the whole pack. Soon they were all barking, baying, and yipping.

* * * * *

Morgan watched the alpha break away from the pack. Things were about to get bloody. He'd already identified the animal as the leader. Alphas always recognized other alphas. The canine moved in for attack.

He didn't want to hurt it if he could help it. The beast was fighting for its pack's survival. Morgan knew a thing or two about that, but he was fighting for more than survival. He was fighting for his mate. He glanced at Gina.

The warmth and assurance he saw in her hazel eyes fueled his conviction. "Let's do this," he said.

Blood painted the sand crimson as Morgan's bones snapped and his muscles reshaped. He fell to his knees and coughed. His blunt teeth tumbled out of his mouth onto the ground, before quickly being replaced with razor sharp canines. Morgan's hair and skin thickened over his vital organs and talons sprouted from his fingertips. He let out a pained scream that fractured into a howl, as he became more wolf than man.

The second the change was complete, Morgan took off toward the alpha, ignoring the rest of the pack. If he could take down the leader, the others would fall. He was counting on Demery to protect Gina no matter the outcome of the fight.

Morgan tackled the alpha. The impact sent them tumbling end over end. Sand flew everywhere. The moment they stopped, Morgan lunged for the canid's ruff. Before he could latch on, the hybrid struggled free and leapt to its feet. Its big head whipped around with surprising speed and its powerful jaws caught Morgan's arm.

Blood welled in the beast's mouth and it shook its head, attempting to tear off the limb.

Morgan cried out and clamped down on the canine's ear.

The animal yelped, releasing him in the process and jerked its head away. Blood ran down the side of its face as it licked the bits of flesh from its teeth. The fur on its back rose higher and its tail stiffened, then the animal attacked again.

This time Morgan was ready for it. He felt the impact and allowed it to carry him over so he could roll the canine beneath him. Morgan grabbed hold of the alpha's throat and sunk his sharp teeth into its neck.

Blood poured into his mouth. The coppery aroma filled his lungs, making him...*hungry*. Despite his instant revulsion, Morgan swallowed the warm, tempting liquid. The sweet taste hit his system like a laser blast to the gut. A sharp rush of power followed it.

The feeling spread through him until his body trembled from the onslaught. Morgan clamped down on the animal's throat even harder. The alpha whimpered beneath him, but Morgan didn't care as his senses sharpened and the world around him came to life.

What was happening to him? Was this a side effect of Raphael Vega's vampiric blood pulsing through his wolf veins or was this something else entirely?

Fear slowly replaced Morgan's euphoria. He had lived with his wolf through war, loss, and pain. His feral nature was as natural to him as breathing. He didn't know what he'd do if it went away. His wolf was what kept him bound to Gina. If Morgan lost that tie, then everything they'd sacrificed, everything they'd worked to protect would be for naught.

Without his wolf, who was he? *What was he?*

The animal stopped struggling beneath him and tucked its tail between its legs. A moment later, it exposed its abdomen in defeat. Morgan growled low and deep, then slowly released the canine. It staggered to its feet and dropped its head in submission. The pack's excited yipping stopped. The silence that followed was unsettling.

Morgan shifted until he could stand like a man, then made eye contact with each of the animals. In turn they ducked their heads and kept their gazes averted. He threw back his head and howled. When Morgan finished, the pack scattered into the darkness. He slowly turned to face Demery, expecting to see the same submission.

The vampire's red eyes glowed, then Demery grinned, flashing sharp fangs and deep dimples. "Way to go, wolfman," he said, then clapped.

Some of the tension in Morgan's body deflated, but not all. He grabbed a canteen and swished water around in his mouth before spitting it out, then he took a drink and swallowed.

"Is it over?" Gina asked.

"It's done." Demery glanced back at Morgan. "At least that part," he amended. "I think I'm going to scout ahead. Be back in a few."

Blood smeared Morgan's body as he stared at Gina. He needed to see for himself that his mate was safe. Needed to reclaim what was his, so no one and nothing could ever take her away. Only then would he stand a chance of getting his beast under control.

* * * * *

Red watched Morgan's body contort. When it finished, the man she loved was standing before her naked.

"Come here." His guttural voice raked the air, scoring the night.

Her knees quivered and she felt her body tighten in anticipation.

"I said come here," Morgan repeated. This time his words weren't nearly as garbled.

Red hesitated, then slowly approached him.

Morgan circled her, much like the pack had earlier. He stuck his nose in her long, black hair and inhaled deeply. "You smell nice," he growled.

Red wanted to point out that she was in desperate need of a shower, but one look at Morgan's face stilled her tongue. Raw hunger etched his features and desire burned in his amber eyes, turning them molten gold. Her breath caught in her throat as she waited to see what he'd do next.

"Mine," Morgan said, then whispered, "I need you to take your clothes off." A plea and a demand.

Her fingers trembled as she unbuttoned her shirt. Red wasn't scared, but she was nervous. Between fighting murder charges and Morgan's false imprisonment, they hadn't been able to spend a lot of alone time together.

She glanced around at the sand dunes surrounding them. Not exactly the place for this or the best timing, but Red wasn't about to deny him pleasure—or herself. She pulled at the last two buttons and they popped off, dropping onto the ground before being swallowed by the sand.

Tension thrummed between them, creating waves of heat that electrified her nerves and ratcheted her need. Morgan's breathing deepened and his muscles quivered.

"I'm afraid if I touch you, I'll ravish you," he said.

Red's gaze locked on his mouth and she licked her lips. "You don't see me stopping you. Do you?"

Morgan groaned. "Take off the rest of your clothes before I rip them off you."

The air rushed out of her lungs as Red's world narrowed on the feral male in front of her. One taste of his skin and she'd be lost.

She inhaled, catching his musky scent on the hot breeze. She shucked her shirt and seductively shed the rest of her clothes.

Morgan tongued his long, sharp canines in anticipation. "I can't wait to taste you. I've dreamed about it. Ached for it. I'm done waiting," he said. "Get on all fours."

Red's stomach fluttered with anticipation and she dropped instantly.

* * * * *

The second Gina's knees hit the sand, Morgan was on her. He pushed her onto her hands, did a quick check to make sure she was ready, then entered her. One thrust into Gina's tight warmth and Morgan was home. The only home he'd ever need.

It seemed like forever since he'd last lost himself in her body. He trembled, caught between savage need and emotional overload. "Please forgive me," he rasped. "I didn't want it to be like this."

"There's nothing to forgive." Gina wiggled closer.

There would be nothing gentle about this taking. Morgan was too far gone. He pulled back and drove into her. Flames raced along his spine as her tight sheath gripped him. Morgan held her narrow waist so he could watch their bodies join as he pounded into her. He couldn't seem to get deep enough. He wanted to crawl inside her until they were one heart, one being.

Morgan brushed a kiss against her neck and felt Gina tremble beneath him. She pushed her long hair aside to give him better access.

At the sight of her bare skin, his canines lengthened into fangs. He should've been horrified, but Morgan was too out of control to care. He could smell the blood coursing through Gina's veins. It would be sweet. One taste, that's all he needed.

His mouth watered even as revulsion filled him. Morgan had promised himself he wouldn't bite her again. Gina's delicious scent wafted in the air and desire swamped him. His gaze fastened on his mark at the curve of her neck. The mark he'd left so the world would know that he'd claimed her. He tongued the spot, licking the salty sweat from her skin.

"I'm sorry," he murmured, *but I have to…*

Morgan needed to mark her again to reinforce his claim. He

kissed Gina once more.

"Do it!" she demanded.

Morgan growled, then latched onto her shoulder, biting deep where he'd bitten her the first time they'd made love.

* * * * *

Red gasped and her legs nearly gave out as pleasure swamped her. It had always been great between them, but tonight seemed different. More intense.

Morgan rumbled deep in his chest as his rough tongue lapped at her tender flesh. Red could hear him swallowing as he drank in her essence. Her blood set fire to something inside of him.

He moved like a beast, driving his hard flesh into her. Skin slapped heated skin, bonding two bodies, while repairing wounded souls. He needed this. She needed this.

Red needed him.

A chorus of grunts and moans punctuated his movements as Morgan conquered her flesh and laid siege to her heart. "Mine," he ground out, taking one last drink before licking the wound to seal it. "And I'm yours."

"Always," she said.

Morgan cupped her sensitive flesh, then squeezed.

Red exploded on a long, drawn-out gasp, taking him with her into oblivion. Strong hands clamped down hard and he bellowed as his body jerked.

Spent, they collapsed onto the sand.

"I don't deserve you." The hot brush of his breath bathed her neck as tears silently fell from his eyes. His fingertips glided over her skin lovingly as if he were trying to memorize every inch of her.

Red hugged him.

"I'm sorry I bit you. I promised myself I wouldn't, but..." his voice trailed off.

She tried to see the tender spot. "You know I love it when you bite me."

Morgan frowned. "You don't understand. I'm different now. I'm not sure what's happening to me. Raphael's blood... It's changed me somehow. I'm a wolf, but my desires have *altered*."

Red stared into his amber eyes. "You are still the man I love. I'll take you in any form I can get you," she said.

Morgan slid out of her.

The loss of warmth was acute.

"Just don't ever leave me again. Okay?" She touched his cheek.

"I won't." Morgan pressed his lips to her palm.

"Promise?" she asked.

"On my life." He tenderly brushed the hair off her forehead. "I'll die before I allow anyone to separate us again."

Red smiled. "Good, because I'll kill you myself if you do."

Morgan laughed, a big belly of a sound, then pulled her close. "I wish we could stay here like this forever."

Red snuggled against him. "Me, too."

"But I doubt Demery will wait for us much longer and we don't want to lose the cover of night," he said.

"Are you guys about done?" Demery called out from nearby as if on cue. "I'd like to walk for a few hours before we make camp."

He didn't sound three dunes away. If the shifting sand was any indication, he was on the other side of the dune they were lying on. Morgan looked like he was trying not to smile.

"You better have just walked back," Red warned. "Or I'm going to kick your ass."

Demery was silent.

Morgan chuckled and gathered his clothes. He slipped on his pants, then picked up her clothes and handed them to her.

Red wrinkled her nose. "I'm never going to get the sand off me."

"Are you two coming or do I have to come over there and get you?" Demery asked, amusement in his voice.

"He wouldn't dare." Her eyes widened as she looked at Morgan.

He grinned. "I learned a long time ago it's a bad idea to encourage a vampire."

* * * * *

CHAPTER TWO

Red had thought the Republic of Arizona was barren, but two days of wandering in no-man's-land had changed her mind. This place made the backside of the Mars look subtropical. She wiped at the sweat clinging to her face. There wasn't as much as there had been yesterday. Didn't take long for dehydration to set in.

She glanced at Demery. His white protective suit glowed in the sunlight. He looked nice and cool despite the hideous temperature. For a moment, Red was jealous, but the emotion passed quickly.

There was nothing to envy about Demery's situation. His body didn't change temperature—thanks to the genetic alterations he'd received during the last war—unless it was exposed to the sun. If that happened, he'd die.

Morgan trudged along beside her. The heat didn't appear to be affecting him either. At least not as much as it was getting to her. Of course, he was used to living in the town of Nuria, which had never had a protective biodome.

Red had always considered herself prepared for anything, but nothing could've prepared her for the harsh, unforgiving desert landscape that lay before them. She'd never seen so much sand. She was beginning to hate it.

"Should we seek shelter before the sun gets too high?" She hoped they'd take the hint without her having to admit that the heat was making her tired.

Morgan scanned the horizon. "I don't see anyplace we could

hole up for the day," he said. "Demery, do you know of any shelter nearby?"

"Might find something over the next rise," he said.

"Where did you rest the last time you crossed?" Red licked her chapped lips and came away with a mouthful of sand.

"I didn't come this way. Too barren," Demery said.

Red stopped walking. If the place was too barren, then why in the hell were they going this way? Unease rippled through her, but she forced herself to shrug it off. Demery had always had her back in Nuria. He'd risked his life and freedom to help them escape. He'd given her no reason to stop trusting him now.

"You do know where you're going, right?" she asked. "If you're lost, just admit it."

"I'm not lost." Demery chuckled. "I know where I'm going...more or less. We went this way to throw off anyone who might be following. They wouldn't think to look for us here. They'd assume we'd head west where supplies are more plentiful." He pulled out a canteen and tossed it to Red. She caught it without thinking. "Take a drink. It'll make you less grumpy. I've enhanced the water with minerals that will counteract some of the dehydration."

"I'm not grumpy!" Red muttered.

Morgan and Demery laughed.

She was uncomfortable. There was a difference. Red took a drink. When she finished, she secured the lid and handed it to Morgan, who took two big swallows before sealing it and giving it back.

"We have to find someone we can trade with. We need more provisions," Demery said. "Should make it a few more days, but after that..."

They'd die, Red thought.

Nothing turned out to be over the next dune or the one after it. Grit covered Red's face and hands until it became part of her skin. They walked through the heat of the day and into early evening. The sun was dropping below the horizon when Red spotted firelight flickering in the distance.

"Am I seeing things?" she asked. Hallucinating wasn't out of the question.

"No." Morgan stepped forward. "I see it, too." He sniffed the air. "Purebloods."

"Get down," Demery said. They all three hit the ground without question. "We need to figure out if these are squatters, drifters, or Sand Devils."

"What are Sand Devils?" Horned creatures with forked tongues and red skin flashed in her mind.

"Bands of outlaws who rove the dunes in search of unsuspecting squatters and drifters. They're seriously bad news," he said. "Though they can be reasoned with on occasion."

"Think we can sneak around them without them seeing us?" she asked.

"Doubt it," Demery said. "Even if we could, these are the first people we've encountered. We should try to trade with them if we can."

Red reached for her pistol.

"Relax." Demery touched her shooting hand. "Let's find out who we're dealing with before we kill them all. Okay?"

She shrugged casually, but her gaze slid to Morgan. His entire body was tense.

"If they're squatters, they'll have two lookouts. One stationed on each side of the group. They check in by signaling each other. The signal changes from group to group, but we should be able to catch something within the next few seconds," Demery said.

Red watched the inky horizon, waiting for a sign to tell them they wouldn't have to fight their way past this group. She was tired and hungry, and doubted she'd have the energy to put up much resistance if the situation called for it.

Tension increased as they waited. An orange fireball rose into the night sky, then exploded with a thunderous boom. A minute later another occurred in a different location. Demery exhaled loudly and grinned.

"Looks like we've found our first band of squatters." Demery climbed to his feet. "They should have sufficient supplies to trade. At the very least, we'll be able to get enough supplies to make it to the next encampment."

Red and Morgan were slower to stand, since they weren't in a hurry to become an easy target for a nervous lookout.

* * * * *

The camp sat a couple hundred yards away. Circular tents and lean-tos were huddled like melted marshmallows in the center of a ring of fire. Morgan couldn't tell what they were using for fuel, but the flames burned steady and were a good barrier moat between the inhabitants and any intruder that might wander by.

"How do you want to do this?" Morgan asked.

"We'll take a direct approach," Demery said. "If we're out in the open, they'll have plenty of time to see us coming."

Gina frowned. "What if they shoot us on sight?"

Morgan squinted. "I'll be able to smell the guns before we're in range." He didn't add that his acute senses wouldn't help if they had a sniper in their midst.

They headed toward the vagabond group. Loose rags covered the people who were by the firelight, leaving very little skin visible. A few wore big cat and coyote hides. Morgan had seen similar clothing before. It had been worn in the Middle East by nomadic tribes. It was one of the few things that had survived from that area after the last war.

"What are they wearing?" Gina asked.

"Whatever they could scavenge or kill," Morgan said.

"Doesn't seem practical," she said, but her hazel eyes were wide in wonder.

Despite the danger they were in, she was absorbing it all like a kid who'd just spotted her first flying shuttle. Something melted in the vicinity of Morgan's heart.

"Actually," he said. "Those outfits are great for this harsh climate. It cools you during the day and keeps you warm at night. The key is layers. They can be removed or added as needed."

Demery watched the people. "Hey mon, I think I know this group," he said.

"Is that good or bad?" Morgan asked. The last thing they needed after their long trek was to run into hostiles—or worse, someone Demery had crossed in the past.

"It's all good," Demery said. "The Sand Moles welcome traders. Wait here and I'll make contact."

Morgan tensed. "Thought you said we should go in together?"

"That was before I recognized who they were," Demery said. "This particular band is a little skittish. If anything happens to me, head south."

They ducked back down to watch. Morgan didn't like it. The idiot was going to get himself killed. Could he lead Gina across the desert on his own? Morgan didn't like the answer that popped into his head.

"What do we do if they kill him?" she asked, following the same train of thought.

"It won't come to that," he said.

"But what if it does?" Gina asked.

Morgan slanted her a glance. She'd gone from amazement to fear in record time. Her golden skin paled despite the heavy amount of sun it had received the past couple of days.

"We run," he said. "And eventually head south like Demery said."

They watched the vamp slowly approach the encampment. He held his hands in the air so the lookouts could see he wasn't armed. A horn sounded. It was followed by the blast from another. People rushed to their tents and came out carrying guns, bows, and pipes.

Morgan took a quick look around. Other than the ridge of sand they were perched on there was no cover. If he and Gina had to make a run for it, they'd be easily picked off if the lookouts were a half-decent shot.

"What are they holding?" Gina asked. "They look like weapons, but I've never seen anything like them."

"Those are rifles."

"Laser rifles?"

Morgan shook his head. "No, those are antique rifles. They're made out of wood."

"Do they fire metal?" She inched forward to get a better look

"I wouldn't do that if I were you." Morgan caught her leg and pulled her back. "The bullets can travel quite a distance. Getting hit hurts like hell."

"You've been shot with one of those." Her tone was incredulous.

"Not that exact model, but yes. It's an experience I'd like to forget." He rubbed his shoulder where he'd taken a bullet. It still ached when it rained Fortunately, on the dead world, that didn't happen often.

"How did they get them? The International Police Tactical

Team confiscated all of the weapons after the war. Houses were checked, buildings were scoured," she said, sounding bewildered.

Morgan grinned. "They obviously missed a few."

"Are our laser pistols any match to those weapons?" Gina pulled her gun out of its holster.

"Yes, but those have us on distance. We'd need a laser rifle to compete."

She slumped against the dune. "I should've brought a rifle."

Morgan kissed the tip of her nose. "We could only carry so many weapons. We had to leave room for food and water."

"I know." She sounded dejected.

Demery reached the group and stopped.

One of the men in the group stepped forward and patted him down. "All clear," the man said, then quickly rejoined the group.

The murmur of voices rose.

"I'm here to trade, but I also seek shelter," he said. "My name is Demery Wilson. Does anyone here know that name?"

There were more murmurs. This time louder as his name rumbled through the crowd on a tide of voices. Finally a single voice rose above the rest.

"I do." An older man with silver at his temples stepped forward. He wore similar clothes as the rest and had a scruffy beard that started at one ear and ended at the other in a smile of hair.

"Gray?" Demery stepped forward.

The guards notched the rifles against their shoulders.

"It's okay," Gray said. The man smiled, showing a gap in his teeth. "Been a long time, dread man. Didn't think I'd see you around these parts after your last encounter with Reaper."

Demery shrugged casually, but Morgan could see the tension in his large frame. His scent changed, too. It was subtle, but the sour tang of fear was still there.

"You know me, mon. Nothing can keep me away from a good trade." Demery grinned, showing the dimples in his dark cheeks. His body relaxed as he slipped on the jovial, happy-go-lucky mask he used freely around others.

Morgan wondered—not for the first time—what the real Demery was like. It had taken him fifty years to understand Raphael and what motivated him. It had only been a week and change with Demery. A long way to go before the word "trust" would enter the picture.

"This man is known to me. Show him Sand Mole hospitality." Gray stepped forward and lowered his voice. "For your sake, I hope you brought Reaper what you promised."

Demery patted his shirt. "I have it right here."

Gray frowned in confusion, then threw his head back and laughed. "It's nice to know your sense of humor survived intact." He clapped Demery on the back.

"What's he talking about?" Gina asked.

Morgan shook his head. "I don't know. Now shh, let's listen to see if we can find out," he said.

"Do you know where I can find Reaper?" Demery asked Gray. "He still has something of mine."

"We don't run with the likes of him. You know that." Gray's brow furrowed at the mere suggestion of association. "We are a peaceful people unless we're provoked or deceived."

Demery smiled. "I know, mon, but you always seem to know where the devil hides."

Gray grinned back. "That I do. That I do. Speaking of which, tell your friends they can come out now."

Morgan tensed and Gina slipped backward into the darkness.

"Could never get anything past you, old man. It's okay," Demery called out. "They won't harm you. Come on out."

"What do you think?" Gina thumbed her pistol.

Morgan looked at the darkness squeezing in around them. "I think we don't have a choice. We need provisions and shelter or we won't get much farther."

She grasped his arm. "I don't like it."

"I know, but down here Demery's the expert," Morgan said.

Gina shook her head. "It's not Demery I'm worried about."

She put her gun away. Morgan followed, positioning his body between her and the armed men.

When they got close, Morgan said, "My name is—"

"Hunter," Demery provided, cutting him off. "And this is Red." He pulled Gina close.

The gesture was both friendly and possessive. Perhaps a warning. Morgan couldn't tell, so he said nothing, even though his first instinct was to rip the vamp's arm off and use it for a chew toy.

We are outnumbered, he reminded himself. If Demery's little act would protect Gina, then he'd go along with it...for now.

"I'm Gray. And these are the Sand Moles. Welcome."

* * * * *

The group turned out to be quite hospitable. They offered Red and Morgan food, shelter, and water in exchange for a laser pistol.

Red was hesitant to give up one of their weapons, but it wouldn't do them any good if they died of thirst or hunger. Despite the circumstances, the people and their customs fascinated her.

Women danced around a crackling fire in the center of the compound to music that was created using scraps of metal and wires. Red had never heard anything like the high-pitched pings and pops, but found herself tapping her foot and swaying to the music.

One woman with a thick braid of blond hair approached. She tried to coax Red into joining the other women in the dance. Red begged off. She'd never danced a day in her life and wasn't about to start now. But she was tempted. It looked like *fun*.

The men watched avidly. All the men except Morgan. He kept staring at one of the digital diaries they'd found hidden in his cousin Kane's home. He hadn't listened to any of the recordings yet. The loss of his only family was still too fresh in his mind.

"Why don't you put that away and try to relax?" Red pointed at the digital recorder in his hand.

Morgan looked at the device and pain momentarily hardened his austere features. In a flash, it was gone. He shoved the recorder in his pocket, then stared at the fire. He didn't seem to notice the women, but Red couldn't keep her eyes off them.

Maybe when this was all over she'd learn how to dance. She continued to watch as activity went on around them. The Sand Moles seemed so poor, yet moved with such freedom that for a moment Red envied their lot in life. The thought brought her up short.

These people were criminals. She'd have shot them if she had come across them on patrol with IPTT. Now she was relying on their generosity and goodwill. Shame warred with duty and weighed heavily on her conscience. She was so distracted by her thoughts that Red nearly missed Demery as he passed her on his way to a nearby tent.

"Where are you going?" Red thought it prudent to know where everyone was just in case they had to leave in a hurry.

His brown eyes sparkled mischievously and his dimples deepened. "To get a little refreshment." Demery nodded at the woman who'd just poked her head out of the flap.

She'd momentarily forgotten all about his need for blood. "Sorry," Red said.

He took another step.

"Wait, I have a question for you," she said.

Demery paused, his impatience showing, along with his fangs. He must really be hungry. Or maybe he was just horny from watching the women gyrate seductively around the flames.

"Who's Reaper?" she asked.

Demery's cheerful expression faded. "Nobody."

"Then what did Gray mean earlier when he asked if you brought the item for Reaper?" she asked.

"Nothing, mon. Just old business that needs tending to while I'm here," he said, then kept walking.

Morgan waited for him to enter the tent, then whispered in her ear. "He lied."

Red kept her eyes trained on the flap. "I know. His scent soured before he opened his mouth."

"You want me to go after him?" he asked. "I can find out the truth."

"No, this isn't the time or the place to interrogate him." She shrugged. "He may just be overly hungry. I am willing to give him the benefit of the doubt. Besides, unless his business directly involves us, it really isn't any of our concern what he does on his own time."

"You're right." Morgan nuzzled her neck. "I'm probably being paranoid."

Red pulled back so she could look at him. "What's going to happen to us?" she asked softly.

His brow furrowed. "What do you mean?"

A couple strolled by within earshot. She closed the distance between them, hoping the music would help mask her voice. "We are fugitives. How are we going to prove our innocence if we're on the run and don't even know if we'll make it out of here alive?"

"I won't let anything happen to you." Morgan brushed her cheek with his palm. "Once we locate a communications device and find out what Roark Montgomery's up to, we'll make a plan. If nothing else, we'll broadcast about our innocence until someone listens."

"I don't need you to protect me," Red said. "I need you to make sure nothing happens to you." She could handle anything no-man's-land threw at her as long as Morgan was by her side.

He was silent for a moment while his molten eyes searched her face. "I'm sure that Raphael Vega and the others are working on a way to help us from their end."

Red shook her head. If only that were true... Nuria had turned on her during Morgan's absence. No doubt their opinion of her was worse now. Raphael, Takeo Yakamura, and Juan Sanchez were the only ones who'd tried to help, but three men couldn't take on Roark Montgomery's army. If the politician decided to have another go at Nuria, they'd be massacred.

She thought about Raphael's brother, Michael Travers. What would become of him? As Roark's assistant, he'd been their only chance to keep one step ahead of the politician and he'd failed. If Morgan was correct, Roark had gotten to him. Hell, for all she knew Michael was dead.

The thought saddened her. Not over the loss, but what Michael's death would mean to poor Raphael. He'd just found his brother after years of separation and believing he was dead. Now he may have lost him all over again. She closed her eyes and tried to mentally call him.

Can you hear me? Raphael, it's Red.

Silence met her.

Red tried again.

Still nothing.

She opened her eyes to find Morgan staring at her.

"Did it work?" he asked.

"Did what work?" she countered, feeling self-conscious.

"Calling Raphael," he said as if it were obvious.

Had he heard her thoughts or guessed? Red could live with guessing, but she wasn't sure how she'd handle another invasion of

18

her mental privacy. It was bad enough knowing Raphael could hear her thoughts whenever he felt like it. "How did you know?" she asked.

"I've been trying to contact him, too," Morgan said.

"No luck?" she asked.

He shook his head.

"Do you think he's okay?" she whispered, afraid to voice the question any louder for fear it might be true.

"Raphael is a survivor. He's been through far worse than what Roark can throw at him," he said.

Her shoulders slumped. "Then I guess we're too far away to reach him. I don't even know if I'm doing it correctly."

"Me either," Morgan said quietly. "But we have to keep trying. There's no other option." His gaze grew distant. "I need to know that Nuria is okay."

Even after everything they'd been through, Morgan continued to take responsibility for Nuria's wellbeing. For his sake, Red hoped the town was still standing. He wouldn't survive its fall. The guilt would be too much.

She went back to watching the dancers twirl this way and that, their skirts flowing out away from their graceful bodies. After a few minutes, Red tuned out the music and focused her mind.

Raphael, where are you?

* * * * *

CHAPTER THREE

Raphael Vega sat in his rented room above the water trader bar in the town of Nuria. The plush room lay in shadows thanks to the heavy burgundy drapes covering the windows and the sun's slow demise.

It had been a week since he'd tried to find his brother, Michael Travers. He'd attempted to telepathically contact him multiple times to no avail. He was still alive, but that was all Raphael knew for sure.

Red and Morgan should be across the boundary fence by now, if Demery had kept his end of the bargain. He'd checked the remains of Kane's house to be sure they'd gone and hadn't found any trace of them.

Raphael didn't fully trust the vamp, not that Demery had given him any cause not to, but there was just something off about him. For one thing, he was too damn cheerful. It wasn't *natural* to be that happy. Not after the war. In addition to that personality flaw, it was dangerous having another genetically engineered vampire bouncing around town.

Vamps were territorial. It was part of their bioengineering. The governments had wanted solitary assassins when they created vamps and they'd gotten them. Raphael should know—he was the most territorial bastard of them all.

He rolled his shoulders. He had other things to worry about. Morgan would take care of Red. Not that Red couldn't take care of herself—she could, but she was out of her element. She'd gone from a world of rules to one of utter chaos. She would need her inner wolf now more than ever.

A smile flitted over his lips as the word "chaos" crossed his mind. Raphael glanced at the shadowy naked figure lying in the middle of his well-used rest pad. Catherine Meyers' hair was a tangle of short red curls as she lay on her stomach, giving him a tantalizing view of her pale back. She made soft snuffling noises while she slept.

Raphael could make out the curve of her luscious spine as it snaked down to reveal the arc of a ripe rump and a firm thigh. Those same thighs had clutched his hips as he slid inside of her. The room still held the scent of sex and hot, moist woman. His abdomen clenched and he groaned.

He'd taken his little Chaos an hour ago, but Raphael wouldn't know it by his body's eager response to her nudity. He thought by now he'd be tired of the woman. Instead, his need had only grown, along with his hunger, which was a constant throbbing ache.

He'd derived great pleasure in memorizing the location of every freckle and secret spot on her. The urge to explore them again had him rising from his chair. Raphael forced himself to sit back down.

If he were prone to worry, he would be concerned about his building attachment to the woman, but Raphael had learned a long time ago to take life as it came.

His dark gaze caressed her once again and possessiveness welled inside him. He couldn't keep her, but Raphael wasn't quite ready to let her go. He stood and gathered his clothes, then silently dressed. A couple of minutes later, Raphael slipped out of the room, leaving Catherine fast asleep.

He pressed his palm to the door and punched several buttons. When he was done, the only way the door would open was with his code and handprint. A twinge of guilt tugged at him. Raphael quickly squashed it. It was too late for guilt, too late for a lot of things.

Raphael made his way down to the bar. Evening kept the shadows in the water trader long and deep. Its faded walls and pillars showed its true age. A few tables had been scattered throughout the room and were mainly used for customer overflow.

He looked around at the last of the patrons bellying up to the long bar to fill their orders as if nothing had changed in Nuria. Raphael didn't know whether to be glad or upset. He settled on the latter.

The least Nuria could do was mourn the loss of its sheriff—their alpha. Morgan Hunter had led these people well. Protected them with his very life. In the end, he'd given up his freedom and so had Red. Did anyone in here acknowledge their sacrifice? No.

Raphael stared at the people standing around the bar laughing and visiting. His scowl deepened. He was about to head back upstairs to his room when Juan Sanchez and Takeo Yakamura entered. The two men had taken on responsibility for training a new Nurian Tactical Team in Red's absence.

Juan, an average-sized man with dark cropped hair and an unnerving ability to divine the future, gave him a wave, then indicated an empty table near the back.

Raphael hesitated, then joined them.

"Any news?" Takeo asked, his almond-shaped eyes narrowing on the crowd in suspicion. He'd dumped his trench coat onto a chair and tied his long, black hair into a tight queue. His powerful Asian frame practically vibrated with unused adrenaline—thanks to the chimera living inside him.

"Nothing yet," Raphael said. "We would've heard if they'd been captured."

"How can you be so sure?" Juan asked. "Roark has done a good job of controlling the news thus far."

"They would've tried to mentally contact me or at least send out a distress signal. I don't think Morgan and Red would go quietly this time," Raphael said. "Not after what they went through. Their bodies would've turned up by now if Roark had found them."

The men's gazes met in silent agreement.

"It's been over a week, when are you going to release Chaos?" Juan asked.

Raphael stiffened. "When I get good and ready."

"You can't keep her forever. She's not a puppy. She's a woman. A woman who happens to be a member of the International Police Tactical Team." Takeo absently fingered the ends of his long, black ponytail. He motioned to the man standing behind the bar, then held up three fingers. Three synth-beers arrived a minute later.

Raphael's jaw clenched. "Don't you think I know that?" he snapped. He didn't want to talk about Catherine. She wasn't their business. She was his responsibility.

"IPTT will eventually send in a squad to look for her. I'm surprised it hasn't happened already. Do you really want them raining down upon Nuria again after what just occurred?" Juan asked.

Raphael thought about it. No, he did not.

The International Police Tactical Team had swarmed the town looking for Red and Morgan. They'd arrested Red, claiming she'd been behind Morgan's escape from prison. It had all been an elaborate ruse organized by Roark Montgomery in hopes of leveling the town. If it hadn't been for Red's peaceful surrender, he would've succeeded.

Raphael reeled in his temper. He wasn't mad at the men—he was mad at himself. "Have you seen anything in your visions?" He didn't take much stock in psychics, but Juan had been right about some things, so he couldn't dismiss him outright.

"No." Juan stared at Raphael with a pained expression, then picked up his beer and took a drink. "Nothing like that," he said, but didn't elaborate further.

Raphael watched him closely. There was something the psychic wasn't telling him. He could see it clearly in Juan's eyes. He opened his mouth to ask, but then closed it and exhaled loudly. Truth was Raphael didn't want to know what the future held. He'd already considered all the possibilities, including IPTT intervention. None of the scenarios he'd spun in his mind had ended well.

"I'll make sure she's returned," he said.

"When?" Takeo asked.

"I told you I'd handle it! Now enough with the questions." Raphael shoved his chair back from the table. It hit the wall behind him with a bang.

Everyone in the bar stopped what they were doing and gazed toward the commotion.

Raphael glared at the weathered faces around him.

Wariness overrode their initial curiosity and they went back to chatting, but the volume had dropped considerably.

Satisfied, Raphael turned his attention to Takeo and Juan. "You both worry about building the new tactical team and let me handle the woman."

Juan and Takeo looked at each other, then Juan held up his hands. "You know we wouldn't say anything, if the circumstances were different, but you've kidnapped an IPTT member. It'll be a miracle if you aren't arrested on sight."

Raphael's gaze cooled to a slow burn. "Don't you think I know that? It couldn't be helped. She'd been sent to kill Morgan and Red," he said. "Hell, she tried to kill me. If I hadn't subdued her, she might have succeeded."

"We know." They snickered. "What we don't get is why you slept with her, when you should've killed her and dumped her body near the boundary fence."

Raphael's gut clenched at the thought of any harm coming to Catherine. He flashed his fangs and hissed.

"Knock it off, dumbass," Takeo said. "You aren't the only one in the room with fangs." He opened his mouth wide enough to expose his large feline incisors.

A deep sound rumbled out of Raphael's chest.

"Terrific," Takeo snapped. "You've woken the chimera. You happy now?" A hiss punctuated his words as the viper uncoiled from his back and slipped out from beneath his shirt. A forked tongue slashed the air and the snake's head rose over his shoulder in preparation to strike.

"What's next? You going to whip off your shirt and show me the goat's head poking out of your rib cage?" Raphael dismissed the threat.

"The only goat trait I have is in the form of my libido." Takeo smirked.

"I'm sure it's just as quick, too." Raphael snorted.

"Fuck off," Takeo shot back.

"Children, play nice," Juan said. "Or you can't sit at the big kids' table."

"Put your toys away, chimera." Raphael wiggled his fingers. "I'm in no mood to tangle." He pulled his chair away from the wall and dropped into it.

He wasn't mad at Takeo for stating the obvious. Raphael had

been asking himself the same question since he'd found out the truth about Catherine's murderous deeds. She'd killed two people and tried to frame Red for murder.

Why hadn't he killed her?

She was trouble in more ways than one. His nature warred with his compassion and his nature had lost. Badly. It was a first. Which was why he'd resorted to picking fights and grasping at straws for answers.

"He started it," Takeo said.

"I'm ending it," Juan said.

Raphael sipped his beer as he gathered his thoughts. "Catherine helped us break Red and Morgan out of Roark's prison. I don't think she's going to be quick to turn me in for detaining her, since she'd have to implicate herself."

Takeo shook his head. "I wouldn't bet it on it. She tried to kill you once. What makes you think she won't do it again?"

Raphael considered his question. "A feeling."

"You're joking, right?" Takeo laughed. "Do you really think you should base your future and the future of this town on a feeling?"

"No, but I'm going to anyway," Raphael said.

"You are kurutta, man," Takeo said.

Juan quietly watched the exchange, then glanced at Takeo to silence him. "He's not crazy, but I do believe our vamp has a case of bloodlust happening."

Raphael flushed. Not an easy feat for one such as him. "I do not...I-I am not...It's preposterous," he denied.

Lust was definitely involved in his decision to detain Catherine, but there was more to it than that. An elusive more that didn't have a name as of yet. Whatever it turned out to be, Raphael wouldn't be discussing it with the likes of these two.

"I'd better get back to the room." He downed his beer and rose from the table. "I don't want her to wake without me being there."

Takeo's brow arched and he glanced at his watch. "Has she been asleep all day?"

Raphael grinned. "Not all day. I woke her up a time or two."

"How much blood did you take from her?" Takeo asked.

Raphael's smile widened. "It wasn't the blood loss that wore her out."

Juan and Takeo laughed, then quickly covered the sound with coughs as people at the bar looked their way.

"Enjoy your beers," Raphael said, then left to go back upstairs, but not before snagging a canteen of water off the bar.

Let them have a laugh at his expense. It didn't matter. They did not understand that the situation with Catherine called for care and finesse.

* * * * *

When he was out of view, Takeo turned to Juan. "Man, he has it bad."

Juan nodded in agreement. "Vamps are normally detached from their food," he said.

Takeo chuckled. "She means more than food to him. Did you see how he nearly took my head off at the mention of killing her?"

"Yep." Juan played with the label on his beer. "I've seen this in the wolves. Not a surprise given they are pack animals. But never in a vamp."

"Seen what?" Takeo asked. "Insanity?"

"Some may call it that. Others call it the drive to bond—to mate."

Takeo looked back toward the stairs. "Do you think he knows?"

Juan laughed. "Nope, but I do think he's beginning to suspect something is up. He's wound pretty tight."

"What'll happen if she leaves him?" Takeo asked.

"Depends." Juan shrugged.

"On what?" he asked.

"On where she goes and if she plans to come back. I'm pretty sure he'd be able to track her blood anywhere on the planet, now that he's tasted her. And if Raphael is bonding to her like I suspect, he won't let her go easily—if ever."

Takeo shook his head. "Better him than me," he said, as a shiver sliced down his spine. If he were a gambling man, he'd say it was a sign. Lucky for him, he wasn't, but it still took several seconds for the sensation to fade.

Raphael was a fool to let a woman get under his skin. He should know better given how many years he'd walked this planet. Takeo lifted his beer to his lips. No thanks. He didn't want any woman sinking her claws into his hide. He'd avoided feminine traps thus far. He should be able to hold out for another fifty years or so.

Juan canted him a glance. "I hope I'm around to see you fall, big guy. From the look on your face, it won't be long now. That woman won't know what hit her, and neither will you, when it happens," he said.

Takeo glared at him. "Don't hold your breath. It hasn't happened yet and there's been plenty who've tried to tie me down in the past." He held up two fingers. "Tender, bring us another round of synth-beers."

Juan's dark eyes sparkled knowingly.

Takeo didn't like the way Juan was looking at him. It was as if Juan knew something he didn't. Damn psychic! They could be wrong sometimes. Right? Right!

"I'm not going to end up like that miserable bastard Raphael," Takeo said. "Mark my words."

Juan laughed softly.

"What's so funny?" Takeo asked.

"I'm sure Raphael thought the same thing, before encountering Chaos."

* * * * *

CHAPTER FOUR

Roark Montgomery sat behind his desk in his expansive office and stared out the window at the illuminated biodome that kept everything inside bright, lush, and green, while everything outside the dome shriveled and died.

As a political representative for the Republic of Missouri, he was used to working late, but it wasn't work that kept him here tonight. He shifted in his padded leather seat and winced. Despite being put in a healing vat, his sides were still tender from where Gina Santiago had sunk her claws into him. Roark could still recall the shock of that particular discovery.

Up until that moment, he'd thought Red was a pureblood like her grandfather, Commander Robert Santiago. His mistake nearly cost him his life. He'd been lucky that the bitch had missed his vital organs.

One inch to the left and he wouldn't be sitting here. Whether she'd missed on purpose or by chance, wasn't important. The only thing that mattered was that she pay for her treachery.

He spun his chair away from the darkness beyond the dome to face his assistant, Michael Travers, who stood nervously clasping his hands. His pale skin was pastier than usual and his black eyes never stopped shifting.

"What do you mean they haven't found them yet?" Roark's thumb hovered above a small green button on a small, innocuous device in his hand. "I told you to double the IPTT patrols."

"I did as you asked. Please," Michael begged, his gaze darting to Roark's hand. "I've done everything I can. It's like they've disappeared off the planet."

His oily black hair normally molded his scalp like a second skin, but today it stuck out in random tufts around his head. He backed away, clutching his skull as fear contorted his expression into a macabre fleshy mask.

Roark smiled. "Obviously you haven't done everything or we'd have Gina Santiago and Sheriff Morgan Hunter by now. There are only so many places they can hide."

"I've had every place I can think of scoured, but they aren't there. The satellites are no longer picking up their registration chips," Michael said.

Roark frowned. They should've been able to pick up the identi-chips. There were ways to mask the signals and temporarily block them, but it was impossible to stay hidden for long. So where were they? Why hadn't they found them?

His hard gaze landed on Travers. "I will not tolerate incompetence." Roark pushed the button. Not because he had to, but because he *wanted* to.

Michael Travers screamed and fell to his knees. "Keep them away." He swatted at thin air, fighting off invisible attackers that only he could see.

"Are you going to try harder?" Roark chuckled as his assistant squirmed helplessly on the floor.

This was more entertaining than an underground clone fight. He should've implanted the frontal lobe A.I. chip long ago. If he had, Roark would've never had to worry about his assassin turning on him. It would have saved him a lot of sleepless nights. Of course, had he known from the start that Travers was a bloodsucking Other, an abomination that should've been eliminated long ago, Roark would have.

"I will. I promise," Mike pleaded, curling into fetal position "Just make them stop. They're everywhere." He covered his head with one hand while the other scratched blindly at the air.

Roark lifted his thumb and Travers stopped screaming. He lay on the floor, panting helplessly, his body trembling. Sweat covered his pale face.

"Get up. You're embarrassing yourself," Roark said.

Michael laid there, his hands still clutching his head.

"Don't make me ask you again or I'll give you something to whine about," Roark said. "And you better not have soiled my rug. You know how much it costs to get it cleaned."

Michael unfurled, then grasped a nearby chair. He pulled himself to his feet with a wheeze. "I'll try harder," he said. "The rug is fine. See?" He stepped away so Roark could look.

"The next time you come in here to report you'd better have some news or I'll keep that button down until you pray your brain explodes."

"Yes, sir." Michael backed away, his gaze wary and unfocused.

"From this moment on, I want you to conduct the search yourself. I don't trust Commander Robert Santiago to send out his best men to find his granddaughter. Oh, and Travers, if you don't find them, do not bother coming back," Roark said. "Now go before I change my mind."

Michael rushed out of the room, shutting the door behind him.

With any luck Travers would die soon and save Roark the trouble of killing him. He should probably interview people for the position now, he mused. When Roark had first found out that Michael Travers was an Other, he had been outraged. His secret would've ruined his political career had it come out.

Roark had done the only thing he could think of and had Michael's brain chipped. With the touch of a button, a small electrical current would stimulate his frontal lobe, causing delusions, paranoia, and best of all—pain.

According to the people he'd paid to do the procedure, a person with this particular chip would slowly be driven insane as the artificial intelligence linked to their brain and made its own demands. Erratic behavior was the first sign of deterioration. Eventually, the link would eliminate impulse control.

Until the A.I. kicked in, Roark had to use a remote to trigger the chip. Travers had already begun to mentally deteriorate. Roark just needed him to hold it together until the election was over. After that, he could stay in his imaginary world where shadow people lurked around every corner. He deserved it. They all did.

The image of a freckle-faced girl popped into his mind. Roark could still hear her laughter and see her bright smile as she professed her love for the dark-haired boy she'd brought home to meet him.

I love him, Daddy.

Roark had been happy for his daughter. It wasn't until he'd held her broken, bloodied body that he'd discovered the dark-haired, innocent-looking boy that she'd loved so much was actually a monster disguising himself as a pureblood human being. A monster that shouldn't have existed.

On the day Amanda's body was recycled, Roark made his daughter a promise. He'd vowed to fight until he'd eliminated all the "Others". No parent should have to go through what he had. Roark scrubbed a hand over his face, wiping the painful memory away. His office slowly came back into view.

He took a deep breath and opened his desk drawer. Roark pulled out an unmarked navcom and punched in a series of numbers, then waited. The second the transmission was answered he stared speaking.

"Scarlet," he said, praying the influ-gas he'd administered to Private Catherine Meyers and Lieutenant Bannon Richards nearly a month ago still worked.

"Yes," a sleepy voice said.

Roark grinned. "I have a job for you to do. I need an insurance policy."

There was a pause. "I do not understand."

"Just listen," Roark growled. "I want you on standby. When the opportunity presents itself, you are to assassinate the woman known as Gina "Red" Santiago. Got it?"

"Kill Red. Understood, sir."

"Good," Roark said. "Have you recovered from your trip?"

"Not yet, sir."

"Be sure that you do. I need you in top shape for this mission. I'll be in touch." He disconnected the call and put the navcom in the drawer. Roark sat back in his chair and stared at the digital map projected on the wall. "Where are you hiding?"

His gaze scanned the areas that had already been searched. It was possible that Travers had missed his targets, but Roark didn't think so. He was thorough when it came to hunting, even under duress. His eyes dropped to the boundary fence. Would Morgan and Gina be stupid enough to cross into no-man's-land?

Roark considered what he'd do if he were being hunted. First he'd remove his republic identi-chip and store it inside something that blocked the signal, then he'd disappear. There was no better place to disappear than into no-man's-land. Satellites didn't even track movement there.

It was the one place Morgan and Gina could go where they'd be sure the IPTT wouldn't follow. Fortunately for Roark, he wasn't with the International Police Tactical Team anymore.

He activated the comlink. Michael Travers answered on the first ping.

"Get your gear together. You're going on a trip," Roark said. "But first, I want you to send out a communiqué."

"What should it say?" Michael asked.

"Grant immunity and registration to the first Unknown who brings me Gina Santiago or Morgan Hunter. If they can get them both, I'll add an additional fifteen-thousand-credit reward. We can't have them turning up unannounced before the election. We're in the home stretch." With his backup plan in place, Roark wasn't feeling nearly as stressed out.

"Where do you want the message sent? The Northern Hemisphere republics? Southern Hemisphere republics? Or both?" Michael asked.

"I want it sent to no-man's-land. Better yet, tomorrow you can go there yourself to make sure the message has been delivered."

Michael was silent for a moment. "Do you really think they've crossed the boundary fence? That would be suicide."

"It's what I'd do," Roark said.

"Very well, sir. Should I add anything else to the communiqué?" Michael's voice sounded small, like the man.

"Such as?" Roark asked.

"Do you want them dead or alive?"

"Glad to hear you're thinking ahead, Travers. Have the Unknowns surprise me." Roark grinned. Having unregistered individuals, Unknowns, pursuing Morgan and Gina was a stroke of genius. Even if they succeeded, the Unknowns would have no recourse if he decided not to pay because in the eyes of the republics they didn't exist. "You might want to think about getting to them first, if you ever want that chip out of your head."

"Sir?" Hope filled that simple question. "You'd really take it out?"

Roark let the silence stretch.

"Sir?" Michael asked.

"Bring them to me alive, Travers and we'll talk about it," he said, then disconnected the comlink.

He'd never remove the chip, couldn't now that the A.I. had attached itself to Travers' brain, but his assistant would work harder if he believed that were the case.

Roark looked back at the map. Gina and Morgan thought they could hide from him by crossing the boundary fence, but they were about to learn nothing and no place was out of his reach.

* * * * *

It was getting worse. Michael didn't know how much longer he could go on before his mind simply refused to return. The power inside of him was building. He could feel it in his limbs, a sort of itching pressure that never subsided. Michael had no idea if he'd be able to control it. He feared for his safety and that of those around him.

"Raphael, my brother, what will become of me?"

As usual, there was no one here to answer.

A flash of movement caught Michael's eye. Gray, amorphous, and threatening, the shadow rose to taunt him. They were growing weary of waiting on the fringes, lurking in the corners of his mind. Soon they'd become emboldened. A few more presses of the green button and they'd have him. He'd be too weak to fight. Everything he'd worked for, everything he'd recently found would all amount to nothing. What would happen then?

Michael knew the answer, of course. Madness and death. The question was how many would he take with him before they silenced him forever? A dozen? A few hundred? A thousand? Death would be preferable to genocide.

Perhaps he should spread his arms and welcome death now. Save it the trouble of courting him. Death would make a most fascinating lover. There'd be no lies or deception. Only truth.

Michael found its whispered promises of pain-free peace more seductive than any human caress. Not that he had many to compare it to. A few brief encounters where credits were exchanged could hardly count as having relationships.

That said a lot about the choices he'd made in his life. Existence more like it. He had stopped living a long time ago. His brother, Raphael, was the only thing that kept him in this world. Without him, he'd be lost.

* * * * *

CHAPTER FIVE

I sat in the darkness holding the navcom in a white-knuckled grip, unsure of what had just happened. Conflicting images raced through my head. The pictures didn't make sense. My thoughts morphed into crimson blobs as the orders tumbled round and round in my mind.

Kill Gina Santiago.

That couldn't be right. But there was no mistaking the directive. I needed to move. My body was restless, full of unused adrenaline. Despite my initial misgivings, my target was clear. The urge to hunt ate at my insides until I was a sieve of seething emotions.

I had to do my duty.

The world would be better off without Red in it. She'd brought shame to the International Police Tactical Team. The second-string force she'd formed in Nuria had been created out of spite.

Nuria. I snorted in disgust. What a piss-ass excuse of a town. It's crumbling down before everyone's eyes and no one was doing a thing about it. The desert blight should've been leveled long ago. Perhaps I'd do that once I took care of her.

Gina didn't deserve the rank of lieutenant. It should've been stripped the second she handed in her resignation. That was normal procedure for anyone processing out of the IPTT. If it hadn't been for Commander Robert Santiago, I had no doubt the rank would've been removed. He protects her at every turn. Ignores her mental incompetence and the deaths that have occurred on her watch.

Maybe he was the key to finding her...

A plan started to form, the details still amorphous and too general.

A direct approach wouldn't work. The IPTT commander—like Roark Montgomery—was too smart to fall for any obvious ploys. Robert Santiago would be suspicious, as would anyone in his situation. Divided loyalties could be easily toppled.

Fortunately, he wouldn't suspect me. I am the kind of person who's easily overlooked. I'm not above reproach. No one was at IPTT. But I was underestimated. And because of that, I'd be able to get him to drop his guard. Convince him it was in his best interest to trust me.

If he knew or even suspected where Red was hiding, I'd find out. I'm good at uncovering secrets. I've learned to make myself useful. I take my responsibilities seriously. And once I got out of here, I intended to prove my loyalty to the team.

My fists clenched in frustration. Waiting was intolerable. I preferred action. Always had. Always would. It was one reason I was so good at my job.

I glanced around, unseeing. Nothing seemed familiar or real. Yet I knew it was. This room. The furniture. All solid, not a dream, nor were they figments of my imagination. They were as real as the orders I intended to carry out.

In my present predicament, accomplishing them would be difficult, but I'd figure out a way. I had before. I would again. No man, no matter how powerful and intimidating, would stop me.

* * * * *

Catherine sat on the rest pad, wrapped in sheets, clenching her navcom. She slowly set aside the communicator as Raphael entered. He paused, his attention split between her actions and a distant voice whispering frantically in his mind. It was too faint to make out the words. So faint that Raphael wasn't even sure if it had been real.

Was he hearing things? Had his brother, Michael, tried to contact him? Whatever the voice was, it was gone now. He shook his head.

"Are you going to give me my clothes back?" She glanced at her watch. "It's been one week, two days, and nine hours. But who's counting?"

He shut and sealed the door behind him. "You weren't in a hurry to have them an hour ago."

Catherine blushed and ran a hand through her tangled hair. "I'd like them now," she said, ignoring his statement.

"Who did you call on the navcom?" he asked casually, feeling anything but.

"I didn't contact anyone. I received a call," she said as if it were of little importance.

"From anyone I know?" Raphael was shocked by the surge of jealousy pounding in his blood.

She shook her head. The move made her red curls bounce. "I'd rather not discuss it." Catherine's gaze dropped to the rest pad and color rose up her neck.

Raphael wondered how long he had before IPTT arrived. "We need to talk." He stepped deeper into the room. "I think you and I can help each other, if we can come to an agreement."

Catherine scooted back, exposing a pale thigh in the process. Raphael's gaze locked on the skin he'd lavished with attention and he felt himself harden. She must have noticed because she flipped the sheet over to cover herself.

"I could talk better if I were clothed," she said.

"That's unfortunate," Raphael said, "because I like you naked. Preferably under me."

The pink in her cheeks deepened in color. "That's not going to happen again."

Raphael arched a brow. "Don't be so sure." He was nowhere near done with her. The thought that he might never be left him shaken.

Catherine tightened the sheet around her. "What occurred between us was a mistake. You...you...overwhelmed me."

Her words slapped him across his face. Raphael flinched, then something dangerous coiled inside his gut. "Are you saying that I forced you?"

Her green eyes widened. "Not exactly."

"It's a simple yes-or-no question," he said. "You cannot preface your answer."

37

If it were possible for his blood to boil it would be doing so now. How dare the little minx accuse him of forced seduction? He'd never raped a woman in his life. He'd never had to. They'd all come willingly to his rest pad. Catherine might have protested in the beginning, but she never once uttered the word no. He would've known. Wouldn't he? The thought that he might be wrong horrified Raphael.

"I'm waiting," he said, trying to remain calm, while feeling anything but.

She sighed. "No, you didn't, but I was at a clear disadvantage. One you were more than happy to press."

"Disadvantage?" Raphael snorted in derision. "Was this before or after you tried to kill me?"

"I was doing my job," she snapped, but her voice cracked, giving way to nervousness.

"So was I," he grit out. "I recall subduing you with minimal force. As for the rest, I believe we both achieved mutual satisfaction, or were you screaming my name for show?"

Catherine crossed her arms over her ample chest. "There's no need for vulgarity."

His eyes narrowed. "You're the one who accused me of rape."

"I did no such thing. All I said was that you had the advantage. You are a vampire after all."

He threw his arms up in frustration. "It was daylight. I had very little sunscreen on. My skin was frying and my strength was compromised." Raphael waved his hand in the air. "You'll forgive me if I disagree with your assessment."

She rolled her eyes. "Whatever."

"Juan and Takeo seem to think that I should let you go." He wasn't about to tell her they'd wanted her dead.

"You should listen to them," she said. "It'll go easier on you during your tribunal sentencing."

Raphael's brows rose to his hairline. "I'm afraid I can't allow that to happen," he said casually. He caught the fear in her eyes before she masked it and immediately set out to reassure her. "Don't be ridiculous, woman. I have no plans to harm you."

"You threatened to kill me," Catherine said. This time she sounded petulant...and utterly adorable.

"And you tried to kill me," Raphael said. "I'd say that makes us even."

She glowered. "I was drugged with influ-gas and given orders I couldn't resist."

"Are you sure it's out of your system?" he asked.

Her forehead crinkled. It was easy to read her concern, but Catherine ignored the question. "You kidnapped me. Tied me to a chair and seduced me, then spent the week doing more of the same."

"I detained you for murdering several people and trying to frame Red. Not to mention killing any Other you happened to find. As for the rest, I was distracting you from your mission." He smirked. "And doing a fine job of it. I think."

"Distracting me! Of all the arrogant, self-centered, egotistical things I have ever heard, that one takes the synth-tart." She scowled. "I didn't have control of my actions when I killed those people. Had I been in my right mind, I never would've tried to frame Gina Santiago. She's the commander's granddaughter. It would be career suicide."

"Can you prove it?" Raphael watched her closely. "I mean if you could, then I'm sure Commander Robert Santiago would be more than happy to listen."

Catherine huffed. "Did you not hear a word I said?"

"I heard you clearly. Now answer the question," he said.

Catherine's expression soured a second before her body sagged against the headboard. "No," she muttered, then her chin rose in defiance. "Can you prove that I did?"

Raphael shook his head. He was enjoying their bickering far too much. He kept his expression bland. "No, but that does put us in a similar bind, you and I."

She scowled. "How do you figure?"

"You claim that I kidnapped you. I don't see it that way," he said. "I was protecting the alpha and his mate. I know that you murdered those men. I saw it in your mind the second I tasted your tainted blood. Then there's the little fact that you tried to kill me."

"But—" she said.

He held up his hand. "I'm not finished," Raphael said. "You claim diminished capacity. Perhaps a few of the tribunal members will take pity on you and believe you, but I wouldn't count on it since the influ-gas isn't detectable in your system. The tribunal must uphold the law for the sake of the republics. Add in the fact that Gina Santiago is the IPTT commander's granddaughter and it doesn't look good for either of us."

She crossed her arms. "They won't believe a vamp," Catherine said confidently.

"Silly girl, vampires don't exist." Raphael grinned, flashing his fangs. "Do you really want to stand before a tribunal and blame an imaginary creature for all your woes? You'd have to reveal the little secret you've been keeping in order to prove it."

Catherine chewed on her bottom lip, drawing Raphael's eyes away from her troubled gaze. He'd kissed those lips, drank from the sweetness like a man lost in the desert.

Raphael had never thought anything could taste better than blood, but that changed the second he parted her thighs. And he'd do so again, despite her claims otherwise. She couldn't deny what had occurred between them, what was occurring between them right now. If the sexual tension in the room got much worse, they'd both combust.

"Would you out me?" Catherine's green eyes widened and she drew into herself.

"I wouldn't have to," he said. She'd do that herself by talking. She must've realized the same thing because her expression turned bleak.

"Can't we make a deal?" she asked after a moment of silence.

Raphael glanced at his hands and made a show of thinking about it. "Depends," he said. "What do you have in mind?"

"You let me go and I forget all about the whole kidnapping thing."

"That sounds reasonable, but do you think kidnapping—which you can't prove—is comparable to murder? Seems like I'm on the losing end of this deal." He stepped closer to the rest pad.

Catherine sighed loudly. "Shouldn't Roark Montgomery factor into all this? I mean, he's the one who gassed me with Scarlet and sent me on my murderous rampage. I wouldn't have done any of that without the influence of the mind control drug. And let's not forget, he imprisoned your friends. I'd say the blame rests firmly on his shoulders."

Rage boiled inside him. "Roark will be dealt with, but not until we can prove Red's and Morgan's innocence." His voice was cold enough to freeze the air around them. "Until then, it's just you left to hang in the desert wind for his deeds. Your only option is for us to work together."

"Terrific." She snarled. "What do you want me to do, since I obviously have no choice?" Catherine clasped the sheet tighter and scrambled to the edge of the rest pad.

"Everyone has a choice, including you," he said, tonguing the tip of his incisor. Raphael needed her help. Catherine could get into IPTT headquarters. She could meet with the commander and ask for his assistance, if need be.

"Not this time." She shivered under his regard.

Raphael assumed the action was based on fear, until he inhaled and the scent of ripe, moist woman surrounded him. He wanted to shout in triumph, but he didn't dare. Instead, Raphael swallowed hard and shoved his hands into his pockets to keep from reaching for her. "That is a matter of perception," he said.

"Are you going to tell me what you want me to do or do I have to guess?" she asked.

"So cute, but so short tempered," he said. "You must've been a handful for your parents."

For a second, Catherine looked pained. He wasn't sure what he'd said to upset her, but Raphael had no doubt he'd struck a chord. Her hurt expression vanished, quickly replaced with a dagger-shooting glare.

"I'm waiting." Her tiny foot tapped the floor.

"I'll tell you what I want. I want you to help me clear Red and Morgan's names and help me locate them." Raphael's gaze flicked to the thin material covering her. "But first, I want you to lose the sheet."

* * * * *

Raphael's smile turned feral. He flashed both fangs, then took a step forward. Chaos had no doubt he'd done it on purpose. The move should've repulsed her, but instead, it ignited her blood. She hadn't expected the quiver of anticipation to course through her body or the rush of renewed heat that moistened her core.

Damn him.

After she'd discovered that he'd locked her in the room, Chaos had promised herself she wouldn't sleep with him again—no matter how pleasurable she'd found it to be. And it had been pleasurable. She'd never experienced anything like their lovemaking. It took great sex to a level few could achieve.

Her anger was why she'd implied that he hadn't gotten her consent when he'd seduced her a week ago. But the truth was that she'd allowed the seduction to go ahead. Partly out of curiosity and partly out of need.

Raphael had intrigued Chaos from the beginning. When they'd met, she'd only given him a taste of what she could do. He still didn't understand how powerful she was. Had she wanted him to stop, Chaos would've simply used her powers to melt his brain.

Just because she'd decided not to kill him, didn't mean that she trusted him. Of course, there was no telling her body that. The demands it was making couldn't be ignored for long.

Chaos glanced down in time to see the sheet hit the floor. She glared at Raphael, but he hadn't moved. *She'd been the one to discard the material.*

His black eyes simmered with hunger, scorching her flesh wherever they roved. Her nipples hardened under his perusal, turning a bright rose.

Raphael grasped his shirt and pulled it over his head.

The man was magnificent, long and solid with dark, brooding looks that drew her. She'd never known anyone so comfortable in his sexuality. He had every right to feel so given his talent in the carnal arts.

Raphael had brought her to release three times with his mouth and tongue before he'd ever entered her. And from the look on his face, he planned to do it again and again, even though he had nothing to prove and everything to lose.

Chaos squeezed her thighs together and kept her expression blank. She didn't want him to know how much she wanted this. Wanted him. A girl could get addicted if she wasn't careful.

She'd entered Nuria with no clue that Others existed. Now Chaos was willingly giving herself to a vampire. She should be committed. Most people would be screaming right about now, but not her. No, she went looking for trouble and had found it—all six foot two of it.

He tongued his fangs sensually and she felt her neck and thigh tingle where he'd bitten her earlier. This was so wrong. Wanting him was wrong. The logical side of her knew that, but the tactile being didn't care. It wanted another taste of this man, this creature, who could infuriate her one minute and made her crave him the next.

What was the matter with her? She couldn't be thinking clearly.

Chaos needed some space. Yep, that would take care of everything. She opened her mouth to tell him no. In the same moment, Raphael dropped his pants, revealing his straining erection. Veins corded the thick length, leading up and up to a flushed crown. Her mouth went dry.

Nope, nothing to prove.

It would be easy to blame Raphael for the predicament Chaos found herself in, but he hadn't been there the day she went to Roark Montgomery's office with Lieutenant Bannon Richards. She'd gone on her own accord. Raphael also hadn't drugged her with influ-gas and programmed her to kill. That had been Roark, too. And he wasn't forcing her now to lie back on the rest pad and open her legs in preparation for him. Nope, she was doing that all on her own.

Raphael gave her a triumphant grin as he slid inside her. He'd won this round and he knew it.

* * * * *

CHAPTER SIX

The sun rose less than thirty minutes ago and already Michael could feel his brain baking inside his skull. Sizzle. Pop. He didn't know how far he'd walked since crossing the boundary fence. Probably not far. Too bad his body didn't agree. It felt weighted, sucked down by the sand pooling around his feet. For all his strength, there was an underlying frailty. Even without the chip in his frontal lobe to remind him.

He gazed out at the barren abyss. Miles and miles of sand and not a drop to drink. It stretched as far as the eye could see. He glanced down. Footprints were impossible to follow. The sand swallowed them up, always greedy for more.

Michael inhaled. Hot air singed his nostrils, burning his sinuses. Red and Morgan's wolf scent remained elusive. Like the sand and the sun, the air's aroma toyed with him, whispering promises it had no intention to keep.

A shadow slipped past Michael in his peripheral vision. He turned, but there was nothing there beyond vast emptiness. There was never anything there, yet Michael continued to see them. The shadows followed him, waiting like vultures for him to drop so they could pounce and pick his bones clean.

Once again Michael wondered if he should make it easy on them. The vampire inside of him roared in defiance.

"Stay the fuck away from me." He swung his fist wildly, connecting with nothing but hot air.

Michael refused to sit down. That's what the shadows wanted. He'd be damned if he would give in. His gaze locked on the horizon. Waves of heat rode the dunes, surfing them into oblivion. He focused on putting one foot in front of the other.

"Where are you?" he shouted.

He'd put out the bounty just like Roark had asked. Michael hadn't wanted to do it, but he'd had no choice. Roark would've found out had he not and he would've pressed the button. Couldn't afford for him to press the button again. The button was bad. Bad button. Made Michael hurt.

He needed to get the chip out. That was the only way to prevent the pain and madness from taking over. He could feel the chip digging in, anchoring itself somehow. Michael clawed at his skin until blood ran down his face, blinding him. It was no use. The bone wouldn't give. The only way he'd succeed was if he found Morgan and Red first. Then, and only then, would Roark remove the blasted chip.

Michael stumbled and dropped to his knees. For a second his hands looked as if they'd been dipped into a scarlet puddle. *Splashy. Splashy. Licky. Licky.* He blinked, clearing the mirage. All that remained was dried blood.

Fighting the urge to shove his fingers in his mouth and suckle, Michael forced himself to stand. He needed to find shelter before the sun evaporated the last of his sanity. His clothes wouldn't protect him during the worst heat of the day, not with his telekinetic power drained.

Scanning the area, Michael spotted a dark mass in the distance. He couldn't tell what it was from here, but anything beat the endless sand.

Forging on, Michael climbed dune after dune until he lost count. The dark form was beginning to take shape now. At least he hoped it was. He couldn't afford for his shelter to be a figment of his imagination.

The sand continued to talk to him. It beaconed him to rest, like a siren luring weary sailors to their death. Michael plugged his ears and screamed to drown out its insidious voice.

Not much farther now.

He was almost there.

Michael could see the rock up ahead, its corpulent noggin

protruding from the sand in defiance. A giggle burst from his parched throat, morphing into a hacking cough. He threw himself against the rock grateful for the tiniest increment of shade. Michael patted the giant mammoth and crooned to it, stroking its hard surface.

So pretty and welcoming, almost like it had been left here for him.

He plopped down, putting his back against the rock face and dug into his pack for the canteen. The water did little to quench his thirst. Only fresh blood could do that now. Michael decided to wait here and rest until evening came. The dark would make traveling much easier. His only hope was that Morgan and Red would do the same. It was the only way he'd eventually catch up to them.

* * * * *

CHAPTER SEVEN

"I'm going to take you back to International Police Tactical Team headquarters today." Raphael buttoned his shirt, then fastened his pants.

Chaos put aside her breakfast and looked at him unsure she'd heard him correctly. "Why?" Suspicion clung to the word. There had to be a reason for his sudden change of heart.

"It's what you wanted. Or have you changed your mind?" Irritation grated his voice as he yanked his dark hair back into a tight, painful-looking queue.

She shook her head. "No, I haven't changed my mind. I need to get back to IPTT before they send a team after me. I'm just curious, what changed *your* mind?"

Raphael's jaw clenched. "Just be happy I did. Do I need to remind you about our agreement?"

Ah, so that's why he was letting her go. Chaos' heart sank. She'd hoped it was because he was developing feelings for her, not because she'd agreed to help him. Chaos had even convinced herself that she'd seen more than passion burning in his dark eyes on a couple of occasions. She should've known better.

You tried to frame his friend for murder and would've killed her given half the chance. Did you really think that he could care for you after that? Your own parents didn't want you. Why would he?

Chaos looked away when her eyes burned. She wouldn't turn

47

him in for kidnapping no matter how tempting the thought. She'd go back to IPTT headquarters and do damage control. While she was there, she'd check on Bannon Richards. He'd been with her when Roark Montgomery gassed them. Perhaps he was suffering the ill effects of the influ-gas, too.

She had gone with Raphael and the Nurian Tactical Team to help break Gina Santiago and Morgan Hunter out of Roark's secret cell below his office. Not that Chaos had had much choice at the time. Raphael had made it abundantly clear she had to go. Partly so he could keep an eye on her and partly to pay for the lives she'd taken while under the gas's influence.

Chaos hadn't seen the filth, but she'd heard the cell described by the other men. She shuddered at the thought of being locked away without a fair tribunal hearing. She'd watched the history vids. It had taken place in the past, but Chaos had thought that the dead world had moved beyond that stage in its evolution.

"Are you going to get dressed or am I going to have to dress you?" Raphael asked. The bite in his tone caught her off guard.

What was he mad about? Chaos had given him her word last night that she wouldn't have him arrested.

"I can do it myself," she said. "Just give me time to use the cleansing unit."

"Don't take too long or you may find yourself walking. I've asked Jim Thornton to take you and I'm not sure how long he'll wait."

Chaos stopped halfway to the cleansing unit door. She'd thought when he'd said he was letting her go that Raphael meant he'd be taking her back. "You're not coming," she said, confused and more than a little disappointed.

Disappointed? She should be happy. She'd be out of here soon. Isn't that what she wanted all along?

Raphael's harsh expression softened a fraction. "I have to go find my brother. He works for Roark and I haven't been able to contact him."

She bit her lip. "Do you think what Morgan and Red said about the A.I. chip was true?"

"I don't know and I won't know until I talk to him. Their word combined with your experience with the influ-gas has given me many reasons to be concerned."

Chaos ached for him, but she wasn't about to let Raphael know. She didn't think he'd believe her after everything they'd been through. She walked into the cleansing unit. For over a week, all Chaos had wanted was to see the backside of him, but now that the time had come to leave, she didn't want to go.

Maybe she'd developed Stockholm syndrome. Could great sex cause that?

She didn't really have a point of reference. She'd had decent sex in the past, but nothing like what she'd experienced with Raphael. Chaos wasn't sure what she was more surprised about, the sex or the fact that she'd stumbled upon a town full of Others.

She'd never met anyone like herself. Not that she was like Raphael or the men and women she'd encountered here. Her ability to disorient and disrupt human thought was rare even for this town. She wasn't an Other—at least she didn't think she was. There was no way to know for sure.

But Chaos definitely understood the need for discretion. She had spent her entire adult life hiding her powers and running from a past that she neither understood nor cared to explore.

She showered quickly and got dressed. Chaos didn't think Raphael would change his mind about releasing her, but she didn't want to take the chance that he might. When she opened the door he was gone. Her belongings had been placed on a chair in the corner. The same one he'd tied her to right before bringing her pleasure that she'd never known existed.

Chaos could still smell sex and his manly scent wafting in the air, but the musk was fading quickly. She inhaled, trying to store the memory.

You're pathetic.

She shook her head in disgust, angry she was even thinking about what they'd shared. There was something seriously wrong with her if she believed there was more to their romp than manipulation.

"He's moved on already. Deal with it," she muttered under her breath.

The door to the room was no longer locked. Chaos opened it and poked her head out to look around. The yellow hall with flowers painted on the walls was empty. The ache inside her grew.

She stepped out and shut the door behind her. All the other

doors remained closed as she picked her way down the hall, her footfalls silent on the fur-covered floor.

Raphael waited at the water trader bar with a portly redheaded man whose thick glasses made his brown eyes look enormous. He motioned for her to come over when her foot hit the bottom step.

"Catherine, this is Jim Thornton. He's the director of the local dissecting lab," Raphael said. He sounded so normal. Nothing like the man who'd had her stripped bare an hour ago and crying out for release.

"Nice to meet you." Chaos forced a smile.

Raphael placed his hand on the man's shoulder and squeezed. "Jim is going to take you back to IPTT."

Jim eyes widened and his gaze shot to Raphael, who casually released him. His attention turned back to her and he smiled broadly. "It'll be my pleasure, my dear."

"Thanks." Chaos opened her mouth to ask Raphael if she could have a word with him, but he beat her to the punch.

"I'd better get going," he said. "Like you, I have a long ride ahead of me." Raphael barely glanced at her before he strode toward the door.

Chaos stared at Raphael's retreating form. He put his sunshades on at the door and slipped out into the early morning light. She waited to see if he'd look back. Just one glance to confirm that last night—and all the other nights that came before it—weren't just another blip on his sexual radar, but he didn't. The rejection sliced her deep, but she refused to reveal her pain.

Instead, she turned back to the man who was going to give her a ride. "I hope I didn't keep you waiting long," she said.

Sympathy filled his gaze as Jim adjusted the thick glasses perched on his nose. "Not at all. I like to start my patrols early. Got to get to the bodies while they're still fresh and recyclable."

Chaos inwardly grimaced, then gave the water trader one more look around before heading out the door. There was a very good chance she wouldn't be back. Nuria held too many memories. Many of which she'd rather forget.

* * * * *

Raphael stayed in the shadows and watched Catherine and Jim

climb into the hydrogen car. Her head was down and she looked determined, if not a little lost. Other than a few covert glances out the window, Catherine showed no emotion whatsoever.

What did you expect? You've been holding her against her will. Not exactly the way to a woman's heart.

His body shook as Raphael forced himself to remain rooted where he stood. Every fiber of his being wanted to go after her. Stop her. Keep her.

The last thought brought Raphael up short. He didn't *keep* women. He bedded them and then he moved on. If they were donors, then he'd visit them a few times, but he always broke it off before an emotional attachment could form. It had been easy. An ingrained habit that was second nature...that was until Catherine came along.

The closest he'd come to breaking his self-imposed rule was with Red, but Raphael realized that what he'd felt for Red was nothing compared to the riot of emotions raging through him now. And it was all due to a short, voluptuous redhead who'd tried to kill him. Life did have its surprises.

Raphael could still taste her essence on his tongue, feel the squeeze of her body as she gripped him, milking him until he'd collapsed on top of her. He'd loved every inch of her compact frame, but her mind truly fascinated him. Raphael had never encountered anyone who could do the things she could.

Michael's powers were the closest, but even he couldn't cause the confusion and memory loss Catherine was capable of. Raphael was going to miss his little Chaos. The question was, now that he'd finally released her, would she ever return?

The thought of never seeing her or touching her again made him edgy. If Catherine didn't come back, would he be man enough to accept her wishes and walk away?

* * * * *

CHAPTER EIGHT

Chaos waved good-bye to Jim Thornton as he drove off. He'd left her at the entrance to the International Police Tactical Team Headquarters, a pyramid-shaped structure built to withstand bomb blasts. Jim was a pleasant enough man, if you could get past the hours of dissection lab shoptalk. At least she'd been able to tune him out long enough to formulate a plan.

She'd made up her mind to keep her word, even though Raphael had coerced her into doing so. She would help him find proof that Red and Morgan were innocent, if proof existed. He may not believe in keeping his word, but she did.

Chaos had been betrayed many times throughout her short life by people who promised one thing and delivered another that she never gave her word lightly. She also wasn't stupid enough to believe that everyone else in the world felt the same.

If Raphael decided to go back on his word and turn her in for her crimes, Chaos hoped by then she would have a get-out-of-trouble-free card she could play. She prayed it didn't come to that, since it would mean choosing between her freedom and her job.

Chaos cursed the sexy vampire under her breath. It was his fault she was in this mess. It was easier to put the blame on him than to look too deeply in the mirror at the real culprit.

Somehow she had to garner the commander's cooperation without exposing her secrets. Chaos didn't want to lose her job. It was all she had, but there was no way the commander could let her keep it if the truth about her nocturnal activities in the town of Nuria came out. Even he couldn't look the other way when it came to murder.

She could only think of one way to do that. Chaos had to convince the commander that she believed in Gina Santiago's innocence. She didn't, not entirely. The evidence of her guilt was overwhelming. They had her on video visiting Morgan at the Taos Detention Center minutes before he broke out.

But she supposed it wasn't out of the realm of possibility that Red had been framed given what Roark had done to her in one office visit. Ultimately, it didn't matter what Chaos believed. All that mattered was that the commander be convinced of her sincerity by the time she left his office. That way she'd cover her butt and keep her word to Raphael.

Chaos rolled her shoulders and groaned at the stiffness, then glanced at her watch. She had time to go back to the dorm and grab some shut-eye before heading to the commander's office. Chaos wanted to be sharp when she presented her highly unethical and slightly illegal proposition to Red's grandfather.

If all went well, she would secure her job, garner her get-out-of-trouble-free card, and not have to worry about the deaths in Nuria coming back to bite her. The last thought caused a tingle in her neck that was answered by one on her thigh.

For a moment, Chaos could swear she felt Raphael's lips glide over her taut skin. The sensation made her body flood with heat. She shivered and touched the side of her neck.

"Get your head in the game," she muttered under her breath. "Stop mooning over the vampire. He doesn't give dung about you. He just wanted to get his way. Now pull it together and look out for yourself."

A few hours later, Chaos walked into the main building of headquarters. Sunshine filtered through the sloped windows as she approached the security checkpoint. She was quickly scanned for contaminants and explosives, then ushered forward.

She'd managed to get a few hours of sleep, so her head wasn't quite so fuzzy. She was as prepared to talk to the commander as she'd ever be. Chaos walked deeper into the building and noticed Bannon Richards sitting at his metal desk. His shoulders were hunched and he appeared to be writing reports.

He glanced at her, then looked back at the compunit screen as if she hadn't been missing for a week. Strange. Chaos diverted from her course and stopped in front of his desk.

Bannon didn't immediately acknowledge her. He kept his blond head down, focused on his work.

Chaos cleared her throat.

"It's about time you graced us with your presence." Bannon glanced at her. "I thought I was going to have to report you for being AWOL."

She bristled. "I've been on the job for the past week. You were there. You know that."

He snorted. "Yeah, sure you have. It's protocol for team members to put in their time without checking in regularly."

"Roark ordered me to seek out enemies, while you were strong-arming Gina Santiago. You didn't notice because you were too busy getting your rocks off."

His blue gaze darkened. "Watch your tone, Private, or you may just find your bags packed with a one-way ticket home."

She flinched at the threat. Chaos had no place to go. Her parents had dumped her on the steps of a cloning lab as an infant. She had no family to speak of. No home. No one. Raphael's handsome face flashed in her mind.

Chaos pushed it aside and checked her temper, before trying to speak again. "I'm not here to fight. I stopped by to ask how you're feeling."

"What are you talking about?" Bannon's face flushed. His eyes dropped away for a second, unable to meet her gaze. "I'm fine. Why are you so concerned all of a sudden?"

Chaos studied his expression. He didn't seem fine, if the sudden tremor in his hand was any indication. And why was he getting so defensive? She'd asked a simple question. Maybe like her, Bannon had experienced bouts of missing time. If she'd been sent to kill strangers, what had Roark ordered him to do?

Unease set in. Bannon was constantly around headquarters and the commander. He had unfettered access to everyone and everything. Chaos opened her mouth to ask him about missing time, but closed it as his expression turned murderous. Screw him. She didn't have time to worry about Bannon. He could take care of himself.

"Just curious," she said instead. "Thought I'd come down with a bug after leaving Roark Montgomery's office. The illness left me a little confused. But if you're fine, I guess I caught it somewhere else. Probably just something going around."

For a second, fear flashed in Bannon's ice-blue eyes, but he quickly extinguished it. He leaned back, angling his body away from her. "If you're sick, don't give it to me." He covered his nose and mouth with a beefy hand.

Chaos leaned over his desk and coughed. "I wouldn't dream of it," she said, then strolled away as he muttered something under his breath about crazy rookies.

She continued on until she reached Commander Robert Santiago's office. Chaos pressed her eye against the optical scanner and waited. A moment passed, then the wooden door slid open.

"What can I do for you, Private?" he asked.

She started to answer, but stopped short when she took in his appearance. His white hair was disheveled as if he'd been running his hands through it repeatedly. His normally sharp eyes were bloodshot and his chin held growth that hadn't seen a razor in at least a couple of days.

"Sir?"

"Are you going to stand in the doorway or are you going to come inside?" he asked, his impatience clear.

Chaos stepped into the room and waited for the door to close behind her. She'd only been in the commander's office once before and not much had changed. It was still filled with creepy holograms of dead species and musty old books—made out of paper of all things. The odor of the books alone would suffocate her if she had to stay in here all day.

"I won't keep you long, sir." She tried to avoid looking at the holographic animals. Their hungry eyes followed her no matter where she stood in the room.

"Are you here to give me your report on Nuria?" He looked up from the synth-documents in front of him.

"No, sir. There's nothing to report," she said unable to meet his all too knowing gaze.

"You've been gone over a week, Private. What have you been doing all this time?" Robert Santiago asked.

Chaos blushed to the roots of her red hair as she pictured Raphael and all the carnal things they'd done. There was no way she'd discuss that with the commander. "I've been searching the Nurian water trader depot and the town, sir." It was almost the truth. She had searched Raphael's room, when he'd stepped out to get her food. "I have reason to believe that Gina Santiago is innocent."

"What brought you to that conclusion?" he asked calmly, but his gaze had sharpened.

"New evidence has come to light, sir. Evidence I want to keep to myself until I've verified it. In the meantime, I'm here to make you an offer."

His white brows shot up. "Exactly what kind of proposal do you have in mind?" The commander sat back in his chair and placed his hands casually over his firm abdomen, but his expression remained leery.

"I'd like permission to seek more proof of her innocence and retrieve her for you," Chaos added quickly, expecting him to toss her out of his office and off the tactical team at any moment.

His red eyes narrowed. "Why would you want to do such a thing? What's in it for you?" He watched her closely. "Are you looking for a promotion in rank? Or are you after something else?"

Chaos shook her head. "Not rank, sir. I know it has to be earned. No one on the team will respect you if you're bumped without putting in your time."

She thought carefully about what to say next. Chaos did not want to upset him before he agreed to her terms. She didn't know if it would be enough to keep her job in the end, but it was a better chance than she had at present if the truth came to light.

"I'd appreciate it if you'd consider giving me a get-out-of-trouble-free IOU for future use if I succeed," she said.

His heavy brow thickened like fat thunderclouds above his dark eyes. "An IOU seems like an odd request. What have you done that would require such a thing?" he asked, instantly seeing through her ruse.

"Nothing," she said in haste.

Calm down. He doesn't know anything. He's just guessing.

Chaos twisted her fingers. "I am hoping I never have to use the IOU, sir, but I'd like it all the same. Just in case."

His gaze assessed her. "Why should I trust you?" he asked. "For all I know you're working with Roark."

Chaos' chin shot up and a flash of anger warmed her cheeks. "That will never happen," she grit out between clenched teeth. Again was left unsaid.

"What's really going on here, Private?" he asked.

What could she say to him? She'd been drugged and used as a weapon to frame his granddaughter, then forced to break Red out of Roark's prison? Yeah, that would go over really well. She could see it now: *Commander Santiago, I broke one law to cover up my other crimes.*

Chaos snorted and quickly covered it with a cough. She wouldn't believe that story if she were in the commander's position. And if by chance he did believe her, Robert Santiago would arrest her on the spot.

The only way out of this was to prove to the commander that she was innocent. Unfortunately for her, Roark was smart and had left no evidence behind.

Raphael was adamant that influ-gas was undetectable in her bloodstream. There was no reason for him to lie. It would end up being her word against Roark Montgomery's and Chaos had no doubt who would come out on top if she sought legal action. She sighed, knowing she'd have to stick with lies and half-truths.

"Given Gina Santiago's record with IPTT and the fact she was the highest-ranked female officer, her behavior seems uncharacteristic. It casts a negative light on the remaining female tactical team members," she said.

There were still a lot of people in the world who believed the tactical team should consist solely of men. The commander was well aware of that, too. It had to have crossed his mind. And if it hadn't, it wouldn't hurt to remind him.

"While I was in Nuria, I could find no evidence that she'd planned to break Morgan Hunter out of prison. If she's not guilty of that transgression, then perhaps she's not guilty of any of the other charges. I'd like the chance to find out the truth. If I'm successful, then Gina's name would be cleared and the future of female IPTT officers would be secured."

If there was a Hell, she'd be going there for sure with that whopper.

He considered her for several beats. Chaos toed at the floor with her boot. What if he turned her down? What would she do then? Would she still go after Red or would she stay in the barracks and pray that Raphael kept his word and no one found out the truth?

"I can respect your need to protect your job, since I know Lieutenant Santiago would do the same. You know I can't sanction your actions, if you choose to investigate and try to locate my— Lieutenant Santiago. You'd have to do it on your own time," he said. "The International Police Tactical Team is under strict orders to apprehend on sight."

"I understand, sir." Chaos nodded. "With your permission, I'd like to take a personal leave. I promise to keep a low profile."

"How low?" he asked.

"Low enough that only you and I would know what I was up to," she said.

Robert Santiago steepled his fingers under his chin and rocked back in the chair. "If I find out that you're trying to set me up so Roark Montgomery can come in and take over IPTT, you'll be sorry. Getting rid of all female officers would be his first order of business. He'd follow it by getting rid of loose ends."

Chaos' mood blackened. She could feel the power inside of her rising. She tamped it down. The last thing she needed was for the commander to forget why she was here. *Breathe, he's agreeing to your plan.* All she needed to do was stay calm a little longer.

"As I said before, there's absolutely no chance of that happening, sir."

The commander must have seen something he liked in her expression because he nodded and a smile hovered over his thin lips. "Where do you plan to start?"

Chaos hadn't thought that far ahead. Gina and Morgan weren't in Nuria. They'd talked about hiding out at Kane Hunter's home and possibly no-man's-land, but Chaos didn't know where they'd ended up going. They may have said that just to throw everyone off their scent. She would've in their position.

She considered contacting Raphael, strictly for information— not because she wanted to hear his voice. But Chaos doubted he'd willingly share that kind of information with her. He may have fucked her, but he damn sure didn't trust her. Raphael would've never *made* her agree to help him absolve Red and Morgan otherwise.

Robert Santiago must have correctly read her panicked expression because he tapped his cheek and said, "I don't know about you, but I've heard a rumor that Roark and Gina may have been traveling north in a shuttle when Sheriff Hunter attacked them and helped her escape. Shuttles aren't small and they're difficult to hide. I wonder how hard it would be to find that vehicle outside of the Republic of Missouri…"

Chaos cleared her throat. "I'll let you know," she said, then pivoted on her heel and strode out the door.

* * * * *

It was going better than I'd expected. I watched as tactical team members brushed by me on their way home or off to patrol. Once again the urge to go with them swept over me.

Gina Santiago was out there somewhere, hiding, mocking IPTT.

Several officers gathered in the entryway near the mammoth fountain. They stood next to the sloped walls that glittered in the sunlight like lethal incisors. The team checked their weapons and verified their patrol routes, then marched in unison out of headquarters. Their black boots echoed under the pyramidal-shaped roof. Each thump sounded in my chest and I found myself picking up the pace. I had to force my feet to slow before anyone noticed. No need to hurry. The commander still didn't suspect a thing.

I slowly made my way to my workspace, winding through a maze of steel desks. Some were still occupied, while others now stood empty. The air held a hint of vanilla. The aroma should've soothed my nerves, but it didn't. Nothing would until I got out of here.

"Be patient. Everything is going according to plan," I whispered under my breath.

I needed to log in to my compunit. Make sure I hadn't received any new intel. The chances were slim, but still possible. A few heads turned as I neared. The officers seemed surprised to see me. I ignored the curious stares from the worker drones and sat down.

A quick press of the screen showed that the files in my compunit were empty. I tried not to let my disappointment show, but a curse slipped past my lips before I could stop it. A couple of officers at nearby desks glanced at me, then quickly went back to work.

They didn't understand. How could they? No one had ever tasked them with something as important as saving the reputation of the International Police Tactical Team. I knew what my duty was and was proud to be tapped for such a job. Not everyone was trusted with this kind of sensitive information.

My chest puffed out. I wouldn't let the team down. I'd find Gina Santiago and silence her once and for all.

* * * * *

CHAPTER NINE

Raphael stood outside of the Republic of Missouri biodome and attempted to hail Michael via their mental link. Static filled his mind. He couldn't tell if the crackles and pops were interference or the sound of Michael's thoughts. The latter brought a shiver to his spine. No one was powerful enough to control his brother—not even with an A.I. chip implanted in his brain. His powers were god-like.

Morgan and Red had to be wrong. They'd only seen Michael for a few minutes. Not nearly enough time to assess his condition.

Raphael climbed back into his maglev shuttle. The sun was beating down on him, but the military-grade sunscreen kept his sensitive skin protected. He wouldn't burn, but it didn't stop the pain. Of course he'd take the pain over the other option any day. Most vampires exploded when exposed to sunlight. He and Michael were different. Had always been different. He glanced at the sun and winced as its harsh rays did their best to fry him. He couldn't stay out here any longer.

He'd wanted to avoid entering the biodome city, but with Michael not answering Raphael didn't have a choice. The soft blue dome glowed as he approached the gates. He wondered not for the first time if Catherine or Roark had bulletins out for his arrest. Raphael took a deep breath and released it slowly, knowing he'd find out soon enough.

The clean-cut guard at the gate perked up as Raphael's shuttle approached. He pressed a button so the maglev vehicle would hover in place.

"I.D. please," The guard wore a bored expression, as if he could barely be bothered to do his job.

Raphael wasn't fooled. Even now the man was taking in details about his appearance just in case his chip and I.D. came back stolen or invalid. He handed over the paperwork and exposed his neck. It took a minute for his Republic of Arizona chip to register. By the time the light turned green and the guard waved him through the gates, Raphael was sweating.

That was twice he'd been caught perspiring. First with Catherine and now here. He'd have to check himself into the emergency care center if it didn't stop. Vamps shouldn't sweat, especially ones as old as him.

Raphael drove past the green manicured parks and rising skyscrapers straight to Michael's home. He couldn't afford to stop by his brother's office. Couldn't take a chance that Roark Montgomery might see him. Raphael wasn't sure if the politician could identify his face as being one of the men who'd come to break Red and Morgan out of his prison, but he had no doubt he'd recognize him as Michael's brother. Raphael would just have to try to contact Michael via comlink if he wasn't home.

Michael's home was a modest two room unit—inside a multistory steel and concrete building—that had a private cleansing room attached for convenience and comfort. The amenities were rare given the communal bathing facilities located throughout the city.

He used the code his brother had given him after their reunion a couple of months ago. Though the term reunion hardly described their encounter. His brother had been about to assassinate Morgan Hunter when Raphael came upon him in the desert.

Until that point, Raphael had thought Michael was dead, along with the rest of their family. It had been a happy moment and one of utter disbelief. So much pain endured and years lost, but that was over now. They'd found each other once again and Raphael wasn't about to let anything or anyone tear them apart.

The lights were off when he entered Michael's living quarters. Normally obsessively neat, his home lay in utter disarray. Had someone ransacked the place?

Clothes and rest pad linens lay strewn across the floor. Empty blood bags had been tossed haphazardly next to toppled furniture. If anyone had been foolish enough to rob Michael, then the thief was probably buried out in the desert by now. His brother had little patience for thieves or anyone else for that matter.

Raphael looked around, but didn't immediately see any broken items. He inhaled, but didn't scent any blood other than what was in the empty bags. The scene didn't make sense unless...his brother was behind the destruction.

What could've occurred to make Michael do this to his home? Why hadn't he contacted him if he was in trouble?

Raphael had done everything in his power to find Michael after the impromptu prison break, but had been unable to locate him. He realized now he should've tried harder.

Morgan had said that he'd heard screams when Roark chained him to the wall. He'd also told Raphael that Michael seemed *different*. He walked over to the storage bins under Michael's mini-water dispenser where he kept his "equipment bag" as he called it. The assassination kit contained a laser rifle, a knife, and at least one pistol. He opened the bin. The bag was gone.

There was no need to call Roark's office now. Michael wasn't there, but Raphael had a pretty good idea where he'd find him. Why would he go through the trouble of saving Red and Morgan only to hunt them down later? Something was wrong. Very, very wrong.

Raphael pictured Morgan and Red running for their lives. There would be nowhere safe they could hide. Not with his brother on their trail. Michael was an efficient hunter, and an even deadlier assassin. The old military had trained them well, but Raphael's skill was nowhere near his brother's level.

Working for a man like Roark had only honed Michael's awesome skills. Couple that with his telekinetic abilities and he was unstoppable. But Raphael had to try.

Panic and fear gave his gut a one-two punch, leaving him breathless. After everything they'd been through and all the time they'd lost, only one question remained.

Why?

* * * * *

It took the whole afternoon, but Chaos finally located the maglev shuttle wreckage. Someone had gone to a lot of trouble to keep it out of sight. Whether it was Roark, Red, or Morgan she didn't know. The craft was half buried in the sand and from a distance resembled a boulder. No wonder IPTT hadn't been able to find it. It was like looking for a penny in the sand.

Chaos approached the shuttle with her weapon drawn. A hole the size of two laser cannon blasts gaped obscenely at the desert sky, its metal teeth frozen in a perpetual roar. The twisted metal radiated heat, but there was no sign any of the electronics were working. Chaos ducked inside with her pistol raised, but the shuttle was empty. She holstered her weapon and pulled out a solar light, then slowly searched.

At first glance, the only damage appeared to be the hole in the side of the shuttle, but upon closer inspection Chaos found that the navigation system had been carefully removed, not yanked out like she would've expected if someone were trying to disable the vehicle. The instrument panel and tracker cell were also missing, almost like the parts had been harvested to sell. But that didn't mesh with the facts that had been presented.

Why would someone take the time to do that, when the whole point of the attack was to escape or at least make it look like Red had escaped? Did they need credits? Who would they take the parts to if they did? It wasn't like Red or Morgan traded in this area. It didn't make sense.

She pushed charred pieces aside with the toe of her boot. They crumbled under the pressure. After several minutes of futility, Chaos was convinced she was on the wrong track. No one had left any clues behind, only an empty shell filled with more questions.

She was about to leave when an exposed wire caught her attention. Chaos brushed the debris aside and found the remains of a navcom buried beneath. It was an old model and severely damaged, but definitely IPTT issue.

Chaos carefully picked up the pieces and placed them into a preprogrammed courier pouch. She punched her I.D. number into the side of the pouch and addressed it to Commander Robert Santiago. The courier would fly directly to IPTT. He'd have to put in his I.D. number and thumbprint to get it to open, which would keep it from falling into the wrong hands once it arrived at headquarters.

The pouch also generated its own electromagnetic field to prevent it from being shot down outside of IPTT. Every security measure had a countersecurity measure to ensure the contents' safety.

Chaos stepped outside of the shuttle. It was only then that she noticed the sun was setting. She shook the contents of the pouch to make sure it was secure. The bag was silent. It may not be anything, but it was all she'd been able to recover. Chaos set the courier pouch on the ground and pressed a button on its side.

The pouch took off like a guided missile, which was apt, since that's where the technology originated. She watched the pouch rocket through the air, leaving a fiery contrail behind. When it was out of sight, she turned back to the shuttle to reexamine the hole.

What had Morgan used to make it, since a laser cannon was far from portable? He'd been on the run, so he'd had to travel light, but there wasn't anything out there to her knowledge besides the cannon that could do this kind of damage. Was that when Roark had captured him or had he already been imprisoned? She should've asked when she helped Raphael break them out.

Chaos ran her finger over the edge of the opening. It wasn't sharp. It had been fused, which meant heat. Roark should've had this hauled in as evidence when he reported the incident. It would've backed up his story and been damning to IPTT. *Unless he didn't want it to be found.* It was one thing to show a vid of the damage. It was quite another to produce examinable proof. Nothing would surprise her at this point.

"What are you really up to?" she said aloud.

She used her solar light to disperse the growing shadows, so she could continue to examine the blast pattern. There was no way Morgan could've done this on his own and Red wasn't known for her demolition skills.

Besides, now that she'd reexamined the hole it was clear from the edges that the blast had come from the *inside*. No wonder Roark hadn't wanted the vehicle to be found. The portable equipment IPTT held in its vault wasn't capable of this kind of damage. The only thing that could've made a hole this size was a blast cannon and they weighed two hundred pounds. She doubted very much that Roark had allowed Red to carry one with her.

Chaos looked around, but didn't immediately spot anything that could hide a weapon of that size, which meant whoever brought it had taken it away. Perhaps what she'd told the commander had been right all along. The facts weren't adding up. Maybe Red *was* innocent after all.

She stilled. If Roark was willing to drug her, a total stranger, how far would he go to get someone he knew? Someone like Red or Morgan?

Chaos shivered as the answer stared her in the face in the form of a manufactured hole. She punched the shuttle coordinates into her navcom and sent them to the commander. He could decide how to proceed.

What did Morgan and Red have on Roark that made him so desperate to silence them? Chaos wished she knew. It would go a long way to solving this mystery. Despite her assurance that she'd find Red, Chaos wasn't entirely convinced she could do it.

What if Roark found her first? It didn't bear thinking about. Chaos couldn't let him. He'd already gotten a hold of Red once. She wouldn't survive a second time. Finding Gina Santiago was her only guarantee that she'd keep her job and avoid arrest. She had to find her before anyone else did. For that, she'd travel to hell and back to get her.

Chaos bent over to examine the entry one more time and a warm breeze washed over her, raising the fine hairs on her arms. Her hand automatically moved to her weapon. There was no sound, no scent, nothing to alarm her, but she knew she wasn't alone. Worse yet, Chaos had no doubt who was with her.

She scanned the area around her. Chaos couldn't see Raphael, but she felt him like a caress of fingertips across her bare skin. She looked again. Nothing stood out. The desert remained quiet. Abnormally so. Like it knew a predator hunted in the area. She wasn't sure how Raphael had found her. Chaos was positive he hadn't followed them to IPTT. The motion sensors and radar at headquarters would've detected a shuttle stationed nearby.

The sensation of being watched intensified and she unconsciously touched the spot on her neck where Raphael had bitten her. Despite her resolve to forget about him and the whole incident in Nuria, her body remembered with a vengeance. Even now Chaos could feel an ache building inside her, where moments ago there'd been none. She growled in frustration and glared at the growing darkness.

"Come out where I can see you," she said. "There's no point in hiding. I know you're there."

The shadows shifted and suddenly Chaos found herself staring at her seductive kidnapper. His dark hair lifted from his broad shoulders as a warm breeze caught it. His black eyes were flat until they landed upon her, then they took on a predatory glow that she felt all the way to her...soul.

"As you wish." Raphael's gaze scrolled over her.

Her breath caught. "I don't appreciate being followed," Chaos said. Ire and desire mixed to form a volatile cocktail inside of her.

"Hmm, I was thinking the same thing. If you wanted to see me again all you had to do was comlink me," he said smoothly.

Her eyes widened. He had not just accused her of chasing him like some lovesick moppet. She did not chase men and she especially wouldn't chase him. Chaos hadn't even known he was there until a minute ago.

"Your ego is astounding." She huffed. "I'm amazed there is room to stand next to you."

"It's funny, I don't recall you complaining about the size of my...*ego* this morning or the night before or the night before that and the night before that—"

"Enough! I get it." Chaos felt a flush of heat fill her face. "We're not discussing that anymore."

"If you don't want to talk about our..."

"Raphael," she growled his name in warning.

"Nocturnal activities," he continued, "then perhaps you'll tell me what you're doing here out in the middle of nowhere. Anyone could've come upon you. You left yourself vulnerable." There was accusation in his voice, along with something she couldn't identify.

Why was he angry? It wasn't like she'd snuck up on him. "I'm armed," she said, tapping her laser pistol.

Raphael moved with blinding speed, quickly disarming her. "Weapons are of little use, if you're caught unaware." He handed her pistol back to her. "Now I'll ask you again, what are you doing here? What were you looking for?"

Chaos tensed. She didn't want to discuss why she was here. She'd given him her word that she'd help. That should be enough. As for her other reasons for being here, those were none of his business. Chaos didn't want him to know she was trying to work around their agreement by bringing in the commander from the start. She wasn't sure how Raphael would respond to the news. "I'm on patrol."

He looked at her clothes. "You aren't dressed for patrol."

"How would you know?" she asked.

"Do not play me for a fool, my little storm." He stepped closer, crowding her, and inhaled. "I can smell the truth—and the lies before they leave your succulent mouth. If you like, I can steal them off your lips with a kiss."

She saw his eyes close and his face relax. Almost as if being near her calmed him, which was ridiculous, since they'd only met a week ago and not under the best of circumstances. She smiled as she recalled their hand-to-hand combat. It had been fun, albeit dangerous. Raphael could've easily hurt her, but he hadn't.

The battle had ended in a bite. Chaos had never been so surprised in her life. Despite the savagery, there'd been something overwhelmingly erotic about the moment. Not that she'd ever tell him. She looked up and realized his eyes were open. Raphael was watching her, a smile playing on his sinful mouth.

Chaos broke eye contact first, then cleared her throat. "A kiss won't be necessary." She was not disappointed. She glanced at his mouth, taking in his savage lips. Nope, not disappointed at all.

She'd have to tell him the truth or at least some version of it if he could detect a lie so easily. Chaos still wasn't sure how he could do it, but the how wasn't nearly as important as the fact that he could. She'd tried confusing him and look where that got her, fanged and banged. She sighed in resignation.

"I'm going to find Red."

Raphael's expression changed from flirtatious to suspicious in a breath. "Why?"

"It's what we agreed to, remember?" she asked. "Find proof of their innocence, then find them. I'm doing both at the same time."

"Yes, I recall our agreement, but I doubt that's what brought you out here in the middle of the desert." He cocked his head and looked at her, studying her as if she were a new species. Chaos couldn't tell what he was looking for, but after a while, he relaxed. "Whose orders are you following?" He straightened the sleeves of his shirt casually while he waited for her answer.

Chaos scowled. "I don't know what you're talking about."

He sighed dramatically. "That's two lies," Raphael said. "Do not make it three."

She growled in frustration. "Fine! I'm here on the commander's behalf." Chaos hesitated. "Well, he didn't exactly give me any orders. More like permission to go."

"I see." Raphael didn't say anything else. Instead, he slowly looked around as if someone might be listening.

"I'm alone," she said.

"I know you are," he said, as if it was obvious to anyone who wasn't a simpleton.

Chaos rested her hand on her hip. "Look, I know we had an agreement. I haven't gone back on my word. I just added my own twist to it," she said. "Now are you going to tell me what you're doing here? Because I'll be honest, this whole conversation is beginning to bore me."

She glanced at her short nails and did her best to hide the fact that her hands were shaking. She'd definitely have to stop biting them when she returned to IPTT headquarters.

Raphael gave her a withering look. "Nothing has changed since we last spoke. I'm still seeking my brother. I'd like to find him before he gets into trouble."

Disappointment washed over her. That wasn't the answer she'd expected—or hoped for. Chaos had thought he'd say he was out here looking for Morgan Hunter and Red. Or better yet, he was searching for her. But Raphael hadn't. He was after his wayward brother. Jealousy burned through her, unwelcomed and unwanted. It was wrong to feel that way, when Raphael was only looking out for his family. So why did she?

And why in the hell was she disappointed? It wasn't like she wanted him here. He was already in the way. Raphael would only impede her search further once he found out she didn't care what happened to his friend Morgan Hunter.

The fact that Raphael was here for his brother brought home what she lacked in her own life. If she went missing tomorrow, no one, not even IPTT, would look very hard for her. No one would care.

* * * * *

CHAPTER TEN

Red turned over to find Morgan gone. The tent flap was closed, keeping the light at bay, which was probably why she hadn't noticed. She stretched, then glanced down at her watch: five o'clock.

She jolted out of bed. How had she managed to sleep so long? She never slept all day, especially surrounded by strangers. The Sand Moles had kept their word and provided shelter for the night. They'd even shared their food, although Red still had no idea what she'd eaten. She'd been so hungry and so sick of nutri-bars she didn't care. Whatever it was had tasted good and managed to stay down despite the oppressive heat.

Even now her body lay covered in a fine sheen of sweat and grit. She dressed quickly, strapping on her laser pistols before untying the flaps to the tent entrance. The sun and the heat smacked her in the face, causing her to flinch.

She squinted, cupping a hand over her eyes, and scanned the encampment. She spotted Morgan seated next to Demery at a makeshift table under a lean-to not far from a cooking fire. It wasn't much shade, but it was better than none.

Demery was back in his white protective suit. He waved when he saw her and motioned for her to come over.

"Why did you let me sleep so long?" Red asked.

Morgan looked up from his steaming drink and grinned. "You needed it after last night's hike and exercise."

Red opened her mouth to ask what exercise, then quickly shut it. Heat flooded her face and she cleared her throat. "What are you drinking?" she asked to change the subject.

Morgan's amber eyes twinkled, but he let the change slide. "It's some kind of tea, or so Gray told me. Tastes more like gasoline."

"Gas what?" Red asked.

Morgan shook his head. "I keep forgetting that you were born after the gas disappeared." For a second his ruggedly handsome features showed his true age. He wiped a hand over his face. "Years ago cars and just about everything else ran on fossil fuels. Gasoline was one of the byproducts. Wars were fought over oil. Countries destroyed. Races obliterated. That's how the last war started, but it quickly morphed into something bigger. It's not important." He brushed his dark thoughts away with a wave of his hand. "The only thing you need to know is that gas burned and tasted like shit, if you happened to get it in your mouth."

"Thanks for the warning," Red said. "I'd still like some."

Morgan chuckled. "Sure. Take a seat." He patted the bench beside him and poured her a cup.

Red took one sip and nearly spit it out. Heat scalded her throat and seared her nose as she breathed in sharply and exhaled. Her face puckered and she coughed. Morgan slapped her on the back until she stopped.

"I tried to tell you," he said.

"I should've listened," she said. "It'll definitely take some getting used to." Red raised the cup to her lips, but this time tipped it slowly. "Find out anything while I was asleep?"

Demery leaned forward. "Gray thinks he may know of a place that might house the type of equipment we're looking for."

"Either he knows or he doesn't." Red coughed.

"Someone woke up on the wrong side of the tent today," Demery said.

She ran a hand through her hair. "Sorry, I'm just used to having solid intel. I don't like guesses."

Demery nodded. "Understood. Unfortunately, we won't know for sure until Gray's scout returns. He's the one who's encountered the group Gray's talking about."

Red met Morgan's gaze. "And exactly when will that be?" she asked.

"Sometime this evening," Morgan said.

"I don't like the idea of losing travel time." She glanced around at their hosts. "We don't want to overstay our welcome."

"We'll lose a lot more than walking time if we go off on a wild boar chase," Morgan said. "This is the last place you want to get lost."

"Agreed." Demery grinned through his faceplate. "No sense in wandering around in this heat, mon. Won't get far if we're baked. Sun will be down soon enough."

Red nodded and finished her drink. Morgan handed her a plate of food, none of which she could identify. "What is this?" she asked. She wasn't as hungry today as she'd been last night, so the food didn't look near as appetizing.

"It's better if you just eat it and try not to think about it," Morgan said.

"Fair enough." It couldn't be worse than some of the things she'd eaten in her life. She'd gnawed on a few bodies when she was in her Other form and didn't even know it.

Red picked up a piece of mystery meat and plopped it in her mouth. It was dry. Really dry. She poured herself another cup of tea in order to wash the food down. She doubted the drink was the real thing, considering how rare and expensive tea was these days. Good thing, too, since this beverage would likely kill any bacteria lingering in the food.

She took a sip to knock back the flesh clogging her throat. "It doesn't get better," she said, swallowing hard. "So what are we supposed to do until the scout arrives?"

Morgan's smile turned seductive. "I can think of a few things."

Red snorted. "Not going to happen. The tent was hot when I left. I can't imagine what it's like now that the sun's hitting its side."

"Spoilsport." Morgan teased. "I guess we'll just have to occupy ourselves by trading for more goods."

"What are you going to do, Demery?" she asked.

"I have some business to take care of. Plan to make a few trades of my own. Need to locate Reaper if possible. Still hoping Gray knows how to find him. After that, I'm going to entice a few of the men into playing a game of zigzag quartz." He pulled out a worn deck of metal cards. "I'm feeling lucky."

"Is Reaper nearby?" Morgan asked.

"Probably not. He doesn't get along with Gray's group or any other for that matter. I'm hoping he'll be camped along our next route. If so, we can drop in for a quick trade."

"We'll see," Morgan said. "Don't have a lot of time for side trips."

"It's important that we make time." Demery didn't elaborate further.

Morgan shook his head. "That wasn't part of our agreement."

Demery stilled. "I didn't realize we had one, mon." He left them sitting at the table, staring at his retreating back.

"Looks like we'll be stopping," Red said.

Morgan met her gaze. "Looks like."

While they waited for the scout to return, Red and Morgan managed to trade extra charges of ammo for a few canteens and a portable food storage case. Red hoped they weren't out here long enough to make use of the case. She wanted to find someplace to get a communiqué out, not learn survival tips for no-man's-land.

Morgan went back to the tent to rest. There wasn't much else to do. Red found Demery under a lean-to collecting what looked to be valuable stones from a couple of the Sand Mole men. They didn't look happy, which meant Demery had obviously won the zigzag quartz game.

"Did you find out about your friend?" she asked.

"Friend?" Demery frowned. "You mean Reaper?"

"Yes."

"The man isn't my friend. He's the most vicious snake I've ever encountered and a hell of a zigzag quartz player. Far better than me." His brown gaze dropped to the metal deck in his hand and his full lips thinned.

"I thought—" Red stopped midsentence. "Then why are you looking for him?"

"He's been keeping something of mine. I told him the next time I was down here I'd stop by and pick it up."

"You said the Sand Devils were thieves. Couldn't he have just smuggled it to you?" she asked.

"Not this particular item," he said.

"Sounds serious." She kept her voice light.

Demery gave her a strained smile. "Not really," he said. "With

74

all the tactical team training, I haven't had the chance to return and retrieve it."

"What is 'it'?" Red couldn't imagine anyone leaving anything of value in this place

"You could say it's a family heirloom. It's of personal value to me, but wouldn't mean much to anyone else," he said. "Reaper's been keeping it safe for me, while I've been away. I don't want to impose on his hospitality any longer."

"The way you made them out to be yesterday, it didn't sound like they were the type of people to be hospitable," she said.

"Anyone will be hospitable for a price," he said softly.

What did he mean by that? Red thought about asking, but one look at Demery's face told her the conversation was over. If someone had something that was dear to her, she'd want it back, too. Of course if it were something really valuable, Red wouldn't have let it go in the first place. So why had Demery?

* * * * *

Night descended on no-man's-land, bringing the predators with it. Morgan caught glimpses of movement by the sand dunes, but the fire moat surrounding the Sand Mole encampment kept them at bay. Not for the first time, he wished they were on their way.

The scout arrived shortly after eight. He was a wiry man with a thin beak of a nose and small dark eyes that took in everything, but gave little away. His scraggly brown hair curled at odd angles around his head, making him look as if he'd been hit by lightning more than once in his lifetime.

He entered the encampment after giving a two-bark signal followed by one clap. One of the women broke away from the group and rushed forward with a canteen in her hand. She threw herself in his arms and kissed his cheeks repeatedly.

"Welcome home, Jeb." She led him over to the center table which turned out to be the communal gathering place for the Sand Moles.

"I bring news," he said, exchanging greetings to those he passed. People gathered close so they could hear what he had to say.

"Do tell," Gray said, clapping him on the shoulder. "We could use some good tidings."

"Word has arrived that—" The words caught in his throat at the sight of Red, Morgan, and Demery, choking him into silence.

Gray frowned. "Jeb? What's wrong?"

"Who are they?" Jeb stabbed a finger at them accusingly.

Gray motioned for them to approach. "This is Hunter, Red, and you know Demery."

Jeb nodded at the vamp, but didn't acknowledge Red or Morgan's presence. "Have they joined our group?" He assessed their clothing.

"No." Gray shook his head. "They are just passing through. They've been enjoying our hospitality, while awaiting your return."

Jeb blinked, then his beady eyes narrowed. "Why were they waiting for me?" His wiry body coiled, ready to spring.

"They hope you can help them. I fear I've bragged about your extensive travels. I told them that if anyone knew where communiqué equipment could be found, it would be you," Gray said.

An uneasy smile touched Jeb's face. "Why thank you, brother. I do believe I can be of assistance to the strangers. I know of such a place south of here."

"That's wonderful," Gina stepped forward before Morgan could stop her. Waves of excitement poured off her.

Morgan didn't want to dampen her enthusiasm, but something was wrong. He could smell it in the little man's sweat. It stank of deceit and lies. Jeb's body twitched and Morgan closed the distance between him and Gina.

"Where is this place?" She inched nearer, not noticing the change in his demeanor.

Jeb watched her closely, his eyes cold and calculating as if he were waiting for the perfect opportunity to strike.

Morgan's muscles tensed, ready for an impending attack.

Jeb noticed Morgan's close proximity and casually shrank back. The move was casual. Morgan doubted anyone noticed but him.

"It's two days' journey to the southwest about an hour from the old coast," Jeb said.

Gina turned to Demery. "Do you think you can find it?"

"Are you talking about the ruins near Verde?" Demery asked.

"No." Jeb shook his head. "You'd need to head an hour south of there once you cross the mountains."

"Okay," Demery said. "I know the general area. I think I can find it." His attention was caught by the woman he'd slept with the previous night. "Be back in a minute," he said, not waiting for an answer.

"Who do we contact once we arrive?" Gina asked.

The man looked at her as if he were considering his answer carefully. "You need to speak with Razor. Tell him Jeb sent you. That should at least get you past the towers."

Gina smiled. "Thank you."

"Don't thank me yet." Jeb turned his attention back to Gray. "Mind if I have a word with you in private?"

"Of course," Gray said. "Excuse us a moment. Feel free to continue to enjoy our hospitality until I return to see you off." He nodded in the direction of the musicians, who began to play.

Morgan watched the two men walk several yards away. He couldn't hear everything they were saying with the music playing, but he could make out a few words. He caught enough to confirm his suspicions. There was definitely a problem. Jeb knew who they were and why they were here.

"What's the matter?" Gina brushed a hand over his arm.

"You need to start using your senses," Morgan snapped, staring at Gray and Jeb, who kept their backs to them.

Gina slowly drew her hand away. "Why? What's happened?"

"That man, Jeb. He was lying about something. I could smell it reeking from his pores. Even if he hadn't, his body language screamed deception. He knows who we are and he's up to no good."

"I—" was all Gina had a chance to say before he cut her off.

"No excuses," Morgan said. "Our lives are in danger. Don't let their hospitality cloud your judgment."

Gina's jaw clenched. "Do you think he's lying about the location?"

"No." Morgan stared at the men, who were now looking back at them. "It's something else." He ran a hand through his hair, disheveling it. "Something having to do with us."

"But no one knows we're here," she said.

"I can't hear them over the blasted music." Morgan's hands shook in frustration. How was he supposed to protect Gina if he couldn't even hear himself think?

She stepped closer. "Do you think Gray made them play on purpose?"

"Maybe." That would imply he knew *what* they were. Morgan took a deep breath. The scent of the people nearby hadn't changed. Whatever was happening was coming directly from Jeb, and now Gray. "Get your things together. We may need to leave in a hurry." Morgan kept his attention on the men and the group around them. He sniffed the air every minute to make sure nothing had changed.

With luck, they'd be able to leave without any problems. So what if Jeb knew their real names? It didn't mean anything. Or at least it shouldn't. They weren't the only fugitives in no-man's-land. Everyone living here was considered one.

Jeb and Gray assessed them once more. This time there was no mistaking the speculation in their eyes. Something Jeb said had changed Gray's opinion of them, and not for the better.

* * * * *

Red watched the exchange for a moment, then walked off toward the tent they'd stayed in the night before. Demery caught her right before she stepped through the flap.

"What's going on?" he asked, wiping traces of blood from his mouth.

Red shook her head. "Not sure. Morgan is spooked about something. Said Jeb was lying. He knows who we are."

"That shouldn't matter." Demery glanced over at Morgan. "Did you pick up anything?"

Red face flushed. "I didn't think to try."

Sympathy filled Demery's warm brown eyes as he tore his gaze away from the men. "It takes time," he said. "You'll get it eventually." He cupped her elbow and squeezed, then released her.

Would she? Or would she end up dying before she learned how to use her abilities? Red didn't have a good track record when it came to embracing the wolf inside of her.

"What are you doing?" Demery asked.

"Morgan said to pack our things. We may need to get out of

here in a hurry."

"Right." Demery slipped around the back of her tent toward his own. He returned in minutes, bag in hand.

"That was quick." Red shoved the supplies into the extra tote they'd brought along for this purpose. She filled the food case next.

"If Morgan says we may need to leave in a hurry, I'd like it to be with my things. Wouldn't want to get caught without my protective suit." He grinned. "I'm going to find out what's going on. Maybe I can defuse the situation before it gets any worse."

Red hoped he could. She packed the rest of their belongings into the bags and dragged them to the center of the compound. Red placed them on the ground near her feet and nodded to Morgan to let him know they were ready.

Gray and Jeb had returned to the group. They were now seated at the long metal table, while Jeb ate. Something in Gray's demeanor had changed. He still wore an easy smile, but it didn't reach his eyes, and tension filled his lean shoulders, making them stiff beneath his baggy clothes.

Demery tried to speak to him, but Gray didn't seem interested in conversing.

Morgan was right. Something was wrong. What had Jeb said to him? Red had never seen the man before today. Yet she was detecting hostility. They needed to get out while they still had the chance.

"We're leaving now," Morgan said to no one in particular. "Thank you for your hospitality."

Red watched Gray and Jeb pause as she hoisted two of the bags onto her back. The music stopped abruptly.

Gray rose slowly from the table. "I'm afraid we cannot allow you to go," he said.

Red's ears were ringing from the blood pounding in her head. Her hands slipped to rest on the pistols strapped to her thighs.

"We aren't asking," Morgan said, his voice raspier than it was moments ago. His fists were clenched at his sides.

The wolf was riding him hard. Even now his eyes were changing color and his hair was beginning to thicken to a rough mane.

"The situation has changed." Gray nodded to the people around them, who slowly pulled out their weapons.

Red stepped forward. "We don't want any trouble."

"I appreciate that, Ms. Santiago. It is Gina Santiago, isn't it?" Gray asked.

Red felt the blood leach from her face. She glanced at Morgan, who'd stiffened at the sound of her name being mentioned aloud. He'd been right. Jeb did know their true identities.

"I don't know what you're talking about," she said calmly. "My name is Red."

"No." Gray shook his head. "Your name is Gina Santiago and that there," he indicated to Morgan, "is the ex-sheriff of Nuria, Morgan Hunter."

"You're wrong," she said, sounding desperate.

"There's a fifteen-thousand-credit bounty on your heads that says I'm right."

"What?" Red couldn't have heard him correctly. Did he say bounty?

Who would've placed a— She stopped short. Roark. Only Roark would do something like this, which meant he'd figured out where they'd gone. Bile rose in her throat. Now not even no-man's-land was safe. Safe? She laughed to herself. They'd been anything but safe from the second they crossed the boundary fence.

"Jeb here says news of the bounty is spreading fast. The Sand Moles deserve those credits more than most. We're the ones who've put you up and been hospitable."

"Yes, you have," she said. "So why stop now?"

Gray shrugged. "Credits are credits. Besides, you owe us."

"We traded in good faith," Morgan said. "We owe you nothing."

"That's not how we see it," Gray said.

"Then that's your problem," Morgan said. "Not ours."

He sighed. "Did I mention that the credits are good whether you're dead or alive?" Gray asked.

That was all Red needed to hear. She drew her pistol before she could reconsider and fired. The laser shot out, dropping Gray where he stood. A cauterized hole smoldered where his heart had beat only seconds ago. The smell of burning flesh and intestinal waste polluted the air. Someone screamed and there were a few muffled cries, but no one moved.

"We're going to leave now." Red hoped the shock of her actions kept everyone in place for a few minutes longer. "Anyone tries to stop us and they'll end up like Gray with their blood watering the ground."

Demery's brown eyes were wide, but he didn't say anything. Like Morgan, he'd drawn his weapon and pointed it at the lookouts before they could raise their rifles. He quickly gathered his tote and slung it over his shoulders.

"Let's go," Red said.

They retreated into the desert, keeping their eyes and guns trained on the small group until they cleared a big dune and disappeared out of sight.

"What were you thinking?" Morgan asked when they were a safe distance away.

"That we weren't going to get out of there without a firefight. The way we were placed, there was a pretty good chance we'd end up shooting each other in all the commotion. I didn't want to risk it, which meant that either Jeb or Gray had to die."

"You're crazy, mon." Demery shoved his dreadlocks away from his face. "You could've gotten us killed."

"I took a calculated risk that the loss of Gray would shock the group. I prayed it was enough to keep them from acting. Jeb's loss wouldn't have been as great. Gray would've ordered his people to fire. In the end, it was an easy decision." Red said the words dispassionately, but inside she was chilled at the ease with which she'd taken the man's life. When she shot, she hadn't felt anything but the need to survive. Like a trapped wolf ready to gnaw its own leg off, she'd acted quickly and without remorse.

"Gray was good people, mon," Demery said. "As good as people get on this side of the fence."

Red's eyes narrowed. "He was a threat and planned to turn us over to Roark. You heard him. We're wanted dead or alive. Personally, I'm partial to breathing."

Demery slowed. "You don't know Roark was the one who put a bounty on your heads, mon."

Red rounded on him. "Don't be naive. Who else would've done it? My grandfather?" she shouted. "Doubtful. Not many people can afford to part with that many credits. Roark can. He's amassed a fortune while he's been in politics."

"I'm not the enemy," Demery said. "I still think we could've worked something out with the Sand Moles. Now I'm never going to be able to trade with them."

"I'm sorry we messed up your commerce and gambling opportunities," she said sarcastically. "Fifteen thousand credits hanging over our heads make me a little twitchy on the trigger. Who knows how many people have heard about the bounty by now. We aren't going to be safe anywhere."

Morgan came over and put his arm around her. "It'll be okay," he said. "All we need to do is reach the encampment Jeb spoke of."

She gave a pained laugh. "Who's to say that they don't know about the bounty, too?" Red asked. "It stopped being okay a long time ago. We don't even know if Jeb was telling the truth."

"He was," Demery said. "I know the place. It's real. I've been by there on my travels, though I've never stopped."

"For our sakes, I hope they weren't the ones who told him about the reward." Red ran a hand through her loose hair. She'd been in such a hurry to pack and leave that she'd forgotten to tie it back. Maybe she should cut it. Long hair wasn't meant for these conditions. Like compassion, it only got in the way.

CHAPTER ELEVEN

"As much as I love these little chats we have, I'm going to take off now." Chaos gathered her investigative equipment, then headed back to her shuttle. She'd spent most of the night scouring the area, but hadn't turned up anything else. The sky would be lightening in a few more hours.

"Where are you going?" Raphael asked.

"I have some more things to check out," she said. If she was lucky, he wouldn't notice that she hadn't answered his question.

He lifted her tote onto his shoulder. "Perhaps I can come along and help?" Raphael suggested.

"You said you were looking for your brother," she said. "I don't want to keep you any longer."

"I am. Nothing has changed. If we are going in the same direction we could keep each other company." His hand brushed her arm, the move casual but intimate. A subtle reminder of what they'd shared this past week.

His warm scent washed over her and Chaos' breath caught. When she realized what she'd done, Chaos growled in frustration. "I work better alone," she snapped. "I don't need a distraction."

"If I make you uncomfortable, all you have to do is tell me," his voice teased, but there was no mistaking the challenge behind his words.

"You don't." It was a lie. Truth was Raphael had her coming out of her skin. "That would require feeling something for you."

"Exactly." Raphael flashed her a grin that made her knees weak.

Chaos didn't know how she felt. One minute she wanted to punch him. The next she had to fight to keep from throwing herself in his arms. "You are impossible!" She groaned in frustration, then jumped into her maglev shuttle and started the engine. "I better not see you following me or I'll shoot you out of the air."

She slammed the shuttle into gear. It rose two feet off the ground and took off. Chaos arced to the left, purposely traveling in the wrong direction to confuse him. She'd circle back as soon as she was sure he wasn't following, then head to the boundary fence crossing.

* * * * *

"You won't see a thing. I assure you," Raphael murmured as she drove away.

He didn't know what the little minx was up to, but he'd find out. Raphael hadn't asked her to contact the commander of IPTT about Red and Morgan. He'd only planned to do so as a last resort. She'd taken it upon herself, which knowing how Catherine's mind worked didn't bode well for him.

Raphael thought he'd come up with a clever trap, one that would work out for the both of them, when he'd gotten her to agree to help him. But he obviously hadn't been clever enough. Raphael had considered reading her thoughts, but he wanted Catherine's trust. For some reason her trust was important to him.

Torn between the need to locate Michael and the need to go after Catherine, Raphael hopped into his shuttle. Thanks to the eye replacements he'd had during the war, with a blink he could see as well at night as he could during the day.

Catherine zoomed farther east. Raphael threw the shuttle into high gear. He killed the lights and all unessential electronics. She'd never see him back here. As long as he kept a couple of miles between them, the sensors on her shuttle would never detect him.

Raphael followed at a steady pace, sipping on a packet of blood. Catherine had turned south ten minutes ago and was be on a direct course for the boundary fence. The thought of her crossing into no-man's-land alone curdled the blood in his stomach. What was she thinking?

She may be powerful, but Catherine was no match for no-man's-land. It didn't matter that he'd intended to go there himself. She had no business putting herself in danger. He had the overwhelming urge to turn her over his knee and paddle her delectable bottom. His body liked that idea far too much. Raphael shifted to ease his burgeoning erection.

Catherine stopped at a lot a quarter of a mile from the official boundary crossing station and parked her shuttle. Raphael had hoped he'd been wrong about her destination. She disembarked from the shuttle and gathered a pack that was almost as big as she was, then struggled to pull it onto her back. He shook his head as she nearly toppled from the weight.

He should just go back to Nuria and leave her. That was the smart thing to do. It wasn't as if he was prepared for a trip into no-man's-land. Raphael stared out the window as Catherine stumbled toward the crossing checkpoint. He hit the wheel in frustration, cracking it, then scrambled out of his vehicle. He grabbed the single blood bag he had left and shoved it into his pocket. Stubborn woman. She'd get herself killed if she wasn't careful.

"Wait up," he shouted.

Catherine ignored him and kept walking. Raphael secured his vehicle and jogged over to the crossing. She had thrown her pack on the table and presented her neck for scanning.

"State your purpose," a guard wearing a navy quadrant inspector's uniform said.

"Business," Catherine said.

"Pleasure," Raphael added.

The guard looked at him askance. "Anything to declare?"

"She's insane." Raphael glanced at Catherine.

The guard snickered. "Move ahead." He ushered them on.

"You are the most bullheaded human being I've ever met." Raphael grabbed her arm and yanked her around to face him.

Catherine looked down at his hand and waited for him to remove it. Raphael pried his fingers open and glared at her.

"I thought I told you not to follow me." She showed her I.D. to the next set of guards at the checkpoint. "What are you doing here?"

"I told you," he said. "I'm looking for my brother, Michael

Travers."

Her green eyes narrowed in suspicion. "What would he be doing at the boundary crossing?" she asked. "This isn't exactly a travel destination."

"Probably the same thing you are," Raphael said, exasperated. "I thought you said you were looking for evidence."

"Who said I'm not? You don't know what I'm doing," Catherine said, before quickly lowering her voice. "Unless you've read my mind."

He rolled his eyes. "I don't have to read your mind to know what you're up to. It's written clearly on your little cherub face." Raphael pulled out his I.D. He had expected to have time to return to Nuria to retrieve supplies before crossing into no-man's-land, but Catherine had blown that plan into space. Now he'd have to buy what he needed from the trader store and they always marked things up.

She shook her head. "You're seeing things that aren't there," she said.

"Am I?" he asked, ushering her forward.

"Yep."

"Fine, have it your way." Raphael exposed his neck to the scanner. Two beeps later he was walking down the long gray, sparsely lit corridor that would eventually open up into no-man's-land. Catherine strode in front of him, her pack swaying from side to side like stacked plates ready to fall.

"It seems to me," he said, breaking the silence, "that we'd probably get a lot further if we worked together."

"I told you I'd keep our bargain and I meant it," she said. "I don't need your help."

"I have no doubt that's true, but I could use your help finding my brother. You must have met him when you went to Roark's office."

Catherine stopped dead and her shoulders tensed. "He showed Bannon and me into a waiting room. I never saw him after that. He certainly wasn't there when we left. Do you think he had anything to do with drugging us?" she asked casually, but Raphael heard the apprehension in her voice.

"No," he said. "I'm sure that was all Roark."

There was no doubt in Raphael's mind that had Michael

participated in something like that he would've let Raphael know. That knowledge should've stopped doubt cold, but it kept crawling forward, whispering insidiously in the back of his mind.

"Why would he be in no-man's-land?" she asked. Catherine's expression told him she hadn't quite believed his assurances.

"That's what I'm here to find out," he said.

Raphael dropped into the outfitting shop and picked up a pack, canteens, food, a tent, industrial-grade sunscreen, and protective clothing. His credit account took a major hit, thanks to Catherine's impromptu trip, but it was necessary. He could stay out in the sun fairly long for a vamp, but he didn't think he'd make it all day. He did have his limits, although Raphael rarely copped to them.

Despite all her protests, Catherine had followed him into the store and was browsing the items. She picked up a hat and an extra canteen. He noticed that she bypassed the tents, so either she had one in that enormous pack of hers or she didn't anticipate being out here long.

It was too much to hope that she planned to share his tent with him. Raphael had never cared for camping, but he could get used to it if Catherine were his tent mate. He looked at her as he considered the possibility.

She scowled back.

Perhaps it would be better if they had their own space.

Catherine hadn't told him what she was doing here. Sure she'd mentioned getting permission from the commander of IPTT, but permission for what? It was one thing to look for proof, quite another to pursue fugitives.

Raphael didn't know what Catherine planned to do once she caught up with Morgan and Red. It was just one more reason he needed to go with her. He shoved his overpriced supplies into his pack and stared longingly at Catherine's bare neck. Just looking at her stoked his hunger.

What he wouldn't give for a canteen full of blood. Thanks to the need she evoked, he'd finished all but the last of his supply on the ride down here. His one blood bag wouldn't last long in the heat. Hell at this rate, he wouldn't make it out of here before he devoured it.

Catherine tipped her head and he glimpsed his teeth marks on the side of her nape. They looked more like love bites in this artificial lighting. Raphael licked his lips as his incisors lengthened and the material on the front of his pants strained. He'd just have to improvise, when it came to feeding. The thought of what that would entail had his temperature rising.

She caught him looking at her and flushed bright pink. Obviously his expression had been patently transparent.

"All done," Raphael said.

"About time," she countered.

He laughed. "I didn't realize you were waiting for me. Had I known, I would've hurried," Raphael said to get a rise out of her, since her actions had been blatantly obvious. "I take it you've reconsidered my offer."

She shrugged. "We can travel together and hope to find your brother along the way, but we go in the direction I want," she said. "No arguments."

"Of course," Raphael agreed, since they'd be heading in the direction he needed to go. That didn't stop him from hoping he was wrong about Michael. Maybe Roark had sent him somewhere else. The man had a lot of enemies. It would explain his brother's absence.

Even as the thought flitted through Raphael's head, it was unlikely.

He hoisted the pack onto his back and indicated for Catherine to lead the way. She did, but stopped when they reached the final gate. There she hesitated.

"Having second thoughts?" he asked, in hopes she'd call the whole thing off.

"No, just adjusting my pack." Catherine made a show of shifting her pack, then she stepped forward and pressed a button on the wall. Nothing happened for a second so she pressed it again harder.

"Give it time. You are so impatient, my little storm," Raphael said. "Don't you know good things come to those who wait? Besides, the sun will be up soon. We'll have to camp at the crossing until dark."

Catherine rolled her eyes. "Shut up, cliché man. It's your fault that we aren't on our way already."

The final door slid open with a hiss. A blast of warmth greeted them with a dry embrace. The gaping maw that was the endless desert stretched out before them, waiting to swallow them whole. There were so many directions to go in. They could be anywhere.

Raphael tried to ignore Catherine's delicious scent as they proceeded into the fleeting darkness. It was difficult given the lack of distracting odors. The sand gave under his booted feet. This would not be an easy journey—his gaze fell upon his petite traveling companion—for either of them.

Good thing she had a day to reconsider her folly.

* * * * *

Chaos felt him watching her. Raphael did that a lot. She didn't know if he was waiting for her to attack again or if he was sizing her up as a snack. She didn't want to think that it might be sexual. It was hard enough walking this close to him without her body betraying her at every turn.

They waited at the gate for the rest of the night and all through the next day. There'd been nothing to do but sleep and talk. Raphael had regaled her with stories from his childhood. He'd charmed her, weakening her resolve to keep her distance.

It took forever for the sun to set. Even after the fiery ball sunk below the horizon, it was still unbearably hot. The heat didn't seem to affect him like it did her. Chaos was already sweating and they'd only been walking a few minutes. She'd be a puddle by the time an hour had passed.

It didn't help that her pack weighed a ton. She'd wanted to be prepared, so she'd requisitioned everything required for outdoor survival. Chaos had no idea what they might encounter on this side of the boundary fence, but she was determined to be ready for anything.

Her hand moved to the pistol strapped to her thigh. Its weight was reassuring. In the distance, a big cat yowled. The hair on her neck prickled. She glanced back at Raphael to make sure he was still there. He was, but his expression remained deceptively placid. So either he hadn't heard the cat or he wasn't bothered by its presence.

Fine, two could play that game. Chaos straightened her pack and kept her hand on her weapon as she scanned the area around them. She wasn't afraid of any animal, even one that might turn out to be four feet high and five hundred pounds.

The lights from the checkpoint were a dim memory glittering in the distance. If a predator lurked behind a dune there was no way they'd make it back to the gates before it attacked. She took a deep breath and let it out slowly. No reason to be concerned. It was more afraid of them than they were of it.

Raphael touched Chaos and she jumped, letting out a startled yelp.

"I'm sorry. I didn't mean to frighten you," he said.

"You didn't," she shot back. "What do you want?"

His lip canted, but he didn't contradict her. "I wanted to tell you that the cat we heard earlier is stalking us from the west."

Chaos spun around so fast the weight of her pack teetered, sending her crashing into the dune. She struggled out of the straps and came up with her pistol in her hand. "Where? Do you see it?" She tried to look everywhere at once.

Raphael laughed and couldn't seem to stop. His shoulders shook and he clutched his stomach.

"What's so funny?" Chaos glared at him, giving Raphael her best withering glance.

"You." He pressed his lips together, trying to keep from laughing again. He didn't succeed.

Chaos brushed her clothes off. "You said a cat was stalking us. I don't think that's a laughing matter."

"Yes, it is," he said, trying to catch his breath. "You should've seen yourself, jerking your gun this way and that way. I'm lucky you didn't shoot me."

"I wanted to be ready," she ground out through clenched teeth.

"It would help if you were facing the right direction," he said, casually pointing to a spot over her shoulder.

Chaos turned and searched the darkness for movement.

"You need not worry," Raphael said. His lips brushed her ear, sending goose-bumps down her spine.

Chaos hadn't even heard him move, his footfalls were so silent. Like the cat that was determined to have them as a meal.

"I will not let the feline touch you. You are mine—*to eat*," he said.

Heat flooded Chaos' face as his words singed the panic out of her mind. She shivered and swallowed hard, forcing herself to meet his black gaze. He was smiling at her, his white teeth glowing in the darkness. At that moment, she didn't know which was the more dangerous predator, the cat or Raphael.

"Don't make me shoot you," she warned. "I only agreed to allow you to tag along because you said we were headed in the same direction. I can easily change my mind and send you on your way."

Raphael snorted. "Whatever you say, little storm."

"Let's get moving before the cat gets any closer." Chaos lifted her pack from the sand dune and brushed it off. "I'd hate to have to kill it."

"You are absolutely right." Raphael dropped his pack and raced to the ridge of a nearby dune so quickly she barely tracked his movements. When he reached the top, he slowly turned his head to the west. When he spotted his target, he stopped. A rumble rose from inside of him, building in ferocity. When he released it, the sound came out as a primal roar.

Chaos heard a feline's answering snarl closer than she would've cared for it to be. Raphael spread his arms wide and hissed, exposing long, sharp fangs. There was another yowl, but this one seemed less sure than the previous one.

The cat was having second thoughts about attacking. Hell, she was having second thoughts. Raphael roared again and strode off in the direction the snarl had come from. Chaos frowned. What was he doing now? Surely he wasn't crazy enough to confront the animal unarmed.

He disappeared into the darkness. Chaos listened carefully, but couldn't hear much over the pounding of her heart. She charged her weapon with the press of her thumb.

"Raphael?" she called out.

He didn't answer.

Chaos dropped her pack and climbed to the top of the dune. It was so dark that she could barely see her hand in front of her face. Damn him. Where had he gone? The thought that the cat might have gotten to him and dragged him off stilled her movements. The disturbing image was followed by a wave of sadness that nearly upended her.

"Raphael, this isn't funny. Where are you?" she said in a hushed tone in case it decided to hunt her next.

She squinted into the darkness as if that would somehow help. Chaos raised her pistol and pressed a tiny button on the side of the barrel. A night-vision scope popped into place. She put her eye up to it and slowly scanned the area.

There was no movement or heat signature lingering anywhere. For a second, she couldn't breathe. Her hand went to her chest as she tried to calm down. What if something had happened to him? What if she never saw him again? Panic and something akin to fear overwhelmed her.

"Where are you damn it?" Her voice broke. She swallowed back the sudden grief.

"It's nice to know you missed me," the whisper was so soft it barely registered.

When Chaos did, anger flooded her. She spun around and slammed her tiny fist into his face. The punch must have caught him off guard because Raphael rocked back on his heels and fell onto the sand.

Chaos leaned over his prone body and jabbed a finger in his chest. "Don't ever do that again. Do you hear me?"

"Loud and clear, *ma petite*," he said. Not even the blood on his lip could detract from the stupid grin he wore on his handsome face.

"What are you smiling about?" Chaos snarled, getting madder by the second. She'd been so scared that she'd lost him it hadn't crossed her mind that he might be playing with her.

"You wouldn't have hit me if you didn't care." He stood gracefully and brushed off his clothes.

"You're making too much out of it," she said, hoping to misdirect him. "I just didn't want to have to fill out a report listing cause of death as cat food."

"If you say so." The smile refused to leave Raphael's face. In a flash of anger, she'd as good as shouted her feelings for him.

"I swear." Chaos growled, her fists clenching at her sides. "If the cat doesn't get you next time, I will."

* * * * *

CHAPTER TWELVE

Somehow he'd lost a day, sleeping in the half-shadow of the rock. The sun had drained Michael more than he realized. Without the sunlight, he could move more quickly. Not that the sand sucking at his shoes helped. He'd emptied them twice already, but had finally given up on ever getting the tiny granules out of his socks.

A slight breeze picked up from the south. It wasn't cool, but it did relieve the stifling heat that the still air created. Michael moved steadily, trying to sense Red and Morgan. He hadn't picked up their scent, but was convinced they'd come this way.

Going to either coast was useless. Nothing survived near the poisoned seas. The boundary fence lay to the north, which left only one direction: south. Roark was convinced they'd gone to no-man's-land. Their desperation was even greater than Michael's if they had.

Deciding to give it a few more days, he trudged on. Michael scanned the dunes for any sign of life. Nothing moved but the sand, forever shifting and reshaping, erasing all trace of those who dared tread upon it. Seas of beige cascading waves, tumbling, tumbling down.

A mile farther Michael came upon a pack of wild dogs eating what appeared to be a small deer. It was only when he got closer that Michael realized it was a child, not a doe, wrapped in brown clothing, its tiny limbs ripped from its body and spread across the desert floor.

His senses went into overdrive. If a child was here, then that meant people couldn't be far away. Michael picked up his pace, the thought of fresh blood driving him. Licking his dry lips, he skirted by the ravenous pack. If the kill hadn't been old, he would've joined in on the feast or taken it from them. Nothing like a feeding frenzy to remind him that he was alive.

It took another four and a half hours, but eventually Michael stumbled upon what looked to be a nomadic settlement—tents huddled in the middle of a rise surrounded by a flaming moat. There was one walkway that led in, but Michael was sure there had to be another. No one was stupid enough to trap themselves without the possibility of escape, especially people living in no-man's-land.

Dropping to the sand, he belly-crawled forward. People were rushing from place to place within the compound, their movements frenzied. Had they been recently attacked? He thought of the dead child lying in pieces. Tension gripped him as he inhaled deeply. The last thing Michael needed was to be caught off guard by an unseen enemy.

A flash of movement to his right made his head turn. The shadow disappeared before he could get a good look at it. Not now. Michael slammed his eyes closed, squeezing until the lids hurt. The pain helped him focus. Reminded him of who he used to be.

"Go away," he hissed under his breath.

Michael's head throbbed and he felt movement under his skull once again. The chip was burrowing deeper, which was an impossibility, so it had to be his imagination. A shock zapped him, painfully contorting his muscles. Michael gasped. Roark was nowhere near. He would've sensed him. That meant the chip had acted on its own.

It took Michael a moment to digest the gravity of the situation. He didn't like the conclusion he came to. What had Roark done to him?

Michael watched the shadows retreat, but how long they'd stay gone was anyone's guess. Shaken, he continued forward, dropping lower in the sand. The gentle *shoosh* as his clothes brushed the grains would be lost to human ears. He didn't want them to see him before he was ready. He licked his chapped lips. So thirsty. The raw ache for blood burned his insides, demanding to be filled.

Guards flanked the encampment, their eyes alert, almost fevered. The faint coppery scent of blood tickled Michael's nose, teasing him with the promise of sustenance. The blood was old, but Michael's body didn't care. His stomach growled loud enough for the guards to notice. They both turned, weapons raised.

"Come out," the one nearest him shouted, unable to pinpoint his exact location.

Michael considered not complying for a moment, then slowly rose to his feet, putting his hands in the air. It was all for show of course. He could kill them both in a blink and not strain a muscle.

The chip in his brain flared at the thought, flooding his body with endorphins, encouraging him to act on the impulse. Michael fought the urge and a wave a pain swiftly followed. He gulped in air and staggered forward.

"I'm unarmed," he said.

It was the truth and a lie, since Michael had dropped his assassination kit on the ground where he'd been hiding moments ago. The real weapon lay within him dormant, but ready for use at a moment's notice. It was the reason he'd survived for so many years. The reason Michael had found his brother, Raphael. And the reason Roark had him chipped.

"Come forward and don't try anything or we'll shoot," the guard shouted. That wouldn't happen, since Michael was quite capable of stopping a bullet.

He did as the guard asked because it suited his purpose. Michael needed to find out whether Red and Morgan had passed this way. The only way to do that was to get closer.

"Do you have any water?" Michael asked. "I ran out an hour ago." It wasn't water he needed, but he figured they'd be far more accommodating than if he asked for their blood.

"Keep your hands where we can see them," the guard said, not answering.

Michael walked across the small entryway while flames licked at his flesh from both sides. Sweat beaded on his forehead. Unusual, but not unheard of for his kind. The fire crackled, fed by some kind of liquid fuel and rags.

"I could really use your help," Michael said, repeating his

request for water. His meek act slipped easily onto his narrow shoulders. Once again he became Michael Travers, lowly assistant.

One of the guards nodded to a woman, who placed a canister of some sort on a table. She pointed to it and then stepped away.

"Thank you." The water burned Michael's raw throat, causing him to choke. He wasn't even sure it was solely water, but at least it was wet. Michael put it down and took a couple of deep breaths, while forcing himself to remain as unthreatening as possible. It wasn't hard. He was not a big man.

Despite the changes in him, Michael had small hands and delicate features. Most people didn't see him as dangerous until he killed them. It was one of the many reasons he was such a good assassin. Michael took another drink of water. This time it soothed.

The guard stepped forward when Michael finished, weapon raised. "State your business."

Michael watched him, paying special attention to the slight tremor in his hands and the laser pistol strapped to his thigh. It looked new, unlike the weapon in his hands, which had seen better days. Despite the varnish, the wood of the rifle had rotted from age. The inside of the barrel looked clean, but rust dotted the outside in red freckles.

"I told you. I ran out of supplies and need assistance," he said.

"You don't look like a trader. Where did you come from?" the man asked.

"The boundary fence."

"You're registered?" He sounded surprised.

"Yes." Michael didn't bother to ask him if he was since anyone living on this side of the fence had chosen not to or couldn't afford the credits it took to go through the process.

Michael turned his head to show the man where his chip was implanted.

His brown eyes narrowed in suspicion. "Why would so many Regs want to suddenly journey into no-man's-land?"

Michael arched a brow. Why indeed? He took another deep breath and caught a familiar scent. It was wild and feminine just like its owner. "Where is she?" he asked.

The guard stilled, his gaze growing wary. "Where's who?"

"Don't play dumb with me." Michael advanced on a tent not far from the table.

"Stop or I'll shoot," the guard shouted, then fired. A blast landed near Michael's feet.

He stopped, anger and energy rising inside of him. "That was a mistake," he said softly, turning to face the man. So softly Michael doubted he heard him.

"The next shot will be in you," the guard warned. His bravado was admirable, but it did little to wipe the stink of fear from his skin. The man knew now that he was staring at death.

Michael watched the other guard off to the right raise his weapon. He was still a good distance away. Smart man. Too bad it wouldn't help him.

"The last man who pulled a gun on me didn't live to take his next breath," Michael said. The chip in his brain pulsed in approval. Suddenly the need to resist the impulse to kill didn't seem all that important.

"Huh?"

Michael reached out with his mind to the nearest guard and yanked the gun from him, tossing it into the fire beyond. The man stood dumbfounded, gawking at his empty hands. Before the other guard in the distance registered what had happened, Michael mentally grabbed his weapon and slowly turned the muzzle on him. It became a battle of wills. Michael's was stronger. When the muzzle rested against his chest, Michael blinked and the gun fired, sending a loud crack rumbling through the air.

Screams filled the night as people ran out of their tents and lean-tos, weapons drawn.

Michael became a killing machine, disarming them all at once. He smashed their bones and piled the bodies up near the fire like human kindling. Others he let fall where they stood.

The physical drain was immense. Michael's power weakened, but no one noticed. When there were only two people left, the first guard and a woman, he stopped his bloody rampage. Once again the chip in his brain flooded him with endorphins. A reward for a job well done.

"Now, I'm going to ask you again. Where is she?"

The woman whimpered. Tears streaked down her grit-covered face, leaving clean trails behind. She glanced at the corpses of her people. "They killed Gray and left," she said.

The man shot her a censorious look meant to silence her, but the woman was too far gone to notice.

"Where did they go?" Michael asked, barely containing the urge to taste her throat.

"Southwest," she said, then dropped to the ground and rocked.

"You come here." Michael summoned the guard.

The man shook his head. Defiant to the end. "Go to hell," he ground out between clenched teeth.

"I'm not going to ask you again." Michael raised his arm, directing his telekinetic power toward the guard. The man's feet left the ground and he floated toward him. Michael's power faltered and the man's toes dug into the sand.

The guard shrieked, the fear inside of him exploding like a cork under too much pressure. He struggled against Michael's mental bonds, but it did him no good. He may be weak from lack of blood, but he was still stronger than any being currently walking on the dead world.

Michael set the man down in front of him and looked into his leathery face. His gray eyes were wide and he'd wet himself. The acrid odor of urine nearly overpowered the scent of blood coming from the bodies.

"Bring me the canteen," Michael said to the woman. For a second, she didn't move. Her mind had created a safe haven for her to escape in.

"I said bring me that canteen," he repeated, but this time louder. Michael pointed to the object on the table.

She blinked as if waking from a dream, then rose to do as he bade. The woman handed him the canteen, then quickly backed away. Her fingers shook violently as she plunged them into her pockets.

"Thank you." Michael's fangs lengthened in anticipation.

The man's eyes got even wider if that were possible and his struggles increased. Michael brushed his scraggly hair away from his neck. His skin was dirty, but it mattered not, because what Michael was after wasn't found on the outside.

It was difficult to hold the guard with need riding him so hard, but somehow Michael managed. He stared at the man's neck and concentrated, watching his pulse jump beneath his skin. The movement was hypnotizing.

A small tear opened the guard's throat, gradually growing

larger and larger, then deeper and deeper, until it found the carotid artery. The man's cries turned into terrified whimpers. Michael mentally plucked at the vein and it opened, exposing glorious fountains of crimson. They showered him, covering his face, blanketing his clothes. Michael closed his eyes in ecstasy and licked his lips. So warm. So salty. So delicious.

Michael placed the canteen against the man's neck and waited for his heart to do its job. It didn't take long to fill. When it was finished, he sealed the lid.

"Do you have any more?" Michael asked the woman, but she didn't hear him. She was already in shock.

The man's color faded. Michael moved quickly and covered the opening with his lips, sucking hard. The coppery taste exploded on his tongue. So good. So sweet. More. He needed more.

He drank and drank until Michael was convinced his stomach would burst. The man tasted so fresh. If he didn't stop, he'd be blood sick. But the thirst remained, driving him to gluttony. Or maybe it was the chip.

Michael released the man and he fell. Deceased before he hit the sandy ground.

The woman was staring in his direction, but Michael didn't think she could see him. He searched the tents and found two more empty canteens. The rest were full of water. He'd take as many as he could carry. Michael returned to the woman. She hadn't budged. The merciful thing to do was to kill her.

He plucked her off the ground. She didn't struggle or cry out. She simply lifted her matted blond hair off her neck and tilted her head, so he'd have better access. Fang marks glared back at him. Someone had fed from her before. Michael didn't recognize the vamp's earthy scent. A twinge of guilt hit. It was wrong to poach on another vampire's food source, but guilt had no place in no-man's-land.

"Thank you," he said, then clamped onto her throat with his teeth and ripped.

She didn't make a sound as Michael filled his canteens and then left her to bleed to death. It seemed like such a waste of blood, but he couldn't carry anything else. Michael's power surged, striking her heart. By the next beat it stopped and the woman was dead...just like the rest of her people.

He went back into the tent where he'd found Red's scent. It mingled with Morgan's. They'd stayed here, and not long ago. A day perhaps, two at the most. The scent was too strong to be old. They were still alive.

Michael left the tent and its contents behind and gathered the canteens, making his way back across the entrance and out where he'd left his weapons. He added the canteens to his supplies, then climbed the ridge of the nearest dune and looked out at the horizon. The black had been steadily replaced with light gray. The sun would be coming up in a matter of minutes. There was no time to waste.

The breeze increased, bringing with it a familiar odor wafting on the air. It stopped Michael in his tracks. He turned his face into the wind. The scent was there again, stronger, closer. Michael inhaled deeply to be sure he was not mistaken.

He wasn't.

He was still far away, but the wind confirmed Michael's fears. "Raphael, what are you doing here?" he asked the night, not expecting an answer.

The spicy odor of his brother taunted him. Made Michael long for his company, when he needed no man. Raphael's scent was tangled with a lighter one, sweeter almost. One that seemed vaguely familiar. His brother wasn't traveling alone.

Michael debated for a moment whether to contact him, but decided against it. There could be only one reason Raphael was out here. And that was to stop him. Michael went back into the compound and grabbed a lean-to to take with him. The thought of burning the remaining tents crossed his mind, since it would eliminate his scent, but the flames would draw Raphael straight to this location. If he didn't burn the place, there was a possibility his brother might miss the compound. Michael decided to leave it standing.

The best thing his brother could do was stay as far away from him as possible. Michael loved Raphael, but right now he was a danger to him and anyone who might be traveling with him. And he would remain so as long as this chip stayed in his head. Raphael's blind devotion prevented him from seeing the truth. For both their sakes, Michael prayed that never changed.

* * * * *

CHAPTER THIRTEEN

They smelled death before they saw it. Raphael and Catherine approached the camp, spotting the pile of bodies immediately. The fire burning in a deep trench was almost out. It wouldn't be long before the predators approached.

Catherine put her hand over her nose and mouth. "What the hell happened here?" she asked, gagging.

Raphael could tell she wasn't really looking for an answer. He inhaled, catching his brother's scent. It was faint due to decomp, but strong enough to let him know that he'd been here recently. Michael had been close enough to hear his call.

He made his way around the pit and walked into the middle of the tents. He picked up three more familiar scents—Red, Morgan, and Demery. Every muscle in his body clenched. Had they all been here at the same time? Were they among the dead? He'd have to check all the bodies to be sure.

"This one's throat has been ripped out." Catherine stood over the body of a woman. "And that one's been slashed." She pointed to a man lying nearby. "I don't see any marks on these others. It's like they just died."

"I doubt very much that they all laid down in a pile and died. Have you spotted Red or Morgan?" he asked.

"No." She shook her head. "Not yet. I'll keep looking."

A wave of relief hit. "Let me know if you find anything," Raphael said.

She scowled. "Other than Red and Morgan, what am I looking for?"

"Signs of trauma." Raphael wasn't about to share his insights into what had happened here. This carnage wasn't the work of shifters. The only creature who could kill like this was a vamp, which meant either Demery or his brother, Michael, had been behind the killings. The question was why? Had these people tried to attack Red and Morgan? There was no reason to assume so. Yet this was no-man's-land. They didn't exactly operate by the rules, nor did they need a reason to kill.

After a few more minutes of searching, Catherine approached him, looking paler than she'd been only moments ago. The sun had barely peeked over the horizon. Soon it would be beating down upon them and they'd have to take shelter. This place was as good as any.

"Are you okay?" He stroked her cheek.

She swatted his hand away. "I'm fine. What are we going to do with the bodies?"

"Move them out into the desert, so that the predators don't come in here while we're sleeping."

"I'm not staying here." Catherine gaped, looking around at the destruction. "This is a dead zone. We don't even know what happened. What if whatever killed them comes back?"

"It won't." Raphael had no doubt the killer or killers were long gone. "The sun is coming up. We won't get far in the heat. This place has shelter and probably a few supplies we can make use of. It's not like they'll need them anymore. Rigor has come and gone in all the bodies. They've already begun to decompose."

"What if something in their supplies killed them?" she asked. "We have tents. We should go."

He hadn't thought of that, but this clever woman had. Raphael walked over to the pile of bodies. He hated to do this, but he had no choice. He leaned over them and breathed deep. The scent of decay hit, rolling his stomach, but beneath that he smelled nothing unusual.

Raphael lifted one of the victim's arms. It crumpled, bending in an abnormal way. He started at the wrist and felt up to the elbow. The bones were like gravel beneath his fingertips. He dropped the limb. Definitely a vamp's work.

"I don't think they were poisoned," he said, slowly backing away from the bodies.

"Then what killed them?"

More like who, he thought.

"I'm not sure what happened here." That was the truth. Raphael had seen only one sign of shots fired and the slug was still in the ground.

"Do you think Red and Morgan did this?" Catherine's green eyes were wide as she looked around cautiously. Her hand moved unconsciously to her pistol.

He shook his head. "No, I'm certain they didn't have a hand in this slaughter."

"If not them, then who? Do you think your brother came this way?" she asked casually. "You said you were following him."

Raphael tensed, but kept his features calm. "I doubt we'll ever know what was behind this massacre. Now help me with the bodies before the sun gets much higher," he said. "My eyes are watering from the stench."

"Why don't we burn them?" she suggested.

He shook his head. "The animals we encountered are starving. These bodies could keep them fed for a week or more."

Catherine frowned. "But they're people," she said, as if that explained everything.

"Yes, they were, but they're dead now. They won't feel a thing and their deaths will help ensure the survival of others," he said softly. "I know you find this distasteful, but I could really use your help."

Raphael looked at her. He could see the battle raging behind her soulful eyes. She wanted to fight him on this, but part of her understood and agreed with his reasoning. In that moment he realized how young Catherine really was, and he'd never felt so old.

"Fine, let's get this over with." She marched toward the bodies. Catherine grabbed the smallest one and dragged the corpse over the walkway that led out of the compound. Raphael didn't speak. He walked over, picked up two of the bigger bodies, and followed.

They dragged the bodies out fifty yards from the moat of fire and scattered them over a hundred foot area. Raphael took out a knife and sliced through the corpses' clothes, wrenching them off.

"What are you doing?" Catherine shouted, her color high. She was out of breath and itching for a fight. It was her way of dealing with the death surrounding her.

"I'm making it easier for the animals. This way they won't have to eat their way through clothes. And if anyone wanders by in need of clothing, they'll have it readily available."

Catherine shot him a look of disgust. "You're creepy sometimes, you know that?"

"I know," Raphael said quietly. Her assessment hurt more than it should. "Now come here and stick out your arms." She did as she was told. Raphael cut the clothes away and piled them in Catherine's arms. When the pile reached the top of her head, he told her to go back to the compound. He finished what he'd started and collected the remaining outfits.

He could already hear the predators approaching. They were silent, but not silent enough. There was a pack heading in from the east and a big cat coming from the north. Maybe even the same one they'd encountered earlier. It wouldn't matter. There was enough food here for all of them.

Raphael straightened and headed back to the compound. He could feel the sun's needle-like rays beginning to sting his skin. He hadn't bothered putting on sunscreen because he'd planned to be inside by now. He hurried, dropping the rest of the clothes on a table near the center of the compound.

He found the fuel the group used to keep the fire in the pit going, a combination of rags and various flammable liquids that Raphael had never seen before. He wondered where they'd gotten their hands on such a thing, but quickly released the thought as the pain in his skin intensified. He replenished the moat until the flames once again rose high, then grabbed their packs and slipped into a tent. There was no time to set up one of the ones they'd brought with them.

Chaos watched Raphael rub his arm and seek shelter. She glanced out over the horizon. The sun was higher now and so was the heat. It was like someone had tossed flame onto the ground and set everything alight.

She missed the climate-controlled dome at IPTT. Even the shuttles were cooler than this and the air only worked half the time in them. She started to turn away when movement caught her attention.

A pack of canines had found the bodies and began to feed. There were coyotes with them, which let out excited yips before joining in. A big cat with black and gold stripes came in from the opposite direction. The pack tried to run it off, but didn't succeed

Despite the bones sticking out of its sides, the cat was large and powerful—easily big enough to kill every canine. Chaos rubbed her arms to ward off the chill skating over her spine. She couldn't think about what the animals were eating or she'd scream. She gave the horizon one last look and followed Raphael into the tent.

He was lying down, holding his arm when she entered. Raphael sat up quickly and dropped his hand.

"Let me see your arm," Chaos said.

"It's nothing," he said. "Just a little burn. It'll be gone by nightfall."

"I'll be the judge of that." She pushed his hand away. Blisters covered his arm where it had been exposed to the sun. Chaos gasped before she could stop herself.

"I'm fine." He winced.

"Like hell you are. This is bad." Chaos looked around the tent for her pack. She saw it perched against the wall and left him to retrieve it. She dug into the bottom and came out with a white tube, then rummaged inside the bag once more for a disinfectant capsule.

"Really, it's nothing." He sighed. "At least it will be in a few hours."

"Yeah, you're a big tough guy. I get it. You may want to close your mouth and shut your eyes," she said.

"What?" He looked at the items in her hand. "What are those?"

Chaos set the clear capsule on the floor of the tent and pressed the center of it. "Close your eyes and mouth now!" she shouted, then shut her eyes.

There was an explosion and a thick mist filled the air.

Raphael cursed and grabbed his canteen. He took a deep swallow of water and wiped his mouth with the back of his hand.

"Told you to close your mouth and shut your eyes," Chaos said, then walked over to where he lay. "This should help your burn." She opened the lid on the white tube and squeezed some of the clear substance onto her fingertips. Chaos took care applying the ointment. "It'll hurt a little at first, but it should take the pain away."

His eyes narrowed with suspicion. "What was the other thing?"

"Disinfectant," she said. "Should be dry by now. I wasn't about to stay inside this tent without it. Dung knows what biological things were lurking on these furs." She shivered dramatically.

Raphael watched her, his dark gaze unwavering. When she was done, Chaos popped the lid back onto the tube and dropped it into her pack.

"Try not to move," she said. "It takes a couple of minutes to set."

He nodded.

She ignored the heat she saw banked in his black eyes and rose to explore the tent. The space wasn't big, about fifteen feet across, but there were hides and rags tossed around that indicated at least eight people slept in here. Chaos wondered which of the bodies had called this place home.

Raphael lay on the center mound facing the entry flap. Even in repose, he was watchful. "Get some rest while you can." He patted the empty spot beside him.

"I'll sleep over here, thanks." Chaos ignored the heat rising inside the tent.

"Suit yourself." Raphael grinned, then rested one arm over his eyes.

After a moment she asked, "How can you think of sex after hauling dead bodies around? That's sick, even for you."

"I've been called worse." Raphael held her gaze. "Despite what you think of me, I am not a monster. I've seen more death in my lifetime than any man should. I learned long ago that you can't do much for the dead. It's why I choose to concentrate on what makes life worth living. Surely you can understand that." He closed his eyes, effectively ending the conversation.

She could, but she didn't say so. Chaos didn't feel like giving him the satisfaction of knowing that she agreed with him. She waited for a moment, watching him rest. When she was sure he wasn't peeking, Chaos looked him over. She hadn't been able to do so before because he was always watching her. Now she could look her fill.

He had a lean body made for swift movement and stealth. He'd walked up on her so many times without her hearing him that she was convinced Raphael somehow floated. His fingers were long, pale, and tapered. He could do wicked things with those hands. He'd brought her pleasure unlike any she'd ever experienced with just the brush of his thumb.

Even now she could feel his hands caressing her flesh, seeking out the hidden places in her body, exploring moist openings. She allowed her gaze to venture down his long, hard length.

Chaos paused at the bulge protruding at the juncture of his thighs. Raphael may have a lean body, but he was a big man. She'd nearly fainted at his size, convinced there was no way he'd ever fit inside her. But fit he did...repeatedly.

The bulge grew before her eyes. Her gaze swept to his face, where a smile danced over his sensual mouth. Even resting, Raphael toyed with her like he knew her every thought, her every fantasy. Maybe he did. Maybe that bite delivered more than orgasmic release. Maybe something entered her blood, even as he feasted.

Her nipples hardened under her shirt and Chaos nearly groaned aloud. Her body ached—and not from the long hike they'd made or the heavy lifting. She wasn't going to let her hormones get the best of her. Chaos punched her pack before settling against it. It was going to be a long day.

* * * * *

Raphael kept still, although it pained him to do so. He could feel Catherine's curious gaze, studying him. He wanted her to look. Liked that she'd spent so much time doing so. His shaft ached incessantly and he wanted nothing more than to strip those dirty clothes off her petite body and give Catherine a tongue bath starting at her toes and working his way up.

Despite her protestations, he could smell her need. It permeated the tent, making the hot air even more stifling. Raphael thought about reaching out to take her, but he'd done that enough in Nuria.

It was Catherine's turn to do the taking. She needed to be the one in control, even if it was an illusion. That would be the only way they'd ever move past him detaining her against her will.

She believed he felt nothing for the dead, but Catherine was wrong. Despite his years spent on the battlefield, Raphael had never gotten used to the casualties. Of course, these nomads hadn't lost their lives due to war. They'd simply had the misfortune of encountering his brother.

Michael, what have you done? Sadness welled inside of him.

Raphael pushed it aside and waited, but still she didn't move. What was taking Catherine so long? The ache in his groin had intensified to out-and-out pain. Damn it, at this rate he'd have blue balls before she ever got the nerve to act. He peeked out from under his arm, opening his eyes just wide enough to see. She was propped against her backpack, arms crossed over her chest...*sleeping?*

Raphael sat up abruptly. What the hell? He looked at her again. Catherine's eyes were closed and her mouth had fallen open. Her knees were bent to keep her upright. She had to be toying with him. Surely she hadn't gone from lust to sleep that fast. He leaned closer, expecting her to yell "gotcha!"

Catherine snuffled, then she let out a loud snore.

Raphael fell back onto the rags with a scowl. So much for spending the afternoon rolling on furs.

* * * * *

CHAPTER FOURTEEN

They had kept their brisk pace throughout the night to cover as much ground as possible. Demery took the lead, while Morgan brought up the rear. All watched for potential ambushes.

Demery slipped his white protective suit on as the sun peered over the horizon. "It'll take another day or so to reach the outpost the scout spoke of," he said. "Do you want to keep going or rest?"

Red looked at Morgan. He tilted his head as if to say it's up to you. "Let's go a little farther. I want more distance between us and the Sand Moles." The nomads had every right to want to retaliate.

Demery nodded and strode on.

Movement to the left caught Red's attention. Something brown scurried over the dune, leaving an "S" shape in the sand behind it. "What's that?"

Morgan came forward as Demery stopped. He smiled when he saw what had caught her attention. "It's a lizard."

"I didn't think there were any of those alive outside of captivity," she said.

He grinned at her. "I guess someone should've told the little guy."

Red watched in fascination. She'd read about lizards and all the other creatures that used to live on Earth before the last war. Most were extinct. The ones that weren't either lived in captivity or struggled with starvation. But not this one. It was wild like the animals her grandfather told her stories about. She followed it up over the ridge and watched it disappear inside a tiny hole in the sand.

"He went in a hole," she said.

Morgan laughed. "That's what they do when a predator is after them."

"A predator?" She frowned and glanced around, but didn't see anything that would eat the small lizard. Red looked back at Morgan, whose smile had grown. "Oh, you mean me." She laughed as she stepped off the dune. It felt good. She hadn't done much laughing lately.

He hugged her. "You are amazing," he said. "You know that?"

"Why?" she asked.

"Even in the middle of this hellhole, you can still find time to be fascinated by the simplest thing."

"Thanks." She squeezed him back. "Guess I've spent enough time terrifying lizards."

They trudged on. Sand filled their boots and abraded their faces. They journeyed for another hour without spotting any other signs of life.

"Do you think they'll have the equipment we need?" Red asked Morgan as they sat to rest in the shade of a dune.

"I don't know. I'm not expecting much." He looked grim. "The good thing is that even if the equipment is old school I should still be able to do something with it."

"Old school?" she asked.

"From my time," he explained.

Once again Red was reminded that despite appearances, Morgan was older than her grandfather. "Let's hope the ancient equipment still works," she said tartly.

He grabbed her side and squeezed. Red wiggled away from him before returning to rest her head on his shoulder.

Demery watched them with something akin to envy in his eyes. "You better get some sleep, mon. We have a lot of miles to travel before we reach the outpost."

Red nodded and closed her eyes.

* * * * *

Morgan waited until Gina's breathing had deepened, before

propping her against the pack. He stood stretching his legs and back. Despite exhaustion, sleep evaded him. He'd pulled out Kane's diaries, but still couldn't bring himself to listen to them. He was too distracted, too worried.

The scene from the previous night kept replaying in his head. Gina had shot the leader of the Sand Moles with little to no thought. Something she wouldn't have done outside of patrol a month and a half ago. Was the wolf changing her or was he to blame?

The latter thought disturbed Morgan. He'd brought her into a hostile world. She'd been naive in so many ways, her life sheltered by her grandfather and IPTT. Morgan didn't want Gina changing because of her association with him. He loved her the way that she was, even before she knew what lurked inside of her. Gina was a brave, fearless, sensual woman. His match in every way.

Morgan leaned down and pressed his lips to her forehead. She murmured, but didn't wake. He sensed her wolf lurking close to the surface. So close that he wondered if it was finally ready to come out on command.

Part of him longed for her to let go, allow the wolf free rein for a while. The wolf in him wanted its mate. Another part of him feared it. What if she couldn't control herself in her other form? She'd finally controlled a partial shift. It had taken months and Roark trying to kill him to do it, but she'd managed. He'd been so proud of her.

Morgan didn't want to take that sense of accomplishment away, but there was more to being a wolf than just controlling the change. There were responsibilities she'd have to accept if they ever returned to Nuria. Responsibilities he wasn't sure she'd be happy about. Was she ready to step into the position of alpha female and bear his young? Her existence had already brought Nuria hope. That hope would solidify if she were able to have a family.

The thought of Gina carrying his child hit Morgan in the gut, then slowly rose to sit comfortably on his heart. If he closed his eyes, he could almost picture her rounded belly and heavy breasts. She'd be beautiful with her body bursting with new life.

Morgan choked on the swell of unexpected emotion and had to walk away before he embarrassed himself. The thought was too overwhelming for him to contemplate when there was a very good chance they wouldn't make it out of here alive.

He scanned the horizon. It wasn't the first time he'd wondered why they hadn't been followed. It could be that killing the leader of the Sand Moles had scared the group into inaction, but it didn't seem likely.

People living in no-man's-land didn't scare easily. They were used to death hanging around, patiently waiting for one of them to make a mistake. So where were they? Where was the scout? Jeb wasn't following. He would've smelled him.

Demery lumbered up beside him. "Is there a problem, mon?"

Morgan rolled his shoulders and squinted behind his sunshades. "Something isn't right," he said.

Demery tilted his head and slowly made a 360-degree turn. "I don't sense anything," he said once he'd finished.

"That's just it. Why aren't they following us?" Morgan asked. "We shot their leader. They should've at least sent the scout out to keep an eye on us."

Demery frowned behind the mask of his protective suit. "You're right. I haven't sensed anyone out there. No one behind or up ahead."

Morgan scratched his head. "Between the two of us, we should be able to sense someone or something. I realize this place is dead, but this is something else." He stared at the sand until his eyes watered.

Demery continued to scan. "It's like we are the only living creatures for miles around."

Morgan nodded in agreement. "I don't like it. It feels wrong. Could be a trap."

At the word "trap," Demery stiffened. "You're being paranoid, mon."

"You heard what the scout said. We have a bounty on our heads. I realize that doesn't include you, but I doubt that would stop anyone from shooting first and asking questions later," Morgan said.

"You're right. I am in danger as long as we're traveling together." Demery glanced at Red. "But I can't abandon her yet."

"Yet?" Morgan tensed. "Is that your way of telling me that you're going to eventually leave us out here?"

"No, mon. I won't be leaving you. At least not until you're settled somewhere." Demery grinned. "Maybe it's a coincidence we haven't run into anyone. Try not to look a gift lizard in the mouth," he said.

Morgan snorted, but his stomach continued to churn.

* * * * *

It was late afternoon by the time Red woke. The light had begun to turn the sand crimson and orange. Morgan and Demery were huddled beside her in the shade, sleeping. She stood and stretched, reaching her arms above her head before rolling her shoulders. She needed to move. Itched to run, but she couldn't in the heat. Red placated herself by crawling to the top of the dune. She kept her head down, so she could peek over the ridge and scan the area. There was no movement. Red squinted in the direction they were heading.

"Hey guys, I think it flattens out over there," she said.

The two men came awake with a start.

"What?" Morgan asked.

"I think I see a flat area in the direction we need to go." Just the thought of being out of these dunes made Red giddy. She had sand in her boots, pants, hair, and teeth. Pretty much any bit of exposed flesh was covered in grit.

The men rose and joined her at the top of the dune. "Did you spot anything else?" Morgan asked.

She shook her head. "No, nothing."

"Then let's go. The sun will be setting in a few hours," Morgan said.

They gathered their equipment and started walking. Just as Red had thought, the dunes gave way to a flat desert valley. The skeletal remains of cactus dotted the area like sentries from the past, their ghostly white bodies a reminder of the fallen. She'd never seen anything more beautiful or more frightening.

Red stopped to empty her boots. Morgan did the same. Demery didn't have to worry about it, since sand couldn't get into his suit during the day. Night was a different story.

She turned to the vamp. "How much farther?"

"Another day's walk from here," he said. "Remember Jeb said

113

that we have to go over the mountains, but I don't think it's a good idea to cross them in the dark. The hiking trails are treacherous and there are a lot of places for people to hide."

The craggy ridge of sienna-colored mountains stood majestically in the distance. They appeared small, but they'd be imposing once they got closer. At this pace it would still take several hours to reach them.

"We better get going," she said. Maybe they'd get lucky and make good time without being spotted.

She judged the time before sunset. If they went now, they just might make it to the foothills before dark.

* * * * *

They were two hours into their walk when Red spotted a puff of dust rising in the distance. She squinted, watching the plume grow as it drew nearer.

"Something's coming," she shouted and looked around for a place to take cover. There was none. "Keep your heads down." She took off running toward the foothills.

Red judged the distance between the plume and the mountains and realized they wouldn't make it, unless they ran faster. They sprinted, keeping low to the ground. Red had hoped they'd blend with the terrain, until she glanced over at Demery's white protective suit. It glowed like a beacon against the flat beige desert floor.

Morgan followed her gaze and cursed under his breath, then ran faster. "We may have to shift," he shouted.

Red nodded, even as her stomach protested. She'd only managed a partial shift before now. The only time she'd ever successfully shifted was when she was asleep. She wasn't like Morgan, who could shift with a thought. Her process took time and concentration. And frankly, had yet to be totally successful. It must have dawned on Morgan at the same moment because he looked at her with fear and concern in his eyes.

The cloud of dust grew larger. Red could see a glint of metal reflecting off some kind of vehicle. She could also see something else—it wasn't alone. There were many vehicles traveling in a convoy. She looked up at the mountains ahead of them. They were closer, but not close enough.

"Shift and get out of here," she shouted to Morgan.

He looked at her like she'd lost her mind.

"We may need your help when these people catch up with us. It's better if they don't know you're here."

Demery looked over at the approaching band. "I think I know these people."

"You said that last time and look where it got us." Red was panting. The heat made it hard to catch her breath.

"We were doing fine until you killed the leader," Demery retorted. He was slower in his suit, which made him still faster than Red and any pureblood around.

She shot him a sharp glance. "I saved our asses from getting turned over to the authorities."

"Well whoever these guys are, there are a lot of them. We're out-manned, out-gunned, and out-maneuvered. If this is who I think it is, running won't help." Demery slowed.

Fear coiled in her gut. "Who are they?"

The vehicles seemed to multiply by the second. Even Morgan looked worried as he pumped his fists harder. His hair had already thickened and the muscles in his back and legs corded as the change ripped through his body. His clothes tore away, leaving flesh exposed and vulnerable to the unforgiving sun.

Red's lungs burned and her side ached like a tactical drill sergeant had kicked her. She wasn't sure how much farther she could run before she collapsed. Between the heat and the weight of the pack, her body was dehydrating at an astonishing rate. Soon her muscles would cramp and the race would end.

Don't give up now, you're almost there, Red chided herself.

She pressed her thumbs to the stocks of her pistols. It wasn't much, but Red found the weapons' presence soothing. Children had blankets, she had her guns. She heard a beep. She had enough time to charge the pistols, but did she have enough ammo to take out an entire band of armed enemies? Not a chance.

Red tried to focus on the change, calling to it. Her hands burned as claws forced their way through her fingertips. A burst of energy shot through her, but didn't give her enough added speed to beat the motorized pursuit.

"Demery," she shouted. He didn't answer her immediately.

"You said you knew them. Who are they?"

He stopped to face the approaching vehicles. "It's Reaper and the Sand Devils," Demery said, smiling. "We found them at last."

Red looked at the dark cloud of dust that the vehicles were kicking up in their wake, then back at Demery. Why in the hell did it feel like that wasn't a good thing?

* * * * *

CHAPTER FIFTEEN

Raphael awoke to something tickling his stomach. His first reaction was to swat it away. Only when it happened again did he realize what the tickle was...Catherine's lips.

He stayed very still, waiting to see what she'd do. She pressed her mouth to his abdomen and slowly made her way down to the front of his pants. Raphael's breath caught.

"I was wondering when you were going to wake up," she said.

His lashes fluttered open to half-mast so he could see her. She was straddling him, her knees resting next to his thighs. She'd pushed his shirt up, exposing his chest. Her lips were slightly swollen like she'd been kissing him for a while. The fact that he hadn't woken was a testament to his exhaustion and the level of trust he had in her.

"Don't let me stop you." Raphael licked a fang in anticipation.

Catherine's full lips quirked and she leaned forward to lay another open-mouthed kiss on his chest. Her tongue peeked out, tasting his flat nipple, hardening it instantly.

Raphael gripped the rags and furs beneath him to keep from reaching for her. This one was for her. Catherine needed to be in control. Needed to realize that there was more going on between them than bargains and threats. His head dropped back and he tried to relax, but her sensual mouth wouldn't let him.

Catherine teased his flesh, biting, nibbling, and licking like he was covered in synth- honey. His body bowed beneath her as she brushed the waistband of his pants with her tongue.

He wanted her to open them and take him deep into her mouth. Raphael wanted to feel Catherine's lips surround him. Her tongue stroking him. The suction of her mouth, when she drank from him. He was so hard he felt near bursting. One touch, one caress, and he'd spend himself like a teenage boy next to his first naked woman.

Her warm breath caressed the hairs that disappeared beneath his waistband. Raphael's stomach clenched as she slipped her tongue over them and slowly licked. He gritted his teeth and grasped the rags tighter. They ripped.

Catherine giggled. "Like that?" she asked.

"You know I do," he said between ragged breaths.

She leaned down and kissed him again, trailing her lips along his abdomen. His eyes followed her every move. Her fingers deftly found the opening to his pants and unfastened them, spreading the material wide. Warm air hit his rising shaft and he gasped.

"What do we have here?" she asked.

His erection pulsed, growing thicker and longer under her hungry gaze. "Damn it, woman," Raphael growled. "Are you trying to torture me?"

"Yes." Catherine laughed. "I figure it's only fair, given what you've done to me."

She had a point. "Fine," Raphael said. "Do what you wish. I am yours for the taking."

That throwaway statement stopped her. Catherine blinked in surprise and looked at him. Her gaze searched his face. The vulnerability he sensed, rocked him, shattering what little protection he'd had around his heart.

"Why would you say that?" she asked.

He met her green eyes. They shimmered with such intensity that it stole his breath. "Because it's the truth," he said softly.

* * * * *

Chaos stared for a moment longer, then pulled Raphael's shirt over his head. He had such a beautiful body, all strong lines and firm walls. In clothes or naked, he oozed sexuality as easily as most people exhaled. She'd wanted to touch him on her own terms, but didn't think that was ever going to happen.

She still couldn't believe she'd gotten up the nerve to do so while he was sleeping. Chaos splayed her small hand over his chest, running a finger down the length of dark hair that led to his impressive erection. She longed to taste him there and she would, in a moment, after she'd had her fill of exploring the rest of him.

Chaos stood and stripped the boots off Raphael, taking his pants along with them. When she'd finished, he was lying against the makeshift rest pad, gloriously naked. She allowed her eyes to feast, taking in every inch of him. He lounged back so erotically male, waiting to be worshipped.

A smile played on his lips as he watched her. He looked to be getting as much pleasure from this encounter as she was. Why that surprised Chaos, she didn't know. Maybe she'd thought he only got off while using high-handed tactics.

His expression said otherwise. Raphael was a creature of pleasure—both giving and receiving. He wasn't selfish, as she'd initially thought. She'd misunderstood his earlier actions, though she hadn't yet forgiven them. Chaos wondered what else she'd misunderstood about the man.

"Don't move." She slowly undressed.

Raphael's eyes darkened, heating in the low light, and his breathing deepened. The muscles in his arms quivered, but he didn't move. He only watched. The longer he watched, the hungrier *she* became.

"What are you planning to do?" he asked, his voice a rough rasp that puckered her nipples.

His eyes followed her body's responses, taking in every change, every subtle nuance. Like a predator, he was clocking her weaknesses, waiting for a chance to pounce.

Chaos dropped to her knees and straddled his thighs once again. His shaft bucked against his abdomen in anticipation. She slowly kissed Raphael's neck, then made her way down his body. He gasped when Chaos bit his collarbone, then groaned as she soothed the sting with a swipe of her tongue.

With every embrace, the moisture gathering between her thighs increased. By the time Chaos worked her way to his shaft, she was drenched and Raphael's body was covered in sweat, a testament to the fight he'd been waging internally.

She grabbed him at the base, then met his gaze before slowly sucking him into her mouth. His nostrils flared as she drew on him deeply before releasing him and repeating the whole process again.

Raphael let out a strangled cry and his hands bit into her shoulders. He clung to her as she slowly devoured him.

"I never thought I'd feel your mouth around me." He rolled his hips to chase her retreating lips. "So hot. So moist." He groaned. "And so damn good. Please," he said, breathlessly, his entire body tense and quivering with the need for release.

Chaos giggled, then ran her tongue along the underside of his length until she encountered his sac. She sucked one ball into her mouth while gently palming the other. A small amount of fluid shot out of Raphael's shaft and his entire body trembled as he fought to stave off release.

A sense of power washed over Chaos, knowing she had—at least for now—this extremely powerful man under her control and craving her touch. She reveled in the feeling, even though it made her ache.

When she'd started this game, her intention had been to keep her emotional distance while she manipulated his body. It was only fair given what he'd done to her in Nuria. Raphael had tied her to a chair naked and interrogated her. He'd used pleasure as a form a torture. It had been humiliating…and the most thrilling thing she'd ever experienced.

But arousing Raphael had backfired. She'd not only fueled his desire, Chaos had ignited her own. She ground her clit into his hard thigh to get some relief. Instead of taking the edge off, the small movement made it worse. She whimpered around Raphael, then gradually released him.

Raphael's eyes were clouded with raw desire. His gaze locked on her hand as she encircled his length. "What are you doing?" he croaked.

"I'm taking you," she said. Chaos rose, positioning her body above his, then slowly lowered herself onto him, impaling herself.

His lungs heaved, bellowing loudly as Raphael watched.

She rode him slowly, rocking her hips between thrusts. He felt so good, so big and hard, filling her completely. Chaos couldn't remember a better fit or a sexier man than Raphael. He was slowly but surely erasing every man from her memory and she was letting him. But could she trust him with more than her body?

Chaos rose to her knees. The heated glide of his shaft was exquisite as it stroked in and out, hitting just the right spots. The need built inside her until she couldn't take it anymore. Chaos reached for her clit and plucked at her swollen flesh while she bounced up and down, faster and faster. The wet sound of skin slapping skin filled the tent. The world narrowed between them as the primal dance continued.

When she was balanced on the precipice, teetering between awareness and oblivion, their eyes met. What Chaos saw shimmering in Raphael's black depths stole her breath. A moment later, she gasped and plummeted into the abyss. She fell further, faster, and harder than she'd ever tumbled before.

Power rushed out of her body, encircling them in a cocoon of chaotic energy. Raphael convulsed beneath her, his hips jerked, driving him deep inside her. A cry wrenched from Chaos' raw throat and her body jolted on top of him, dimming her vision and deafening her to her surroundings.

By the time the wave allowed her to come up for air, Chaos was sprawled across Raphael's chest and he was stroking her back. Her breathing was coming in great pants and she noticed one more thing—he was still hard as a boulder.

"I thought you..." She tried to get her thoughts together as she looked at him.

"This one was for you." He smiled and continued caressing her with his short nails.

"But I wanted you—" Chaos began.

"And you had me," Raphael said before she could finish.

She frowned. "You didn't climax."

Raphael smoothed her brow. "I need a little something more." he said, without clarifying.

"More?" She was worn out. Chaos didn't think her body could handle more after that orgasm. It took her a moment to realize what he meant. Raphael hadn't taken her blood this time.

His words came back to her. *This time was for you.* He'd purposely held off biting her so she could be in charge. Something in Chaos' heart melted. Something she thought would never thaw. With a flick of her wrist, she brushed her short hair aside.

* * * * *

Raphael's heart stuttered in his chest as Catherine bared her neck to him. He licked his lips before he could stop himself. "No." He shook his head. "This one was for you. If I take your blood, it'll change everything."

"Not if it's freely given," she said, tilting her head a little farther until the muscle bulged.

Raphael's nostrils flared as he fought the urge to yank her to him. Instead, he stroked her back with his fingertip, then threaded his hands into her short red hair. He pulled her mouth to his and kissed her deeply, passionately. Tasting, touching, stroking, and coaxing her tongue to tangle with his.

She'd done a good job of avoiding the intimate act earlier. Perhaps Catherine thought not kissing him would somehow protect her heart, but Raphael would have none of it. He wanted all of her, demanded nothing less than her complete and total surrender.

Catherine was tentative at first, as if she wasn't used to being kissed. Her style was clumsy and endearing. He vowed that would change under his tutelage. He would teach her everything he knew and then some.

He pulled back, letting her take charge and set the pace. Raphael waited for her to relax. They clanked teeth and mashed lips in a clumsy mating that made his heart melt with its purity and sheer innocence.

When things fell into a natural rhythm, Raphael deepened the embrace, tasting her once more with his tongue, worrying her lips with his teeth. He made sure to keep his fangs retracted. He didn't want to accidentally cut her and send himself into a frenzy. Catherine followed his lead, then slowly took charge.

Her swollen nipples hardened as they brushed his chest. Raphael pulled her close and kept kissing her. She tasted so fresh, so clean, utterly wrong for him, but that didn't stop him from taking what she offered.

He wanted her. Hell, he needed her. And Raphael hadn't needed anyone for a very long time. He knew he was in trouble as Catherine's weight settled on top of him. He released her hair and ran his hands down her body, grasping her ass. It was small and compact, much like the woman. He squeezed, grinding her hips into him. He thickened inside her and surged toward release.

No! Not yet, something in his mind screamed.

Raphael broke the embrace, trailing kisses over her eyes and cheeks. Catherine gasped as he made his way to her ear. He nibbled on her lobe, before dipping his tongue inside. Her body clenched him tight. He wasn't the only one anticipating the bite.

"Do you want me?" he murmured in her ear.

"You know I do." She rocked her hips.

"All of me?" He ran his fangs along the column of her throat, but didn't break the skin.

"Yes," Catherine hissed, then slammed her body down on his erection.

Raphael groaned. "You're not playing fair." He nipped her lobe before returning to nuzzle her neck.

"I never do," she said. "You of all people should know that by now."

"I do." Raphael growled and bit down.

Catherine exploded on contact, her body riding another orgasm as her hot blood rushed into his mouth. Raphael's senses came alive, cataloguing the moment like a voyeur. The musk, the sweet taste of her essence on his tongue, the tight grip she had on his shaft, and the need that kept building and building inside of him.

Raphael pumped his hips, driving her down at the same time until she was locked tight. Damn it, he couldn't get enough traction. Without thought, he rolled them, never breaking contact. He tongued her neck, while drawing from the wound.

God, she tasted so good and felt even better. His hips rocked, pumping hard as her blood rocketed through his system and sent him into an animalistic fervor. Raphael threw his head back and roared, then latched onto her neck again.

He was half out of his mind and blood drunk by the time he followed Catherine into oblivion. Spent, Raphael collapsed to the side, pulling her close and tucking her small frame against his chest.

It took some time, but her breathing finally leveled out. Soon she'd be asleep. Raphael stroked Catherine's hip, trying to maintain consciousness, but it was a losing battle. She'd sapped his strength, leaving him deliciously spent in every way.

"That was the most amazing thing I've ever experienced." He'd never be able to let her go. How would he tell her? And what would she do when she learned the truth?

They rose as the sun was beginning to set. Chaos gathered her pack, struggling to get it on her shoulders. Raphael walked over and plucked it out of her hands. He handed her his smaller pack, then pulled hers onto his back.

"Let's switch for a while." He secured her pack into place without waiting for her answer.

* * * * *

Chaos opened her mouth to protest, but closed it quickly, secretly grateful. She shrugged into his pack and then flipped up the tent flap. The fire in the moat had died down, but was still enough of a deterrent to keep the predators away. Not that it would matter, since they'd be leaving the safety of the fire ring soon.

She stepped through the opening and scanned the area around them. Chaos didn't see anything, but waited for Raphael to confirm her observations before going any farther.

He followed her as she walked past the tents toward the thin strip of sand that acted as a safe crossing spot.

"Do you think we'll ever catch up with them?" she asked.

Raphael looked at her, then at the empty area surrounding them. "Yes, as long as they don't encounter any trouble."

"What about us?" she asked.

Raphael caught her chin in his fingertips, his black gaze burning in the fading light. "I won't let anything happen to you," he said with such conviction her heart clenched.

Chaos swallowed hard. "I'd appreciate if you kept yourself out of harm's way while you're at it."

His expression softened, but before he could say anything they might both regret, she said, "Let's go. We have a lot of ground to cover before dawn."

He nodded, but the knowledge she saw in those black eyes unnerved her.

* * * * *

CHAPTER SIXTEEN

Raphael followed Catherine feeling more content than he'd ever felt in his lifetime. He still wasn't sure what that meant, but he was happy to wait for the answer. Once they reached the top of a particularly high dune, Raphael closed his eyes and inhaled deeply.

Michael, can you hear me? he asked, using the psychic channel they'd used as children.

Silence met his call.

Michael, I know you can hear me. You're close. I can sense you near. Why do you not answer?

A breeze picked up, rustling his hair.

Brother, please don't play this silly game. We've been apart long enough. He pleaded.

Raphael? The voice was quiet, hesitant…almost unrecognizable.

Michael, it's me. Where are you? I searched everywhere after Morgan said you were injured. Your silence concerns me. Let me see with my own eyes that you are well.

I'm camped to the south. Where are you?

Not far from a nomadic settlement. Raphael paused, wondering whether he should mention the dead. Michael would sense it if he held back anything. *There were bodies. Lots of bodies.*

Michael ignored the mention of bodies as if they were of no consequence. Raphael's unease grew. He'd protect Catherine with his life, but what if the person he was trying to protect her from was his own brother? Ice filled his veins.

"Are you okay?" Catherine stopped when he hadn't followed. "Is something wrong?"

"I'm fine," Raphael said evenly. "I am trying to contact my brother, using the method *I spoke to you with.*" He finished the last half in her mind.

"Still not comfortable communicating that way," she said. "I'll be over here. Come get me when you're done." She pointed to a spot not far from where she currently stood. It was enough space to give him privacy—not that he needed it.

Michael, are you still there? Raphael called out again.

Yes, you were about to tell me who you are traveling with, he said.

It was Raphael's turn to pause. He hadn't mentioned he was traveling with anyone.

Come now, brother. Don't be shy, Michael teased. *Who is she?*

Her name is Catherine Meyers. She's a member of IPTT.

The news was met with more silence.

We've reached an agreement. I take full responsibility for her. I think it would be best if we met up and traveled together.

How did you know I'd be here? he asked.

Raphael thought about it, then decided to once again answer truthfully. *I searched your home. When I saw your bag was missing, I had a pretty good idea of where you were headed. The only question I have is why?*

Michael sighed mentally, but Raphael heard it.

Long story. Much has happened since we last saw each other.

I've heard some troubling news, but the full story remains murky. Morgan said that Roark harmed you. Is that true? Raphael asked.

I won't wait long. Michael ignored his question and sent him a mental picture of his surroundings.

We'll hurry, Raphael said, breaking the connection. They needed to reach Michael. He could feel it in his gut. His brother was on the edge of being lost to him, but Raphael was determined to save him.

"Did you talk to him?" Catherine rose to her feet.

"Yes." Raphael nodded.

She waited a minute, then added, "And?"

"He is waiting for us to the south. I've seen his small shelter. It's tucked between the dunes."

Catherine looked around and laughed. "Everything here is tucked between dunes."

Raphael smiled. "I've seen what he can see from the top of the dunes surrounding him. I'll feel him when we get close." He looked around to get his bearings.

She hesitated. "It's none of my business, but are you sure this is a good idea?"

"Meeting up with Michael or traipsing out in the middle of no-man's-land without an army?" Raphael asked.

She laughed. "The prior. I mean the guy hasn't exactly gone out of his way to speak to you. And I know you've been trying to contact him."

These were all questions he'd asked himself and had yet to come up with satisfactory answers. What had Roark Montgomery done to his brother to create the screams that Morgan had heard? Why had his brother been avoiding him? Why was his brother after Morgan and Red, when he'd sworn to help them? Until they met up, he wouldn't have his answers.

"It would be safer traveling with my brother," he said quietly, hoping it was the truth.

"No offense, but your brother didn't look like much of a fighter when I met him," Catherine said.

"In this instance, looks can be very deceiving. Michael is the most dangerous man I know."

Her face scrunched. "I thought you owned that title."

Raphael laughed, the sound painful to his ears, and shook his head slowly. She had no idea how very dangerous his brother could be. And he prayed that remained the case for her sake—and his.

Her world was swathed in shades of black and white. There was no gray, only right and wrong. Catherine had no clue how violent a human being could become when survival was on the line, but Raphael and his brother did. They'd lived in hell and walked out the other side, brushing flames off as they went.

"You should know, little storm, that even though I'm extremely dangerous, I am defenseless compared to my brother."

"Good thing you brought me with you." Catherine grinned.

127

"If only it were a joking matter," Raphael said softly.

Her expression grew pensive. "How can you love him if he's such a monster?" she asked, her eyes the size of synth-steaks.

Raphael slipped into her mind and saw she hadn't meant to offend him, so he answered her query with one of his own. "I think the better question is, can you learn to love a monster?"

"I don't have to love him," she said. "We just have to get along."

Raphael looked at her. "I wasn't referring to Michael."

* * * * *

They found Michael exactly where he said he'd be waiting. His campsite was packed up and he was pacing like he could bolt any second. His skin was paler than usual and Raphael noted a slight tremor in his hands.

Raphael put an arm out to stop Catherine from getting any closer. "Wait here." He needed to see how his brother was doing, before he allowed her to approach.

"If you need me, yell." She patted her gun.

"I'll be all right. He's my brother," he said, not sounding as confident as he would've liked. "Michael," Raphael called out.

Michael stopped pacing and turned to face him. For a moment, it was like they'd never been apart. Happiness showed on his face, reminding Raphael of the boy who had followed him to school every day. The joy was gone as quickly as it appeared. His eyes narrowed when they landed on Catherine.

"Brother, it's me," Raphael said.

"I know who you are. Do you think I would not recognize my own brother?" Michael continued to stare at Catherine, his gaze cold and assessing.

Raphael waved his arms, drawing his brother's attention away. His heart hammered in his chest, threatening to batter his lungs into jelly. He stopped a few feet away from Michael, noticing for the first time the dark circles under his eyes.

"What are you doing out here?" Raphael asked.

"The same thing as you, I suspect," Michael said.

"Not likely," Raphael replied. "What happened to you?" He took in Michael's torn clothing and scraped knuckles. He looked as if he'd been on the losing end of a fight. Raphael thought about the dead nomads they'd encountered. If there was a fight, they'd lost.

Michael glanced at him.

Cold swept over Raphael despite the heat. "Tell me, please. So I can fix it," he said, sounding desperate. He hadn't found his brother after all these years only to lose him again. Michael was his only family.

Raphael glanced over his shoulder at Catherine. Her hand rested casually on her weapon, but there was nothing casual about her stance. He willed her to stand down, even though she was only trying to protect him. It was evidence of how shaken Raphael was that he'd forgotten he could mentally communicate with her.

"I can smell the woman on you," Michael said. "Her scent covers you like cologne." His black gaze switched from cold to assessing.

"So? A woman's scent on me is nothing new." Raphael shrugged and kept his expression placid, even though he was feeling something akin to panic inside. Catherine was his. He wouldn't share her body or her blood. Brotherly love wouldn't change that fact.

"True, but this one appears prepared to shed blood in order to protect you," he said. "That is something new." Michael's eyes narrowed as he stared at her. "She looks familiar. Do I know her?"

"No," Raphael said. "But you have run into her in passing."

"Roark's office?" he asked.

"Yes," Raphael said.

Michael grunted in response. "When do you plan on dumping her?" he asked. "She's too small to keep up with the pace we'll set."

"I'll release her when the time feels right," Raphael said. It would never happen.

"Typical," Michael said.

Raphael shook his head. His brother wouldn't understand. "There is nothing typical about this one," he said.

That got a rise out of Michael's left brow. "You'll have to tell me all about it, brother, especially what makes this one so special. She doesn't seem like your...type."

"I have a type?" Raphael asked.

Michael laughed. "Not that I recall." He opened his arms and

129

walked forward.

Raphael stepped into the embrace. "I've missed you," he said, relaxing. Michael seemed normal enough. Contrary to Morgan's assessment, he wasn't showing any signs of distress. Maybe things weren't as bad as Raphael thought.

"Me, too," Michael said. "Now tell your woman to get her hand off the gun stock. I'm not going to bite."

Raphael released Michael, then waved to Catherine to come forward.

* * * * *

Chaos approached cautiously. Raphael's expression was one of relief. She wished she could say the same for his brother's. Something about Michael Travers left her cold. She didn't know whether it was his black eyes or his pale gray complexion.

She glanced at Raphael, who had the same features, but somehow less defined. Raphael was a rough draft to Michael's polished finish. Chaos continued to stare, cataloguing each man's features. She decided it wasn't the color of the eyes that told the real story. It was what she saw in them.

Death.

If Michael Travers felt anything, he didn't show it. Looking into his eyes was like staring into deep water. Chaos didn't like what she saw reflecting on the calm surface. It belied the darkness below. A shiver traversed her body despite the evening heat. He was everything Raphael described and more. How could she have ever thought he was incapable of murder? Michael practically vibrated with barely leashed violence.

Raphael thought they'd be safer traveling together, but Chaos wasn't so sure now that she'd gotten a good look at his brother with his tattered clothes and wild eyes burning with madness.

"Come here," Raphael said. "I know you've met my brother briefly, but I'd like to introduce you properly."

"Catherine Meyers, this is my brother, Michael Vega," Raphael said.

"Thought you said your name was Travers." She stared past Raphael and forced herself to meet Michael's obsidian gaze.

"It is. I changed my last name long ago, when I thought..." his words trailed off as he looked at Raphael.

"We thought we'd lost each other," Raphael filled in. "We only recently reunited. It was a joyous day for us both."

Love shined in Raphael's face. It was so bright that its brilliance nearly blinded Chaos. She'd never had any siblings or parents for that matter. She'd never had anyone to call family besides the clones she was raised with, but she was never really one of them. Chaos hadn't been created. She'd been born. Her parents just hadn't wanted her. She'd gotten over it. But every once in awhile, when she witnessed this kind of love, it drove home all she'd missed.

Chaos stuck out her hand. "Nice to meet you," she said.

Michael grasped her fingers and she felt a mental push that didn't feel like Raphael's gentle presence. *You don't have to pretend*, the voice said. *I sense the truth.*

Michael... How was he able to speak directly in her mind? Did he know why she was really here? The thought terrified her.

For Raphael's sake, I do have to pretend, she said, responding in kind.

His lip canted into what Chaos guessed was supposed to be a smile. "It's a pleasure to see you again." *I know you don't care for me*, he added mentally.

Do you blame me? The last time I saw you I ended up drugged out of my mind. She didn't add that she went out and killed people afterward. *Your boss is a real piece of work.*

I had nothing to do with that, I assure you.

Raphael said you'd say that, she said.

But you don't believe him.

Now that I've gotten a good look at you, no. She shook her head.

It's the truth. I don't act in such covert ways. Once you get to know me, you'll find I'm quite direct. It was said nonchalantly, but his tone didn't lessen the threat behind his words.

Really? Then what are you doing here? Chaos asked. *Taking in the sights?*

Michael gave her a real smile this time. "She's clever, brother," he said. "You'd better watch her closely. I know I will."

Raphael's grin seemed forced. He pulled Chaos close. "You should know that I rarely take my eyes off her."

"That's evident," Michael said, acknowledging their embrace. "I've never seen you quite so taken. She must really be *special*."

A slash of red covered Raphael's cheeks. He released Chaos as if she had singed his fingertips. "We should continue on," he stammered.

"Eloquent as always." Michael chuckled. His warm gaze moved from his brother to Chaos, where it quickly cooled. *You'd better not hurt him,* he warned.

Funny, I was about to say the same thing to you, she said.

* * * * *

CHAPTER SEVENTEEN

The vehicles barreled toward them, causing the ominous brown plume of dust to grow. The sound of the engines rumbled like thunder.

"We have to make a stand," Red shouted to Morgan.

"There's no cover," he said. "It would be a slaughter."

"I'll try to talk with them." Demery gave Red a quick smile, then set out to meet the Sand Devils.

"You said these people were thieves. What if they aren't in the mood to reason?" Red asked. The question stopped Demery. "They may know about the reward, too."

"Probably, but it doesn't matter. The sun is setting," Demery said. "We aren't going to make it to the rocks in time and even if we did, they know this area ten times better than I do. It's where they hunt. Besides, they have something of mine."

Her heart stuttered in her chest at the thought of being hunted. She'd always been the predator, never the prey.

Morgan's gaze softened when it fell on her. She was the reason they couldn't make it to the mountains before the Sand Devil vehicles reached them. Red knew it even though she couldn't detect blame in his amber eyes. Once again her inability to control her Other was putting them all in danger just like it had back in Nuria. Despite all her progress, nothing had changed.

I'm sorry, she mouthed, then looked away, unable to meet Morgan's gaze for fear she'd see condemnation. Red turned to face the group approaching from the west.

They didn't have much left to trade with, but they could part with a few items. She hoped that would be enough to keep them alive, because they didn't have the firepower to fight their way out.

The Sand Devils came to a halt thirty yards away. The windows had been replaced with metal, leaving slits for the drivers to see out.

Red couldn't spot any of the people. They remained tucked in their vehicles like turtles inside of metal shells. Demery stepped forward in his protective suit and held his arms wide. Morgan moved closer to Red, positioning his body between her and the group.

"Who's in charge here?" Demery shouted through his suit.

No one in the steel convoy replied.

"My name is Demery. Perhaps some of you know me," he said, loudly. "I seek Reaper."

A door to one of the vehicles in the rear popped open and a long-limbed beautiful woman with skin like the night sky poked her head out and looked at them.

"Demi, is that you?" she cried and bounded out of the vehicle toward him. She wore a long skirt and top that matched the desert. It flowed around her slim frame. Her feet were bare and callused from walking on the sand.

"Melea?" Demery rushed forward and caught the woman as she leapt into his arms. "I've missed you so much." He held her close.

"You came back for me." She hugged him like she'd never let him go and kissed his faceplate.

Demery pulled back and brushed her long braided hair away from her face. "Are you well? Has he been—" Demery's voice broke. He glanced at Red and Morgan as if remembering that they were still there.

"I'm fine." Tears filled her big brown eyes. "Especially now that you are here. I knew you'd come."

"Melea, time to return to your rightful place," a baritone voice boomed. "Your blood and I have business to discuss."

Red and Morgan looked at each other as a massive man stepped out of the same vehicle Melea had been in only moments ago. Standing head and shoulders taller than the roof of the vehicle, the man's body was corded with muscle. A snake tattoo started at his neck, then curled down around his arm before its head ended at his closed mallet-sized fist.

Metal piercings twinkled in the fading sunlight, protruding out of his shaven head like horns. He was not a handsome man. His pulverized appearance revealed his participation in plenty of fights. The altercations had left his nose winding like a switchback road down his face.

"I'm not going to ask you again, Melea," the man growled, flashing teeth that had been filed into sharp points.

Demery held the woman tighter. "We had a deal, Reaper," he said.

"And I've kept my side of the bargain," Reaper said. "Your woman is in more or less the same condition you left her in."

Demery pulled Melea back to have a good look at her.

The woman was a little underweight and scraped up, but otherwise appeared fine as far as Red could tell.

What in the hell was going on? Who was this woman? Was she the item he'd needed to retrieve? What had Reaper meant by blood? Red didn't like the sound of that, considering that a vampire was involved.

"Demery," Red called out.

He shook his head, warning her to remain silent.

"Who are your friends?" Reaper asked.

"No one of consequence," Demery said. "I believe we have business to discuss."

Tension poured off Morgan. Red didn't like this. Demery obviously knew these people, but why had he left this woman with Reaper? Did he have a choice? She thought about everything Demery had told her at the Sand Mole compound. He hadn't shared much beyond his love for zigzag quartz. He'd made the arrangement with the Sand Devils sound casual, despite calling them thieves. Yet if the woman was involved, their business here was anything but standard.

Morgan grabbed her hand. "We may have to make a run for it," he whispered under his breath. He'd obviously been thinking the same thing she had.

"What about Demery?" Red asked.

"He can take care of himself," he said.

"But he's the only one who knows where the outpost is

located," she reminded him. "We can't leave him with these people."

From his sour expression he must've forgotten and hadn't appreciated the reminder.

"We can't outrun these vehicles." Red judged the distance to the foothills of the mountains.

The man approached Demery and plucked Melea out of his arms. Reaper shoved the woman back toward the vehicle and demanded she get inside. She fell to her knees. Her shoulders were slumped and it looked as if she were about to cry.

Demery tensed like he wanted to stop him, but he didn't act. His hands curled into fists until his knuckles popped under the pressure.

Red's free hand moved slowly to her laser pistol.

"I wouldn't if I were you." Reaper indicated to the armed people who'd left their vehicles and taken up position behind him.

Red flexed her fingers and forced her hand to relax.

"Let's talk." Demery stepped forward, taking Reaper's attention off Red. "I'll be right back," he said.

Morgan and Red watched Demery disappear into a far vehicle with the big man following behind.

"What do you think they're discussing?" Red asked.

"No idea, but I wish like hell I did," Morgan said.

"Do you know what Reaper meant when he referred to Demery and the woman as blood?"

* * * * *

"No," Morgan said, but that wasn't entirely the truth. He had an idea of what "blood" meant, but didn't want to say anything to Gina until he was certain.

He'd known a few vamps over the years, but other than Raphael Vega, they'd kept mainly to themselves. Morgan had heard rumors about blood bonds, but they were rare from what he could gather. Not because of any kind of fear on the donors' part, but because a bond was rumored to make a vamp vulnerable to attack.

Morgan didn't understand how they worked, but knew it was some kind of symbiotic relationship that linked the bonded pair.

Hurt the donor, hurt them both. He just wasn't sure if that meant mentally or physically. He looked at Gina. He may not understand a blood bond, but he was well aware of the pain he experienced when he'd thought he had lost his mate.

"What do we do now?" Gina looked at him as if he held all the answers.

Times like these Morgan wished he did. "We wait." He took a seat on the ground. "And hope that Demery is as clever as he thinks."

"That's it?" she asked.

He grabbed her hand and pulled her down next to him. "That's all we can do until the vamp comes out. I'll scent the air as soon as he returns to see what I can pick up."

* * * * *

Demery sat next to Reaper and waited for the big man to settle. It was difficult to be in the same space with the beast. Even inside his protective suit he could smell the taint of cruelty wafting from the behemoth's skin.

"It's been a long time," Reaper said.

"Yes, it has, mon," Demery agreed. "I tried to get back here sooner, but I had to locate the goods for holding up my end of the bargain."

"And have you?" he asked.

Demery's gut twisted over what he was about to do, but what choice did he have? Melea wouldn't last much longer out here with the Sand Devils, and if something traumatic happened to her while he was so near, Demery would likely die with her.

He had to get her away from Reaper so he could get his life back. He just hadn't had time to broach the subject with Morgan and Red yet. He was sure once they understood the seriousness of the situation they'd be more than happy to help.

"Did you notice the man I'm traveling with?" Demery asked.

"I miss nothing." Reaper eyed him suspiciously.

"He carries what you need, mon," he said, hoping he could at least keep Red and his blood safe.

Demery didn't want to leave the sheriff behind, since he'd been kind to him. And he wouldn't if he could avoid it, but this was no-man's-land. The rules of survival were different here.

"Are we talking wolf blood?" Reaper asked.

He nodded. "Yes."

"He was a wolf soldier?" he asked.

"Yes," Demery repeated. "He's one of the originals, mon."

"What about the woman?" Reaper asked. "She looks like she holds some potential."

Demery kept his expression blank. His protective visor helped conceal the tension thrumming through him. "She is a pureblood I picked up for feeding purposes only."

"Pity." Reaper smiled, his shark-like teeth menacing. "Does the wolf know about our deal?

"Yes," Demery lied, ignoring the bile rising in his throat. He forced his thoughts back to Melea. Soon the sun would disappear and he'd be able to remove this tiresome suit and feel his blood's skin in his hands. Taste her essence on his lips. The moment would be bittersweet given the price of the privilege.

"The wolf doesn't look like someone who'll readily give up his blood." Anticipation softened Reaper's hard features. "I may have to take it."

"Since when has that ever stopped you?" Demery asked.

"Never!" Reaper threw his baldhead back and laughed. "Force makes the blood taste better. It makes a lot of things better." His gaze flitted over the women standing nearby.

Demery's stomach pitched. He did not envy Morgan. He needed to talk to the sheriff. Convince him this small sacrifice was their only way out of this situation. "This concludes our deal," he said. "Melea comes with me and so does the other woman."

Reaper watched him closely. "Getting greedy in your old age."

"No," Demery said, sadly. "Just hungry."

* * * * *

Demery exited the vehicle with a grim expression on his face. The sun had gone down, so he carefully removed his protective suit. He approached Morgan and Red, debating how to tell them the truth.

Perhaps, if he had sufficient time to explain, Morgan would voluntarily give up some of his blood. Demery was sure he could convince Reaper to take less, if he had the time and Morgan's cooperation. He opened his mouth to ask, but caught the sheriff's narrow-eyed expression. His wolf was suspicious—not that Demery could blame him. He'd be if he were in Morgan's position.

"What's happening?" Red asked. "What did Reaper want?"

"It's taken care of," Demery said in lieu of explanation. He couldn't exactly blurt out the truth and take the chance that they'd bolt. He needed a drink. Maybe after a few games of zigzag quartz, he'd come up with the right approach.

"What does that mean?" she asked.

Before Demery could respond, Reaper exited the vehicle. "You will be our guests for tonight," he said. It wasn't a request.

"Demery, what is he talking about?" Red asked. "I thought you were going to get the item and we'd be on our way."

"We will. I'll explain everything later." He clasped her arm and their gazes met briefly. Demery didn't look at Morgan. "You have to trust me. I promise we'll be out of here by tomorrow." He grabbed his pack without further explanation and went toward the vehicle containing Melea. What else could he say to Red that wouldn't upset her?

Nothing.

So he said nothing. She'd forgive him eventually. They both would once they learned why he'd agreed to the deal. Yet even as the thought crossed his mind, Demery knew it wasn't the truth.

Red would kill him the first chance she got. That's what an alpha female did when faced with the threat of losing her mate. And Red would definitely never forgive him. Fortunately, she was in good company.

* * * * *

"I have a bad feeling about this," Morgan said.

"So do I," Red said. "What do you think he did? It's not like Demery to be this cagey."

He shrugged. "Whatever he's up to doesn't bode well for us," Morgan said. "The scent of the big man has changed to one of anticipation. I can smell it and depravity in his sweat. He practically vibrated with excitement when he said we'd be staying the night."

Red inhaled. The rancid odor remained trapped on the hot breeze. "He's not an Other, is he?"

Morgan shook his head. "No, he's something far worse."

"Is that why he smells funny?" Red asked.

"He reeks of perversion and violence," he said.

Her grandfather had warned her that there were worse things out there than Unknowns. Red hadn't believed him at the time. She'd thought he was just being overly protective. She should've listened. Her life was in shambles. They were severely outnumbered by Sand Devils, whose pureblood leader went out of his way to appear animalistic. She didn't know how he'd accomplished such a feat, but she had no intention to stick around and find out. They needed to grab Demery and leave.

The question was, would he go with them?

She trusted this man, this vamp, with her life. Had grown to like him and depend on him as any tactical team member would. He'd stood by her when Nuria had turned on her. It hurt Red's heart to think her trust might have been misplaced.

Morgan was right. The change in Demery did not bode well for them. His explanation had better be a good one.

Red glanced at the shadows of the mountains in the distance. With the sun gone, they looked almost purple against the sky. People set up camp, using the vehicles as both homes and protective walls against the elements. She'd read about circling the wagons, but she'd never witnessed it until now. Except these weren't wagons and this wasn't the Old West. The Old West was civilized compared to this place and these people.

Music played from somewhere on the other side of the makeshift settlement. Women swayed. This music wasn't like what the Sand Moles had played. It was deeper, more primal. It rattled Red's chest with its thumping beat. The women continued to dance, then one by one they shed their clothes. Some playfully hid their nudity, while others boldly flashed their curves.

Red's mouth dropped open at the brazen display.

The Sand Devil men watched the dancers, their eyes aglow. Some had already stripped, baring their bodies so they could join the dance. They were less graceful than the women, but no one noticed. Other men simply touched themselves, while the women shimmied seductively in front of them, bending at the waist.

"What's happening?" Red asked, as the tone of the dancing turned carnal.

The men stroked themselves suggestively. Red had seen plenty of naked men in her time. She wasn't bothered by the nudity, but she didn't care for what they were doing.

One of the men grabbed a swaying naked woman and slung her over his shoulder. His muscles bunched as he twirled her around and laughed. The woman screamed, but not in fright. He slapped her bare bottom, then probed it with his thick fingers. She squealed loudly and squirmed, but didn't try to push him away. If anything, it looked as if she was enjoying the attention.

"You'll do," he said.

The man strode off to lie in front of one of the vehicles.

Rags had been tossed in a pile to form a makeshift rest pad. He dropped the woman onto them and mounted her without prelims. She didn't seem to mind, if the moans coming from her were any indication.

Red flushed and looked around nervously. "What are they doing?" she asked, as couple after couple paired off. No one sought privacy. They simply dropped where they felt like it and rutted.

"It's called an orgy," Morgan said. "It's when couples have sex in a group." He sounded like he was speaking from experience.

"Have you ever participated in one?" she asked.

Morgan blanched. "Not my style, but I have witnessed them before."

Red was silent for a few moments. "I don't think I like the Sand Devils," she said, then scooted closer to him. "They're not like Gray's group." Red wished they were back with the Sand Moles. It didn't matter that she'd shot their leader. They were still preferable company to these people.

Morgan placed his hand on her waist and pulled her close, then leaned in to nuzzle her ear. She thought he was trying to comfort her, until he whispered, "If the situation deteriorates, we may have to leave in a hurry. There won't be a lot of notice. If I tell you to run, I want you to head straight for the mountains and don't look back."

* * * * *

CHAPTER EIGHTEEN

Raphael watched Michael closely, looking for any odd behavior. A twitch, a flash of anger, anything to explain his brother's reluctance to be near them. Thus far he'd seen nothing. Had Roark lied to Morgan? It wouldn't be the first time. But that didn't explain why Michael hadn't contacted him.

His brother hadn't said much since they joined him on his journey. Not that Michael had ever been chatty, but this was too quiet, even for him. The fact that he was keeping to himself and thinking made Raphael nervous. When his brother focused his thoughts, people died.

"Did Roark happen to have any new information on Red and Morgan?" Raphael asked. He had no doubt his brother would know more than him and Catherine. Roark was nothing if not thorough.

Michael glanced over his shoulder. "Nothing beyond the reward for their capture," he said, but his expression told a different story.

Even as kids, Raphael had always been able to tell when Michael was lying. His brother had gotten better at deception over the years—they both had in order to survive, but his eyebrow still twitched when he lied. Or in this case, withheld the truth.

Raphael stopped as Michael's words registered. "There's a reward? What kind of reward?" And why was this the first time he was hearing about it?

Michael's dark gaze flicked to him. "Roark had me issue a bulletin before I left," he said without further explanation.

Dread seeped into Raphael's bones. If people in no-man's- and knew there was a reward for Red and Morgan, then no place would be safe. He thought about the dead nomads they'd encountered. Had they known about the reward? Was that why they were dead?

Raphael quickly dismissed the idea, since bulletins weren't issued in no-man's-land. The fence wasn't the only divide between the republics and this area. Communications were also kept out. For all intents and purpose, no-man's-land was perpetually in the dark.

"What exactly did the bulletin say?" he asked.

"Fifteen thousand credits for the person or people who bring in Red and Morgan." Michael shrugged as if the whole conversation was boring him. Maybe it was. His brother had always been a little different. Even as a child he'd been detached.

"If you needed credits, all you had to do was ask." Raphael frowned, staring at his brother with fresh eyes. He peered beneath his disheveled appearance to the heart of the man.

"Stop staring at me like that," Michael hissed. "I don't need your pity or your credits."

"Red and Morgan aren't in the republics," Raphael said, instead of asking the question he wanted to ask. He'd have to wait until he could get his brother alone. "Why would Roark send that message out? It doesn't make sense."

"The notification wasn't for the republics. It went out to no-man's-land," Michael said.

Raphael flinched. "That's impossible. Not even Roark can broadcast to this area without permission."

Michael laughed, an ugly grating sound that hurt to listen to. "When are you going to learn, brother dear? Roark can do anything he wants and there's not a damn thing anyone can do to stop him."

He shook his head in disbelief. No one had that much power. No one. Acid churned in his gut. "What are you really doing here, Michael?" Raphael watched for the telltale sign to indicate a lie. He'd asked him before, but his brother had brushed off the question with a non-answer. Now it seemed imperative to know.

"Like everyone else in no-man's-land, I'm trying to collect.'

Michael's voice nearly gave Raphael frostbite for all the emotion it held.

"You've never cared about credits," he said softly.

"Things change." Michael's brow twitched.

* * * * *

Chaos wasn't concerned about rewards or Morgan Hunter, but she'd sworn to the commander that she'd do her best to bring his granddaughter back and that's what she planned to do. Roark putting a bounty on their heads made her job that much harder. Greed made even the sanest person crazy. She cursed under her breath and glared at the endless miles of sand before them.

If Michael was telling the truth, then that meant she'd have to go through him to get to Red. Chaos had no doubt she'd lose Raphael if she did. So much for future relationship plans—not that she'd made any. Or even thought about making any plans with Raphael, but they had shared a few precious moments.

Chaos looked at Michael. He avoided her gaze. Something was amiss in his story and she was determined to find out what. "Why would Roark send you in, when he could wait for someone to bring Morgan and Red to him?" she asked. "I mean credits are nice, but there has to be more to it." Roark struck her as someone who loved to delegate duties. Without Michael nearby he had no one to order around.

"I suppose it's because I'll bring them back alive," he said, not sparing her a glance. "Can't say the same for the people who received the bulletin."

Chaos' spirits took a nosedive to her knees. What if Red was killed before she could reach her? What would she do then? She couldn't exactly bring Gina Santiago's body back to IPTT and expect the commander to understand.

Raphael grabbed Michael's arm and hauled him to a stop. "Why does Roark want them dead?"

"They're a threat to his political campaign. Now if you'll excuse me, I have to check in." Michael pulled a navcom out of his pack. He pressed a button and spoke into a small microphone. "Target is still at large," he said. "Repeat, target has yet to be located."

Roark's voice crackled. "You know what needs to be done. Let me know when you find them."

"Affirmative." Michael turned the device off.

"We could've used that earlier," Chaos said. It would've come in handy, since her navcom hadn't worked since they crossed the fence.

"Doubtful," Michael said. "It only works with its twin. It would have to be rewired to send a message out anywhere else."

So much for contacting the commander to warn him about the bounty. The navcom wouldn't do much good if all it could do was contact Roark. Of course, she might get some personal satisfaction from telling him exactly where he could go.

"Do you plan to kill them when you find them?" Chaos asked.

"I already told you, I intend to bring them back alive," Michael said.

Chaos watched Raphael tense. "Back to what exactly? Prison? A tribunal? Will the law be involved in any way?"

Doubtful given Roark's actions to date.

Chaos had the overwhelming urge to shoot something or someone. Her gaze landed on a likely candidate.

"You ask a lot of questions," Michael said.

"And you aren't exactly forthcoming with answers," she said. "You did say you planned on bringing them both back, correct?"

"Are you deaf or are you just trying to annoy me?" Michael asked. "I'm taking them both to Roark. That's clear enough for even you to understand. Honestly, brother, I don't see what you see in this woman." He gave Raphael a censorious look.

Chaos couldn't let him have Red. Before she could tell him so, Raphael squeezed her arm, silencing her.

"Why would you help us break them out, when all along you intended to return them?" Raphael asked.

"I have my reasons."

He looked at Michael. "We'll decide what to do with Morgan and Red, when and if we find them."

"You don't want to fight me on this, brother," Michael said.

"You're right. I don't," Raphael said. "But I will if I have to."

They traveled on in tense silence. No one felt the need to speak, but there was no doubt plans were being made. Even the closeness she'd felt with Raphael before meeting up with his brother had somehow fractured. A wedge by the name of Michael Travers Vega had been driven between them. She missed the connection, missed their bantering. And wondered if they'd ever get it back. Unlikely, if she ended up using her gift to scramble his brother's brain.

* * * * *

Chapter Nineteen

Why must they look so fucking happy? In the middle of nowhere, roasting and still they looked at each other like lovesick buffoons. Catherine's scent was all over Raphael and his covered her. It was impossible to discern where one began and the other ended. Which made being around them unbearable.

Michael questioned his brother's sense of loyalty. Raphael swore he was all about family, but was he? Would he be once things turned ugly?

Michael wanted to tell his brother the truth. Had tried on many occasions, but each time he opened his mouth the chip in his brain sent pain cascading through his body. By the third time it happened, Michael knew it was a warning of some kind. Somehow the chip had figured out a way to protect itself and was behaving like a cornered animal. His gaze moved to his brother.

At least Michael would no longer have to worry about Raphael. He'd be well taken care of, if this trip didn't turn out as Michael planned. He wanted to trust Catherine Meyers, but like him, she had an agenda. Michael could sense it, even though she tried to hide it from him. *Little girl, little girl, don't you know it's not nice to trick a vampire?*

Get back! Stay away!

The shadow slunk out of view, but its laugh rumbled like thunder in its wake, hurting his ears, clouding his mind. Pretty colors, dancing and twirling out of sight. Michael tried to follow them, but his eyes refused to focus.

The wind shifted, erasing the rainbow, bringing contempt and deceit. Michael raised his head and inhaled. His mind cleared enough to ascertain that enemies lurked up ahead. There were three—no, five. They hoped to surround them. They thought because their clothes were not rags that they'd make easy victims. Michael grinned to himself. Fresh blood was so much better than the hot, rancid brew sloshing in his canteens.

A bark of laughter escaped before he could stop it. Michael clasped his hand over his mouth to hide his fangs. "Excuse me," he said absently.

"What's so funny?" Catherine's delicate features pinched in distaste.

She'd probably make the same face if he pulled her head off and drank from her skull. The chip pulsed, urging him to act. Michael's fingers twitched, but Raphael was watching. Always watching her. If he didn't know better, Michael would think his brother didn't trust him. Raphael was so focused on her every move that he didn't notice the real threat, gliding in over the dunes.

"Inside joke. You wouldn't understand." Michael wondered how long it'd take her and Raphael to realize they were being hunted.

It was probably wrong not to say something, but Michael was disappointed that his brother's senses had dulled to such a degree. There was a time when he'd have located them first.

Oh, Raph, stop thinking with your dick for a moment and open your mind.

He didn't of course. Raphael always had odd priorities. Fortunately for him, Michael always focused on the details. The shadows skipped through his mind, a none-too-gentle reminder that that was not the case anymore.

Damn phantoms! Leave me in peace!

A cackle was their only reply.

The delusions were getting worse. The phantoms' visits had increased. Their time spent with him grew longer every day. Roark didn't need to press the button for the A.I. chip to do its job. It continued to act on its own. Roark had probably had it specially developed at one of his research labs. A bioweapon, if Michael were to guess.

Green button, green button go away. Come again some other day.

The threesome continued their journey south as the band of thieves closed in. They were quiet, but the sand gave their location away. It whispered their impending arrival in a time-weary voice.

Catherine stopped. "Did you hear something?"

Michael wanted to say yes, but the chip flared. He shook his head no. Raphael listened. Nothing but the sound of wind and sand answered.

"Let's keep going." Raphael's gaze now moved cautiously over the dunes.

Michael prepared for the upcoming battle by dropping his cumbersome pack onto the ground.

"What are you doing?" Catherine asked.

The attack came from the left. The pureblood moved faster than expected. Michael had a split second to call out a warning before the man slammed into Raphael, sending them both sprawling into a dune. Pain pulsed through his skull. Michael gasped and nearly crumbled to the ground.

Catherine screamed as another assailant came storming out of the darkness like a demon without the virtue of fire. She spun, throwing the pack off in the same movement as a blade sliced the air where she'd stood only seconds before. A wave of power burst out of her, sending the man to his knees.

If Michael hadn't experienced it with his own senses, he wouldn't have believed it possible. His head swam and for a moment Michael was dangerously disoriented, leaving him vulnerable.

My, my, my, aren't we just full of tricks. What are you, little girl?

Michael clutched his head, trying to clear it. There was no time for answers. Three more men sailed in from atop the dunes. They swooped down upon them like turkey buzzards, ready to pick their bones and pockets clean. Raphael's fangs extended and he viciously tore at one of the men attacking him. The other stayed just out of range, waiting for an opening.

Catherine made a grab for her weapon, but she wasn't fast enough. Whatever power she'd had dissipated. The man who'd tried to knife her was closing in for a second go, while the other rushed Michael.

His mistake.

It only took a thought to stop the man's heart. The look of surprise on his face was priceless. Too bad Michael didn't have time to enjoy the moment.

Michael rushed forward to aid Catherine. His brother would never forgive him if he allowed her to die, when her death could easily be prevented. Raphael may not know he loved the woman, but Michael did.

It was etched clearly on his brother's face and verified by deed. The pain of the emotion cut deep and he nearly faltered. Michael had just found Raphael. He didn't want to lose him to another.

He grabbed the thief, tearing his hand off Catherine's throat, then twisted his neck until something popped. The sound was loud enough for all to hear. *Pop, pop. Twist, twist. Crack, crack. And they all fall dead.*

The third man turned away from Raphael and saw his comrades lying at their feet. He hesitated as he looked at Catherine, then headed toward Michael. Perhaps the man thought he could avenge the dead. He obviously believed Catherine was helpless because she was a woman. A stupid mistake that was about to cost him his life. Catherine pulled her weapon and fired, dropping the man next to his dead friends.

Boom!

Raphael was doing a fair job at fighting the two remaining thieves, considering his teeth were locked on the one man's neck, slowly draining him, while punching the other man in the face.

"Need any help?" Michael asked.

Catherine rushed forward.

He caught her before she could do anything foolish like get herself killed.

"Let go!" She struggled to break free.

"No!" Michael's arms locked, restricting her movements. "Raphael will be fine. There are only two of them. What did you do to me?"

"What are you talking about?" she asked. Her gaze never wavered from Raphael.

One of the men managed to chuck Raphael under the chin, but his brother didn't budge.

"He needs help." Catherine pried his fingers, applying moves Michael had no doubt she'd learned at the tactical team training facility. They'd probably be effective on someone who'd never been tortured.

Her movements tickled him. Raph didn't need her help dispatching those two. The one in his arms had just died. The other man simply hadn't realized yet that he'd soon follow. Michael could speed the process up, but what fun would that be? Besides, this scuffle would serve as a lesson to his brother to pay attention to his surroundings.

The remaining thief drew a knife and lunged at Raphael's chest. Raphael twisted, putting the dead man in his arms between the attacker and himself. The man impaled his partner to the hilt, then screamed in outrage. He probably thought he'd killed him.

Raphael dropped the dead guy and swiped his leg out, depositing the remaining man on his ass.

"Enough!" he shouted, bringing everyone to a standstill. "Brother, are you hungry?"

Michael smiled. He knew him so well. "I could use a nip."

"He's all yours." Raphael shoved the man toward him.

"What's he talking about?" The thief's eyes widened at the implications.

"I would think that would be obvious," Michael said, a second before his fangs extended.

"No!" the man bellowed. "Stay away from me." His gaze darted to Raphael. "Kill me like a man, not like an animal."

Raphael turned away.

The thief tried to scramble up a nearby dune, but Michael stopped him by mentally lifting him off his feet and bringing him back. From the fear in his eyes, Michael could see it had finally dawned on him just how large a mistake he and his friends had made by attacking them.

The familiar length of his fangs tickled his tongue as Michael licked them in anticipation. The sensation sent delicious gooseflesh dancing along his spine. He angled the man's neck, while keeping his arms pinned to his sides. His mouth watered as he sank his fangs into the thief's pulsing vein and feasted.

He was yummy. Michael had expected something less appetizing from his worn appearance.

He would've bitten him elsewhere if he'd wanted the man to live, but Michael didn't. As he drank, Michael watched Catherine's expression change from one of curiosity to out-and-out revulsion. Her red hair was tousled from the fight and her clothes were covered in sand. She was sweating and out of breath, but still mustered enough energy to convey her disgust.

Michael waited to make sure he had her undivided attention, then he smiled, allowing the blood to dribble down his chin onto his shirt. The coppery sweetness stuck to his skin, teasing his nostrils with its heavenly scent. Normally he wasn't what one would call a messy eater—far from it actually—but Michael hadn't been able to resist the urge to rattle her. He wanted to scare Catherine off before she could take Raphael away from him.

He liked having her off balance. It was better to keep her that way until he figured out what was behind the disorienting stunt she'd pulled earlier.

Catherine watched for a few more seconds, eyes rounded and mouth gaping, then slowly turned away. Raphael reached for her, but she jerked out of his grasp.

"Leave me alone," she said and kept walking. Catherine didn't look back as she disappeared into the night.

"Catherine, where are you going?" Raphael frowned like a child who'd lost his favorite toy.

How Michael wished that were true, but he'd never been that lucky. He considered the woman threatening to come between him and his brother. He pictured the blood running down his chin. With the vision clearly in his head, Michael closed his eyes and sent a thought slamming into her mind.

Welcome to the family, Catherine Meyers.

* * * * *

Chaos couldn't seem to get the picture of blood dripping down Michael's chin out of her mind. Every time she tried it came back in even more vivid detail, along with Michael's sinister welcome. She had no problem killing if the situation called for it, but she didn't take joy in the act. Not like he did.

She could see it in his black eyes. They'd sparkled as he'd drained the man in front of her. He'd enjoyed it. Reveled in the act

152

of killing. The whole thing had been performed like some twisted dance with Michael as the star. He'd wanted to shock her and it worked. She was shocked—not by the death, but by the method.

Sure, Raphael was a vampire. And yes, he'd killed, too, but she hadn't seen the same gleam of satisfaction in his eyes. Raphael had killed because he had to. Yes, he'd drank from one of the men, but it had come more from hunger and control than from pleasure. He didn't get off by sucking people dry.

Chaos stopped walking. Was she rationalizing Raphael's actions? Possibly, but she hadn't mistaken the joy she'd seen on Michael's face. Killing was second nature to him. He loved it and he was very, very good at it.

She wondered if Raphael had seen the gleam in his brother's eyes, or had he been too blinded by love and devotion to notice? Was this the fate that ultimately awaited Red and Morgan? He could have Morgan on a platter if it made him happy. Let Michael snack on him or take him back to Roark, but she wouldn't let him have Red. Gina was hers to return safely to IPTT. The sooner Michael Travers Vega accepted that, the better.

He saved your life, a little voice in Chaos' head reminded her. It knocked the self-righteous indignation right out of her system. Michael had saved her from being choked to death, when he didn't have to bother.

Was she being too hard on him? Maybe she'd misjudged him just as she'd done with Raphael when they first met. Let's face it— when she tried to kill him. Was she any better than they were?

Chaos had killed without mercy in Nuria. It had been under Roark Montgomery's compulsion, but she had carried out the murders. Suddenly the answers weren't nearly as clear as they'd been a moment ago.

* * * * *

Raphael watched Catherine until she disappeared. Her shoulders were stiff and she held her head high. Waves of anger and disgust radiated off her tiny frame. He'd warned her that Michael was a dangerous man and now she finally believed him. He should be relieved that the blinders had been removed from her naive eyes. So why did he feel like shit?

He turned back to Michael, who finished drinking, then dropped the dead man onto the ground.

"Good to the last drop." He smacked his lips for emphasis.

"Why did you do that?" Raphael asked. His brother had never been a messy eater. He was fastidious by nature. Dripping the blood had been for show.

"Do what?" Michael asked innocently.

Raphael's eyes narrowed. "Play with your food," he said in disgust. "You turned into a movie cliché. Since when do you waste blood by letting it run on the ground?"

"Oh that." Michael shrugged. "I thought she should know what we really are, not what we present to the world," he said. "Catherine needed to experience the truth firsthand and not romanticize it." The censorious look he sent Raphael said everything.

Raphael's jaw clenched. "She already knows. Shocking her was overkill, but then again, you know that. You smelled me on her. You know I've tasted her. Hell, you've seen my mark on her neck."

"Yes, but you're a seducer. You make sure your *prey* is relaxed before you feed," Michael said.

Raphael flinched. His brother made him sound so callous, so calculating. He'd *cared* about the women he'd bedded. Perhaps not deeply, but he had cared…as much as he was able. He'd never given anyone his heart. Had no desire to.

Til now, echoed in his mind.

Michael sighed as if the conversation bored him. "I don't want to see you get your heart broken by a woman who can't handle a little blood."

Raphael stiffened. What did he mean by that crack? His heart wasn't in any danger of being broken by Catherine. A myriad of emotions filled him. Raphael opened his mouth to issue a denial, but the words tangled in his throat and came out sounding like a snarl.

"What is she anyway?" Michael wiped the blood off his face with the back of his sleeve. "I don't sense Other in her."

"I told you, she's unique." Raphael thought of Catherine's smart mouth and fiery temper. He'd kiss that mouth right now if she'd let him. Thoughts of Catherine took his mind off the glee he'd seen on Michael's face as he'd killed the men.

Raphael had never enjoyed killing, but he'd accepted that it had to be done on occasion. What he'd witnessed moments ago had frightened him more than any surprise attack.

"Your pet almost knocked me on my ass when she was attacked," Michael said. "My head wouldn't stop spinning. I've never felt that kind of power from anyone."

"It's why they call her Chaos at IPTT. She's like a microburst waiting to descend," Raphael said. "I'm not sure she even knows where her power comes from or how to control it completely. We haven't discussed it in detail. We've had more important things on our minds."

Raphael was already losing interest in the conversation. He didn't want Catherine to wander too far ahead of them. What if another predator came upon her? His heart had nearly stopped when he had seen that thief go for her throat. If it hadn't been for Michael, she'd be dead.

"I have to go after her." Raphael gathered his gear. "Thank you for saving her life."

Michael snorted. "She really has you wrapped around her finger, doesn't she? Do you ask how high when she says jump?"

Raphael stilled, his hands clenched at his sides. He had the overwhelming urge to punch his brother in the face. "What are you implying?"

Michael toyed with the strap on his pack. "There was a time when this woman would've been falling at your feet, trying to figure out ways to please you. Not the other way around. She has you bowing and scraping before her."

He scoffed. "You don't know what you're talking about," Raphael said.

"Don't I?" Michael asked. "When we met up, you implied Catherine wasn't special. You let me believe you'd get rid of her once you grew tired of her company. But that's not going to happen. Is it, brother?"

Raphael's body tensed. Through the years he'd been an ass to a lot of women. Oh, he'd left them satisfied. He wouldn't have been able to call himself a man otherwise, but he'd still used them. Sometimes for shelter, other times for sex, but mostly he'd used them for blood like Michael implied. A woman in the throes of passion tasted better than anything on the planet. He should know—he'd sampled a veritable smorgasbord.

It wasn't until he'd met Red that Raphael realized something was missing. She was so strong and powerful, yet naively vulnerable. The wolf inside her was beyond alluring. He'd made his move on her and she'd been tempted, very tempted, but in the end Red had turned Raphael down. Her heart belonged to another. The rejection had hurt, but he'd respected her all the more for it. That's when Raphael knew for sure she was the right woman for Morgan.

The trouble was that now he wanted more. The thought of a quick roll on the rest pad for blood and sex had left him cold. The afternoon he'd made love to Catherine had turned his world upside down. She'd brought him to life, when Raphael hadn't known he was dead inside. Catherine, and only Catherine, had filled the emptiness swallowing him whole. He couldn't lose her. It had taken too many years to find her.

His gaze returned to his brother. "Times change, Michael. And so do people. You should know that better than anyone. Now I'm going to walk away before I say something I truly regret," Raphael said.

Michael's lip curled in disgust. "I do know better, brother. I'm staring at the proof and it nauseates me. You've gone from a proud warrior to a groveling snit. You should see yourself."

"You just don't get it, do you?" Raphael shook his head and felt a pang of regret.

Michael never would understand what it felt like to give his heart to another. To want to be with that person as much as possible because the time apart made you ache. No, his brother would never understand. He was too caught up in the chase, in the kill. It was all a game to him. To be won at all costs.

"I'd better go find her before she gets lost," Raphael said softly.

"Do you want me to bring her back?" Michael's tone implied he'd be perfectly happy to let her wander the desert forever. "It would be quite easy to lift her. It's not like she weighs a lot. Might even be funny to see the look on her face, when invisible hands pick her up and carry her over the dunes." He chortled.

Raphael glanced over his shoulder. "Thanks, but I think I can handle it." He looked at his brother. Really looked at him. He ignored the bloodstained skin and the rumpled clothing. Looked past them to the face beneath the civil mask. His true face.

Michael wasn't the same man Raphael had known and loved a lifetime ago. The years of torture and the assassinations he'd performed had eaten away at his humanity and changed him. The question was into what?

* * * * *

CHAPTER TWENTY

Red awoke to a callused hand covering her mouth. She struggled until her eyes managed to focus in the predawn light. Morgan stood over her with his finger pressed to his lips. She nodded in understanding and he released her. Red stood, trying not to make a sound. The group had been drinking and partying all night. They'd only stopped as dawn approached.

Demery had stayed close to Reaper and his blood for most of the night. He'd pulled out the metal deck she'd seen him playing with at the Sand Mole compound and gambled until she couldn't hold her eyes open. That was the last Red had seen of them. She scanned the area, but didn't immediately spot him.

Red mouthed, where's Demery?

Morgan shook his head and shrugged. He pointed to the mountains, which had turned gray from the fast-approaching dawn. He splayed his fingers and mimicked a running movement.

"Time to go," he whispered.

Everyone appeared to be asleep or passed out from the revelry. Red didn't see Demery or his white protective suit anywhere. She also didn't see Reaper or Melea. She leaned in close to Morgan and pressed her lips to his ear.

"He didn't get a chance to explain what's happening."

Morgan met her gaze with a sharp one of his own. "He had all night. We gave him every opportunity. At one point, I even cornered him after a game of zigzag quartz. Demery didn't say a word. He just gave another excuse, then went off to relieve himself behind one of the vehicles."

"We can't just leave him," Red said. "He wouldn't leave us."

"After what you witnessed last night are you sure?" he asked.

Red hesitated as she thought about it. "Yes, I am."

His brow furrowed. Morgan scrubbed a hand over his face, his frustration evident. "I looked all over, but I couldn't find him I don't like the idea of leaving him any more than you do, but now is our chance to get out of here unscathed and we're going to take it. Demery is a big boy. He knows these people. He'll be fine."

Red shook her head violently. She wouldn't leave anyone behind. It had been drilled into her since day one at IPTT.

"We don't have time to argue." Morgan grabbed her arm and tugged her away. "We have to make it to that outpost before anyone else hears about the bounty. Do you really think these people will let us go once they do?"

Her heart sank. He was right. Red knew Morgan was right. If they didn't make it to the outpost and try to contact the outside world to warn them about Roark, they could end up dying here in no-man's-land. Red didn't want to die in this place.

"Okay," she said. "But promise me we'll come back for Demery when we're done, if he hasn't reached the outpost by then."

Morgan kissed her. "I promise," he said. "Now let's go."

They crept out of the campsite as silently as possible. Red's heart was pounding so hard she doubted she'd hear it if anyone sounded an alarm. She expected to see lookouts, but there were none. Their absence spoke volumes about Reaper's savage reputation. When they got a hundred yards away, they ran for foothills. They reached them within minutes and ascended.

"I don't feel right about leaving Demery," Red said.

"I know. Keep going," Morgan said climbing faster.

"I'm really worried about him," she said. "What if they kill him when they find out we're gone?"

Morgan frowned. It was obvious from his expression that it hadn't occurred to him. "Why would they do that? The deal he had going with them didn't have anything to do with us, remember? Demery had been looking for Reaper. It was sheer luck that the Sand Devil's found us first."

"Bad luck," she muttered.

Red understood, but she still wasn't convinced that the mysterious deal was enough to keep him alive. The situation definitely involved Melea, but something told her that they somehow factored into the equation, too. Why or how? Red had no idea. They didn't have anything to bargain with other than their pistols, and the Sand Devils had plenty of weapons. They didn't need more.

Damn it, Demery! You should've explained the situation you were in.

The mountains grew rapidly steeper and Red had to pull herself up to reach the next outcropping of rocks.

"You doing okay?" Morgan asked. Sweat dripped down his rugged face, leaving his hair curling into his neck. His amber eyes watched her closely as he gave her a leg up here and pulled her up there.

"I'm fine. Just a little winded. Not used to this altitude. Do you have any idea where we're going?" Demery was the only one who knew the exact location of the outpost. The thought of wandering around the desert for days, weeks, or months in search of it was decidedly unappealing.

"The Sand Moles had said it was located southwest of their position. I figure as long as we keep traveling in that direction we'll run into either it or another group who can help us pin down the location," he said.

"Those are a lot of ifs." Red strained to climb.

"What choice do we have?" Morgan asked.

"We could've located Demery and found out what was really going on. He'd said we'd be leaving today. I don't think he meant without him," she said.

Morgan sighed and ran a hand through his hair. "I'm sorry. I really tried to find him. I snuck all around that place and didn't see him or smell him anywhere. The suit would've stuck out against the sand if he'd been there. Maybe he went off with one of the women."

"Without telling us? Seems unlikely," she said.

"Not sure if you noticed, but he wasn't exactly acting normal once we ran into the Sand Devils."

She grasped the rock above her. "It was obvious that it had

been awhile since he'd seen his blood, Melea. Maybe he was nervous."

"Possibly, but we gave him every opportunity to come clean. Nerves alone do not explain his odd behavior. He was up to something. I don't know what, but I smelled deception on his skin when he took the protective suit off. Staying in the Sand Devil camp any longer was not in our best interest," he said. "Now keep climbing."

Red scowled, but did as he ordered. It was too late to turn back. By now they would've discovered them missing. She hoped that Morgan was right and that Demery would be okay. If not, she'd never forgive herself.

* * * * *

Morgan struggled to pull himself up onto the next cliff face. He hated mountains. He'd been camped in them, when his wife and child were killed. He could still remember the helpless sensation of trying to get down from the ridge he'd been on and reach his family in time.

It had taken so much longer than it should have. That mountain had been covered in trees, back when real forests still existed. It hadn't been dead like this one. He'd been too late. They'd died waiting for him to arrive, waiting for him to save them. He wouldn't go through that with Gina.

Morgan's hand slipped, slicing his palm on a jagged rock. He grunted, then forced his arm to change. Claws and fur appeared, then disappeared quickly, leaving a pink line where the cut had been. He continued climbing.

"We'll stop at the next outcropping of rocks," he said. "Make sure no one is following us."

"What if we spot Demery?" Red asked.

Morgan grunted. "As long as he's not with friends, we'll wait."

She looked over her shoulder at him. "And if he is?"

"Then we'll keep moving and pray we can outrun them," he said.

"Do you really think he'd betray us?" she asked.

Morgan met her gaze. "Men do awful things when they're desperate. I should know."

* * * * *

They reached a small ridge that gave them enough flat space to stand on, but there wasn't room for much more. The sun was higher now, but the mountain kept them from being exposed. That would change once they made it over the top and had to make their way down the other side.

"How long until we get out of here?" Red asked.

"No idea," Morgan said. "I'm not sure how wide this range is."

"Do you think we'll make it out before dark?" she asked.

Red looked at the tiny ledge they were standing on. It was a sheer drop on one side and a rough slide on the other. Both would ensure injury if they fell. There was nowhere to sleep and no way they'd be able to traverse the terrain in the dark, even with their enhanced eyesight. They were wolves, not mountain goats.

"We have to," Morgan said.

They had at least thirteen hours of daylight to make it to the other side. "Let's get going. No time to lose."

Red and Morgan reached the top of the final mountain. They stood looking out at the valley below. Much like the one they left, the desert had taken over everything, leaving slopes of sand behind. At least these dunes didn't seem quite as high as the ones they'd traversed to get here.

A warm breeze blew over them. Red closed her eyes and inhaled, taking in everything around them. The mountain had an earthy smell, almost as if water clung to it, when there hadn't been rain in months. She didn't scent any people or death, even though it waited for them around every corner.

She opened her eyes. In the distance, something glinted, flashing in the sunlight like a diamond faceted by fire.

Red shielded her eyes and peered at the object. "What's that over there?" she asked. The object flashed again, bursting with life in the valley of the dead.

Morgan grabbed a monocular and pointed it at the shiny object. "It doesn't look like much. Hang on." He adjusted the lens. "Correction, I think we may have found the outpost."

"Are you serious?" Red squealed, unable to contain her enthusiasm. They'd made it. Somehow they'd managed to find the elusive outpost. "Let me see."

Morgan handed her the monocular. "If it's not the place, they may know how to get there."

Red could see what looked like a single building. She almost wept in relief. Her body ached from all the hiking and climbing. She never realized how easy she'd had it at IPTT. Given another opportunity, Red would never take her boring life for granted again.

She stared at the outpost in the distance. If she hadn't been looking in the right direction at the right time, she would've missed it. The thought chilled her to the bone. They could've easily spent days wandering aimless in the desert had she not looked up.

Red shook herself. She couldn't think about that now. They'd still have to get down and hope the place held the equipment they needed, but at least they'd made it this far.

"Don't get too excited," Morgan said. "That's a lot of open space to cover. A lot can go wrong. We still have to get from here to there without being spotted by the Sand Devils. And it may not be the right place, though it's in the area they talked about." He double-checked the coordinates to determine the exact location of the outpost.

"Do you think they're following us?" She glanced over her shoulder at the route they'd taken through the mountains. Her muscles trembled from exertion.

His lips thinned. "I have no doubt they will be soon, if they aren't already. So we need to get going."

They descended quickly. Once they reached the bottom of the range, they'd have to stick to the base of the mountains, while they made their way west.

* * * * *

Demery awoke on the ground, sprawled out next to the woman he'd fucked the night before. Her blood had fed him, while he sated her needs. She was naked. Her ripe nipples stabbed skyward, a bountiful offering if he'd ever seen one. Too bad the suit prevented him from taking advantage.

Light splashed her skin, making it appear striped. She was

making tiny snuffling sounds each time she exhaled. Demery smiled in remembrance, then stretched, rolling his stiff muscles.

The ground was harder here. He'd gotten used to sleeping on the sand. Demery had decided to take the woman away from the main camp because he hadn't wanted Melea to sense what he was doing.

He rolled his neck. His head ached from the Sand Devil wine, leaving him woozy. Demery couldn't remember the last time he'd drunk so much. He'd spent time with Melea, making sure she was okay. He had only taken a little of her blood. Just enough to test their connection. It was still intact, even though he'd hoped otherwise.

Demery hadn't wanted to be greedy, so he'd sent Melea away before his body could make further demands and found another willing donor. She was now lazing in the sun like a satisfied cat. He'd even managed to win a few hands of zigzag quartz. Perhaps his luck was finally changing.

All and all it was a good night with the Sand Devils. Reaper had been surprisingly hospitable given the debt he owed him. He supposed he would be, too, if someone laid a gift of powerful blood at his feet. He had to find Morgan now and explain before Reaper got to him.

Demery inhaled deeply and froze. He turned his head slowly, inhaling again expecting to catch the musk of wolf on the air. Perhaps he was too far away. Demery jumped to his feet and stepped outside. He sniffed again. He'd always been able to smell them, but he didn't now. This couldn't be happening. Not when he was so close to gaining everything. But his senses didn't lie. Red and Morgan were gone, leaving him and Melea as good as dead.

* * * * *

CHAPTER TWENTY-ONE

Staring at the endless sand only brought home how vast the world was and how many places there were to hide. Red was out there somewhere. Perhaps shielded by misguided individuals who'd fallen prey to her lies. I felt helpless. It didn't matter that I was doing everything I could to find her.

Surrounded by curious eyes, I couldn't make any sudden moves. The men were skilled and could easily stop me. Even if I managed to lose them for a time, they'd eventually catch up with me. I wouldn't be able to travel fast enough over the terrain to outrun them.

It was definitely hard to wait. Seemed like all I'd been doing these past few days was bide my time. My hand moved to the laser pistol strapped to my thigh. The stock made my palm itch to pull it. I caressed the weapon with my fingertips. So cool and deadly. It would be easy to pick them off. I drew back appalled by the direction my thoughts had taken, but the guilt didn't last long.

Soon, I thought, picturing Gina "Red" Santiago in my mind.

If I concentrated hard enough, I could see myself pulling the weapon, taking aim at her chest, and firing. I could almost smell the seared flesh as the laser shot out from the muzzle and blew a hole in her body. Red wouldn't have time to respond because she'd never see it coming. She would never suspect a thing.

* * * * *

165

CHAPTER TWENTY-TWO

Robert Santiago sat behind his desk at IPTT headquarters blindly staring at synth-reports. He hadn't heard from his granddaughter, Gina or Catherine Meyers since she'd notified him that she'd crossed into no-man's-land.

Given the place's reputation, he didn't know if Gina was alive or dead. He shook his head, sending white hair onto his forehead. That wasn't true. He'd know if she was dead, but that didn't stop the worry or the fear of losing her.

He had to do something to clear her name. He felt helpless sitting behind his title, doing nothing. Robert thought about Private Catherine Meyers. He shouldn't have let her go after Gina. She wasn't experienced enough to head into no-man's-land alone. It was only desperation that had made him say yes and now he deeply regretted it. If anything happened to Meyers, it would weigh heavy on his conscience.

The door to his office chimed. He hit a button on his desk and an image of one of the tech support men came into view. Robert pressed another button and the door opened.

"Sir," the young man named Tucker said.

"Do you have anything for me?" Robert asked, dispensing with small talk.

The tech department had the remains of Gina's navcom, Rita, for several days now, and surely they'd been able to come up with something in that time period.

Tucker's face pinched like his pants had shrunk. "Nothing yet, sir."

"Then what are you doing here?" he asked, barely leashing his temper, which had gotten worse in Gina's absence.

She was the only family he had left. The thought of losing her forever was unthinkable. He'd already lost his daughter due to her love of an Other. He wasn't about to lose his granddaughter, too.

He fidgeted. "We aren't sure we're going to be able to fix the navcom, sir."

Robert rose, towering over the much smaller man. "What do you mean you can't fix it? I thought you were the best."

"I am," Tucker said. "I mean we are. The thing is, the navcom is pretty banged up. Crushed really. Red has broken Rita plenty of times, but never like this."

"Gina didn't break Rita," Robert bellowed. "Not this time."

He swallowed hard. "If you say so, sir."

"I do."

Tucker shuffled his feet and looked at anything but Robert Santiago. "We have one more thing to try, but if that doesn't work, then there's nothing we can do," he said. "I'm sorry."

"Did you bring me any good news?" Deflated, Robert sank into his chair.

"We can tell there is something on it. We don't know what it is yet, since we haven't been able to retrieve the data."

Robert perked up, feeling hope for the first time in weeks. "Keep working on it. Let me know when you have something."

"Yes, sir." Tucker turned toward the door.

Before he could reach it, Robert stopped him. "Oh, and Tucker."

"Sir?"

Robert leaned forward. "This project is considered top secret. No one but you and the other tech guy working on the navcom are to know what you find. As soon as you have the information, I want you to come to me immediately. Day or night. Understood?"

"Understood, sir." Tucker nodded, then left the office.

There could be anything on the navcom. It wouldn't necessarily be something they could use. Robert just had to hope that Gina had been smart enough to try to record her last moments with the politician and that Roark wasn't smart enough to watch what he was saying.

How likely was that? His head dropped into his hands. Those were a lot of ifs and maybes. Too many for his peace of mind. There had to be another way to catch Roark Montgomery in his lies. He just wasn't seeing it because he was too close to the situation.

Robert stacked the reports he'd been reading. The buzzer at his office door went off again. He looked down at the monitor and saw Bannon Richards standing outside.

"Enter." He pushed a button to unlock the door.

Bannon strode in as cocky as ever, wearing a shit-eating grin on his face.

"Lieutenant, how can I help you?" Robert asked.

"I was wondering if you have any new orders for my team, Commander."

Robert tilted his head. "Such as?"

Bannon cleared his throat. "We still haven't located the fugitives. I thought maybe you had a new area in mind for us to search. Roark says he's covered everything to the west."

Robert's eyebrows shot to his hairline. "Since when do you work for Roark Montgomery? I had the impression that you were a decorated tactical team officer under my command. Did you resign from your post without notifying me?"

Anger vibrated through him, tensing his muscles. He clasped his fingers to keep them from shaking. Robert was well aware that some of his men moonlighted for Roark on their days off.

Roark's IPTT record garnered him a lot of respect and adulation. But he didn't like the idea that Roark had somehow infiltrated IPTT and had took command. He inhaled deeply, then slowly let the breath out.

"No, sir. I didn't resign." Bannon's jaw jutted. "I just thought that pooling our resources would allow us to cover more ground."

"You aren't paid to think, Lieutenant. You're paid to follow orders. I suggest you get back to patrolling for Unknowns, before you find yourself busted back down to private."

Bannon's face flushed and his blue eyes chilled to ice chips. "Yes, sir." The words dripped with so much venom that Robert Santiago found himself leaning back.

"Dismissed." He watched Bannon stride angrily to the door and made a mental note to keep an eye on him.

The lieutenant slipped out, shooting him a dirty look before the door closed. Robert had known about the rivalry between Bannon and Gina. He'd had no idea that the animosity ran so deep until now.

Bannon was a good officer, but he was going to be a problem, especially if he'd already taken orders from Roark Montgomery. His ambition must have gotten the better of him. He still couldn't believe the gall of the man. How dare he come in here and question his orders.

Who did he think he was? Commander?

His head pounded. Robert pinched the bridge of his nose and rubbed his temples. This was one more thing to worry about on top of a mountain of others. He opened a drawer, brushing aside his toiletries, and took out a dissolving patch to slip under his tongue. The headache would be gone in a matter of seconds thanks to the medicine. If only his other problems could be remedied as easily.

* * * * *

CHAPTER TWENTY-THREE

Morgan and Red kept their weapons holstered as they approached the outpost. The building they'd spotted through the monocular looked like an upside-down metal bowl up close with a door and three windows carved out of it. The windows didn't hold glass. Instead, metal had been pounded and tied together in primitive shutters.

Three towers with crude rope ladders formed a triangle around the outpost, giving the guards an unobstructed view of the area. Like the first group they'd encountered, a pit surrounded the whole compound. Unlike that first group, this pit was filled with razor-sharp glass and pieces of metal that had been molded into spikes. There was no way of crossing it without being cut to pieces. They'd obviously found the right place.

"State your business," the guard to their left shouted.

Morgan and Red raised their arms in the air.

"We are looking for Razor," Morgan said. "The Sand Moles sent us. They said you might have some communication equipment we could use or barter for."

"Who told you such a thing?" the guard to the right hollered.

"Jeb," Red said.

The two guards looked at each other, then back at Morgan and Red.

"Jeb wouldn't do that," the guard on the left said. "He knows better."

170

"You must be Razor," Morgan said.

"I am," he said.

"How else could we have found you, if not for Jeb?" Morgan asked. "We are traders who have never been to this area."

The guard on the right said, "Maybe we should ask Jonah."

Razor didn't look happy about the prospect. "What do you have to trade?" he asked.

"Weapons. A few supplies. And electrical skills. We will pay for anything we use," Morgan said.

"With what?" the guard on the right asked, suspicion clear.

"Credits," Red said.

"Show me," Razor said.

"Let's see the equipment first," she said.

Razor pondered their proposition while the guard on the right waited.

"Okay," he finally said. "Drop your weapons and come across the bridge. If you make any sudden moves, you're dead."

Red glanced at Morgan, who nodded for her to comply. She unbuckled her holster and let if fall to the ground. She felt naked without her laser pistols, but she wasn't exactly helpless. She could partially shift in a pinch.

They walked across the small bridge with their hands held high and stopped when they reached the other side. Razor had managed to scurry down the rope ladder and was waiting when they arrived.

"Remove your packs and drop them on the ground."

Red looked up and saw that the guard on the right had them covered from above. She shrugged and did as they asked, dropping her backpack onto the sandy ground. Morgan followed suit.

"Now can we please speak with Jonah?" She didn't know who Jonah was, but she hoped that he was more intelligent than the two guarding the entrance. She looked at the towers and caught movement. There were four more men than she'd initially counted. Red looked again. Make that six guarding the front and back entrances.

Razor motioned them forward with the barrel of his rifle. Morgan told Red to lead the way. It seemed the gentlemanly thing to do, but that wasn't why he'd offered. Morgan wanted to put his body between her and the gun.

They walked to the reinforced metal door and waited. Razor hit a spot on the ground with his boot heel and something clanged. Red looked over her shoulder at Morgan and frowned. His expression was placid. Deceptive under the circumstances. He waited patiently for the door to open.

They didn't have to wait long. The big metal door slid open with a scraping noise that Red had no doubt came from sand buildup. Darkness greeted them.

"Get inside." Razor nudged Morgan with the rifle.

Morgan looked at the gun, then grinned at the man. Razor's eyes widened and he took a step back, forgetting he was the one who was armed. Red faced the darkened entry and stepped over the threshold. She waited for her eyes to adjust before going any further. It didn't take long. The place looked like a warehouse of some sort, but for what she couldn't tell. Morgan walked forward and stopped at her side.

"Where's is Jonah?" he turned to ask Razor, but he was gone, shutting the door behind him.

Morgan rushed forward, but couldn't stop it in time. "Damn!" He pressed his hands all over the door. "I can't feel a handle. There doesn't seem to be a way of opening it from the inside."

"We're trapped?" Red's skin itched at the thought of being stuck in here. The wolf suddenly wanted out. She rolled her shoulders and tried to relax.

Morgan inhaled. "No, I don't think so. I smell a pureblood. The scent is fresh, but he's not in here with us."

"Sure it's not Razor you're picking up?" she asked.

"Positive. This scent isn't malodorous."

She looked around. "Then where in the hell is he?" Red inched forward, her senses on high alert.

Morgan sniffed. She did the same. Despite the dust clinging to the metal crates, the air smelled clean, like it was blowing in from outside. They didn't spot any vents, nor did they see anything out of the ordinary.

"There's something about this place that's familiar," Morgan said.

"Are you saying that you've been here?"

"No, nothing like that," he said.

"Then what do you mean?" She stared at the shadows. From what she could tell the warehouse was full of nothing but rusted junk.

He examined the area. "I've seen this type of building before," Morgan said.

"A warehouse? I have, too. They pretty much all look the same," Red said.

"Shh—" Morgan moved in circles around the room, all the while examining the floor. "I think I hear something."

Red listened, but didn't immediately hear anything. She listened harder and caught a whirling sound coming from the floor. It was followed by a strong vibration. "What is that?" She backed toward the door they'd come through.

"If I'm not mistaken, it's an elevator."

"Here? In the middle of no-man's-land?" Red asked. He might as well have proclaimed that this place was a hydrogen car factory. How could a dilapidated warehouse hold a working elevator? It wasn't possible. There was no power in no-man's-land.

You hadn't thought there'd be vehicles here either, a little voice in her head chided.

Morgan studied the floor some more, tapping his foot here and there.

"What are you doing?" Red asked.

"Looking for the door," he said.

Maybe the heat had gotten to him. It was possible he was suffering from heat exhaustion, even though they'd made an effort to remain hydrated. He continued to bounce and tap on the floor.

"Morgan, you aren't making sense. There's nothing here but mechanical ghosts. Demery was wrong. The guards were just trying to trap us with that talk of Jonah. He probably doesn't even exist." They'd left Demery for nothing. Her heart sank as she realized they'd finally run out of options.

The whirling sound grew louder and Morgan stepped back. "It's coming," he said. A smile flitted across his lips.

Red gasped, as the floor opened up. Her eyes widened as she watched the hole grow larger and larger. Would it swallow the room and them with it? She looked up to judge the distance to the beams that ran along the ceiling. Could they jump and reach them?

A platform appeared a moment later. A blond-haired man stood in the center of it, holding a device in his hand that had a red button and a green button on it. A large pistol was tucked into a holster and strapped to his leg.

"You must be the traders Razor spoke of. Don't get many around these parts outside of the Sand Moles. At least not any who aren't out to cause trouble. Are you looking for trouble?" His gaze slid to Morgan.

"No," he said.

Red said nothing.

"I prefer the lady's response," he said. "It's more honest."

"I didn't say anything," Red said.

"Exactly. You don't talk. You can't lie." The man smiled and beckoned them forward with one tanned hand. The other held the device tight as if he were afraid they'd rip it away.

Morgan placed his hand on the small of Red's back and guided her onto the platform.

"What is this thing?" she asked.

"If I'm not mistaken, it's an old missile silo," Morgan said.

"You are correct, Mr. Hunter." The man pressed the green button and the platform lowered.

"How do you know my name?" Morgan asked.

The man grinned mischievously. "Everyone around here knows your names. Bounties tend to make their own kind of introductions." The man turned to face Red. "And you must be Gina Santiago. I can't wait to hear all about what you've done to warrant such a high price."

Red's stomach dipped from his words and the sudden descent.

"Where are my manners?" He brushed his hand over his gray pant leg. "My name is Jonah. No call for surnames out here." He held out his hand, which was surprisingly clean given the conditions of the warehouse. So were his clothes, come of think of it.

Red felt a twinge of jealousy. She'd give her left boot for a cleansing unit. She stared at the man's clean hand, but didn't shake it. He seemed courteous enough, but she still might have to kill him.

Jonah shrugged and extended the offer to Morgan.

Morgan shook his hand, then they all fell back into silence.

Red couldn't see the bottom of the shaft. She could barely make out the top. How deep was this silo? The doors slowly slid shut, leaving them in complete darkness. Her heart leapt, then slammed into her ribs. The darkness felt like it was closing in, taking all the oxygen with it. She fought the panic clawing at her throat. She couldn't breathe.

"Morgan?" she called out.

His hand found hers with ease and he pulled her into his body. "It's okay. Take a deep breath. We're almost there," he murmured.

"How can you tell?" she asked.

"Most of these things are around 176 to 200 feet deep. Just large enough to accommodate a missile, a well, kitchen, rec area, storage space, living quarters, and a command center. At least the ones I've been inside."

"He's right," Jonah said. "We've arrived."

On cue, the platform stopped with a slight jerk. Red could hear Jonah patting the wall in search of something. She was afraid to move for fear she'd fall off into the abyss.

"Here it is," he said. Something clicked and lights came on all around them.

Red blinked, temporarily blinded. A door stood five feet away. It had a round handle of some sort. Red had never seen one before. "What is that?" she asked Morgan.

He smiled. "It's called a hatch. You spin the wheel to open and close it."

"Really?" she asked. "Why doesn't it just open when we approach?"

Jonah chuckled. "I fear we're a little old-fashioned around these parts. Don't have the modern amenities found in your dome cities."

Red watched him spin the wheel. There was a loud clank and the door swung open on creaky hinges.

Jonah stepped through and waved them forward. "This way," he said.

Morgan went through the door next. Red followed, but stopped to examine the wheel. It only moved in two directions, left and right. She spun it back and forth, using one hand, then both. It was kind of fun.

"Does it do anything else?" she asked, turning it again.

"Nope." Morgan pried her fingers off the hatch. "Let's go. You can play with the door later."

The hallway had lights like she'd never seen affixed to the

walls about every twenty feet. She could see Jonah moving ahead of them. He didn't seem too concerned about his safety. He wasn't even watching them—or maybe he was. Red looked around and immediately spotted digital recorders.

The hall was bare with thick concrete walls and a matching floor. Sound traveled, but quickly muted.

"How thick are these walls?" she asked.

"Very," Morgan said. "The shaft we just came down was used to launch missiles. These walls had to be thick enough to contain the blast."

"What are those?" She pointed to the balls stuck on all the doors.

"Those are called door knobs. You turn them to open and close the doors just like the hatch."

Red approached one cautiously and tried to turn it. The metal felt cool to the touch, but nothing happened. "I think this one's broken," she said.

"Why?" he asked.

"Because it doesn't turn," she said. "See?" She tried the knob again, but it merely rattled in her grip.

Morgan smiled indulgently. "It's probably locked."

Her lips pursed. "I keep forgetting that you're from this world," she said softly.

"I'm in your world now." He grasped her hand.

Instead of giving it a reassuring squeeze, Morgan laced his fingers through hers and held on as they walked.

"I've never been this far underground. Do you think Jonah will have what we need? And if he does, will the equipment work from here?" she asked.

"He should," Morgan said. "Most missile silos came equipped with communication centers. They were made to work underground. We just have to hope that no one looted this one before Jonah moved in."

Jonah waited for them at the end of the hall. He stood in front of another metal door.

"This way." He opened it, and then stepped aside.

Morgan dropped Red's hand and walked forward to look inside. "It's okay," he said, as he passed through the doorway.

She followed. There was a decent-size room and another long

hall, except this one had several doors shooting off from the main hall.

"Welcome to Eden," Jonah said after they were all in the room.

Red looked around at the sparse mismatched furnishings and the metal doors. Nothing about this place reminded her of the biblical Eden. Eden was supposed to be lush, green, and bursting with life. This place was just the opposite with its sterile gray walls, beige, green, and orange furniture, and steel doors. Her expression must have given away her thoughts.

"Don't let outward appearances fool you," Jonah said. He walked over to the nearest door and opened it, revealing a botanical wonderland.

Red gasped. "Is that real?" she asked.

Jonah grinned. "Every last leaf. Go ahead. Check it out."

Red couldn't believe her eyes. She'd seen the greenhouses inside the biodomes. They were organized in neat rows to optimize growth. This place looked like the jungles she'd read about in school. Plants exploded from every direction, cutting off walkways and towering overhead. Bright lights dotted the ceilings. "But how?" she asked, gaping at the multitude of green. So many shades, so many different textures. The beauty was so overwhelming that it hurt her eyes.

"Those are sunlamps," Morgan said from behind her. "They provide the light needed to grow these things. What I don't understand is how you managed all this without any water."

Morgan and Red turned back to Jonah, who looked like a proud father showing off his first child.

"It's spring fed," he said.

"That's not possible." Red sobered. "All the springs in the world were poisoned during the last war."

His brow quirked. "Not all of them," Jonah said. "I test the water daily. So far, it's clean. We even have enough to shower."

Morgan's body practically quivered. "You have showers here? With real water?"

Jonah nodded and grinned. "Yep, we sure do. We use solar panels to heat the water."

"Do you have any idea the kind of gold mine you're sitting on?" Morgan asked.

Jonah's smile withered. "This is my Eden. I share it with whom

I wish and no one else. A few people have tried to take advantage of my good nature and hospitality. They are buried out back in unmarked graves," he warned. "Now let me show you where you'll be staying."

Red didn't want to leave. There was something about this room that felt so peaceful, so relaxing. It reminded her of the photos in her grandfather's books. The green world he'd spoken about on so many occasions.

She touched the petals of a yellow flower. They were soft and dewy. The fragrance coming from the blooms perfumed the air. "Amazing," she murmured.

This place truly was Eden. Red had the overwhelming urge to stay. Chuck her old life, leaving Nuria and Roark behind for good. The thought scared her. She released the plant and followed Morgan and Jonah through the door.

They were led farther down the hall to another set of steel doors.

"You'll find showers and extra clothes in there. Let me know if you need anything else. When you're done bathing, just come out and I'll show you to your room. The halls are monitored, so don't get any funny ideas. One blast of the alarms and the guards have orders to eliminate all outside intruders."

Morgan stopped him before he left. "We need to use your communication equipment, if you have any."

"Later." Jonah opened the door to a tiled room.

Red stepped through the doorway and looked around. The room was plain with white walls and metal benches bolted to the floor. Several showerheads protruded from the far wall. Metal cases of some kind flanked the row of showerheads. She ran her hands over the metal, examining the dials attached to the outsides.

"Those are called lockers," Morgan said after Jonah shut the door. "You put your clothes inside while you shower."

Red frowned, spinning the dial. "Why doesn't it open?" she asked. She spun the dial the other direction just like the doorknob, but nothing happened.

"You have to pull up." Morgan showed her.

The door to the locker swung open, revealing towels. Red picked one up and placed it on the bench. "Do you think we're safe?" she asked, her gaze moving to the closed door.

"Not as long as we're in no-man's-land," Morgan said.

"He's been so accommodating—too accommodating if you ask me."

"Jonah's behavior is definitely unusual, but I think we're okay for the time being. I scented no deception. If he wanted us dead, he wouldn't have bothered to give us the grand tour. He could've just ordered the guards to shoot." Morgan walked to the door and pressed a button.

"What did you do?" Red asked.

"Locked it," he said on his way back.

"Why?" she asked.

"Privacy," he said.

Morgan walked into the shower area and turned a knob on the wall. Water shot out of the showerhead. He held his hand under the stream and adjusted the knob, then played with the water, cupping it in his palm.

"I can't believe this." He grinned at her. "I haven't had a real shower in years."

He stripped his dirty clothes off. Red watched the layers peel away, revealing bronzed skin. Within seconds he was gloriously naked. Her mouth went dry. She sat on the bench and gazed at Morgan as he dipped his head under the water, sloshing it down his back.

Sand and grit turned the water brown at his feet, but he didn't seem to mind. He was like a child experiencing his first chemical pool. He splashed and laughed, flicking water over his shoulder at her.

Red giggled as moisture hit her in the face. It felt incredible. She undressed, watching the man she loved enjoy himself for the first time in weeks. It was good to see him smile. He hadn't done that in a while because there hadn't been a lot to smile about.

"Is the water warm?" she asked, expecting him to say no.

"It's perfect." He splayed his hands, allowing the water to wash over his fingers. "Come see for yourself."

Why not? Red thought. *What harm could it do?*

Morgan was whistling now as he rubbed cleanser on his body. By the time she stepped near the spray, he was covered in foamy suds. Red ran her hands over his smooth skin, then dipped her head under the water.

"This feels so *weird*," she said.

She'd spent her whole life taking chemical showers. Never once had she experienced water other than to drink it. It felt strange. The liquid didn't immediately cleanse her parched skin. Instead, it slowly eroded the dirt, before washing it away.

Morgan cupped the water and let it rain over her head. Red laughed and closed her eyes as water splashed on her face. He grabbed a bar of something. "This is soap," he said. "It's what we used to use before they developed cleanser."

Red had read that soap used to come in bars, but she'd never seen one. Morgan rubbed the bar over her skin and she watched as bubbles formed.

"This seems like an antiquated way of doing things," she said. The words had barely left her mouth when Morgan ran the soap over her nipple, causing it to pucker.

"Antiquated, eh? I don't know about that. From here, it looks like we might've been missing out on the good stuff by using technology."

* * * * *

Gina's breath caught as he swirled the bar of soap over her other nipple. Gooseflesh rose on her skin as he began a slow glide along her length, washing away the sand and grit, leaving clean skin and awareness behind.

"We shouldn't be doing this now," she said.

"Now is all we have." Morgan couldn't take his eyes off her. She looked so beautiful with her long black hair hanging down her back and her breasts jutting out proudly from her chest. Her stomach quivered when he brushed a hand over it.

The soap left streaks of suds that were immediately washed away by the water sloshing over their bodies. He brought the soap to her head and lathered his hands. When the suds were thick enough, he plunged his fingers into her hair and massaged her scalp.

Gina groaned. Her head fell back and she closed her eyes.

"That feels so good," she said.

Her body turned pink from the warm water. Morgan longed to taste her skin. She looked like a sprite playing in a fountain.

Positively delicious. She shifted her legs, giving him tantalizing glimpses of her firm thighs and the black curls that hid something far more appetizing.

Morgan's mouth watered at the thought of dropping to his knees and devouring her. She'd be sweet. She always was when her juices flowed. Gina was everything he could ever ask for in a woman—a mate. He wouldn't lose her, couldn't lose her again. Not without losing himself in the process.

"Lower," she growled, shifting her head around so he could reach her fragile neck.

His fingers slid down, guided by a force outside of himself. Morgan felt his body respond with every knead, every stroke. Round and round he rubbed, making sure he hadn't missed a spot. He trailed kisses over her collarbone, followed by gentle nibbles. "I'm just getting started."

Morgan guided Gina under the spray and rinsed the soap from her hair. The strands felt like silk in his hands. He ran his fingers through the length, carefully detangling it as he went. He continued his downward slide, even after he ran out of hair, until he was cupping the lush globes of her bottom. His strong hands molded her flesh, taking care not to rub too hard.

She groaned, resting her forehead on his shoulder as his lips once again found the curve of her neck. Her spicy scent rose above the fragrance of the soap, enticing his senses.

Morgan stroked her supple thighs. He loved her legs. They were so long and luscious. The feel of them wrapped around his body was as close to heaven as he'd ever get. He clasped her thighs and slowly lifted.

"I love you," he murmured. Morgan wanted those words to sink so far inside her that she never forgot.

Gina instinctively encircled his neck, her taut breasts crushing into his chest. When her legs were around his waist, Morgan's knees locked and he leaned forward.

She gasped, when her back made contact with the wet tiles.

"Cold?" he asked.

"Yes," she said, her voice a mere whisper.

"Won't be for long." Morgan nuzzled her neck, finding the spot where he'd claimed her.

Her hips rocked, sending her core over the top of his erection.

Morgan's breath hissed from his lungs as he fought for control. When he was sure he had a hold of his wolf, he went back to the mark. His teeth grazed her tender flesh, then he lapped the spot with his rough tongue. When he played with the spot, it drove Gina crazy.

"You taste incredible. You've always tasted incredible. Is it any wonder I fell at your feet?" he asked.

"Mmm..." Gina rotated her hips again. The movement slotted his hard shaft at her entrance. "I don't recall things going so smoothly."

"Honey, you had me the moment you sashayed into the dissecting lab." Morgan growled and bit down on her shoulder.

Gina's head fell back and she moaned, as pleasure took her over the edge. Her body shuddered in his hands. He couldn't seem to get enough of her blood. Like the finest liquor, she burned going down his throat and made him crave more. Morgan took another deep swallow, then forced his mouth to release her.

He'd always liked the taste of blood during sex, a nibble here, a scratch there, but it had been more primal screwing than anything else. And he'd never marked anyone. Now he could hardly orgasm without blood being brought into the equation. That damn vamp, Raphael had a lot to answer for.

* * * * *

Red couldn't get enough of Morgan. His body was so rough, hard, and hot it nearly singed her. She still couldn't believe that she'd climaxed when he bit her. Even now her body rode a wave of sheer exhilaration, waiting to tumble once more.

She rocked her hips and Morgan slid an inch deeper. He was so thick, she could barely catch her breath. Her gaze met his and she froze. His amber eyes were shadowed and tinged with a ring of red.

"What's wrong?" Red brushed his forehead with her thumb to smooth the lines.

He didn't say anything as he licked the wound on her neck, then guided her under the warm cascading water.

"Morgan, talk to me. You're not worrying about the blood thing again. Are you?"

He stared at her, his gaze seeking reassurance.

Red held him close, comforting him the only way she knew how. Morgan thought he was losing himself to the thirst for blood, but she knew better. Once an alpha wolf, always an alpha wolf. The vampire blood coursing through his veins only enhanced his abilities.

He shook his head and the wariness faded. "It's nothing. I'm sure it's just the stress of being on the run."

She tilted his chin and kissed him, allowing her lips to linger. "Talk to me," Red said.

"You still feel connected to me, right?" he asked. "I mean your feelings haven't diminished since Raphael shared his blood." Morgan subconsciously brushed his thumb over the spot on her neck.

Red's eyes widened. How could he think such a thing after all they'd been through? "Why would you think that?" she asked.

"Because *I* feel different," he said softly, still looking at her. "Not about you. But inside here." He pressed a hand to his chest.

Red stared at him. "If anything," she said. "The bond I feel for you has grown." Even now she yearned to feel his teeth in her flesh, the brush of his tongue, the gentle pull of his lips as he sucked her blood.

His smile was slow to come, but when it appeared it was lopsided and wolfish. "Glad to hear it's not one-sided. You probably think I'm overreacting, but my tastes have changed. I have *cravings*. Cravings for things that I wouldn't normally crave. Things I shouldn't crave. I know vampires are not like the creatures in the entertainment vids. They aren't magical. They aren't the undead. They're genetically engineered like I am. Nothing about their history explains the changes I've experienced. It's like Raphael somehow infected me with some of his DNA."

Red listened, paying attention to what he wasn't saying. Raphael was a vampire, so naturally he needed blood. He could go outside, but most vamps couldn't. Morgan was afraid he was becoming like him. But despite his fears, in her heart he hadn't changed. Now all she had to do was convince him.

"You bit me and took my blood long before Raphael saved you," she said. "So the wolf part of you must be inclined to do that."

His eyes met hers and his pain turned them molten. "That was different."

She tilted her head. "How so?"

"Unmarked females aren't allowed to stay in Nuria. They disrupt the pack. I was marking you," he said softly.

Red tried to squirm out of his arms, but he wouldn't let her. "You can't tell me you did that just to keep me safe." For some reason that thought hurt.

"No." Morgan shook his head.

"Then why?" Red asked.

"For me." The words were so faint that she barely heard them. "I wanted you so badly I never considered your feelings. I was determined to have you no matter what. I'm sorry." He brushed a hand over her arm soothingly.

"So you didn't mark me because of the rules?" Red was relieved to hear him say so.

"That's the reason I gave myself when I decided to do it." Morgan snorted. "But I was only trying to justify my actions. I hope someday you can forgive me."

There was a time when Red would've been angry after hearing his confession, but that was before she almost lost him to Roark Montgomery.

She sighed and gently stroked his hair. "There's nothing to forgive. We've both done things we aren't proud of. There's no changing the past."

Morgan tilted his chin. "You aren't mad?"

Red shook her head. "No, but I am curious."

"About what?" he asked.

"You said you bit me in order to mark me as yours."

He nodded.

Red nibbled on her lower lip. "Does it matter that I never bit you back?"

A genuine smile played at his sensual lips. "Yes and no. To Nuria, you're still considered my mate. But *I* need more than their acceptance. I need to know—my wolf needs to know—that you want us."

The vulnerability she saw in his eyes was something Red had never witnessed from Morgan. He'd always been fearless and aggressive. Every inch an alpha werewolf. This moment was different. He was laying his heart in her hands to do with as she pleased. If she chose to, she could crush him and walk away. But if Red did that, she would be hurting herself, too. In the end, the choice was easy.

"How can I claim you?" she asked.

"With a bite, but it must be your decision. I've disrupted your life enough. I will not take this choice away, too."

She lowered her mouth to the spot where his neck met his shoulder.

"Wait!" Morgan cried out, halting her mid-motion. "There is one more thing you should know before you bite."

Red nodded for him to continue.

"If you bite me, it's irreversible. You won't be able to take anyone else to your rest pad without suffering extreme discomfort. So think about it carefully. There is no going back," he said. He closed his eyes and waited for her to decide.

She kissed his firm lips tenderly. "I've already made my decision," Red said. And she had. She'd made it the moment she'd broken the law and crossed into no-man's-land.

Morgan's eyes opened. "Are you positive?" he asked.

She could see the hope blossoming in his rich amber depths, but he kept it tightly leashed.

"I am," Red said and continued her descent. Her lips brushed Morgan's throat. Despite the soap he'd used earlier, his skin still held a hint of salt and a rich earthy aroma.

Red licked the spot she intended to bite, then concentrated on producing fangs. Pain shot through her jaw and blood filled her mouth as her teeth were ejected by sharper incisors. She spit them out, rinsing quickly with water to cleanse her palate. She wanted to taste him and only him.

She returned to the tendon bulging at the base of Morgan's neck. It strained beneath her lips, so enticing, so inviting. Red could no longer resist. The world flashed brilliant colors the second she bit down.

Morgan's body jerked, driving his hard shaft deep.

Red gasped at the sudden invasion, but it didn't take long for her body to adjust. She placed her lips against his skin and drew deep, filling her mouth with his blood.

Morgan's whole body trembled beneath her and he slowly sunk

to the ground, still cradling her against him.

Red rocked her hips, taking him deeper, while her tongue worked the tender flesh at his neck. Corded muscle bunched every time she sucked, but Morgan made no move to stop her. His eyes were closed and his jaw remained clenched as he teetered on the verge of release. Red had never felt more powerful in her life. She rose up onto her knees, then slowly glided back down.

Morgan groaned, his hands curling into fists as he let her have her way.

She swiped her tongue over the bite mark to seal it, then rode him in earnest. He didn't touch her, but she could tell it pained him to do so. She rode Morgan steadily until they were both panting for relief. Red reached down between their bodies and stroked.

Morgan's rib cage cracked as his body attempted to shift, but he managed to pull his wolf back.

Red smiled. It was the first time she'd ever seen him this out of control. She ground her hips into him and it nearly sent her over the edge.

Morgan cried out as claws sprang from his fingertips. His eyes changed to a deep gold and his fangs came out. He tongued them and growled.

The sound hardened her nipples. Red felt the first ripple of release rush through her system. She squeezed him, refusing to orgasm without him.

Morgan was so far gone that one squeeze was all it took. He bellowed and thrust wildly before emptying himself inside her.

Red shuddered, enjoying the wave after wave of pleasure lapping against her skin. Her wolf quickly faded.

"I don't think I can move." He kissed her tenderly as his wolf receded.

"Try." Red laughed. "The water's getting cold."

They rose and rinsed one last time, before shutting off the shower. Morgan grabbed the towels and dried her off.

"I can do that myself," she said.

"I know." He grinned. "But I can't seem to keep my hands off you."

Red brushed his scruffy face lovingly with her fingertips. "I feel the same."

He finished drying her, then handed her the clean clothes he'd found in one of the other lockers. They didn't fit. The shirt was too tight and the pants were too loose, but they'd do until she could clean her others.

"Now let's go talk to our host," Morgan said, then got dressed.

* * * * *

CHAPTER TWENTY-FOUR

They found Jonah waiting in a nearby room. He was staring at something that held wires and circuits. "I was about to send the guards in to get you two." He snickered.

Heat flooded Red's face and she looked away before he could see. "I'd never seen a water shower before," she said in way of explanation.

"I doubt all that groaning and moaning was due to the shower." He gave her a look that said she wasn't fooling anyone. "Relax, I'm teasing."

"What are you doing?" she asked, changing the subject.

He pointed to the flat board in front of him. "Trying to get this to work."

"What is it?" she asked.

"A circuit board," Morgan answered.

Jonah glanced at him and raised a brow. "How did you know? Most people these days have never seen a circuit board outside of a museum."

Morgan looked uncomfortable for a moment. "You make do with what you have," he said by way of an answer.

Jonah's gaze sharpened, but he didn't persist. "I think this one is shot, unless you can get it working," he said.

Morgan stared at it. "I can take a crack at it," he said. "Do you have a computer to attach it to?"

"What's a computer?" Red asked.

"It's like a compunit, but much, much more primitive," Morgan said.

Red stared at the equipment. Morgan had said they might be able to piece something together in order to contact the outside world, but now that she'd seen the circuit board, she was having doubts. Five years' worth of rust covered the flat board, along with a layer or twelve of dust. It would take a miracle to get it working and Red was fresh out of believing in those.

"My dear," Jonah said. "Perhaps you can help me gather some vegetables for a meal."

Red looked at Morgan. She could tell by his expression that he didn't want her to go, but she was of no use to him here. At least picking vegetables was something she could do. She hoped. Red had never actually picked anything that didn't come out of a food-dispensing machine.

"Don't worry." She brushed a lock of dark hair from Morgan's handsome face. "I'll be fine." Her gaze swung around, pinning Jonah where he stood. "Besides, if he tries anything, I'll rip his heart out and eat it."

Jonah laughed, but Red didn't. She kept her expression neutral and waited for him to squirm. Great host or not, she meant every word.

* * * * *

Red followed Jonah into the greenhouse. The room was hot and moist, a sensation she'd never experienced before. She was used to hot and dry, but the moisture was different. It clung to her skin, beading on her lip and forehead. Her clothes became weighted after a few minutes, clinging to her modest curves.

"What is this called?" she asked, feeling the air with her fingertips.

"Humidity," Jonah said.

"Is it always this sticky?"

"Always." He grinned. "The vegetables are over here. Once we gather some, we'll head over to the fruit trees."

Red glanced around, trying to take the place in. The space was so large that it was impossible to see everything from one spot. The air was rich, almost as if it couldn't be contained by the room.

She'd seen pictures in the vids and read stories about the planet in its green years, but nothing could've prepared her for the sensory overload of this wild place. This place that was so foreign, yet oddly comforting.

"How long did it take you to grow all this?" Red touched a leaf. It was smooth and moist, its fine "hairs" tickling her fingertips.

"Years," Jonah said. "We lost a lot of crops at first, then we worked out the proper temperature and environment. After that, things took off rather quickly. Now come over here and help me pick carrots."

Red walked over to where he stood. The tufts of green stuck out of the ground every few inches. "I've read about carrots, tasted synth ones, but I've never seen a real one. What should I do?"

"Follow my lead." Jonah grabbed one of the green stalks at the base and pulled. An orange root appeared. He dusted off the extra dirt and shoved it into a basket crooked at his elbow.

"This." He pointed to the orange bit. "Is a carrot."

"You eat the orange part?" Red eyed it like it might bite. Didn't look very appetizing. Synth-carrots were purple.

"Yes." He wiped off more dirt, then brought it up to his mouth and bit down. The root crunched as he chewed. Jonah smiled, flashing orange teeth, then swallowed. "Here." He held out the carrot. "Give it a try."

Red hesitated, then leaned forward and inhaled. It didn't smell bad. Strange, but not bad. She stuck her tongue out and touched it. The texture was weird. Hard. Much harder than anything she'd ever eaten. She took a bite and chewed. The first taste was sweet, but it was quickly followed by a tang of bitterness. Red made a face as she swallowed. She wasn't entirely convinced that real carrots were better than synth ones.

"What do you think?" Jonah asked expectantly.

"Not bad." Red analyzed the taste that remained in her mouth. "It would take some getting used to." She didn't want to hurt his feelings.

"They're a lot better once they've been stir-fried. They soften up quite a bit and the bitterness goes away."

Red nodded in agreement, even though she had no idea what he was talking about.

Her confusion must've shown because Jonah added, "Stir-frying is when you cut up the vegetables and toss them in a very hot pan that's been placed over a fire. It's one of the many ways we cook things out here."

No food dispensers or protein packs. Everything done by hand, over a fire no less. So primitive. It was almost too much to fathom. Could she live like this? Would she want to if given the choice? Red didn't know.

"Why are you helping us?" she asked. The question had been nagging her since they'd met.

"You mean why help two fugitives?" Jonah retorted.

Her stomach clenched, twisting the carrot she'd just swallowed. "Yes," Red said, wondering if she'd have to kill Jonah after all. If she did, who would tend the plants? She looked at the basket of carrots and frowned.

"As a rule, I've never liked politicians and I don't believe half of what I hear."

"Good policy, but there has to be more to it than that," she said, unconvinced those were the only reasons for his assistance.

His gaze grew distant. "I didn't always live here, you know. I had a wife and family once upon a time. Back in the days when they used to hunt you down and force the chip into your neck. Not everyone took the time to do it right. A lot of people died during the implantation process. People were afraid to help." Jonah shook his head to clear away the bad memory. "I realize governing bodies are a necessary evil, but I don't have to like them. Never believed in folks being chipped for their own good. Thought it violated the basic right to privacy. Still do, but I'm in the minority."

"Morgan feels the same," Red said.

Although he'd preferred to fight for changes from the inside. Or at least he had before the trouble with Roark cropped up. Running away to live as Unknowns had been their only option at the time, but it wouldn't be their first choice.

Things weren't as black and white as she'd once thought. Red inhaled, smelling only leaves and earth. She could detect no deception on Jonah's part. But she worried that the soil was fooling her senses. Or, maybe she was just seeing things clearly for the first time.

Jonah's eyes crinkled. "I knew I liked Morgan. Now I know

why," he said with a wink.

* * * * *

CHAPTER TWENTY-FIVE

Morgan spent the next two days trying to piece together enough equipment to fashion a transmitter and receiver. It was difficult, given that most of the computers hadn't been touched since the early twenty-first century. There was no telling whether it would work. And if by some miracle it did, Morgan could only think of one man who might be able to hear them. He wasn't sure if Coleman Parker would listen after everything he'd done.

The Eye of God, as Coleman liked to be called, had welcomed him on his first day of work at the Santa Fe Cloning Lab Corporation. He'd invited him out for drinks and dinner, which Morgan had happily accepted. The man wanted more than friendship and he'd used Coleman's attraction to get close enough to his electrical equipment at work to jam it.

At the time, Morgan had thought he was doing so in order to retrieve the DNA of his late wife, Sarah, and son, Joshua, who'd died during the last war. According to false bulletins, they were to be cloned for pleasure use and cheap labor.

After the explosion at the lab that Roark Montgomery had arranged, Morgan realized that he'd been set up to take the fall. The politician had made sure he was spotted near the blast. Roark had arrived shortly after the bomb detonated and carted him off to the Taos Detention Center, while the Eye of God watched in disbelief.

Morgan ran a hand over his freshly shaven face. It wouldn't be long before the stubble returned. He sat back and stretched, trying to loosen the kinks in his back from being hunched over circuit boards.

Gina had gone to sleep hours ago. He should've joined her, but he couldn't keep his mind off the equipment. He'd put her through so much. She'd given up everything she'd ever worked for, and for what? To go on the run? Become a wanted criminal? To follow a man who abandoned her when she needed him most? Morgan vowed once again to be a better man. The kind of man Gina deserved.

The only way he was going to be able to keep his word was if he got them out of this mess. His eyes lit on the diaries he'd found at his cousin, Kane's home when they'd been hiding out.

Morgan had thrown them into his pack, but hadn't listened to them yet.

The thought of hearing Kane's voice again was too painful to bear. He still had nightmares about killing the only family he had left and probably always would. Morgan hadn't told Gina about the dreams because he hadn't wanted to upset her. She had enough on her mind without tossing his guilt onto the pile.

Morgan picked up the first digital diary and turned it over in his hands. Listening to it was the only way to connect to the man he once loved like a brother. He stopped spinning it and pressed play. A hiss erupted. It was followed by Kane's deep baritone, discussing inconsequential things. Kane quickly moved on to describing the last time he and Morgan had shared a woman.

He flushed and looked around to ensure he was still alone. He didn't want Gina to overhear anything about his past exploits. Morgan fast-forwarded to see if there was anything else on the device, but it ended with Kane's thoughts about the evening and ideas for future encounters.

Sadness welled. Not for their past, but for the future they were denied.

Even if his cousin hadn't died, Morgan had moved beyond sharing women now that Gina was in his life. He dropped the recorder and picked up another. There were thirteen diary entries total. Morgan hoped they weren't all like this one or he'd definitely have to go find Gina.

Unfortunately, he got his wish.

The next ten recordings were barely comprehensible rants about Morgan's leadership or lack thereof and the need for a change. By the time he'd finished listening to the eleventh recording, Morgan's chest hurt as if he'd done twelve rounds in a ring with a prizefighter. They'd been so close at one time.

How could he have missed all the signs of his cousin's unhappiness? Maybe Kane was right. Maybe it was time for new blood to lead Nuria.

Morgan glanced at the two remaining recordings and debated whether to toss them into the trash. Instead, he pushed them aside and went back to work on the transmitter. Morgan got his first signal shortly after dawn. It was crackly and didn't sound like much, but he hoped it would be enough.

The Eye of God had powerful equipment at work and at home. He'd talked about being able to pick up signals around the world. Morgan prayed he hadn't just been bragging to impress him.

He soldered two more wires together and tried speaking into the jury-rigged device. Morgan waited and listened, hearing only pops and squeals. He put his mouth to the mic.

"Eye of God, can you hear me?" he asked again.

Static answered with an angry hiss.

"Coleman, I know you're always listening to rogue communications. Please pick up. It's Morgan."

More garbled signals came back, some so high pitched only his wolf could hear them. What had he expected? A welcome back? Glad to hear your voice? Oh, by the way, thanks for fucking up my equipment and making me look bad on the job?

Morgan sat back in his chair and ran a hand through his hair. It needed a cut. Maybe he'd take care of that before they left here. He'd been at it all night and for what? Static. Gina was still asleep, but wouldn't be for much longer. He decided to let her rest. No sense in waking her with the bad news.

He continued to listen to the high-pitched whirls for another hour, while his hope faded. Morgan picked up one of the two remaining diary entries his cousin had made. This time when he pressed play a different voice appeared, replacing Kane's rich baritone. Whether from lack of sleep or disbelief, it took Morgan a moment to recognize the other voice. When he did, he nearly fell out of his chair. He grabbed the device and hit replay.

No, he wasn't imagining it. The voice was Roark Montgomery's. Why did Kane have a recording of the politician?

Morgan listened carefully. He could hear the sound of the emergency care center in the background. Kane had been at work when he recorded this. It was the next words out of Roark's mouth that nearly shattered Morgan's composure.

I want you to take care of Gina Santiago.

Morgan jumped back to the beginning of the recording again, but the words were the same. This time he let the recording continue, listening in horror as Roark ordered a hit on his beloved Gina and openly discussed the Others.

"We have you now, you bastard," Morgan muttered under his breath.

He looked at the jumble of multicolored wires lying on the table in front of him. Morgan picked up a few and started detangling them. If he could only get this blasted machine to transmit, they may just have found a way out of this mess. And their chance had come from the most unlikely source.

* * * * *

Demery tumbled down the short ridge, then struggled to his feet. Reaper had beaten him for hours after discovering Red and Morgan missing. It was only his promise to return Morgan to the asshole that had kept him and his blood woman alive.

Even now, he could hear Melea's screams tearing at his eardrums and see the tears streaming down her face as Reaper tied her facedown onto a battered old truck and sliced her clothes off with a wicked blade.

His chest clenched in pain as the memories flooded his mind. Demery had thought for sure that Reaper was going to kill her. Perhaps he should have. It would've been kinder than what he'd put them through for nearly two days.

Demery would never forgive Reaper. Never forgive Morgan for causing it or for forcing Red to leave. And he had no doubt that Morgan had been behind her leaving without him. Red wasn't the type to leave a man behind.

He willed his body to go on, pushing past the agony that came with each step. They couldn't have gotten much farther than the mountains. Maybe Reaper already had them. He shook his head, knowing that wasn't the case.

There was no way Morgan would've gone down without a fight, and Demery would have heard the laser fire crackling on the wind. Instead, all he'd heard was the drone of vehicles as the Sand Devils made their way to their other compound and the constant ringing in his ears from Reaper's right hook.

He could've ridden with them, but Reaper had demanded he take the mountain route. It was his way to extend the punishment to his body. He'd warned him that if he failed, he'd kill Melea.

Demery swallowed hard, his throat parched from lack of blood. He should've been fine after feeding two nights ago, but trying to repair the beating had used up his reserves. He hadn't seen a living creature for the past three hours, but he'd seen plenty of dead ones. Fortunately, none of them had been Morgan or Red.

He could see the foothills up ahead. It had taken longer than it should have, but he'd finally made it through the mountains. He was too tired to celebrate the small victory. Too hurt to even shout.

He'd been lucky. Reaper had let him live. Barely. The only thing that mattered was that Melea was still alive. As long as she lived, he would. She'd pleaded with him to stay. Pleaded with him to save her when Reaper mounted her and rutted in her bruised flesh like a mongrel dog.

Demery could still hear her muffled wails as she uselessly struggled to escape the monster's grasp. He felt her pain and humiliation, then as if that weren't horrifying enough, he'd experienced the sudden invasion. Felt it tear at his flesh as if it were he who'd been violated.

Damn the blood bond.

Reaper's knowing gaze had locked onto Demery and he'd laughed. "Enjoying it as much as I am, vamp?" he'd asked, pumping harder.

Demery had closed his eyes and gritted his teeth, shutting out Reaper and the shocked pain of what was happening. He'd willed Melea to do the same, but it was hard since Reaper wasn't a little man.

Hours passed before the Sand Devil was finished defiling her and Demery. Once he realized he was no longer getting a reaction out of either of them, Reaper ordered Melea to be removed to their other compound.

The beatings had begun shortly thereafter. Demery had been grateful that Reaper had not forced Melea to watch and experience the pain like he'd forced him to do. Through the years he'd suffered worse *physical* injuries, but the blood had always been there to ease his pain. Now nothing outside of vengeance would.

Reaper was sadistic and knew that the best way to torture him was through his weaknesses, the need for blood and Melea. Demery tripped and fell halfway down one of the foothills before coming to rest against a boulder. Everything ached and it hurt to breathe. He laid there for a few minutes, then forced himself to his feet. Demery checked his suit to make sure it hadn't ripped in the tumble.

Anger pushed him on, fueling his muscles. He had to find Morgan and Red. They'd have come through here at some point. This was the only trail leading out of the mountains. The only track smooth enough to traverse.

The land was beginning to flatten out. The foothills became smaller and smaller the farther away from the mountains he got. The scent of blood caught his attention. Demery followed it, his senses springing to life.

He didn't know if an animal had been wounded or perhaps it was those he sought. Thirty minutes later he found the remnants of a small crimson puddle that had long ago dried in the heat. It contained Morgan's essence and held the strong scent of wolf.

Demery glanced around the area, examining the clearing. Nothing else had been disturbed, which meant there hadn't been a struggle. He inhaled deeply. The blood was at least a couple of days old. Morgan had shifted, which meant he could've covered far more ground than normal.

He cursed aloud, using languages he hadn't spoken since his childhood. Slowly reason returned. Morgan would never leave Red. The blood meant they'd headed this way. Had they found the outpost?

Demery hadn't been entirely honest when he'd told them he knew exactly where the outpost was located. He did know its approximate location. Since he'd been the one guiding them, he had to wonder if they'd gotten lost. They wouldn't last long if that were the case, especially with the Sand Devils on the move south. They were bound to come across them if they were caught out in the open.

His gut told him to head to the outpost. If Morgan and Red stopped there for supplies, he'd find out...or he'd torture everyone he encountered until he did. Melea was counting on him. This time he wouldn't let her down.

Several hours later, Demery came upon the compound. He dropped to his knees, half out of exhaustion and half to avoid being spotted. Pain shot through his body. He waited for a wave of nausea to pass. The outpost was heavily armed and situated in a location that gave them good visibility. They'd see anyone approaching no matter which direction they chose.

He stared at the three towers, gauging his chances of making it under one without being spotted. Demery decided they were nil. He'd have to take a direct approach and hope he got close enough to get his hands on one of the guards.

Demery looked down at his protective suit. He'd have to be careful. He couldn't chance one of them shooting a hole in it while the sun was high in the sky. He burrowed deeper into the dune to plan his approach.

Demery did his best to ignore the constant growl of his stomach and steady ache in his ribs. His dreadlocks were matted to his head where Reaper had kicked him, the lump that remained a reminder of the asshole's displeasure.

Reaper wanted a pet. One he could bleed when it suited him. Demery was determined to deliver the wolf. By the time Reaper was finished with Morgan, Demery vowed the sheriff would feel every last ounce of pain he and Melea had endured.

* * * * *

CHAPTER TWENTY-SIX

Robert Santiago stared unseeing at his bookcase. The fact he hadn't heard from Tucker yet was a bad sign. Repairing the navcom had been a long shot. He knew that, but it didn't ease his pain or his sense of guilt. He should've done more to protect Gina. If he had, she wouldn't be in this predicament.

Even as the thought crossed his mind, Robert knew it wasn't true. It had always been only a matter of time before Gina discovered the truth about her family history, about her true nature. There was no way he could've predicted the path that knowledge would lead her down.

He rubbed his temples, attempting to fight off a headache. He should've grabbed a couple of hours of sleep, but these days he rarely slept. And when he did, nightmares haunted him. His navcom beeped, then immediately fired medication into his bloodstream. It wouldn't help. Hadn't helped the four previous times either.

The vidscreen on his desk activated. Robert walked over to his desk to see who it was. Tucker was standing outside his office door, holding something.

He pressed a button on his desk to open the door.

"Commander." Tucker rushed inside. "I've found something." His clothing was rumpled and his brown hair poked out from all sides. Despite his disheveled appearance, excitement added lift to his gait.

Robert held a finger to his lips, immediately silencing the tech. He pointed to the door, which hadn't closed yet. Tucker nodded in understanding and waited. The door slid closed with a hiss.

"You were saying," Robert said.

"You're never going to believe it," Tucker said. "We found something on the navcom, but it doesn't make sense."

"Play it for me," Robert said.

Tucker did as he was asked. Roark Montgomery's voice came out of the small speaker.

You'd have been dead...now... Kane hadn't fallen for you ...up. He had orders to kill you.

What you're doing is illegal... (Gina's voice) If the tactical... (static) ... discovered ..., you... (hiss) ... arrested.

But... (pop) ... aren't going to find... (static)... I'll report your escape. . . like I reported. . . Hunter's.

Roark's threat was as clear as if the politician was standing in the room with them. Robert Santiago trembled, not from fear for himself, but for what his granddaughter had gone through. She must've been terrified sitting in the back of that shuttle.

The recording stopped abruptly.

"What happened to Rita?" he snapped.

Tucker's face flushed. "Sorry. That's all we could recover. The crystals were crushed."

It wasn't a lot, but coupled with the shuttle they'd towed in thanks to Catherine Meyers' GPS coordinates it would be enough. "I want a copy of that before you leave this room," Robert said.

"I anticipated as much." Tucker took out a miniature dig-recorder from his pocket. "It's already on there. What would you like me to do with the original?"

"Seal it in the vault as evidence, then repair the navcom. I want Rita up and running a.s.a.p."

Tucker shook his head. "It's in so many pieces I'm not sure that's going to be possible."

Robert smiled at him. "You've already proven to me that you can do the impossible."

Tucker grinned. "I'll do my best." He walked toward the door. "Sir?"

"Yes?"

"Was that Roark Montgomery on the recording?" he asked.

He debated whether to answer truthfully. "Yes, it was."

"But he's running for office on a reform and unity platform," Tucker said, unable to comprehend why the man would do such a thing.

"Tucker, I trust you'll keep what you found in the strictest of confidence," Robert said. He didn't want the information leaking before he was ready to act. "This is an active case."

"Yes, sir." He looked stricken.

Robert had seen that look before. The last time had been on his own face, when someone he'd looked up to had fallen from grace. A man didn't get over that kind of thing, but he did learn from it. "Once you've placed the evidence into the vault, take the rest of the day off. You've earned it."

Tucker's expression brightened again. "Thank you, sir."

"Dismissed." He had him. Finally he had the proof needed to have the charges against Gina dismissed. Robert Santiago couldn't wait to see what Roark had to say for himself now.

* * * * *

Lieutenant Bannon Richards ran into Tucker coming out of Commander Robert Santiago's office. The man was distracted and didn't notice he'd stepped into his path. The tech guy ran straight into him as Bannon had planned.

"Heads up, Private Tucker," Bannon said. "A commanding officer is present."

The man's eyes widened and he stiffened to attention. "Sorry, sir. I didn't see you there."

"That's because you weren't paying attention. Where were you headed in such a hurry?" Bannon asked. He needed to know why the tech had been visiting the commander. The thought that the reason could be innocent was quickly dismissed when Tucker's expression grew wary.

Tucker took longer than he should've to answer. "Nowhere, sir. Just back to the lab." His gaze dropped, leaving little doubt that he'd lied.

Bannon nudged him, moving into Tucker's personal space. "What were you doing in the commander's office?" he asked, his tone demanding the truth.

"N-nothing. He'd wanted updates on some repairs I've ɔeen working on," Tucker said.

Bannon's eyes narrowed. What was the commander up to⁑ He never asked about regular maintenance. "Repairs on what?" he asked, not expecting an answer.

"A junked navcom," the man said. His gaze darted down the deserted hallway. "If you'll excuse me, I'd better get back to work." Tucker swallowed hard and sweat broke out along his temples.

Bannon reluctantly moved aside to allow him to pass. Tucker had gone five steps when Bannon called out, "Did you succeed?"

He stopped and slowly looked over his shoulder. "Yes, I did." Tucker rushed off without another glance.

Bannon didn't know what was going on, but he figured the navcom must be pretty important if Robert Santiago was requesting the tech department to report directly to him. He thought about the talking navcom unit Red used to wear and realized he should've asked the tech guy more questions.

Roark had told him to keep an eye on things. Mainly to let him know if he'd seen any sign of Gina Santiago. He hadn't. But something told him that Roark would want to know about this.

He walked away from the commander's office and pressec a button on his navcom. Bannon didn't want to be overheard. It took a few seconds to receive confirmation that the private connectiɔn had indeed been made. A moment later, Roark's voice boomed cut of the tiny speaker.

"Sir, this is Lieutenant Bannon Richards. I hate to interrupt lunch, but I may have something."

"Has Gina Santiago tried to contact her grandfather?" Roark asked.

He shook his head, forgetting Roark couldn't see him. "Not that I'm aware of," Bannon said.

There was silence. "Then why are you contacting me so close to the election?" he asked. "I told you the only time you should call is if you spotted Gina or Morgan."

Bannon was beginning to think he'd made a mistake. He'd been so damned determined to earn a position at Roark's side that he'd acted hastily. If he weren't so concerned about angering Roark further, he'd disconnect now. Instead, he brought his lips closer to the mic.

"I just ran into a tech guy who was leaving the commander's office."

"So?" Roark said. "That's fairly common as I recall."

"Yes, sir. Normally it is." Bannon stopped speaking for a moment when a private walked by. When the man was gone, he continued, "He said the commander had him working on a busted navcom. Seemed kind of odd, since the commander doesn't care about broken equipment beyond viewing repair request reports."

Roark was silent again. "Did this tech tell you where he got the navcom?"

Bannon experienced a flush of embarrassment. He hadn't bothered to ask, but he wasn't about to inform Roark of his incompetence. "No, sir."

A buzz sounded on the line.

"What was that, sir?" Bannon feared someone had intercepted their communiqué.

Roark didn't immediately respond.

"Sir?" Bannon repeated. Maybe he hadn't heard him. The buzz grew more insistent.

"It appears that your commander is trying to get in touch with me. I better see what he wants. Keep your eyes and ears open, Lieutenant. Good work."

* * * * *

Roark cut the transmission and straightened his tie. The vidscreen glowed, then buzzed again. He pressed a button on his desk and Robert Santiago's weathered face appeared on the screen.

"Commander, I was just on my way out to grab lunch," he lied. "Are you calling to congratulate me?"

"Hardly," Robert said. "The election isn't until tomorrow."

"A formality and you know it. So what can I do for you?" Roark gave him a bored expression. It was no coincidence that the commander contacted him now. He must have found something really important.

Stay calm. No need to panic. Find out what he wants.

Robert's dark eyes sizzled with barely leashed fury. "It seems a navcom has been recovered from your old shuttle," he said.

"My shuttle?" Roark's heart pounded. What kind of game was Robert Santiago playing?

"Yes, you know the one you said Morgan Hunter bombed in order to help Gina escape."

Roark forced a smile. "Ah, that shuttle. A total loss. I haven't thought about it since the incident. How did you find it by the way?"

Robert waved the question away. "It's not important. What is important is the navcom that was recovered."

"Why is that?" Roark tugged at his tie.

Surely there had to be more than a navcom if he was contacting him. Roark had thought his man had taken care of everything when he'd hauled the shuttle farther out into the desert and blasted a hole in its side. Obviously he'd forgotten to search the inside thoroughly. Or maybe he'd thought the laser cannon blast would take care of any lingering evidence. He'd been a fool and Roark planned to make sure he never had the opportunity to repeat his stupidity—after he dealt with the commander.

"Did it reveal your granddaughter's whereabouts?"

The commander didn't rise to the bait. "The navcom recorded the most interesting thing," Robert said. "At least I found it interesting. I'm sure a tribunal will, too."

Roark was beginning to sweat. The man was bluffing. "I doubt there'd be much left on a destroyed piece of equipment," he said. His brain worked overtime as he tried to recall the conversation he'd with Gina Santiago.

The commander grinned and Roark's skin tightened to the point of discomfort.

"We've recovered enough," Robert said. "Certainly enough to raise a few questions about your version of what transpired."

"Is that so?" Roark asked. "Navcom recordings can be faked."

"True, but I believe under further examination this one will be easily authenticated."

Roark tugged at his collar. "Mind elaborating?"

"Not over the vidscreen." Robert sat back calmly, placing his hands on his abdomen.

"Then I suppose all that's left to do is for us to meet, so I can hear this mysterious recording for myself," Roark said.

He had to find out what the commander knew. The election was too close for his character to be called into question now. If Robert Santiago somehow managed to find something to implicate him, Roark would simply have to have Bannon destroy it and the man protecting it.

"Tell me where and when and I'll be there," Robert said.

"Today, at my office." Roark glanced at his watch, wondering if he'd have time to get things into place. He thought about his prison below the building. It wasn't as if it would need to be cleaned. "Let's say we meet at two. I'll type you in for a couple of hours. That should give us more than enough time to cover the important points."

"See you then," Robert said.

"Look forward to it." Roark disconnected.

He had a lot to do before the commander arrived. He wished his assistant, Michael Travers was around. He didn't want to get his hands dirty. Unfortunately, Roark had little choice. If Robert Santiago wanted to play games, he'd let him. One thing he would guarantee was that this would be a visit the commander of IPTT wouldn't soon forget.

* * * * *

CHAPTER TWENTY-SEVEN

Jonah knocked and stepped into the room. "There's a man outside asking to see you," he said.

Morgan jumped, dropping the screwdriver he'd been using onto the floor. It clattered and rolled under his chair. He hadn't realized he'd dozed off. He scrubbed a hand over his face and yawned.

"Did he give you a name?"

No one but Demery and the Sand Moles should know where to find them. He pictured the hole Gina had left in Gray's chest and the shock on the Sand Moles' faces. He didn't want to bring trouble to Jonah's door, if he could avoid it.

"He's wearing a white protective suit and says his name is Demery," Jonah said.

Despite telling Gina otherwise, Morgan hadn't expected to see Demery again. The Sand Devils were the type of people who didn't forgive mistakes. That was why he'd been so determined to get her out of there. Had Demery managed to escape, too, or were the Sand Devils waiting nearby?

"Is he alone?" Morgan asked.

"Looks to be. I put the guards in the towers on high alert. If anyone is sneaking around out there, they'll spot them long before they get here. You expecting company?"

"No one I want to see." Morgan debated how much he should share with Jonah. They'd been through a lot. Made some hard decisions. Morgan had no doubt that he'd understand, but would

Jonah want to anger the other groups when he had to live here? "Have you told Gina?"

"No." Jonah shook his head. "She's playing in the garden. I didn't want to interrupt her. Besides, he was asking for you. Didn't mention the girl."

The hair on Morgan's neck rose and his muscles tightened as his wolf brushed his flesh. "Did he say what he wanted?"

"Said something about needing your help." Jonah scratched his head. "Not sure what he meant by that. Do you know?"

Morgan ignored the question. "How does he look?" he asked instead.

"Can't tell." Jonah rubbed his whiskers. "Can only see his face in that suit he's wearing. Looks okay, I guess."

That was a good sign, wasn't it? The Sand Devils wouldn't have allowed Demery to leave with his suit if they'd wanted him dead. But that didn't explain Melea's absence.

"You sure Razor and the others didn't see anyone else with him?" Morgan asked.

"Not unless they're invisible. My men have him covered. Mind telling me what's going on? I'm beginning to get that twinge in my side that tells me trouble's coming."

"It's a long and complicated story," Morgan said. "If I knew there was going to be a problem, I'd warn you."

"Appreciate it." Jonah leaned against the doorframe. "Is this fella really a friend of yours?"

"Not exactly, but we were traveling together until we ran into the Sand Devils. Parted company unexpectedly after that," Morgan said.

Jonah let out a long whistle. "Never did care for that bunch. They have a camp about ten miles south of here. They leave us alone, but it's not by choice. We give them incentive to stay away." He patted the weapon strapped to his leg.

"Do they know about Eden?" Morgan asked.

Jonah eyed him suspiciously. "No, and I'd like it to stay that way."

Morgan's chair screeched as he scooted back to stand. "Then I'd better get out there and see what he wants. If Gina comes looking for me, tell her I'll be right back." He paused. "But do me a favor."

Jonah waited.

"Don't tell her where I've gone or who I've gone to meet," Morgan said.

He wanted to find out what was going on before he brought Gina into the mix. If it turned out he had to kill Demery, Morgan didn't want Gina to have to witness the vamp's death.

"Thought you said you weren't expecting trouble." Jonah's face pinched with worry.

"Nothing I can't handle." Morgan met his gaze fleetingly, then looked away.

A moment of silence stretched between them.

"Did you get that thing working?" Jonah nodded at the mass of wires and circuits that passed for a transmitter.

Morgan was relieved by the change of subject. "Don't know. I have a signal, but I'm not sure if I'm able to broadcast. Haven't received a reply yet." He rolled his neck to relieve the stiffness "If this takes longer than I anticipate, please give this to Gina and tell her to keep trying to contact the Eye of God. He'll know what to do with it." Morgan handed Kane's recording to Jonah. "I'll be back soon."

"Make sure that you do. I'm not going to be the one to break bad news to your woman. She's liable to take my head clean off." Jonah grinned and walked out of the room.

Morgan rode the lift up to the opening of the missile chamber, listening to the steady hum of the hydraulics. His nerves were taut. He'd gone over their encounter with the Sand Devils multiple times in his mind.

He'd had no choice but to leave Demery and escape. Morgan hoped the vamp understood why. He would've done the same given the chance, or so he told himself as he stepped into the blistering heat.

The sun was high in the sky, causing the temps to soar. He took a deep breath and slowly exhaled, scenting the air for traps. When he was sure he wouldn't be ambushed, Morgan exited the dome.

Demery stood on the other side of the moat with the guns in the towers trained on him. His hands were in the air. When Morgan got closer, he saw that Demery's hands were trembling, but it wasn't from fear.

Morgan waved to Razor and the other guards, then signaled

Demery to lower his arms. They came down in a rush. The protective suit he wore was no longer white. Dirt and sand tarnished it, leaving only fleeting glimpses of the color it used to be. It looked as if he'd been rolled down a hill and then stuffed into a sand dune.

"Didn't think I'd ever see you again." Morgan approached cautiously. Demery may be in a protective suit, but he was still a vampire.

"I'm not surprised, since you left me to twist in the sun, mon," Demery said. His words were hoarse, but they still held a bite.

"I looked for you before we left. Checked everywhere I could think of. You weren't in any of the vehicles."

He swayed and winced, clutching his side. "You mustn't have looked too hard, because I was there," he said. Demery's gaze flickered to the guards.

Morgan reached out to steady him. "I'm telling you, I looked everywhere."

"Don't touch me." Demery shoved his hand away.

Morgan stepped back. "After what we'd witnessed the night before, I had to get Gina out of there as soon as possible. You would've done the same," he said.

Demery laughed. "No, I wouldn't, mon. I would never leave a man behind. Every soldier knows that. It's the first thing you learn. Obviously you forgot, or maybe you were the type who saved his own hide and didn't worry about your men."

Morgan flinched. "You would if it meant your mate's life," he said. He'd already lost Gina once. It wouldn't happen again. He had felt bad about leaving Demery, but he wouldn't change a thing.

"Melea and I have a blood bond," he said.

"True," Morgan said, "but she's not your mate or you wouldn't have left her the first time."

Demery's expression sobered. "I guess we'll never know, mon. Did you find what you were looking for here?" He nodded at the dome.

"Maybe," Morgan said. He needed to know more about what happened before he shared information. For all he knew, Demery had come here to gather intel for the Sand Devils. "How did you escape?"

"Easy." Demery grinned, flashing stained fangs. "I waited for Reaper to get bored with beating the shit out of me, then I grabbed Melea and ran. Of course by then, he'd already raped her repeatedly in front of me. Since we are blood, I got to share the experience with her." He drew a pair of pants out of his pack and tossed them on the ground at Morgan's feet—the back was covered in blood.

Morgan winced at the savagery.

"You ever experience anything like that in the war, Hunter? Know what watching and feeling something like that does to a man?" Demery's face contorted with anguish that quickly morphed into rage.

"My cousin Kane, a man I loved like a brother, attacked and killed three women. I knew two of them personally. His intention was to go after Gina next and force her to be his mate. He would've used any means necessary, including rape, to get what he wanted. If it hadn't been for Jesse Lindley, the owner of the water trader you were staying in, he would've succeeded. I found Gina beaten and lying on the floor with a sack shoved over her head." Morgan took a deep breath as he relived the nightmare. "Jesse was an old wolf and was in even worse shape, since she'd fought Kane off. He killed her while she lay helpless in the emergency care center because he was angry that I'd claimed Gina as my mate. I didn't see or feel any of these things happen, but I know how helpless I felt afterward. I imagine it was the same for you, not being able to help Melea."

"As you can see," Demery indicated to the pants, "it was so much more than a feeling. I experienced every thrust, every tear. I felt her disbelief, her fear, her horror, and eventually her disappointment in me."

"I'm surprised you let him live," Morgan said. He'd have killed the man, even if he died in the process.

"I didn't have a choice. It was leave or die," Demery said.

Morgan understood Demery's outrage. No, he'd never been sexually assaulted, but he had been repeatedly violated at the genetic labs. His body had been subjected to extreme pain and psychological torture. There were times Morgan had thought he wouldn't live through it, but he had. And had come out the other side a changed man.

"Where is Melea?" he asked.

Demery indicated to the foothills in the distance. "I had to leave her against that outcropping of rocks. She was too exhausted to continue and my injuries prevented me from carrying her. That's why I came here. I figured if you'd made it to the outpost, you would be able to help."

"And if we hadn't been here?" Morgan asked.

"Then I would've asked the guards for assistance," Demery said.

Morgan glanced at the rocks and tried to gauge the distance. The wind moaned as it picked up sand, carrying it from dune to dune. "You left her unprotected? What if there's a predator around?"

"She's safe for now, but she won't be if Reaper finds her." Demery looked around, his gaze darting nervously over the sand.

He was right. They needed to get to her fast. "The guards reported that the Sand Devils were making their way around the mountains," Morgan said.

"Reaper sent some of his men ahead to prepare the encampment south of here. While they were doing that, I saw my chance to escape and I took it." Demery's dark gaze dropped to the sand at his feet.

"So they're not out looking for you?" he asked. "I find that hard to believe." Morgan scanned the horizon for movement.

"They have scouts in the area, but the group has moved on," he said.

Morgan glanced at the sun. It wasn't getting any lower. If there was even a chance that what Demery was saying was the truth, then helping him was the least he could do after leaving him.

"We'd better get going," Morgan said.

He debated for a moment whether to retrieve his pistol, but decided against it, since using the lift again might alert Gina. Besides, if Demery tried to pull anything, all Morgan had to do was grow a claw and rip a hole in his protective suit.

"Lead the way," he said.

"Thank you." Demery turned and wobbled.

Morgan's hand shot, but stopped short of touching him. "Are you sure you're up to making this trip?" he asked. "You can wait here. I can get Razor to come with me. Between the two of us, we should be able to carry Melea."

Demery's eyes narrowed and he shook his head. "You've left me little choice, mon. After what she's been through, Melea's unlikely to come to anyone but me. She knows to hide if she doesn't see the white suit."

Morgan's hackles rose at his tone, but he let it slide, given what Demery'd been through. He owed him that much. Contrary to what the vamp thought, Morgan had never left a man behind before.

If the circumstances were different, he wouldn't have in this case either, but it wasn't all about him anymore. He had to keep Gina's welfare upmost in mind. He'd noted the Sand Devil leader's predatory gaze when it fell upon her. It wasn't a matter of if he acted, but a matter of when. And Morgan would die before he'd let Reaper lay a finger on his mate.

They made good time crossing the desert floor, despite Demery's injuries. Within a couple of hours, they reached the outcropping of rocks. They were much smaller than they'd appeared in the distance. There weren't many places to hide.

"Where is she?" Morgan inhaled in an attempt to catch Melea's elusive feminine scent. The hot oppressive air refused to give up its secrets. He walked a few more paces ahead and looked around. "I don't sense her presence." Unease prickled Morgan's scalp. He looked around and readied himself for a possible ambush.

"She's over there, behind the cluster of boulders," Demery said.

"I should be able to smell her by now," Morgan said. "Especially if she's injured."

"She's there." Demery took the lead. "I cleaned her up the best I could. Can't exactly have her running around smelling of blood, when I'm in this shape."

Morgan followed, his senses alert. If this was a trap, as he was beginning to suspect, he needed to be ready. Claws sprung from his fingertips. He welcomed the pain.

"Melea," Demery called out, then ducked behind a boulder.

Morgan frowned and approached cautiously. He still couldn't detect her scent. He sniffed again, finally catching a faint musky odor.

Demery was still hunched over. "It's okay, I'm here. You can come out now," he said.

Morgan waited.

213

When Demery straightened, he had a scarf in his hands. Morgan recognized it as being one that Melea had worn. His muscles relaxed and his claws retracted. Morgan thought getting him out here had been a ruse, when he'd been unable to smell her. Had been expecting one, which was why he hadn't wanted Gina to come along. He was relieved to be proven wrong.

"You know what I love about wolves?" Demery laughed.

He shook his head. "No, but I'm sure you're going to tell me." Morgan's unease came back in an instant, along with his claws.

"It's that they rely on their sense of smell and ignore what's right in front of them." Demery turned and the scarf floated to the ground.

Morgan didn't register the laser pistol in the vamp's hands until it was too late. The shot rang out, catching him in the chest, knocking him onto the rocks. His skin burned as if a torch had been taken to it.

Gina... He'd lost her for good this time.

Morgan glanced down, expecting to see a gaping hole where his heart had been. Instead of a fatal wound, his skin reddened and continued to burn. A stun blast. The son of a bitch had hit him with a stun blast. Morgan's body stiffened and a wave of pain rolled over him, then he felt nothing at all.

* * * * *

CHAPTER TWENTY-EIGHT

Demery unzipped a pouch in his suit and pulled out a short-range comdevice. "It's done," he said. "Come and get your pet."

He put the comdevice away, then picked up the shackles the Sand Devils had left for him. He shoved his blood's scarf into his pocket, then went to work. Within a few minutes, he had a collar around Morgan's neck and his limbs bound. He'd removed his shirt and replaced it with a long silver chain, which fastened at his neck and ran to his waist.

Demery tugged at it, testing the leash's strength. It clanged, but otherwise stayed strong. Perfect for leading the wolf around. If Reaper wanted a pet to bleed for sport, then he'd damn well give him one.

The Sand Devils arrived quickly. Morgan was still out and would remain so for at least another hour, since he'd hit him at such close proximity.

"I've done as promised, mon. Now give me my blood and let me be on my way," he said with more authority than he felt.

Reaper signaled to someone at the back of the caravan. Melea was shoved out of one of the vehicles. She ran toward Demery on shaky legs. Before she could get to him, Reaper snatched her by her braids, stopping her.

"We had an agreement," Demery said, between clenched fangs.

"I will keep my end of the bargain, but not until I'm sure that Other blood runs through his veins." A fat finger pointed at

Morgan's unconscious body. It was followed by a swift kick to the ribs.

Morgan moaned, but did not wake.

"I gave you my word," Demery said.

"And look where it got me," Reaper said.

Demery growled in frustration. "I had no control over their actions," he said.

"Maybe that's true. Or maybe you helped them get away." He shrugged. "Your word doesn't mean much around here. You gave me your word before and you ran off to live on the other side of the boundary fence. If I hadn't taken care of your blood, she would've perished." Reaper cupped Melea's ample breast until she cried out in pain.

Demery shook with fury, his gaze locked on Reaper's hand. "I didn't leave her. I went in search of what you wanted. You said specifically that you'd only accept wolf's blood in exchange for Melea," he said. "Here's your wolf." He toed Morgan.

"If that's true, then our trade will be complete," Reaper said. "But if you've double-crossed me again, I will pass your woman around to every man while you experience her pain. Then I'll bleed her slowly in front of you and watch you thirst to death."

Melea's mocha skin paled at the threat. Blood roared in Demery's head, deafening him to everything but his rage.

"Or maybe if the wolf doesn't suit me, I'll have you take his place," Reaper said.

"Taste him and be done with it," Demery snarled. All this talk about blood and violence was making him hungry. "Stop wasting time."

"You forget your place." Reaper shoved Melea behind him and stood nose to sun shield with Demery. "I will taste the wolf, but not here." He glanced around at the mountains like he expected an ambush. "Let's move this to the encampment."

"How long will it take to get there?" Demery prayed it wasn't too long. He didn't think he'd make it much farther without blood.

"A few hours. Now pick him up and put him in that vehicle. We don't have all day. Just looking at him makes me thirsty." Reaper laughed. "But I don't have to tell you about the thirst. Do I?"

He walked toward a metal monstrosity that resembled a steel

armadillo, leaving Demery to follow. Reaper jumped in the passenger side and pulled Melea onto his lap. He went back to stroking her breasts, all but daring Demery to stop him.

Melea stared straight ahead, her brown eyes wide and unfocused. He'd seen that look before in the eyes of soldiers who'd experienced heavy combat. Given time she might recover from the trauma. Demery looked closer at her vacant expression. Then again, she might not.

Demery bit the inside of his mouth and tasted blood. He swallowed it, praying it would keep him going until he could feed properly and get Melea away from this madman.

The ride to the Sand Devil encampment took awhile. In the distance, he could see the outpost where he'd found Morgan. Demery was grateful that Red hadn't come out to meet him. He wasn't convinced he would've been able to go through with the plan and lie to her face as easily as he'd done to Morgan.

He glanced down at the sleeping wolf, who'd been dumped onto the vehicle floor. Morgan was snoring loudly, which was a side effect of the stun. The collar around his neck had already begun to blister his skin. When Reaper finished with him, he'd be raw. Demery didn't envy him that, but Morgan had brought it on himself.

In the beginning, Demery hadn't intended to exchange any of them for Melea, but he had hoped to bargain for her using some of their blood. He'd almost worked out a deal when Morgan and Red left him. Reaper's fury had changed his mind.

The healing had been slow going. Demery still ached, but not as bad as a couple of days ago. Soon he and Melea would be out of here and they'd leave this nightmare behind.

They hit a rock and Morgan groaned.

When the wolf did come around, he'd have one hell of a hangover, but the pain in his head would be nothing compared to what Reaper would do. The barbarian wanted the blood of an Other.

Demery had made the mistake of bartering his own blood when he'd first come to trade with the Sand Devils. It hadn't taken long for Reaper to discover the advantages of drinking an Other's blood. Soon he had added strength and speed without any of the drawbacks. Eventually Demery's blood wasn't enough. Reaper wanted more and greater variety to feed his unquenchable thirst.

He'd barely escaped with his life. Demery hadn't been able to save Melea. She would've slowed him down. Like a coward, he'd had her deliver a message, saying he'd return with a wolf, then left her with these animals. What survived was a shell of the original woman.

As many times as he imagined different scenarios, he'd do it again if it meant the difference between her life and his. He wasn't proud to admit it, but it was the truth.

They made it to the Sand Devil camp, which consisted mainly of lean-tos and tin shacks. Two men removed Morgan from the vehicle and chained him to a metal spike that had been driven deep into the ground. His arms were pulled out to his sides to form a macabre cross. It wouldn't take long for his lips to crack and his skin to burn.

Demery watched as he came around. Morgan's head shot up and his amber gaze locked on him. A growl sounded deep within his throat, both promise and threat, then he yanked on the chains. They clanged loudly, but held.

"You have no one to blame but yourself," Demery said, brushing aside any second thoughts when Melea slid off Reaper's lap.

Morgan's eyes drilled him in place. "You will regret this, vampire," he said, his voice guttural. "These chains will not protect you."

"It won't do you any good to shift. Those chains are silver laced with steel and that post is sunk six feet into the ground," Reaper said. "You can't break them." He shoved Melea toward Demery, then drew a large knife from the sheath at his thigh and approached Morgan. "This will hurt." He sliced him across the chest. A line of red appeared as his skin opened and blood dripped.

Morgan flinched, but didn't make a sound. His gaze remained on Demery.

"Someone get me a cup," Reaper shouted.

One of the Sand Devils rushed forward.

Reaper pressed the cup below the wound and waited for the blood to fill it. He applied pressure to hurry the process along. When the crimson liquid neared the top, Reaper brought the cup to his lips and drank. Blood spilled out of the sides of the cup and down his face as he swallowed greedily.

His lips smacked when he'd finished. "Ah," he said. "He'll do nicely." Reaper pressed the cup back to Morgan's chest, working the wound once more, then turned to Demery. Crimson sloshed over the sides, spilling onto the ground. "Care for a taste?"

Morgan trembled in anger and his muscles tensed, which only made him bleed more. His taut abdomen was now slick with blood. The sweet coppery aroma filled the air.

Demery's mouth watered. He could smell the blood through his protective suit's air filter. It enticed him, lured him closer, when he knew he should stay where he was. He had Melea back. This was what he wanted. The smart thing to do was go. If they left now, they could be over the mountains by tomorrow night.

Reaper waved the cup under his face shield. "I know you want some," he said. "You're practically drooling."

Demery's eyes followed the liquid's swirling movements, mesmerized by the ebb and flow. He was so hungry. His mouth watered and his fangs extended.

"Blood, let's leave," Melea pleaded, tugging on his arm.

He looked into her ashen face. Abuse at the hands of Reaper had faded her natural beauty. "We will soon." Demery brushed his gloved hand over her cheek. "I promise."

She shook her head. "No, let's go now. I'll feed you. You don't need this blood." Tears welled in Melea's eyes.

She was right. They should leave immediately. But it had been days since he'd fed. His body ached from the hunger. Demery was too weak to go far. He'd never make it over the mountains.

Despite her offer, he refused to feed from Melea, not after everything she'd been through. It would only enhance their bond. He didn't want it to get any stronger. Truth was, he didn't want it at all. His gaze locked on the cup and his stomach roared.

Reaper chuckled. "Your body knows what it needs. As does mine." He slapped his firm abdomen. His hand bounced off the muscle with a loud *thwack*.

Melea tried once more to pull Demery away. "Please, let's go," she pleaded.

"You should listen to your blood," Morgan said. "Go while you can."

Demery's face hardened. "You are in no position to tell me

what to do, wolf." He pried Melea's fingers off him. "All I need is a quick taste before we go." He glared at Morgan. "Then you can get to know your new friend."

Tears fell silently down Melea's cheeks as Demery stepped forward and grasped the cup. The smell of blood grew stronger, drowning his senses. Like Reaper, drinking Other blood affected Others, too.

It was one of the few things that would get them drunk, which was why they rarely touched the stuff outside of the rest pad. He didn't plan on overdoing it. He just needed enough to squelch his hunger, regain his strength, and wipe that look of superiority off Morgan's face.

Demery unzipped a spot on his suit and pulled out a special straw that allowed him to feed during the day. He placed one end of the straw into the cup and sucked. The blood swirled, making a couple of loops before disappearing inside of his suit.

The first taste of the hot coppery substance hit his throat and he choked, nearly dropping the cup. His fingers tightened. Demery managed to hang onto it long enough to empty the container. His head swam and he shook it to clear it.

"Enjoy my blood while you can, vamp," Morgan said. "You're as good as dead."

* * * * *

Morgan had never been so angry in his life. He was angry at the vamp, but even more so with himself. It had been stupid to follow Demery. If he hadn't been feeling so guilty about leaving him, Morgan would've listened to his gut.

Now he was strung up like a sacrificial lamb, waiting to be slaughtered pint by pint. His mind immediately jumped to Gina. What would she do when she found out he was missing? Would she come looking for him?

The thought chilled him. He couldn't let her. Somehow he had to warn her to stay away. Jonah would give her Kane's recording when he didn't return. She could take it and run for the boundary fence. At least that way she'd be far away from this place and out of danger.

He glanced at Reaper. The man's taste for blood ran far deeper than just drinking it. He was a sadist. Morgan wouldn't survive unless he could escape, but first he had to get them to stop bleeding him.

Morgan's gaze moved to Demery. Hatred surged through his body and he tested the strength of the chains once more. With the right amount of pressure applied, they would break. The vampire thought he had him, but he'd forgotten one very important thing. Morgan wasn't just a werewolf. He was an Alpha wolf. Once he released that part of himself, Demery's white protective suit would be of little help to him.

* * * * *

CHAPTER TWENTY-NINE

Red stretched her arms over her head and groaned. She'd been bent over admiring the plants for hours. She was surprised that Morgan hadn't come looking for her by now, but he was probably still preoccupied with fixing the equipment.

She made her way to the showers. Red wanted to freshen up before lunch. The stalls were empty and the silo seemed unusually quiet. Red shook off her unease and stripped down quickly. The spray felt wonderful, but she didn't linger. She wanted to find Morgan and check on his progress with the transmitter.

Red finished showering and threw on her clothes. She walked down the dimly lit hall, expecting to find Jonah, but he was nowhere in sight. "Morgan? Jonah?"

No one answered.

She continued on until she reached the control room. Jonah sat at a desk opposite of where she'd last seen Morgan. The equipment he'd been working on was still there, but he was gone. Red had found him asleep in the chair earlier and hadn't wanted to disturb him, so she'd gone to the garden.

"Where's Morgan?" she asked.

Jonah swiveled his chair around to look at her. "Enjoy your time in the garden?"

"Yes, it was lovely." Red ran a hand through her wet hair to detangle it.

Jonah smiled, then went back to reading the paper in his hands.

"Morgan should be back soon. If you're hungry, there are snacks on the counter." He nodded toward the food dispensing station, except that wasn't what Jonah had called the room. He'd called it a kitchen.

Red was hungry, but she didn't want to eat until Morgan returned. "Where did he go?" she asked. And why hadn't he asked her to go with him?

Jonah looked uncomfortable.

"What is it?" she asked.

He looked at the time and frowned.

"Jonah, where is Morgan?" Red's heart began to pound. What had happened while she was in the garden? She hadn't heard anything.

"He told me not to say anything."

"Morgan?" Why would he do that?

Jonah cleared his throat. "Thought he'd be back by now."

"Where did he go?" Red asked, as calmly as she could, but her insides continued to knot.

"A friend of yours arrived asking for him. Apparently, he needed help. Morgan went along to assist," he said.

Fear enveloped her. They didn't have any friends in no-man's-land. "What did this friend look like?" Her throat squeezed, cutting off her air supply.

"He wore a white protective suit," Jonah said. "Here, see for yourself."

He pressed a button and a vid popped up of Morgan and Demery. They were talking low, but the outpost recording devices still picked up the majority of the conversation. Demery and his blood had somehow escaped the Sand Devils. The vid ended with Red still staring at the screen. Her apprehension grew.

"How long have they been gone?" She glanced at her watch.

Jonah scratched his head. "It's been a while. Morgan did tell me that he wanted you to man this device." He pointed to the mess on the table. "Said he was expecting to hear back from the Eye of God."

"The Eye of God?" As if on cue, the receiver crackled and a voice tried to emerge from the static.

"... Hunter? ...God....can't hear....might...you."

"Is that him?" Jonah asked.

Red raced toward the transmitter. "What do I do?" She stared at the mess. It looked nothing like the equipment she was used to dealing with at IPTT. How did it work?

"Press that button." Jonah indicated to a black button in the middle of the tangle of wires.

"This is Morgan's mate, Gina Santiago. Over. Can you hear me?"

Static blurred into white noise as Red turned up the volume. "I don't think he heard me," she said.

"Give him a minute," Jonah said. "You're not exactly using state-of-the-art equipment. Morgan wasn't even sure it was transmitting."

A hiss howled out of the machine. "Have news," the garbled voice said.

"Could you repeat that?" She strained to hear.

"Missing...vid shows possible... abduction," he said.

Red's stomach soured. Who was missing? This stupid machine was useless. She touched the mic and the receiver popped again. Red jumped back as the garbled message continued.

"Bad news...Robert Santiago...believed...kidnapped. Announced...min...ago. Blame you. Montgomery...reward. Turn...in."

Red's throat tightened. She hadn't heard everything the Eye of God had to say, but it had been enough to piece together what occurred. Her grandfather had been kidnapped and they were trying to blame her and Morgan. She looked over her shoulder at Jonah, who was staring at her with empathy in his eyes. The room spun and she barely made it into the chair before her legs gave out.

"I'm sorry," Jonah said. "I take it that man's related to you."

She choked down the lump in her throat. "He's my grandfather. I have to go."

"But he said they think you're behind the kidnapping," Jonah said.

"I know what he said." She ground her teeth until her jaw hurt. "But I also know who has him. I should've known he'd do something like this when he couldn't find us." Red jumped out of the chair and kicked a nearby cabinet. The metal sound reverberated throughout the room. "So stupid." She clenched her fists.

224

"You couldn't have known," Jonah said.

Red laughed, the sound maniacal to her ears. "That's where you're wrong. I've been through enough with Roark that I should have known. I have to go get him."

Her mind was already churning over the possibilities. It would take four days minimum to get back to the boundary fence. They could do it, if they moved at a fast enough clip. She needed to get packed and make sure they had enough supplies. She'd taken two steps when the alarms inside the building went off.

"What's happening?" she shouted over the deafening drone. Red clutched her ears.

"Towers have spotted something." His fingers flew over multiple buttons. "Report!"

"Sand Devils sighted on the feed. Approximately four miles out."

"When was it recorded?" Jonah's face creased with concern.

"An hour ago at least," Razor said.

"They must be long gone by now," Jonah said. "Why trigger the alarm?" He looked at Red and shook his head. "The guards are always breaking protocol for no reason."

"We spotted something else when we reviewed the feed," Razor said. "Thought you might like to see it."

Red watched as Razor held some kind of scope in his hands. He placed the camera next to the scope and hit a button. Two small figures appeared on the screen. She couldn't tell what they were until the sun hit Demery's white suit.

A moment later the unmistakable flash of a laser pistol blast appeared and the figure without the suit dropped to the ground. Red's heart stopped and she couldn't seem to breathe. Pain radiated until her limbs twitched.

It could've been anybody. Morgan would've been too fast to get caught by a laser blast. Possible explanations raced through her mind until black dots appeared in her vision. Red quickly blinked them away. Moments later the feed showed the Sand Devils arriving, then everyone was loaded into the vehicles. They raced off and the recording ended.

"Where's the rest of it?" She needed to see what happened next.

"The feed ended," Jonah said without looking at her. "Can you tell where they went?"

"The other feed shows them moving south toward their base camp," Razor said.

This couldn't be happening. Roark had her grandfather and now the Sand Devils had Morgan—thanks to Demery. They wouldn't take a dead man with them, which meant Morgan had still been alive. At least he had been an hour ago.

"Where's their base camp?" Red asked, her brain on autopilot.

"They're about two-hours' journey south of Eden. It's only ten miles, but the terrain is rough going. Of course, they're probably there by now since they're not on foot," he said.

Red thought about her grandfather locked in Roark's prison and her stomach nearly emptied its acids onto the floor. She threw her head back and this time she did scream—a primal piercing sound that brought her wolf to the surface. Her body trembled violently in impotent rage.

How was she supposed to choose between the two men that she loved? She couldn't. Red pictured Morgan's limp form being tossed into a Sand Devil vehicle and her mind splintered.

"No!" she shouted as the alarms died. "Damn you, Demery!" They should never have left him.

Jonah had risen from his desk and backed against the wall. His hands were outstretched, placating. "Calm down. Take a breath. What are you going to do?" he asked softly, almost as if he were afraid to let her know he was still in the room.

Red swung on him wildly, her gaze barely able to focus beyond the crimson haze clouding her vision. What was she going to do? Her grandfather wouldn't want her to come after him. And neither would Morgan. Both would tell her to pursue the other.

Her heart was breaking as she took a shuddering breath. Not since the loss of her parents and sister had Red been in so much pain. Was it possible to die from heartache? She didn't even know she was crying until Jonah held out a cloth. Red snatched it from his hands and violently scrubbed her face.

The room flashed before her eyes again, switching from drab beige to rich color. The wolf inside her was fighting for its freedom. "I have to go." She strode toward the door.

"Where?" Jonah asked.

"To get my mate back." The thought of leaving her grandfather nearly buckled Red's knees, but the truth was that Morgan was closer. She'd just have to pray Roark didn't do anything before she could reach him.

Even as the thought crossed her mind, Red felt what little hope she had die inside.

"That's suicidal," Jonah said. "There are at least fifty Sand Devils. You are only one woman."

"I'm stronger than I look." And a lot more deadly.

"At least let me send a couple of my men with you," he said.

She shook her head. "No, I'll travel faster on my own." Red wasn't about to be responsible for anyone else's death.

A familiar voice whispered in her mind, but she was too far gone mentally to respond. Red changed into baggy clothes, then made her way to the lift. If there was ever a time she needed her wolf, it was now.

"Give me my guns." she growled. She'd use them on anyone and anything she came across on the way to the Sand Devil camp. Once she got there, Red would have to rely on something far stronger and faster to get Morgan out. "I hope you're ready wolf," she muttered.

The guards didn't question her. They simply tossed down the weapons and she quickly scooped them up. Red took a deep breath and sprinted away from the outpost.

* * * * *

Raphael winced and rubbed his temples as pain flashed behind his eyelids. He swayed and Catherine caught him.

"What's wrong? Are you okay?" she asked. Her hand moved to stroke her gun. A nervous habit she'd developed over the last few days.

"I'm fine." Raphael took a steadying breath. "But something is wrong with Red."

Catherine stopped suddenly and he nearly barreled into her. "What do you mean?"

He could see the emotions swirling behind her green eyes. A lovely mixture of panic and something indefinable.

Michael stopped and adjusted his pack. "What's happened?" he asked.

"I'm not sure. She shut me out, but not before I sensed

immense torment."

"Has she been injured?" he asked.

Raphael shook his head. "I don't think so. This felt more like mental anguish than physical." What had happened to cause such a severe reaction? He rubbed his arms to ward off the sudden chill. He tried to reach Morgan, but was met with a wall of pain. "We have to be getting close or her emotions wouldn't have been so strong."

"Let's pick up the pace." Catherine tightened her pack so she could jog.

"It won't do us any good if we collapse from heat stroke before we reach her," Raphael reminded her. He'd donned his long-sleeved clothing to give him some protection, then lathered on the sunscreen, but still felt the heat saw in and out of his lungs with every breath.

They ran anyway, covering the last of the foothills. Michael stopped at the base of the final one and inhaled.

"Do you smell it?" he asked.

Raphael frowned and breathed deeply. His muscles froze the second the familiar fragrance hit him. "Morgan." He sniffed loudly, half afraid of what he'd find next.

Fortunately, he didn't detect much blood, but he did smell something equally disturbing—another vamp. Demery? Or someone else? And there were others around. More purebloods than he could distinguish.

"Do you have his scent?" Michael asked.

Raphael nodded. "Follow me."

He trotted over the desert floor, stopping every few feet to smell the air. Morgan's scent remained strong, but it appeared to be leading off into two different directions. He squinted and caught a flash of metal in the sunlight.

"There." He pointed.

"I see it," Michael said.

"I'm not sure which way he went," Raphael said.

Michael stepped forward and slowly turned in a circle. "His scent is stronger to the south," he said. "I also sense something else. Another wolf, perhaps."

"Is it Red?" Raphael asked.

"Can't tell." Michael shook his head in frustration. "The heat is

228

distracting me."

Catherine raised her arm. "I vote we follow the unknown wolf." She continued on without waiting for an answer.

Raphael looked at Michael and shrugged. "Fine with me."

Michael smirked. "That woman leads you around by your balls."

"You say that as if it's a bad thing." Raphael grinned.

* * * * *

CHAPTER THIRTY

As Red traveled south, she felt more alone than she'd ever felt in her life. Jonah had given her approximate directions to the Sand Devil campsite. A month ago she would've shot and killed him on sight and now she was depending on him to find Morgan.

She ran, stopping every hundred yards or so to see if she could catch Morgan's scent. His musky fragrance tickled her nose, but it was followed by a more sinister odor of fear. Whether it was Morgan's or someone else's, she couldn't tell.

Red's heart thudded painfully in her chest as she picked up her pace. She glanced over her shoulder, but could still see the towers at the outpost glistening in the sunlight. If she could see them, then they could see her, which meant she hadn't traveled far enough. Red raced on until the lookout towers could no longer be discerned from the landscape.

She glanced ahead. The swirl of dust from the Sand Devil vehicles had long since faded. Red prayed she was still going in the right direction. She needed her wolf. Needed its help to find Morgan.

"He's in trouble," she said. "I can't help him without you."

She put her holster down on the ground, then Red beaconed the wolf to come forth. For the first time in her life, she didn't try to hold back, wasn't afraid of what would happen. Red simply let go and embraced her beast.

Pain racked her body. Red clenched her jaw and threw her head back as bones broke and blood splattered the front of her shirt. She cried out again and again, unable to contain the agony as she transformed into a shape she barely recognized.

The world around her faded to black, then suddenly exploded with life. What she'd considered a dead world of beige now took on new nuances of color. There were golds, reds, and coppers mixed with the beige, giving the desert a glistening effect. If she could cry, Red would've wept tears of joy.

Thank you.

Red inhaled smelling the musk of her fur, the coppery tang of blood, and the sharp acidic scent of anticipation. Below all that, she caught the familiar aroma of wolf. Morgan. Her jaw snapped shut with a clack as she ground her incisors together. Claws sharp as razor wire and twice as deadly stretched out where short nails used to be. She flexed them, watching them retract and extend.

Her muscles bunched and Red leapt forward. She grabbed her holster with her teeth and took off running at speeds that would've been impossible only moments ago. Her claws dug into the earth, leaving deep furrows behind. She followed Morgan's scent on the breeze. It led her further south.

Red ran over the uneven terrain, but despite the heat she felt anything but tired. Her mind and body were energized as she took in the world around her. So much to see, so much to do, with only one goal in mind: find Morgan.

She had no time to think about Roark holding her grandfather. She couldn't contemplate the torture he might be enduring or she'd turn around and head back to the boundary fence.

Red came upon the Sand Devil compound in the late afternoon. She dropped her holster and slowly circled the makeshift housing. She sniffed the ground, easily locating the guards who watched over the area.

There were six of them spread out around the compound. Out of those six only two appeared vigilant. The rest were distracted by something in the center of the compound. Her mouth watered in anticipation, but she didn't move. First she needed to locate Morgan.

Red worked her way around the encampment until she spotted Demery's white protective suit. He was seated next to a fire across from the Sand Devil leader, Reaper, and Melea. Demery had risked everything for the woman, a mistake he would soon regret.

The jingle of chains had Red's ears perking. She followed the sound and that's when she spotted Morgan. His bound arms were outstretched and his sunburned chest was bleeding. Chains dangled from his bare neck and waist, binding him to a post.

He wore a makeshift collar. Red had seen those in the history vids. People used to put them on their pets. His eyes were closed, but his breathing was steady. She could sense the anger burning inside of him, which meant he was also conscious.

Red continued making her way in a circle, using small mounds of sand and dried dirt as cover, trying to search for an easy entry. There was none. If she wanted her mate, she'd have to fight her way in, somehow free him, and then they'd have to fight their way out. Despite the overwhelming odds, her wolf raised its head in eagerness.

She watched as one of the Sand Devils approached Morgan with a long dagger. He sliced a fresh wound on his arm and held a cup under the tear as the blood dripped down. When it slowed, the man squeezed Morgan's flesh to increase flow.

Morgan growled, but the man ignored him, intent on doing his job. He filled two cups, then brought them to Demery and Reaper, who drank with gusto. Neither one acknowledged Morgan's presence. To them he was an animal to be used for sustenance.

Red's body trembled in fury and her claws ripped at the earth, scoring it with her anger. If they wanted an animal, she'd give them one. The wind shifted and Morgan's head shot up. His amber eyes glowed as he looked in her direction, then he quickly dropped his chin. The glance may have been short, but the warning was clear. He might not be able to see her, but he knew she was there and wasn't happy about it.

Well too bad. He'd have to get over it. Red looked back at Morgan and caught a quick head jerk. Did he think she'd just leave him here to slowly bleed out? Surely he wasn't that naive.

Red thought about Roark and what he was doing to her grandfather while she hesitated to act. Her resolve solidified. Both she and Morgan would get out of here together or no one would get out alive.

Her wolf dropped its head and stalked the nearest guard. Everyone was so busy celebrating the capture of Morgan that no one noticed when Red took the first guard down with a swipe of her claws across his throat. Blood showered the ground as he dropped to his knees.

The only sound came from a gurgle as he attempted to speak. His mouth opened and closed like a fish exposed to the air. For a second, she worried that Demery might smell the blood, then she saw the cup in his hands. He wouldn't be able to smell anything with blood in his mouth and Morgan bleeding nearby.

Demery laughed at something Reaper said, then held out his hand for Melea to come to him. She did…but not in a rush. Something had changed between them. Red wondered if in his inebriated state Demery noticed. The poor woman was trapped between two powerful men, neither of whom truly cared for her.

Red had only been around the Sand Devil leader for a few hours, but in that short period he'd proven himself a ruthless bastard. She wouldn't feel bad when she killed him. He deserved far worse for what he'd done.

The second guard was harder to take down. He kept shifting positions, which made it difficult to sneak up on him without alerting him to her presence. In the end, Red leapt ten feet, landing on his chest and knocking the wind out of him.

He punched her repeatedly to try to dislodge her, while struggling to gain his breath. The blows hurt, but Red refused to release him. She bit down until he turned blue, then shook her head. His neck snapped and he immediately stopped struggling. She left him lying in the sand, his head twisted at an odd angle, as she moved on to the next lookout.

The third man seemed more interested in what was happening inside the encampment than in what was going on outside. *His mistake*, Red thought. She sliced open his abdomen, gutting him, before he even realized she was there. He didn't scream. He simply stared in disbelief at his intestines lying on the ground at his feet. Red fought the urge to taste her kill, but there were three guards left.

Red saw Morgan cocking his head left and right, listening. Was he following her progress? Her wolf mind couldn't decide. It was too focused on the next hunt, the next kill.

She snuck up on the final three by crawling on her belly. One man was looking around and had finally noticed that the other men were gone. Red surged forward before he could sound an alarm. Her jaws clamped down on his throat while she impaled the other two with her claws. Like knives, they slid in deep, under their rib cages, filleting their hearts as she flexed her paws.

The men dropped, while the guard in her mouth whimpered. His Adam's apple bobbed against her tongue. Red's jaw locked to prevent him from escaping or crying out. She squeezed until his windpipe caved beneath the pressure. Red tasted his hot, sticky blood and quickly swallowed a few gulps, then licked her muzzle as he joined his friends in death.

With the guards down, Red partially shifted until she could stand on two legs. Now more monster than wolf, Red leapt over the small dune and raced toward the leader of the Sand Devils.

Reaper's reactions were slower than she'd anticipated, or maybe she was just faster. Melea screamed as Red stretched out her claws and swiped at him.

Reaper stumbled back, causing her to miss delivering a fatal blow. Red's claws raked him across the chest, leaving deep furrows behind. She wasn't in the right position to try again, so she spun on Demery.

"I trusted you," she snapped, her jaws closing with an audible click. It was difficult to speak in this form.

Anger and outrage erupted from her. He'd trapped her mate. Sliced him. Bled him. And drunk from him. For that he would pay. Red hunched, preparing to leap.

Before she could attack, Reaper rushed her like a maglev tank. "You bitch!" His big hands locked around her as he squeezed her against his chest.

Morgan struggled, pulling at his chains.

The air rushed out of Red's lungs. Reaper was going to break her ribs. Her claws tore into his arms, but his grip didn't loosen. Her vision swam from lack of oxygen. If she didn't break free now, it would be too late.

"Hold her," Demery shouted, trying to get close.

Red kicked at his face and the vamp backed away. Since her claws were useless against the Sand Devil leader, Red opened her mouth wide and latched onto his biceps. She bit down as hard as she could. The move broke Reaper's arm and severed the tendons.

He bellowed and shoved her away.

Red fell to the ground and gasped, trying to catch her breath. Her lungs burned as she rose to prepare for the next attack.

Some Sand Devils watched fascinated by the creature that would dare attack their leader. Others ran, terrified by what they'd witnessed thus far.

Red's claws clacked as she brushed them together. "No one bleeds my mate and lives," she barked. The garbled words were followed by a deep growl. She felt the hair on her neck and legs rise as she and Reaper circled each other.

Reaper was favoring his wounded arm, but he'd pulled a knife from somewhere and now held it out, swiping at the air.

She bared her teeth and growled at him, as she circled slowly in search of an opening.

Reaper jabbed at her abdomen.

Red dodged the blade and sucked in her stomach. The knife hissed in the air, barely missing her. She could hear Morgan pulling at his chains. They clanged as he fought to get loose. Soon he'd be free. But this man would be dead long before that occurred.

"Come on," she shouted. "You're not afraid of the Big, Bad Wolf, are you?"

"Patience, love. I'll get to you in a moment." Reaper never took his beady eyes off her when he addressed Demery. "You were holding out on me. You told me there was only one."

"You only asked for one." Demery moved toward Morgan.

She growled out a warning, which the vampire didn't heed.

"Let me show you how to end this." Demery pulled out a laser pistol and pointed it at her.

Morgan partially shifted. The chain holding his right hand snapped.

Demery's eyes widened. "You're bound by silver. You shouldn't have been able to do that."

"You think this is the first time I've been held by silver?" Morgan asked.

Demery swung the weapon around until it was leveled on Morgan's chest.

Red didn't think. Didn't hesitate. She spun away from Reaper. Her arm arced wide and she caught Demery across the shoulders with her long claws, tearing his suit and ripping the gun out of his hand. She heard him gasp, but it was more out of surprise than from pain. The leader of the Sand Devils took the moment her back was turned to charge.

"Drop!" Morgan yelled.

Red hit the ground. Reaper had so much forward momentum that he ran right over the top of her and straight into Demery, burying his blade deep into the vamp's chest. Demery clutched the knife in shock. The leader of the Sand Devils was so surprised that he didn't try to grab it back.

Red jumped to her feet and launched herself onto Reaper's back. She sank her claws into his meaty sides and twisted, fileting his organs. He bellowed in pain. Red opened her jaws wide and clamped onto his thick neck. She shook her head violently, shredding arteries and muscle. Blood fountained into the air, covering them.

Reaper dropped to his knees, still facing a shocked Demery.

Red released him and stepped back. She spread her claws and swiped, decapitating him in two blows. Reaper's head rolled off his shoulders toward Morgan before coming to a stop.

Morgan tore through the remaining chain and dropped to the ground. "You are even more magnificent than I imagined," he said. "Your wolf is glorious." He brushed his hand over her pelt, then snarled at Demery.

Red gave Morgan a sad smile. There was no time to celebrate her victory. Nothing about this moment brought her happiness. She looked at the knife sticking out of Demery's chest.

"I'm sorry, mon. I didn't mean for any of this to happen."

"I know." Red's jaw clenched and tears burned her eyes. "But you turned my mate over to these animals. I-I saw you drinking his blood."

He laughed, but the sound quickly faded to a cough. "I'm a vampire. What did you expect?"

Red sniffed. "I trusted you." Her body shifted back into its human form, leaving her naked and trembling.

Demery looked pained, whether from the wound or from her words she didn't know. "I would've never let them have you," he said softly. "I've seen what they can do to a woman." His gaze sought Melea. She was whimpering on the ground, rocking back and forth, her cheeks wet with tears.

"Did you make her the same promise?" Red asked.

He flinched, but didn't answer. "I know I don't have the right to ask, but I have to..." Demery's face looked fuller than it had a moment ago. His body swelled, slowly filling his protective suit.

Red watched, horrified by the sight.

"Not much time. You need to leave now." Demery gritted his teeth against the pain. Blood spattered the inside of his faceplate. "Please take my blood back with you. Fulfill the promise I made."

"Get back!" Morgan shouted.

Red looked at him in confusion.

"He's becoming a weapon." Morgan pushed her back.

Red grabbed Melea and yanked her to her feet. She was weeping silently, trying to go to him.

"Let me go!" she cried.

Red pulled her away from Demery and together they ran to the far side of a nearby dune. She glanced back.

Demery was even bigger now. The protective suit ripped at the seams and spread like butter away from his body. His flesh had gone from dark brown to a strange red as blood pushed its way to the surface, forming blistering geysers across his skin.

"Stay low." Morgan tugged them further away.

Demery was unrecognizable beyond his mocha eyes, which bled crimson tears. "I'm sorry," he said, a second before he exploded.

Fleshy shrapnel shot out in all directions, catching a few of the Sand Devils as they tried to flee, killing them instantly. Morgan pushed Red and Melea to the ground and covered them with his body.

When the last of the hardened skin had fallen from the sky, they rose. Morgan stripped clothes from one of the dead and handed Red a baggy shirt. She dressed quickly, then retrieved her pistols. They'd need them for the long walk back.

"This way," Morgan said. He led them in the opposite direction of the screaming Sand Devils, who ran into the desert.

Red looked at the spot Demery had occupied. All that was left was bits of hair and bone. Her stomach lurched. She dropped to her knees and vomited.

Melea fell beside her and curled into fetal position. The woman's eyes were wide and unfocused, as she wailed in torment.

Morgan rubbed Red's back, until nothing more came out. "Feel better?" he asked.

"No." She'd never feel better.

"We have to get out of here," Morgan said.

"Is she going to be all right?" Red asked.

"I don't know," Morgan said. "They had a pretty strong blood bond. I'm actually surprised she survived his death. Normally, when one goes, they both go."

Red wiped the back of her mouth, then nudged Melea with her foot.

Melea flinched, then focused on her surroundings. The wailing stopped.

"Can you walk?" Red asked.

Melea nodded.

"Good! Let's go," Red said.

A mile later, they rounded a first low mound of sand and ran straight into Raphael, Michael, and Chaos.

"Fancy meeting you here in this paradise." Raphael gave them a visual once over, then picked a hardened piece of flesh off Morgan's shoulder. He flicked it away with his fingertips. "I take it we missed all the fun."

"Not quite." Red stepped forward, balled her fist, and punched Michael squarely in the face. "How could you do this to me, you blood-thirty son-of-a-bitch?"

* * * * *

CHAPTER THIRTY-ONE

"What in the hell are you doing?" Raphael helped Michael off the ground.

Gina rounded on him, but Morgan stepped between them and grabbed her by the waist. "Why don't you ask him?" She stabbed a finger in Michael's direction.

Raphael turned to Michael. "Do you know what she's talking about?"

"No idea." Michael brushed off his clothes. "Perhaps the heat has gotten to her."

"It's not the heat, you dung pile. It's my grandfather," she cried.

Morgan pulled her close and stroked her hair. "What about him?"

Raphael looked to Catherine and Michael for answers.

Catherine shrugged and shook her head. Her hand moved restlessly to her weapon. She stared at Gina for a moment, her body tense, then she looked away.

All eyes fell upon Michael.

"Don't ask me. I have no idea why she hit me." He wiped the blood off his mouth and licked it from his fingers.

"I'm surprised to see you here," Morgan said.

Michael frowned. "Why?"

"I heard your screams," he said quietly. "How are you feeling?"

Michael flinched and his dark eyes squinted. "As you can see,

I'm better now," he said.

Morgan stared at him, searching for any sign to contradict his words. He looked like the old Michael, albeit a little sunburned, but he couldn't forget those screams or Roark's glee. They'd address his concerns later. First he had to find out what had happened.

"Gina, honey, calm down and tell me what's going on." Morgan pulled her back until he could look in her face. Her eyes were red and filled with unshed tears.

"I heard from the Eye of God before I left the outpost." She sniffled. "But he couldn't hear me."

"Doesn't matter." Morgan brushed her hair away from her wet cheeks. What he'd found in Kane's audio journals was far more damaging to Roark Montgomery than anything the Eye of God could've located.

"I was about to sign off when he said there'd been a worldwide announcement made. He said—" she choked. "He said Robert Santiago, leader of the International Police Tactical Team, had been kidnapped. Roark is blaming us for his disappearance. He has him, Morgan. The bastard has my grandfather."

Morgan's gaze burned through Michael. "Is this true?" he asked.

Michael scowled. "How should I know? I've been in no-man's-land for several days. The last few with Raphael and Catherine."

Morgan looked at Raphael, who gave him a curt nod, confirming Michael's story. "Roark has fooled us before. Maybe he's at it again," Morgan said.

Gina rubbed her face with the back of her hand. "Do you think so?"

"Only one way to find out." Morgan looked at Michael. "I'm sure Roark sent a communications device with you. Get on it and find out if this latest transmission is true or just another ploy to draw us out of hiding."

Michael pulled out a navcom. "This may take awhile. We're not exactly close by."

Morgan's ears perked at the sound of engines roaring to life. "Save it until we get back to the outpost."

Gina raised her head. "What about her?"

Morgan turned to the woman standing a few feet away. He'd

forgotten all about Melea. The woman's dark skin was pale and her eyes looked too big for her face. Her cheeks were hollowed from the horrors she'd experienced at the hands of the Sand Devils. She trembled and Morgan could smell her fear. It burned his nostrils, making him sick.

"Don't worry, we won't harm you," he said.

"She killed Demery," Melea said, her voice barely above a whisper. "He would've died from the wounds she inflicted, even if Reaper hadn't finished the job."

"I'd planned to kill him. She just got to him before I could," Morgan said.

Melea wrung her hands. "He was only trying to help me," she said, barely holding herself together.

"Had he asked, we would've gladly assisted him, but he chose to betray us. That is something we cannot tolerate. Even when it's done for the right reasons," he said. "I hope someday you'll understand."

Tears streaked down her cheeks and she shook her head, slowly backing away. Her fearful gaze remained locked on Gina.

"You have a choice. You can either go back to the Sand Devils or you can come with us. But if you come with us, know that we will not tolerate betrayal. Take Demery's death as a warning." Morgan was being extremely harsh on the woman given what she'd been through, but he had little choice.

Roark had just upped the stakes exponentially. They didn't need any more surprises. He headed north toward the outpost. Morgan kept his arm around Gina and didn't bother to see if anyone followed. They would. What other option did they have?

"I will come with you," Melea called out, her voice desperate.

"Smart choice." Morgan hoped she wouldn't regret her decision.

* * * * *

It was dark by the time they reached the outpost. No one had said much on the slow walk back and for that Red was grateful. She hadn't been in the mood to talk. She couldn't get the look on Demery's face out of her mind. She'd seen the surprise, regret, and eventual acceptance of his impending death. The sadness lingered, haunting her.

Jonah was waiting when they arrived. The guards disarmed everyone before allowing them to enter. She could've told them it was pointless, but she didn't bother. It made them feel like they were in control. There was no need to shatter that illusion.

"Glad to see you're back in one piece. More or less," he said. "Want to introduce me to your friends?"

"This is Raphael Vega, Michael Travers, Melea, and Catherine Meyers," Red said by way of introduction. "Everyone, this is Jonah. He runs this outpost and has been kind enough to help us."

He shook their hands and showed them to the spare rooms so they could freshen up.

"Let's meet back here in..." Red glanced at her watch. "...forty-five minutes. You need to send that transmission and find out what's going on," she said to Michael.

Thirty minutes later Michael pressed several buttons on his navcom. His normally placid expression looked strained as he thumped the device a couple of times.

"What's wrong?" Red asked.

"It must be the sand. It's working intermittently." He shook it.

"Can you hail Roark?" Red asked as the tension inside her returned.

She needed to know what was happening with her grandfather. Was Roark playing mind games or did he really have him? And if he did, what would she do? She had no problem exchanging her life for his, but would that be enough to appease Roark?

"This is Travers reporting in," Michael said. "Do you read?"

Static filled the air.

"Home base, this is Travers. Please respond."

More pops and crackles blasted the silence.

Red felt so helpless. What if he couldn't reach Roark? She'd have no choice but to return to the Republic of Arizona and hope that was enough to garner his release.

"Travers, report," Roark barked.

Red jumped in surprise. "Ask him."

Michael nodded and held up a finger. "I've received a broadcast claiming the commander of IPTT has been kidnapped," he said.

There was a pause.

For a moment Red thought they might have lost him.

Then Roark spoke. "Are you alone, Travers?"

Michael looked at Red, then at Morgan. They both nodded at him.

"No, sir," he said. "That's a negative."

"Hello, Ms. Santiago. Mr. Hunter." His smug voice grated on Red's nerves. He was gloating. "I see you received the message I sent."

She snatched the navcom from Michael's grasp. "Cut the dung, Roark. Where's my grandfather?"

Roark chuckled. "I don't know what you're talking about."

"Stop messing around," she said.

"He volunteered to keep me company in your absence," Roark said. "I had to ensure you'd comply to my demands."

"What demands?" she asked.

A strained voice as familiar as her own came onto the line. "Gina? Is it really you?"

"It's me, Grandpa," Red said. "Don't worry. We'll get you out of there."

"Don't make promises you can't keep," Roark said.

"Gina?" her grandfather repeated, sounding weaker. There was a scrape, then a loud moan.

"What have you done to him, Roark?" Red asked.

Roark chuckled. "Had to soften him up so he'd cooperate. Old fool actually thought he could come here and threaten me right before the election."

Threaten him with what?

Red brought the navcom to her mouth. "Grandpa, can you hear me?" He had to hear her. He had to know she was coming for him. Had to know how much she loved him. "I'll be there soon. Don't worr—"

"Save it," Roark said. "Speed won't matter. I haven't forgotten what you did to me in that cell."

Fear's cold fingers enveloped her. There was some shuffling, then Red heard the hum of a laser pistol as it charged. "Roark, what are you doing?"

"What I should've done a long time ago," he said.

A shot rang out over the connection. The sound was followed by a frightened male shriek and a loud thud as something hit the floor. They heard a gasp, then a sickening gurgle.

"Help—"

There was another shot, then silence.

For one painful moment Red thought her heart had exploded in her chest. She gasped and forced air into her lungs. Her fingers trembled as she shook the navcom.

"Grandpa? Grandpa? Answer me this second!" she shouted. "Roark! What have you done?"

"Sorry, the commander is permanently indisposed." Roark chuckled.

Red crumpled to the floor.

"One problem down, two to go," Roark said. "Come back so we can finish this once and for all."

This would never have happened if she'd stayed in the Republic of Arizona. She'd been selfish to run. Hadn't thought about what would happen to the ones they left behind.

Red choked back her tears until an eerie calm replaced the pain. "I'll kill you for this," she vowed, clutching the navcom.

"Save your breath," Roark said. "You'll need it for your defense. That is if you make it back to the republics alive."

She cursed loudly, clutching the navcom. It did little to alleviate the pain coursing through her. The sheer agony of losing the last member of her family made it feel like she was being ripped in half.

Red didn't know how she'd survive or if she'd survive. A piece of her heart had shattered as the second shot was fired. Her limbs went numb and her mind retreated to a safer place. She clasped her hands around her knees and rocked back and forth, seeking comfort where there was none.

"You've lost, Roark. You just don't know it yet." Morgan pulled Red close. "We now have the proof to destroy you. One tiny broadcast and your political career is over." He leaned into the navcom. "In the end, you may get your proof that the Others exist, but we're going to take you down with us."

"You'll never get the message out," Roark said, but his voice wavered a bit. "I've made sure of it."

"We'll see about that," Morgan said.

Red glared at the navcom. "You just shot your only bargaining chip."

"Travers?" Roark barked.

"Yes, sir," Michael said.

"Remember your duty," Roark said. "Here's a reminder in case you forgot."

Michael screamed and fell to the floor, clutching his head, writhing in pain. "Make it stop. Please make it stop!"

"Finish your job and I will."

Red tossed the navcom against the wall, cutting off Roark's transmission. Michael's pain had temporarily jerked her out of the shock that had set in. She'd done the first thing she could think of to kill the signal.

Michael stopped thrashing, his breath coming in deep gasps.

"How is the chip in his head doing that?" Red asked.

"I don't know," Morgan said. "I've never heard of a chip that could do that to a man."

She frowned. "Can we scan him to assess the damage?" Red asked.

Raphael lifted the device. "I think you broke the navcom when you threw it."

Red ran a trembling hand through her hair, "I didn't know what else to do. I was afraid Roark was going to kill him."

"I might be able to get the navcom working again," Morgan said. "Give me awhile. In the meantime, get him into a bunk. Try to make him comfortable."

* * * * *

Michael struggled to his feet. "I'm all right," he said. He blinked to clear the shadow people from his vision, but they refused to leave.

He blinked again, this time keeping his eyes shut for a few seconds longer. Michael cracked one lid and saw a gray shadow race across his line of vision. He opened his other eye. He wasn't alone.

The shadows stood like sentries, waiting. For what, he did not know. They'd always been quick to dart out of the way, but not anymore.

"On second thought." He swayed. "A short rest might do me some good."

Michael allowed Raphael to help him down the hall. His

245

brother's face was pinched with worry, but he said nothing. What was there to say? Michael glanced over his shoulder as he entered the area that housed numerous bunks. The shadows waited, their ghostly faces filled with glee.

"What happened back there?" Raphael asked.

He tried to shrug, but couldn't. "It was just Roark sending a reminder of who's in charge," he said.

Raphael grabbed his hand. "We'll figure out a way to fix this."

Michael smiled. "You worry too much, brother."

"Somebody has to." Raphael's voice to cracked. "Now get some rest." He pulled the blanket up.

Michael's chest clenched. "I will," he lied.

* * * * *

CHAPTER THIRTY-TWO

Morgan stared at the broken navcom, unable to focus. He couldn't get Gina's cries out of his mind. Her tears had scorched his soul and no amount of shifting to his wolf form would repair it. The calm she'd shown after listening to her grandfather's murder had been worst of all. She'd shut down before his eyes as if someone had flipped a switch.

He still didn't understand how Montgomery had gotten the drop on Robert Santiago, but there was no denying what they'd heard. Someone had died at Roark's hand. Someone who sounded exactly like the commander. Roark would die for his multitude of sins. Determined, Morgan examined the device. If he could manage to fix it, they might be able to broadcast in time to change the course of the election.

He thought about the recording sitting next to him. If he sent out Kane's message, there would be no hiding for the Others. Questions would be asked. Answers would be sought. This journey wasn't just about him and Gina anymore. Something far greater was at stake. Could Morgan risk the lives of the people of Nuria and the Others around the world for revenge and their freedom?

Freedom—what a joke. He and the Others had been living in self-imposed exile from the rest of society for decades.

Morgan had spent so many years in hiding that he wasn't sure if he could live out in the open. And what if the same people who'd hunted them down before tried to come after them again?

247

The men behind the experiments were dead, but their successors were still around, watching, waiting for the Others to pop their heads up so they could blow them off their shoulders.

He thought about the Nurian trainees. The Other tactical team was nowhere near ready for that kind of altercation. With Demery's death, they'd lost one of the most promising cadets. His mate mourned the vamp's passing. She hid her pain well, but he'd still noticed. It was his fault he was dead. They should've never left Demery behind.

Morgan took out the tools Jonah had loaned him and pulled off the back of the navcom. It didn't look good. In fact, it looked like a mess—thanks to Gina's impromptu rage. He moved a few wires to get to the crystal keyboard that fueled it. At least the crystal was still intact, which was something. Morgan set the tools down on the table.

He brushed a hand over his chest and winced. He was still tender from the stun blast and the knife wounds, but thanks to a quick shift they had stopped bleeding and sealed tight. By tomorrow, the discomfort would be gone. In a week, it would look as if nothing had occurred.

He fiddled with the navcom. Everything was about to change. Morgan hoped the Nurians would forgive him.

* * * * *

Red came upon Melea standing in the giant greenhouse. "Amazing, isn't it?"

The woman jumped in surprise. "I'm sorry. I didn't..." Her gaze roamed the room for another exit, but she quickly realized that Red blocked the only one.

"It's okay. I like it in here, too. It's a good place to think," Red said. "Especially now."

The woman nodded, but didn't relax.

Red looked at her. "Can I ask you a question?"

Melea nodded for her to go ahead.

"Why did Demery call you his blood? I know you weren't his mate. If you had been, he would've challenged Reaper long ago."

The woman gave her a sad smile. "I reminded him of his little sister. The fact that I had her name helped. Obviously he didn't treat me as such, but he did look after me, or at least tried to. Demery was a good man, but he had his faults." Melea shrugged. "I loved him like a brother, but he gambled. And when he lost..." her voice trailed off.

"He lost you to the Sand Devils?" Red asked, trying to imagine the woman's terror. She shuddered at the thought.

Melea nodded, then quickly looked away. "He didn't mean to, but Demery learned the hard way that you can't beat Reaper. He promised to return to get me and he did, even if his rescue was cut short." Her voice turned bitter.

"If he viewed you as his little sister, how did you come to be his blood?" Red asked, steering the conversation away.

The woman laughed, but there was no amusement in her soft voice. "It was an accident. Demery had a little bit too much to drink one night. Thought it'd be funny to see me swallow his blood. I'd been traveling with him for a while, so I didn't think much of the first exchange. Or the one that followed. It wasn't until Reaper forced me to...that Demery found out it could also harm him. I think that's why he ran and left me."

Red thought about Raphael. Could he feel her pain now that she'd tasted him? And what of Morgan? Raphael had fed him his blood to save his life.

"How much blood did you drink?" Red asked.

"Several mouthfuls. I ended up vomiting," Melea said.

Maybe the amount mattered. She'd have to ask. "I'm sorry things turned out the way they have," Red said. "You probably won't believe me, but I really liked Demery. I don't take my part in his death lightly."

"You kept your promise to him." Melea sounded surprised. "Why?"

Red couldn't blame Melea for being surprised. Everyone in her life had either lied or used her. Most did both. "Because he asked."

The woman brushed her face, wiping at the tears that slipped down her cheeks. "That's it? No other reasons?"

"He was my friend." It was a stark admission, but no less than the truth. Red wanted to comfort Melea, but she didn't know how when they were both in so much pain. "I will make sure you get to the Republic of Arizona," she said.

"Because of guilt?" she asked, eyeing her suspiciously.

Red leveled her with a sharp gaze. "Does the reason matter?"

"I guess not." Melea slipped deeper into the greenhouse and disappeared behind the fruit trees.

Red left her to grieve and went to find Raphael. He was standing in the control center looking at all the buttons. His back was to her, when she walked in.

"I haven't seen one of these places since the war," he said softly. "It looks so ancient now, but back then it housed so much destructive power."

"How are you holding up?" Red asked.

Raphael turned. "I could ask you the same thing. You look like you've lost weight."

Red laughed, despite the pain. "Wandering around the desert does wonders for the diet."

He smiled. "Yes, I suppose it takes some getting used to."

"How are Michael and Catherine?" she asked.

"My brother is not well. The chip inside him is causing him pain. He blocks me so I can't tell how bad it's gotten. I fear for his health. Perhaps if Morgan can get the navcom working, we'll have a better idea of what we're dealing with." He sighed. "Catherine." Her name brightened his features, lighting his eyes. "She is still in shock over Roark's transmission, but she is strong and will get through this."

"Roark's caused so much pain and misery. If he gets elected, I fear for our people. I fear for all people," she said.

Raphael met her gaze. "No matter what happens, he will be dealt with. You have my word."

"I hope you're right." Red rubbed her arms. "I better check on Morgan," she said, noticing Catherine at the door.

* * * * *

Chaos watched Gina Santiago leave, then slipped into the room. She hadn't been able to talk to the woman alone. It seemed like every time she tried someone appeared. Chaos had never been good at waiting.

She glanced at Raphael. "I don't know what to do."

He frowned. "About what?"

"I promised the commander I'd bring her back," she said. "If he's truly dead, then there's no one there to return her to." And she had no bargaining chip for when things imploded. She sighed.

"What?" Raphael asked, misunderstanding her mood.

"All she has left is Morgan."

Raphael slowly shook his head. "That's not true," he said. "She has me and several of the townspeople of Nuria to lean on."

"Oh." Chaos' face flushed with embarrassment and confusion. "I suppose as long as she has you that's all that counts." Her tone was a little sharper than she'd intended.

Raphael's eyes twinkled. "What has you so upset, little storm?"

"Nothing," Chaos snarled. "We have no claims on each other. Our agreement was quite clear. Help each other to reach our mutual goals. You've found your brother and I've found Red. We're sorted."

Raphael let the smile spread across his face, exposing his fangs. "Liar," he purred.

Chaos' body responded like Pavlov's dog to a dinner bell. "Knock it off."

"Knock what off?" His footsteps were silent as he closed the distance between them.

She gave him her shoulder. "You know very well what I'm talking about," she said.

Undaunted, Raphael tilted her chin and kissed her tenderly. "You have no need to worry. I care about Red, but not in the way you've assumed. She has chosen her mate. I respect her wishes."

Her power surged. "So what you're telling me is that I'm your default pick. You couldn't get the woman you wanted, so you're settling for your second choice. Nice. I feel so special," Chaos spat. She needed to leave before she got too out of control. When she lost control, people got hurt.

"Hardly." Raphael slid his hands along her arms. "You have held my attention from the moment I laid eyes on you. I find you infinitely more fascinating than the she-wolf." His gaze raked her, simmering with intent.

Emotions welled within her, despite her efforts to keep them tamped down. As much as Chaos would like to deny it, she was falling hard for Raphael Vega. He'd gotten under her skin literally and she'd allowed it with nary a whimper.

She stared at his face, wondering not for the first time what she was going to do with him. He'd come into her life like a tornado and turned her world on its ear. The thought of parting left her bereft, but she couldn't exactly take him with her to IPTT. That didn't leave her with a lot of options.

Chaos had always been a loner, trying to fit in without standing out. It had worked for a while, until her gift raised its ugly head. Now she wasn't sure if she'd even return. What would be the point now that the commander was gone? No doubt she'd already been replaced, especially if Bannon had taken over.

"You'll be the death of me," she said.

"No." He shook his head. "I will bring only light into your life."

Chaos gave him an incredulous look that she hoped said he was full of it.

"You shall see. Just give me a chance." Raphael kissed her again. This time his lips lingered as he deepened the embrace. He ran his tongue along the seam of her mouth until she opened for him. He swept in exploring her thoroughly until her head spun.

Chaos clasped her hands behind his neck and said yes the only way she knew how—by kissing him back and hanging on for dear life as the world dropped out beneath her feet.

* * * * *

CHAPTER THIRTY-THREE

Red found Morgan sitting in front of a desk. "How goes it?"

"I may have the navcom working. It was locked so it couldn't broadcast everywhere, but I changed its settings."

She hugged him. "That's great. Now you can contact the Eye of God and see if he can help us."

Morgan sighed. "I found something while you were in the garden. I'd planned to share it with you before Demery arrived." He pulled out one of Kane's audio journals from his pocket. "Jonah kept this safe while I was detained."

Red recognized the journals instantly. "Did you finally listen to all of them?" she asked, knowing how hard it would've been for him to do so. He still mourned the loss of his cousin.

"Yes, and there's something you need to hear." Morgan pressed play.

Red stood dumbfounded as she listened to Kane and Roark. She couldn't believe what she was hearing. "Can you play it again?" The order to have her killed left Roark's mouth with ease.

Morgan brushed her hand. "I'm sorry."

"What does this mean?" Red's mind raced to comprehend. The implications were overwhelming.

"It means our nightmare is almost over," Morgan said. "At least once we broadcast this and the Eye of God sends it out to the republics."

Red nodded. "Wait a minute. If we do that, then everyone will know about the Others," she said.

Morgan grew silent, his expression grim. "I know."

"There has to be some other way," she said.

He ran his hand over his stubbled chin. "There isn't."

"We can't just send this to the satellites for everyone to hear. You've kept these people safe all these years. They're counting on you to continue."

"I know." Morgan's expression grew apprehensive. "But it's the only way we'll stop Roark for good and gain our freedom. The proof on this recording will seal his fate."

"And the Nurians?" Red asked. "What will become of them?"

He sighed. "They will have to learn to adapt. Just like I will. We've survived worse. Hopefully people will be more forgiving this time around."

Red didn't want the death of the Nurians on her head. "You can't count on that," she said.

Morgan rose from his chair. "What do you want me to do? We have run out of options. You know that as well as I do. And we can't stay here. Jonah has been kind, but he doesn't have the means to support all of us. We have to end this before Roark comes after Nuria, if he hasn't already."

"Now that the commander is out of the way, there'll be no one to stop him." She choked on the pain, clogging her throat. "He may already have control of IPTT." The thought was truly terrifying. Nuria had no hope against a well-trained tactical team force.

"We don't know anything yet. Let's not speculate," Morgan reminded her. He picked up the device. "Now the bad news. I don't think this navcom will broadcast out of this valley. I've checked its signal strength and it's weak. Even if I added it to the transmitter I fixed, I don't think it would reach the Eye of God."

"I swear we can't catch a break." She paced. "Is there any way to boost it?"

"Possibly," Morgan said. "But we'll need to get someplace much higher to try."

Red sighed. "Okay, so we climb one of the mountains."

"There's something else." Morgan touched her hand. "We'll probably only have one shot at this before it fries the crystal."

"Can we still do a scan on Michael?" Red wanted to get the message out, but not at the cost of another life.

Morgan turned the navcom over. "That part of it should still work, but even if it finds something, we don't have the equipment to do surgery here. I already asked Jonah. In all likelihood, we'd kill Michael trying to help him."

"We have to do something. We can't just leave him like this. He's in so much pain," Red said.

Morgan pulled her into his arms. "How is Raphael holding up?"

Red shrugged. "He's hurting, but he hides it well. You know Raphael."

"For his sake, I hope there's something we can do for Michael," Morgan said.

"Me, too." She could tell by Morgan's expression that he was thinking about Kane. He didn't want Raphael to lose his only surviving close family member, too.

They walked into the barracks where Michael was lying on a cot. "Are you awake?" Red asked.

"It's rather hard to sleep when your head is splitting in two." Michael opened his eyes. His skin was paler than usual and his black hair was disheveled.

Morgan put his hand on Michael's shoulder. "We think the navcom has been repaired enough to run a scan on you," he said.

Michael laughed. "It doesn't matter."

"Don't say that," Red said. "We want to help."

Michael met her gaze and shook his head. "You truly are special, but there's nothing to be done. The chip in my head has A.I. capabilities that seem to have taken over. Roark doesn't need to be near for it to activate."

Red gasped. She hadn't meant to, but she didn't realize the situation was so dire. "At least let us try," she said. "For Raphael's sake."

His cheeks flushed at the mention of his brother's name. "Go ahead."

Raphael walked into the room as Red placed the navcom on Michael's wrist. Catherine came in behind him looking disheveled and sporting a love bite on her neck.

"Ah, I see we're having a party." Michael's gaze swept Catherine. "And you obviously started early, Raph."

"Your sense of humor has always been off-color, brother," Raphael said.

Red pressed scan. The navcom beeped, then hummed. It beeped again five minutes later. She lifted the navcom off his wrist and read the results.

"The chip seems to be lodged in the frontal lobe area of his brain. I thought perhaps it had been attached to the bone," she said.

"I told you that nothing could be done," Michael said.

"We have to get it out," Red said. "It's amazing you've made it this far without dislodging it."

Michael shook his head. "You can't remove it without killing me. It's been burrowing into my brain. I've felt it. It's like a continual itch that cannot be scratched."

Red bit her bottom lip as she considered the possibilities. "There has to be a way to block the signal," she said.

Everyone looked at Morgan, who shook his head slowly. "If there is, I don't know about it."

Raphael grabbed the navcom so he could read the results for himself. "It's in a bad spot," he said. "If we try to remove it, he could become psychotic."

"We can't leave it in there," Red said. "It's hurting him. For all we know, it's killing him while we argue about what to do." She paced restlessly. It was easier to think when she was moving.

"Gina," Morgan said.

Red stopped midstride. "Even if we wanted to, I told you we don't have the equipment to take it out. The only hope is to get him to an emergency care center before he dies."

Michael shook his head. "You're not listening."

"Will you be able to travel?" Red asked, ignoring his comment.

"That depends," he said. "Where are we going?" Michael tried to sit up in the cot, but slumped back down.

"Morgan has found the proof we've been looking for to nail Roark. It should be enough to prevent him from winning the election and taking over the republics," she said. "But we can't send it from here. The reception is too bad. We have to get higher. We're thinking that the top of one of the mountains might work."

Michael lay very still in the bed, his expression unreadable. "What kind of proof?" he asked.

Red looked at him, then at the others in the room.

Raphael and Chaos leaned forward, eager to hear what she had to say. No one noticed Michael's lack of reaction but her. She debated whether to continue, but she'd already said too much.

"Kane recorded one of the conversations he had with Roark," she said.

"What did it say?" Raphael asked.

Chaos looked confused. "Who's Kane?"

Raphael gave her a quick shake of his head, silencing any further queries. "I'll explain later," he said.

Red's gaze met Michael's once more. "The message will help clear our names, but it's not all good news," she said. "At least not for the Others."

Raphael frowned. "Okay, now you have me worried. What did the message say?"

"The message was Roark ordering a hit on me. Unfortunately, the recording inadvertently reveals the existence of the Others. So if we send it out, there will be no more hiding," Red said, letting the magnitude of her statement settle in. "For any of us." Her gaze swept to Chaos.

"I'm not an Other," Chaos said in a rush.

"That may be, but you're definitely not a pureblood," Red said. She flushed.

* * * * *

It was Raphael's turn to grow silent. He knew it would happen someday, but not so soon. He considered the ramifications. Was the world ready for the existence of Others? They hadn't been before. Sure, they'd been living side by side with purebloods for over a century, but he could still remember the dark days. When most people heard that term, they thought he was talking about the war, but he wasn't.

The dark days came after the war ended, when their status as war heroes disintegrated and they were hunted like vermin. He could still recall the fear, the pain of discovery, and the years of torture that followed. He and the rest were lucky to escape with their lives.

Lucky? He laughed to himself. The dead were the lucky ones. At least their pain had ended. He couldn't go back to that way of life. And he wasn't sure that enough had changed in the world to avoid repeating past mistakes. Raphael looked at Morgan and Red.

They knew the risks. He could see it on their faces, along with the hope they tried to hide.

"What do you plan to do?" he asked.

"Morgan might be able to come up with more proof if he can reach the Eye of God, but it won't be enough on its own. We need this recording to ensure victory," Red said.

"And what if that chance you speak of brings hell down onto Nuria's head?" Raphael asked.

Red met his eyes. "We've considered everything carefully. The truth is, if Roark gets away with what he's done there won't be a Nuria left to go home to. His goal is and has always been to get rid of the Others. He doesn't care how he accomplishes this goal, only that he does. If you think otherwise, then you are only fooling yourself."

Catherine stepped forward and ran her hand down the length of Raphael's arm. He was trembling. Raphael couldn't help it—the memories of the past were still strong. "And what of my brother?" he asked.

Red's expression turned grim. "We'll get him back to the Republic of Arizona and into the emergency care center. They should be able to get that chip out before Roark realizes what's happening."

"And if they don't?" Raphael asked.

"Brother," Michael drew his attention away from Red. "I have lived through much. I'm sure I can make the journey back to the republics and get through a little surgery."

Raphael frowned. What choice did he have? His brother would die if they didn't return. Nuria's existence balanced on a razor's edge and someone would have to bleed. He nodded his assent.

Michael turned to Red. "I don't suppose you can let us hear this recording."

She looked uneasy, then slowly shook her head. Raphael stared at his brother. Michael gave him a sad smile and something inside of him crumbled.

"The journal is safe with Morgan for now," Red said. "If you're up to it, we'll leave in an hour."

"I'll be ready," Michael said. *Let's hope you are.*

Raphael heard his brother's thought, though he was sure he wasn't supposed to.

* * * * *

Although he had not heard the recording, Michael had no reason to believe what Red had said was untrue. Unfortunately for her, he couldn't allow that recording to reach the mountaintop. Contrary to her beliefs, Roark was the only one who could remove the chip in his brain. The only one aware of what it was capable of doing, if it remained buried inside him.

Deep down Raph knew the truth, too, although he refused to see it. His concern was a valid one. Michael didn't have to read his mind to sense the fear rolling off him. He remembered the dark days. All the Others did. Red had not been born. She never went through the terror of such things. She never had to live through a hunt. She had never been feared.

His head throbbed, but it was no longer from the chip. Realization of what he must do weighed heavily on his shoulders. The shadow men nodded in agreement. If Michael could avoid harming them, he would, but he doubted that would be the case. They were natural fighters. Red and Morgan would do what they must to protect the recording and he'd do what he must to destroy it.

In the end they'd understand. They'd have to. They'd do the same if they were in his situation. Red and Morgan would sacrifice themselves if they thought it would save the Others. He was not so noble. He wanted to live. He had so much to live for now that he'd found his brother. They'd only begun to build new memories and catch up on the years they'd lost. He hoped in the end Raphael would forgive him....

* * * * *

CHAPTER THIRTY-FOUR

The chip's interference was getting worse. Blood took the edge off, but it wouldn't last long.

Red, Morgan, Catherine, and Melea climbed the mountain at dawn. They'd settled on a peak the night before, declaring it tall enough to broadcast the recording. That's if the navcom was still working by the time they reached the top.

"You ready to do this?" Raphael asked.

Michael nodded. He didn't want Morgan to get too far ahead of them.

They scrambled up the rocky face. Michael slipped twice, but Raphael caught him before he could fall. Their gazes met and for a moment they connected.

"Our parents would be proud of the man you've become," Michael said.

"They'd be proud of you, too," Raphael replied.

"No, they wouldn't, but it's kind of you to say." Michael touched him with trembling fingers. "You are the better man, Raphael and I love you for it. Please remember that always. No matter what happens."

* * * * *

Raphael stared at his brother's retreating back. He wasn't sure what just happened, but his gut was twisting with worry. How

260

could words so tender leave him feeling so much pain? He swallowed hard and rushed to catch up.

They crested the top of the peak an hour later. There weren't many places to stand, so each member of the group had to find his footing carefully. Raphael glanced over his shoulder at the drop behind him. It might not kill him, but he'd be in no shape to travel if he slipped.

Catherine stood closest to Red and Morgan. She tried to look casual, but it was a tactical move. He still wasn't sure what kind of deal she'd made with the commander of IPTT—not that it mattered now, the circumstances had changed for everyone.

Morgan pressed the power button on the navcom. The screen glowed, which was a good sign. At least it was receiving some juice from the crystal. He took out the small digital recorder containing Kane's journal, then looked at the group.

"I'm only going to get one shot at this before I drain the power out of this navcom," Morgan said.

"Then you'd better hurry," Raphael said. The words had barely left his mouth when he saw a blur of movement. There was only one creature that could move that fast—his brother, Michael.

Michael's arms snaked around Catherine. In the next heartbeat, he'd pulled her knife and held it to her throat. The sharp blade glistened in the sunlight, its deadly teeth threatening to shred the soft flesh protecting her esophagus.

"No one move," Michael said, his panic-filled voice came out on a harsh rush of air.

"Brother, what are you doing?" Raphael judged the distance between them. He shifted his feet and rocks tumbled down the mountainside, crashing below.

"I wouldn't," Michael said. "Unless you want to lose your woman."

Raphael raised his arms and stepped back. "We're trying to help you."

"I can't let you send that message," Michael said to Morgan, ignoring Raphael.

Morgan's gaze shot to Raphael, who shook his head in warning. "We have no choice. It's the only way Gina and I will ever be able to return to the republics." Morgan went to push the button, but his hand froze above it. "Damn it! Release me!"

Red rushed Michael. She took two steps before her body hit an invisible wall.

"He's using his telekinesis." Red's body shook as she tried to break free.

Raphael focused his attention on Michael. Catherine hadn't moved, although he could hear her thoughts and she was planning an attack. "Don't!" he cried out.

Michael and Catherine jumped, which caused the knife to nick her throat. The smell of her blood filled the air and Raphael saw Michael's eyes lock on the slow, steady drip. The moment Michael's fangs extended, Raphael's heart tripled its beat.

"Michael, no!" he shouted.

Michael tore his eyes away from Catherine's throat. "You are in no position to make demands, brother." He licked his lips.

"Why are you doing this?" he asked.

"You know why." Michael pulled Catherine closer.

Raphael shook his head. "No, I don't."

Michael tapped his brow. "It's in there. It's always in there. It's keeping the shadows at bay. Roark can get it out. He promised if I brought Red and Morgan back he'd take it out. He's the only one who can. Don't you see? I can't let you destroy him."

Raphael frowned and looked around in confusion. "What shadows?"

Michael's black eyes were wildly unfocused. "They think I don't see them, but I do. I really do. They've been following me, keeping just out of sight. I'm surprised you didn't notice that they were waiting for me, when you put me on the cot."

Cold enveloped Raphael. His brother was mad. Morgan and Red tried to warn him, but he hadn't listened. He'd been too focused on getting help. How could he have missed the signs? They'd been there. The subtle clues in his behavior and the not-so-subtle ones like him wiping out an entire nomadic tribe. Raphael had ignored them all. Made excuses for him as...as anyone would do for someone they loved.

The realization that he was partially responsible for this situation struck Raphael to the core. Fear came on the heels of that discovery, numbing him. He shuddered. Catherine was in the hands of a madman and there wasn't anything he could do about it, unless he wanted to get them both killed.

Raphael looked at Morgan and Red. Red's eyes had turned amber and claws had sprouted from her nail beds. She hadn't even cried out, but she was obviously in pain. It was a show of sheer willpower. Soon the change would be complete and there would be no reasoning with her.

Please don't, he pleaded with her and Morgan using their mental connection. *Michael is not well. The chip has left him paranoid. I believe he will kill Catherine if he feels threatened. I cannot lose them both.*

We can't stop the broadcast. It's our only chance. The only chance we'll have to prevent Roark's blood war, Red said.

Give me a moment to talk him down. I believe I can reach him. If I fail, then...you know what needs to be done, Raphael said.

The navcom won't last much longer, Morgan said. *Even now I can see the power draining.*

He is my brother, Raphael said softly. *My only family. And Catherine...she holds my heart.*

Morgan nodded in understanding. *You won't have long*, he said. *This thing only has about three minutes left in it before it dies. He won't let me touch the controls to shut it off.*

Thank you for allowing me to try, Raphael said.

"Let me go," Catherine said, but she didn't try to struggle.

Be still, Raphael told her, but it was too late.

He felt her power building a second before she released it. Morgan, Red, and Melea clutched their heads and dropped to their knees. Michael swayed, then his eyes clouded before quickly snapping back into focus. The power washed over Raphael, harmlessly passing through him.

"I forgot about your little trick." Michael leaned down to lick the blood off her throat. "You try it again and I'll widen this slit until you bleed out."

A growl rumbled in the air. It took Raphael a second to realize that it was coming from him and not the wolves. "Don't touch her again, brother. You test our bond with your actions. You know I love her."

Catherine's eyes widened, then filled with tears.

Raphael forced his gaze away. He couldn't chance being distracted.

"In another minute, it'll be a moot point because the navcom will be dead. Already the screen is beginning to dim," Michael said.

"Has Roark given you so much that you're willing to sacrifice everyone else for selfish gains?" Raphael asked.

Michael's eyes locked on him and he felt pressure build around his throat, threatening to cut off his air. Raphael didn't give Michael the pleasure of seeing him grasp at invisible fingers.

"Selfish gains?" Michael hissed. "How dare you? You know nothing of what I've had to put up with over the years."

"And yet, here you stand still doing your master's bidding," Raphael said. "Seems to me that you've learned nothing."

"My life is worth more than a few Others. Our time together is priceless to me." Michael's grip tightened on the knife handle. "Would you like to see what Roark taught me, brother?"

"No!" Raphael rushed forward as the knife sliced Catherine's throat. The movement distracted Michael and released his hold on Morgan's hand.

Raphael grasped Michael's arm, stopping him from cutting Catherine any further. Her wound was bleeding badly. He pulled the blade a few inches away from her throat and she grasped her neck with her free hand.

Michael had to let her go to get a better grip on the knife. When he did, Raphael shoved her to the side, sending her sprawling onto the ground. Melea rushed forward to help her. Raphael stood face to face with his brother in a desperate struggle to disarm him.

"Michael, stop. This way no one wins," Raphael grunted out between clenched teeth. Kane's voice rang out from the recording as Morgan sent the message, but it was Roark's voice that nearly caused him to drop the weapon.

The recording was short and direct. It ended almost before it began. "Please let me help you."

"It's done," Morgan said.

Michael looked around, his black eyes growing wider. "It's too late. They're coming for me. There is no escape." He struggled to break Raphael's grasp. The fact that he didn't use telekinesis spoke volumes. The knife slipped, cutting Michael's hand. "Keep them away."

Tears stung Raphael's eyes. "Please, brother. Do not do this. Give me the knife. We can help you. We just need to make it to the emergency care center."

Michael's gaze met his and softened. For a moment the world dropped away and they were children again, playing cowboys and Indians in the backyard with sticks and water guns.

"Remember what I said," Michael whispered softly. "Now allow me to help you with what needs to be done."

The words had barely registered in Raphael's ears when the pressure Michael was exerting on the knife ceased and the b ade flipped over. Raphael was still bearing down hard. Without his brother's resistance, the knife slammed into Michael's throat and came out the other side.

Blood sprayed over Raphael's face and down the front of his shirt. He shrieked and removed the knife, pulling Michael into his arms before falling to his knees onto the rocks.

"No, damn you! No!" Raphael cried, shaking Michael hard. "Why? Why after everything we've been through? Why did you do this?"

Michael opened his mouth, but was unable to speak. Blood bubbled out of his wound. Raphael pressed a hand to Michael's throat to stem the flow, but the blood just kept coming, leak ng through his fingers.

"Make it stop." Raphael shook Michael. "You have the power. Make it stop."

Words flowed into Raphael's mind.

Please do not feel any guilt. It was the only way. The only way I could escape once I realized I wasn't going to make it, Michael said.

But we could've gotten you help, Raphael said.

Then what? I'd spend the rest of my life waiting for an assassin to find me? That is no way to live. I tried to make it easy on you.

His words stilled Raphael's breathing. *You set this whole thing up.*

Not initially. Only when I realized it was too late.

Why, brother? Raphael asked.

You wouldn't do it otherwise. The threat to the Others wasn't enough, but your love for Catherine would be. I knew you wouldn't let her die.

Raphael brushed his face and cooed softly to soothe his passage. *No, I couldn't.*

Michael choked, spitting up blood. *I swear on our mother's grave I would never have killed Catherine. The chip made me cut her. I didn't want to. I know how much she means to you.*

You mean the world to me, too, Raphael said. Crimson tears flowed down his cheeks as he rocked his brother in his arms.

Remember me as I once was.

Always, Raphael held him tighter, as if that would stave off death. It didn't.

Death swept in and took his brother away.

Raphael threw his head back in anguish. He raged at the heavens. A century of pain erupted in guttural growls. Michael was gone, leaving only emptiness behind.

It took several minutes for him to notice the warm arms encircling him, comforting, even as the pain threatened to crush his heart. He felt moisture on his back and realized that Catherine was crying with him. Or maybe she was crying for him. He didn't know. And it didn't matter. All that mattered was that she was there doing everything she could to remind him that she was there for him.

Raphael didn't know how long he sat there. His muscles were stiff by the time he released Michael and attempted to stand. He stumbled, but Catherine steadied him.

"Did the message go out?" he asked Morgan.

Morgan shook his head. "It looked like it, but I don't know. The navcom died, so I'm not sure how much made it out," he said. "I'm sorry about Michael."

Raphael wiped the tears from his face. "Not half as sorry as Roark is going to be. He did this. He's the one who made my brother into a monster."

They carried Michael down the mountain and buried him deep under the sand. Raphael stood over the mound, swaying on his feet. The rest of the group surrounded the makeshift grave. Red, Melea, and Catherine had never experienced a funeral. They'd been done away with long before any of them were born. Outdated on the dead world, bodies were now recycled like any other biodegradable object and used as mulch to feed the plants in the hydroponic chambers.

"Do you want to say a few words?" Morgan asked.

Raphael shook his head slowly. "No, we said all we needed to say on the mountain. I hope he found the peace he so desperately sought."

"Amen," Morgan said. "Let's go end this."

* * * * *

CHAPTER THIRTY-FIVE

It took three days for the group to clear the last of the dunes. They could see the boundary fence glowing in the distance, its sight both welcome and foreboding. What if the transmission hadn't made it out? What if the Eye of God hadn't picked it up? What if no one knew what Roark had done? They might be walking into a trap, but they wouldn't know until they got a little closer.

Red couldn't think about that now. They'd made it over the mountains and through the endless dunes without any more trouble. For that she was grateful. There'd been enough death on this journey. It was time to put this conflict to rest. On the other side of the fence the Republic of Arizona waited for them.

They stopped so she and Morgan could put their registered chips back into their necks. It was a risk. A big one. If anyone was tracking them, they'd know exactly where they were once the chips were in place. But it didn't matter—they were done hiding.

Morgan brushed the hair away from Red's face. "You ready?" he asked.

"As I'll ever be." She smiled. "Let's go."

The five of them continued on. Red brushed the dust off her clothes as she scanned the fence line. The blue boundary crackled, the sound carrying on the dry desert breeze. As she watched, something flashed behind the fence.

"Did you see that?" Red asked.

"Yes." Morgan moved closer. "Did you catch what it was, Raphael?"

Catherine stopped, along with Melea. Raphael squinted, then drew to a halt. "It's a laser sniper rifle. If I'm not mistaken, International Police Tactical Team issue," he said.

"Everybody down!" Morgan shouted.

Red's heart slammed painfully into her ribs. Their signal hadn't made it. Their journey back had been for nothing. She took out a monocular and scanned the fence line. A blond head stood out from the rest.

"Bannon," she whispered.

"You sure?" Morgan scanned the horizon.

Red lowered the monocular. "I'd know that shorn head anywhere," she said. "It looks like he's leading the teams."

"Teams?" Chaos asked. "As in plural?"

"Yes, there are at least three of them there. And that's just the ones I can see," Red said.

"What are we going to do?" Melea's eyes were wide with fright. She searched desperately for a place to hide.

Red and Morgan looked at each other, then slowly nodded. "You guys are going to make your way toward the crossing. Morgan and I will turn ourselves in."

"No way," Raphael said. "We didn't walk all this way to have you imprisoned now."

"They don't know about you," Red said. "I'd like it to stay that way. There's a tunnel off to the left. Stomp on the ground to find it. Melea, if you wait until dark, you should be able to make it across with no problem. Raphael will come and get you at midnight."

"I'm not waiting out here by myself," she said. "I'm unarmed."

Red took one of her pistols out of her holster and adjusted the weapon so Melea could fire it, then handed it to her. "Now you'll be safe."

"I'm not going to let you walk into a firing squad," Raphael said. "We can't clear your name if you're dead."

Red sighed. "You said there's a sniper rifle trained on us."

Raphael nodded. "There is."

"Then they've already spotted us. We could probably convince IPTT that we took you hostage," Red said. There had to be a way to protect their friends.

He arched a brow.

"It's worth a shot," she said.

"Not from where I'm laying," Raphael said.

"I hate to break up this argument," Morgan said. "But I just spotted three tanks moving in. I believe the decision has been made for us. We'll have to proceed before they blast us with the heat seekers."

"It's me Bannon wants," Red said. "Maybe if I turn myself in, he'll take me and leave."

Morgan shot her a look that said this conversation was over.

"Fine, have it your way." Red scrambled to her feet and started forward slowly.

The closer they got to the fence the greater her dread grew. There were more than three squads aligned along the boundary fence. Bannon had brought half the teams. Roark must have really been threatened by the information they held. Too bad no one but Roark and them would ever know the truth.

"Who is Bannon?" Raphael asked.

"He's a commanding officer at IPTT headquarters," Chaos answered. "Bit of an asshole, if you ask me."

Red laughed. She couldn't help it. "I see you've had an encounter."

"He was with me when I visited Roark's office," she said. Chaos' eyes widened, when she realized what she'd said.

Red stopped. "And just what were you doing at Roark's office?" she asked.

"It's a long story," Raphael said. "One that perhaps is better shared later."

"Are you vouching for her?" Morgan asked.

Raphael stepped forward. "I am."

Morgan held his gaze and the tension inside the little group rose.

"For you, my friend, I will do this once—and once only," Raphael said, before slowly lowering his eyes in respect for Morgan's position as alpha.

Morgan looked stunned. "I never thought I'd see the day," he said.

Raphael grinned. "I figured since we may not be alive in the very near future it was the least I could do."

The men laughed, sharing an easy camaraderie that Red didn't think she'd ever witness between them.

"Come forward with your hands up where we can see them," Bannon shouted, shattering the moment.

Red's hands shook as she raised them high. Bannon shouldn't be here, leading the teams. Her grandfather should. He was the rightful commander of IPTT. Bannon was a bully as a lieutenant, and she couldn't imagine the power trip he'd be on as commander. The tactical team would lose a lot of good men and women under Bannon's command.

Red forced her feet forward. Morgan still kept his body between her and the teams, but it would do little good if Bannon ordered them to open fire.

"Lower your weapons," Chaos shouted. "It's Private Catherine Meyers. Team member 11174." She pulled out her I.D., but her hand continued to rest on her weapon.

"I'm afraid we can't do that, Private." Bannon's face was grim as they neared the fence. "We have orders to neutralize the threat."

Chaos' gaze locked on Red.

* * * * *

The time to move was now. Once she was in custody, I wouldn't be able to touch her. I shouldn't have waited so long. I should have jumped at the opportunity to take Gina Santiago down when I had the chance.

Panic hit. My orders were clear. Must kill her.

I glanced around at the tactical team members. All eyes were upon me, waiting to see what I'd do next. They'd bear witness to my sacrifice.

My nerves jumped beneath my skin, caught somewhere between fight or flight. No time to back down. I was doing this for the team. My hand brushed my weapon.

Gina stood a few feet away with her head held high. Pride radiated from her. It fueled my anger. *How dare she act like she's innocent.* If she were smart, she'd have recognized the threat that has been with her all along.

My fingers wrapped around the handle of the laser pistol. The weapon recognized my thumbprint and charged. In a few seconds, it would be ready to fire. My hand trembled as I fought the urge to draw the pistol from its holster, but the compulsion to kill was too strong. It drove all logic away, leaving only savage impulses behind.

Red had to die. She was ruining the tactical team, tearing apart what it stood for by creating that abomination in Nuria. Didn't she understand that this was my home?

There was only room for one tactical team and it had been in existence for more than a hundred years.

Kill her.

She needed to get closer. I couldn't take the chance that someone might stop me. I took a deep breath. It was now or never.

* * * * *

Red's stomach clenched as Chaos grasped her laser pistol. She glanced at Bannon. A muscle ticced in his jaw. She'd seen that more than a dozen times. It meant that he was furious. That didn't bode well for them. One wrong move and he'd give the order to kill them.

She glanced back at Chaos. Their eyes met and Red shook her head in warning, but the Private's aggressive stance didn't ease. If anything, it got worse. She was going to get them killed.

Red walked forward briskly, keeping her arms raised. "It's me you want," she said.

"Gina, get back here." Morgan tried to stop her.

"I said hands in the air," Bannon shouted.

Morgan stopped and raised his arms once more.

"Gina Santiago," Bannon yelled. "You are wanted for crimes against the republics. You will be taken into custody the second you cross the boundary fence. If you choose to run, you will be shot." He spoke the last sentence with anticipation.

Bannon wanted her to run. Red had no doubt that he'd take great pleasure in killing her. "I will surrender without resistance," she said. "Let the others go."

"Nice try," Bannon said. "But Morgan Hunter is also wanted. The others will be detained under the conspiracy law."

A dust trail rose in the distance as a vehicle approached from the north.

The power in the fence went down. One by one, Red and her traveling companions stepped forward, only to be knocked to their knees. Power cuffs were placed on Red's and Morgan's wrists, then they were ordered to stand. The vehicle Red had been watching had nearly reached them. She could see now it was a turbo shuttle. IPTT rarely used them because they required so much power.

"Roark," she muttered. It had to be Roark.

Bannon followed her line of sight and smirked. "Just in time."

"In time for what?" she asked.

"You are a disgrace to the uniform," Bannon hissed.

Red flinched. "I did what I had to do in order to save my people and clear my name."

He snorted. "Your name will never be clear." Bannon's large hands closed around her throat and squeezed. "Must stop you," he said.

"What are you doing?" Red kicked out, connecting with his groin, but all it did was make him more determined. Spots swam before her eyes and the world turned scarlet. She gasped, but no air came in. "Bannon, stop."

She could hear Chaos and Morgan struggling beside her, but someone was holding them back. "Why are you doing this?" She choked and fell to the ground.

His glassy blue eyes looked at her, but Red didn't think he could see her. "Why won't you die?" Bannon snarled, leaning over her.

"Stop..." Red gurgled as she tried to breathe. Her vision dimmed.

"That's enough, Lieutenant. Stand down," a baritone voice boomed from behind Bannon's broad shoulders.

He ignored the order.

Red recognized that voice, but even as the thought passed through her mind, she knew it wasn't possible. She must be dying. For that voice had been taken from her in two deafening shots. Bannon turned, giving her a clear view of the approaching tactical team member.

"Let her go or we'll be forced to open fire," the man said.

"No," Bannon bellowed, squeezing tighter. "You can't stop me.

My orders are clear. I'm protecting IPTT."

A flash from a laser blast nearly blinded her. Red felt Bannon's grip ease. She coughed, then blinked several times forcing her eyes to focus. A gaping hole smoldered where Bannon's abdomen used to be. He tumbled, landing beside her. Red turned to see Melea lower the weapon she'd given her, a power cuff hung from one of her wrists.

Shaking, the woman dropped the gun on the ground and slowly raised her hands. "He was going to kill you," she said. Her dark eyes were haunted by the violence she'd been forced to commit.

"Thank you," Red said.

Melea wept.

The tactical team members raised their weapons and prepared to fire.

"I said stand down. That's an order."

"Grandpa?" Red blinked as tears filled her eyes. "Is it really you?" She had to be dead. Either that or she was seeing a ghost.

Robert Santiago rushed forward and pulled her into his arms.

The hug felt real. Red inhaled, taking in the slightly musty odor that clung to her grandfather from handling his book collection. "I can't believe it. You were dead. I heard the shots. I'll never forget that sound of you gasping for breath." Tears streamed down her face.

"I know." He gently pushed her back so he could look at her. "We found the body of an Unknown and the recordings when we searched Roark's office. The audio reproduction was very convincing. It took the tech people a couple of days to figure out he'd hijacked our security feed so he could record my voice. From there it was a matter of editing the right phrases together."

Red burrowed deeper. She didn't allow the power cuffs to stop her. She snuggled into his shirt, breathing in his scent, savoring it.

* * * * *

Robert Santiago gave up trying to move her. "What was going on here?" he asked Morgan. "Why was Bannon choking Gina?"

Morgan's jaw was covered in a short beard and his hair had grown to the middle of his shoulders. If it weren't for his eyes, Robert wouldn't have recognized him.

"He was trying to kill her," he said.

"So I saw," Robert scowled. "But why?"

Morgan shifted, his gaze growing wary. "I don't know, but I'm sure Roark has something to do with it. He always does."

"That's ridiculous. Bannon lives and breathes IPTT." Robert glanced down. "At least he did."

"He was drugged," Chaos said. "With influ-gas."

Robert brushed his granddaughter's back with his palm. "That would be very hard to prove."

"It would be," Chaos said, "if you didn't have a witness. I was there when it happened. He gassed me, too."

Robert gaze moved to the fragile young woman who'd shot Bannon. Her eyes were round with fright and she couldn't seem to stop trembling. He'd considered bringing her up on charges, but that was before he got a good look at her and heard about the extenuating circumstances. There'd been no malicious intent in her expression, only fear for one woman from another...who'd seen far too much violence in her short lifetime.

"We tried to send out a message that could prove our innocence, but I guess it didn't reach you," Gina said, looking around at the teams.

"Nonsense." The commander kissed her forehead. "Why do you think we're here?"

"But I thought..." She held up her cuffed hands. "Bannon said..."

Robert Santiago's gaze shot to Bannon Richards' body. "Richards asked to lead the team. I didn't see a problem with it given his rank. I had no idea it was so he could get his hands on you. I'm so sorry, special one."

"It's not your fault. It was like he was possessed," she said.

"I'll have the dissecting lab run tests on his body to verify Private Meyers' assertions. I'm not sure what he said to you, but we're here because we received your broadcast. The republic leaders asked IPTT to personally meet you and escort you in without further incident."

Gina's brow creased and she shook her head. "What are you saying?"

"I'm saying that everyone heard Roark put that hit out on you. They heard it from you and from your navcom, Rita. We were able to piece together the recording you made in the shuttle. Even without your evidence, we had enough to go to the republic leaders. They are holding an emergency tribunal about Roark's actions and the discovery of the Others. You are both expected to stand before them and tell your side of the story. They are eager to listen."

* * * * *

Red looked over her shoulder at Morgan, who wasn't smiling.

"It's going to be okay," he said, even though his expression said otherwise.

She heard the words, but still couldn't believe it. The message had gotten out. Somehow the broken navcoms had come through for them. She choked and cried harder, this time with happiness. This whole ordeal was over. They'd done it. They had beaten Roark.

"What about Montgomery?" she asked, remembering the election. "Did he win?"

"Yes," Robert said.

Red deflated a little.

Her grandfather's expression clouded and his dark eyes glittered with anger. "Don't worry. We'll find him."

"What do you mean, you'll find him?" Red asked.

"He won the election," Robert said. "But before he could officially take office, your broadcast went out around the world. He knew I'd send someone for him. I'd already informed him of the physical evidence I had against him," he said. "Damn fool thought I'd be dumb enough to come alone, when I shared it with him. He was shocked to see two full teams with me." He shrugged. "Guess he thought he could still use you as a bargaining chip, if he could get his hands on you."

"What evidence?" Red asked. "I'm confused."

"Thanks to Private Meyers, we were able to examine the shuttle Roark claimed was attacked by Morgan. She found it and Rita hidden in the sand. Rita had recorded your conversation."

"But he smashed her," Red said.

"Yes, he did," Robert said. "And our techs fixed her."

Red turned to Chaos. "I owe you an apology."

Chaos shook her head. "No, you don't. I didn't exactly come after you out of the goodness of my heart." Her gaze strayed to Raphael, then to the commander.

Red arched a brow, but she didn't elaborate.

"I gave her permission to find you," Robert said. "I needed to know you were okay. Not that I didn't trust Morgan to take care of you, but I wanted to know firsthand that my special one was alive and well."

Red smiled. "Thank you," she said. "Thank you both." She nodded to Chaos, who responded in kind. "So do you have any idea where Roark might have fled?"

Robert shook his head and a shock of white hair fell onto his forehead. "No, we've checked his office and his home. We even found that cell under his building. Nasty place."

"Yeah, I know," Red said. "Morgan and I received a private tour."

Her grandfather's gaze searched her face. "You're safe," he said more to himself than to her.

"So what happens now?" Red asked, glancing once more at the teams.

"We have to take you in. Don't want it to look like we do not follow protocol. You'll be processed and held at IPTT. You won't be kept in a cell, but your rooms will be guarded. In two days' time, you'll meet with the republic leaders. From there," he said, "it's only a matter of e-filings."

Red still couldn't believe it. They'd traveled so far. Lost so much. And now it was almost over. She thought about Demery and Michael as they were loaded into her grandfather's transport.

Robert Santiago sat on her left and Morgan sat on her right. Raphael, Melea, and Chaos sat across from them. There was a low hum as the turbo shuttle rose slowly off the ground.

"Where do you think he's hiding?" she asked, her voice so low that only Raphael and Morgan could hear her.

Morgan shook his head. "Don't know. He could be anywhere. Someone might even be hiding him. He has a lot of allies."

"Why would anyone do that?" she asked, horrified at the prospect of someone harboring Roark.

"He's a powerful man with a lot of powerful friends. It's not out of the realm of possibility," Morgan said. "You forget, people sheltered us knowing we were wanted."

Red thought about Jonah and the Sand Moles. Morgan was right. Roark may be a fiend, but that didn't mean everyone believed he was in the wrong.

Do not worry yourself, Raphael said, using their mental pathway. *I have no doubt I can find him. His stench permeated my brother's flesh. The odor stays with me to this day. He will not escape justice.*

I've been meaning to ask you something, Red said. *Do you feel pain when I do?*

He frowned. *No, why do you ask?*

Melea said something about Demery being able to feel her pain.

Ah, you mean a blood bond. You and I have not experienced such a thing, Raphael said.

But you drank my blood and I drank yours, Red said.

There's more to it than that. A sexual element. We'd have to exchange blood multiple times for it to occur.

Why didn't she say that? Red asked.

She might not remember. Memory grows fuzzy with blood loss.

Oh, she said.

You sound disappointed, Raphael glanced at Chaos and his gaze warmed.

Not at all, Red said. *More like relieved.*

Raphael laughed.

Morgan's amber eyes met Raphael's black ones, then he looked at Red. He knew they were talking and if his expression was any indication, Morgan wasn't happy about being left out of the conversation.

Roark is ours, he said mentally, slamming the thought into Raphael's mind loud enough for Red to hear it.

Morgan is right. I know you hurt over what he did to Michael, she said.

He destroyed my brother, Raphael said. Gone was the humor. It had been replaced by anguish.

And he will pay, Red said. *I promise. But first we have to get through this.* She raised her cuffed hands in reminder.

Raphael's expression soured, but he eventually nodded. *I will not harm him—much—if I find him. I'll make sure there's some left to chew on.*

As reassurances went, it wasn't the greatest, but it was the best she could hope for under the circumstances. The trip back to IPTT was long and uneventful. One of the few shuttle rides she could say that about as of late. Red was having a hard time keeping her eyes open, so she stopped trying. It wasn't until the vehicle halted that she realized she'd fallen asleep with her head on Morgan's shoulder.

"Sorry," she said as she woke.

He smiled down at her. "It's okay. It was nice."

"Ready to go?" her grandfather asked.

Red nodded. "Let's get this over with."

Over a hundred tactical team members were waiting at the shuttle lot. She didn't recognize many of the faces, which meant most had just come here to get a look at the hottest news to hit the planet in a few decades.

Red held her head high. She wasn't about to cower under their regard. She'd done nothing wrong. And in a couple of days, she'd get her chance to prove it.

Her grandfather and ten armed men led them into IPTT headquarters. There they were processed by more team members. Her grandfather never left her side as images were taken, along with their statements. Morgan turned over Kane's journal. These would be logged into the official compunit banks as evidence. The republic leaders would listen to them and read the files, then conduct the tribunal.

Red had no doubt it would take at least a week before they would hear an official verdict in their case. She hoped that Chaos, Raphael, and Melea were released after they gave their statements. Despite the power cuffs, Chaos was still considered a member of IPTT in good standing. Her grandfather had even discussed promoting her.

As for Bannon Richards, they'd know what had happened to him once the dissecting lab examined him. Red had no doubt he'd somehow become another one of Roark Montgomery's casualties. With any luck, he'd be the last. Red tried to muster sympathy for him, but she was fresh out.

* * * * *

CHAPTER THIRTY-SIX

The tribunal was long and arduous. Red and Morgan were interviewed together and separately. The republic leaders were particularly interested in the existence of the Others and what affect they'd have on the community.

Once Morgan explained that they'd been living with Others for more than a hundred years, they calmed down. At least most of them did. A few worried about the safety of so-called pureblood people, but fortunately they remained in the minority. Of course that didn't mean that they wouldn't keep an eye on them.

Red and Morgan reassured the tribunal that a tactical team made up of Others was already being formed and would be available to begin policing the Other community within the month. This quieted the last of the dissenters. Although they did have to agree to allow regular inspections at least until the republic leaders could determine whether the Others posed a credible threat.

Red supposed that was something. Certainly better than the previous policy of shoot first and ask questions later. The next three days were spent testifying about Roark Montgomery's actions. He'd fled shortly after the broadcast of him ordering the hit and hadn't been seen since. The tribunal assured them that they had people looking for him and it was only a matter of time before he was found.

Red listened attentively because that's what was expected of her, but she thoroughly disagreed. Roark wouldn't be easy to find.

He was used to slipping through nets. And she had no doubt that he had more than a few friends sitting on this tribunal, even if they weren't actively defending him now.

On day six, Red and Morgan walked into the tribunal to await their ruling. Red had spent the night staring at the ceiling of her old quarters. The place felt foreign compared to where she'd been in the last few weeks.

Nothing smelled right or tasted the same. She'd walked around the room picking up objects that should've been familiar, but weren't. They might as well have belonged to a stranger. Well, everything but the navcom that now encircled her wrist.

She still couldn't believe that her grandfather had resurrected Rita. She rubbed the familiar band, resisting the urge to power up. Red hadn't had a chance to see if she still sounded the same.

Her grandfather had assured her she did, but Red wanted to hear her navcom's voice for herself. Unfortunately, that would have to wait until the verdicts were read. She didn't want Rita alerting the tribunal to her elevated heart rate or anything else.

Red grasped Morgan's hand. He squeezed hers back, but didn't look over. Instead, he stared straight ahead, his body at attention. He looked so proud and handsome that once again she was reminded of why she loved him so much.

Robert Santiago walked into the room and Red automatically saluted the commander. Ten years of training drilled into her head was hard to forget.

"All rise," the leader of the tribunal said.

Their chairs scraped as they stood.

Red looked at their faces, attempting to read their expressions, but it was impossible. She inhaled, sifting through their scents. Most gave off clean odors. There were a few that held a slightly sour smell, which could be attributed to nerves or diet. Overall, she didn't sense lies or deception. She hoped that was a good sign.

"Have you reached a verdict?" the leader asked.

"We have, illustrious one," the group said as one.

He nodded. "What say you on the charges of escaping detention and eluding arrest? Guilty or not guilty?"

Red's heart thundered and her ears buzzed as her blood roared through her veins. She swayed. Morgan tightened his hold on her hand until pain shot through her fingers. The discomfort forced her to focus and the panic receded.

"Not guilty with special circumstances," the group said.

Special circumstances was a formal way of saying she and Morgan had just cause to flee.

"The prisoners are to be released effective immediately."

Morgan turned to her and smiled. He pulled her into his arms a second later and kissed her. "Told you everything was going to be okay."

He had, but Red didn't dare hope in case things hadn't gone their way. "I can't believe we're finally free," she said.

"We can go home," he said.

Home. The thought was surreal.

"I found out they released Raphael, Melea, and Catherine a couple of days ago."

"How?" Red asked.

"Your grandfather told me," Morgan said. "They even gave Melea a chip, so she could stay in the Republic of Arizona." He grinned.

"He came to see you? He didn't come to see me." Red had wanted to see and speak to her grandfather so badly, but he'd never stopped by.

Morgan pulled back. "Don't be too hard on him. He wanted to see you. He just didn't want to do anything that could be perceived as giving you preferential treatment."

That sounded like her grandfather. He always followed the book, even when he disagreed with it.

"What else did he say to you?" Red asked, genuinely curious. How many times had her grandfather visited Morgan? And what could they find to talk about besides her? Suddenly Red didn't like the idea of her grandfather visiting without her present.

"A bit of this and that. Mainly guy talk. We had to come to an understanding. If you want to know more, you'll have to ask him, because I've been sworn to secrecy." His lips twitched.

"That's sounds ominous," Red said. What were they up to?

Morgan grinned. "Now that this tribunal is over, I'm sure the commander will have a lot to say to you."

"That doesn't sound like a good thing," she said. "What aren't you telling me?"

"Nothing, I swear." He chuckled.

It was good to hear him laugh. She missed that sound.

Red fought back a smile. "You're a terrible liar."

"Only when it comes to lying to you," Morgan said. "Go spend some time with your grandfather. Now that we're free, I need to contact Nuria to have the credits and seeds sent to Jonah. He kept his end of the bargain. It's time for us to keep ours." He kissed her on the temple, then strolled out of the tribunal.

Red waited for her grandfather, who was shaking the hands of the republic leaders congratulating them on a job well done. It didn't take him long. He came over the second he finished.

"So how does it feel to be free?" he asked.

"Good." Red pressed the power button on her navcom.

A nasal voice came out a moment later. "Gina, where have you been? I've been unable to contact you for... My scanners seem to be unable to recall the date. I will have to run a diagnostic on you and my system to see why."

"It's good to hear your voice, Rita," Red said.

"My system detects dehydration and malnutrition. Administering patch fluids now. You really should take better care of yourself," Rita chastised.

"I was about to ask you if she was working the same," Red said to her grandfather. "How did you ever repair her after Roark crushed her?"

Robert Santiago's bushy white brow lowered over his brown eyes. "It wasn't easy. The tech guys called the job impossible, but they gave it a shot anyway. As you can see, it worked."

Red stood on her toes and threw her arms around him. "Thank you, Grandpa."

He patted her back.

She held him for a moment longer, then pulled back. Her gaze met his and her expression hardened. "It won't be over until Roark is caught."

"Leave that to the tactical team, special one," he said, half pleading and half warning.

"Which team? Mine or yours?" Red asked.

"So you're going back?" Sadness filled his eyes. "After everything that's happened?"

Red nodded. "I have some things to straighten out in Nuria." Besides, it was her home now.

"Speaking of Nuria...Lieutenant Catherine Meyers has requested an exchange with the Nurian Tactical Team," he said. "She thinks it would be a good way to bridge the gap between the teams. Would you have a problem with that?"

Red thought about it. "No," she said. "Chaos has proven herself to be a valuable asset. We'd be happy to have her." Red knew of at least one vampire who would be, too. She couldn't wait to see the look on Raphael's face, when he heard the news. She looked over her shoulder to tell Morgan, but he was gone.

"He loves you, you know. Very much," Robert said. "So do I, Gina."

"I love you, too, Grandpa."

* * * * *

Red and Morgan returned to Nuria the next morning. Strangely, the town looked the same. She didn't know why she'd expected it to change. So much had changed for them. Juan and Takeo met them in front of the sheriff's station.

"Welcome back," Juan said. "I told Takeo you'd return soon."

"Saw that in a vision, did you?" Red shook their hands.

Juan blushed. "Something like that."

"He saw it on the viewer like everyone else in town," Takeo said.

"Some psychic." She snorted. "Where's Raphael and Melea?"

Takeo stiffened at the mention of the woman's name.

"Is there a problem?" Red asked.

Juan grinned at Takeo. "Nothing that won't be resolved with time," he said.

"Don't you have work to do?" Takeo asked Juan.

"Nope, my afternoon is clear," he said, then turned back to Red. "We have ten team members now, not counting Takeo, Demery, and me."

Red tensed. In all the excitement, she'd forgotten all about Demery. The expression on her face must've shown her pain because Takeo asked what was wrong.

"Demery is dead," she said. "I'm surprised Melea didn't tell you."

Takeo suddenly looked uncomfortable.

"She hasn't said much besides 'keep him away from me.'" Juan gave Takeo a pointed look.

Red's eyes narrowed. "You better not be harassing that woman. She's been through hell and she saved my life."

Takeo held his hands up. "I haven't touched her," he said, looking as innocent as possible, but his expression said he would like to. His lovely Asian eyes sparkled with mischief.

She tapped her arm and waited.

"I swear," he said.

Juan laughed. "He's telling the truth—sort of. He might not have touched her, but he's been following her around like a lost puppy for the past two days."

Takeo shot him a warning look. "I have not."

Red pressed her lips together to keep from laughing.

"I wanted to make sure she was finding everything. She's never lived in a town before," Takeo said, as if that was a perfectly reasonable explanation for his behavior.

"Whatever you say," Red said. "But remember what I told you."

Morgan touched her shoulder. "I'm going to head inside. I'm sure there is a mountain of paperwork waiting for me. It'll take time to get reinstated."

"I'll be in, in a moment," she said.

"So what happened to Demery?" Juan asked, turning the jovial conversation somber.

Red didn't know how to break it to them gently so she came straight out with the truth. "The leader of the Sand Devils and I killed him."

The men's eyes widened and they took an involuntary step back.

"What is a Sand Devil?" Takeo asked. "And do I really want to know?"

Juan scowled. "Why would you do that?"

Red hadn't had time to mourn Demery's death. Until now, she'd done her best to forget all about him. But these men deserved an explanation. Demery had been their friend. He had been a friend to them all—at least until things went sideways.

"The trip didn't go exactly like we expected. Life was much harder than we'd anticipated. Demery didn't lie about knowing and trading with several bands of people in no-man's-land. He was known by almost all. He just left out the fact that he'd gambled Melea away and needed Other blood to get her back," Red said.

Juan scowled.

"The leader of the Sand Devils, the group that held her, raped and beat her repeatedly. She's been through so much that I'm amazed she's survived. That girl is a fighter and she deserves our respect." She looked straight at the beautiful Asian warrior standing before her.

Takeo's face morphed into a mask of pure fury. His eyes glistened and his fangs flashed. She heard a hiss and watched the viper move restlessly beneath his trench coat, ready to strike.

Juan looked over at his friend, then asked softly, "What happened?"

Red took a deep breath. "Demery kidnapped Morgan and helped the Sand Devil leader bleed him," she said.

Images of a bloody Morgan strung up at the center of the Sand Devil encampment flashed in her mind. Foolish. They should've never taken her mate from her. She'd have killed them all, if given the chance.

"It's a good thing Demery's dead," Takeo said. *Or I'd have killed him myself* was left out.

His voice was so cold Red shivered. "He paid dearly for his mistakes," she said. "I ripped Demery's protective suit open right before Reaper, the leader of the Sand Devils, tried to knife me. He missed, but nailed Demery in the process."

"So he exploded?" Takeo asked.

"Yes." Red relived the horrifying moment.

Takeo's jaw tightened. "He didn't pay nearly enough, if what you say about the girl is true."

Red met his gaze. "She was nothing but chattel to this group and they treated her as such."

"I will make sure that doesn't happen in Nuria," Takeo vowed.

Red gave him a small smile. "You do that," she said, then turned to Juan. "Have you been able to locate Roark yet?"

He shook his head. "The man seems to have disappeared off the planet, which means he's found a very good hiding place. I've sent two wolves to his old office to check out the prison under his building. If they can get a scent of his blood, it'll be easier to track him. I'm also paying close attention to my visions for clues."

"Keep me posted." Red walked to the sheriff's office, but stopped at the doorway. "I want to thank you both for continuing to build the tactical team and taking care of Nuria while we were gone. I won't forget it."

They shifted uncomfortably under her regard.

Red thought she spotted Juan blushing, but he turned before she could be sure.

"It's nothing," Takeo grumbled.

"If you hear anything else, let me know," she said.

"Will do." Juan still wouldn't look at her.

Red laughed and walked into the sheriff's station. She found Morgan standing in his office. It looked like the place had been hit by a sandstorm.

"What happened?" she asked, staring at the mess.

"My guess is either Roark or the tactical team paid the station a visit," he said, picking up an overturned chair.

"Why didn't Maggie clean after they left?" Red glanced at the open safe door. The yellowed copy of Little Red Riding Hood was still inside. It had been Morgan and Kane's favorite book when they were children…and the inspiration behind Kane's murders.

"She said she didn't want to get in trouble if they came back," he said.

"Right." Red marched out of his office. She'd had enough of Maggie's crap. Morgan might not believe his assistant turned on her when he left, but Red knew the truth. "This stops now!" she shouted.

Maggie Sheppard let out a startled yelp and her eyes rounded. "I don't know what you mean," she said, hiding her trembling hands beneath her desk.

"I put up with your appalling behavior when Morgan was gone, but it ends now," Red said.

Maggie's eyes turned dark amber as the wolf inside her surfaced. She stood, directly challenging Red.

Red's claws came out and her vision faded, before snapping into clarity. "I will not accept anything less than your full submission," she growled. Tufts of hair covered her arms. Bones broke and her teeth ejected. Red screamed, but somehow managed to keep her feet beneath her. "Do you understand?" Her jaw snapped at Maggie, stopping inches in front of her face.

Maggie whimpered. "Yes." She quickly lowered her gaze to the floor.

"Does anyone else have a problem with me running Nuria with Morgan?" Red asked, her voice nearly unrecognizable.

"No," a chorus of deputies shouted.

"Good," she said. "Now get back to work."

Morgan stepped out of his office and surveyed the scene. Pride colored his features. "You heard her," he barked.

Everyone jumped and busied themselves, even the ones who had nothing to do.

She'd finally claimed her spot in the pack—in this town. Red looked at Morgan. His eyes glowed softly, letting her know she'd conquered his heart long ago.

There would be no more defiance as long as they led together. They'd proven ten times over that they were meant to be mates. And no one, not Roark, not Nuria, not even death itself, would ever tear them apart again.

* * * * *

EPILOGUE

Roark Montgomery stood on the front porch of his stone cabin in the Republic of Utarado. He'd found this place tucked inside a dead forest on the side of a mountain range that used to hold twenty feet of snowpack. He'd killed the recluse who owned it and buried him out back. That had been twenty years ago and no one had been any wiser. He'd been coming here to get away from it all ever since.

There was a nip in the air. He held the cup of synth-coffee to his lips and blew on it before taking a sip. It was bitter, but the warmth cut the chill from his bones. The woods seemed eerily calm today. No sounds of scurrying creatures, only a slight breeze that caused the branches to creak incessantly.

He raised the cup again and was about to take another drink when a howl pierced the silence. It wasn't the first time he'd heard the wolves, but they tended to come at night, not during the day.

Roark squinted at the woods, searching for signs of movement in the branches and among the petrified tree trunks. Nothing caught his eye, but he continued to watch as he drank his coffee.

A few minutes passed. Roark was just starting to relax when a second howl came, this time much closer. The hair on his neck rose. The howl was answered by another and another. He put down his coffee cup and reached for his gun.

Where was the sound coming from? It echoed through the mountains, making it hard to pinpoint.

Roark searched the trees, but nothing moved. It didn't matter. He was being hunted. Of that, there was no doubt. He pressed a button on the side of the weapon and a scope popped up. As he looked through it, Roark saw a flash of fur.

"Got you," he said.

The gun was ripped from his hands before he could fire and thrown into the woods. Roark turned to face the new threat. A man with obsidian-colored eyes glared at him. Fury radiated from his body.

Roark stumbled back. There was something familiar about the man's appearance. Had they met? Before he could ask, the man opened his mouth, revealing long, sharp fangs. In that moment, he knew the truth.

"This is for my brother." The man grabbed Roark by the shirt and yanked him forward, then sank his fangs into his throat.

Roark was so shocked by the pain that he didn't even fight back. The man took a couple of swallows of blood, then tossed him off the porch. Roark landed hard, knocking the breath out of him. He wheezed as he crawled into the woods to escape.

He didn't see the second attack coming, but he felt it. Teeth and claws shredded Roark's body, tearing pieces of his life away. He saw dark fur and flashes of amber eyes.

Familiar eyes...

In that moment he experienced true clarity: Roark was staring into the faces of death.

His death.

There would be no mercy. No reprieve. For he'd shown none.

Iron jaws clamped onto his bones, snapping them in half. Roark screamed until he could scream no more, but there was no one around to hear him as the wolves tore him apart.

The world swirled in pools of crimson, then slowly faded to black, taking his dreams of power with it. He gasped, then gurgled. Then Roark did something he'd never wanted to do. He died...with the sound of wolves howling in his ears.

# # #

A Note to Readers

If you enjoyed this book, **LEND IT** to a friend. All my books are lending enabled. If you really loved Red and Morgan's story, then please consider leaving a **REVIEW**.

For more information about Jordan's upcoming books, sign up now for her newsletter:

www.JordanSummers.com/contact

OTHER BOOKS BY JORDAN SUMMERS

AUTHOR BIO

Jordan Summers has thirty-one books to her credit and has sold over 135,000 ebooks. She's a member of the Horror Writer's Association, The Author's Guild, and Novelist Inc. For more information about the author and her work go to:

NEWSLETTER SIGN UP LINK:
www.JordanSummers.com/contact

TWITTER: http://twitter.com/jordanwriter
FACEBOOK: www.facebook.com/JordanSummersWriter
FACEBOOK AUTHOR PAGE:
https://www.facebook.com/authorjordansummersWEBSITE:
www.JordanSummers.com